Jennifer looked at their faces, puzzled yet kindly, and took breath. Alice pushed her cup of tea a little nearer. She split and buttered a warm scone and put it on a plate at Jennifer's elbow. Sudden tears swam in the grey eyes.

'I'm trying to find my family,' she said. 'I don't even know if there's anyone left now, and I don't know for sure that they came from Burracombe. But I *feel* that they did. I feel as if this is somehow my home – the place where my mother and father grew up. There must be someone who knew them. There must be *someone* who knew that I was going to be born.'

BY LILIAN HARRY

April Grove quartet

Goodbye Sweetheart
The Girls They Left Behind
Keep Smiling Through
Moonlight & Lovesongs

Other April Grove novels

Under the Apple Tree
Dance Little Lady

'*Sammy*' *novels*

Tuppence to Spend
A Farthing Will Do

Corner House trilogy

Corner House Girls
Kiss the Girls Goodbye
PS I Love You

'*Thursday*' *novels*

A Girl Called Thursday
A Promise to Keep

Other wartime novels

Love & Laughter
Three Little Ships
A Song at Twilight

Burracombe novels

The Bells of Burracombe
A Stranger in Burracombe

Other Devon novels

Wives & Sweethearts

Lilian Harry's grandfather hailed from Devon and Lilian always longed to return to her roots, so moving from Hampshire to a small Dartmoor town in her early twenties was a dream come true. She quickly absorbed herself in local life, learning the fascinating folklore and history of the moors, joining the church bellringers and a country-dance club, and meeting people who are still her friends today. Although she later moved north, living first in Herefordshire and then in the Lake District, she returned in the 1990s and now lives on the edge of the moor with her two ginger cats and miniature schnauzer. She is still an active bellringer and member of the local drama group and loves to walk on the moors. Her daughter lives nearby with her husband and their two children. Her son lives in Cambridge. Visit her website at www.lilianharry.co.uk.

A Stranger in Burracombe

LILIAN HARRY

An Orion paperback

First published in Great Britain in 2007
by Orion
This paperback edition published in 2007
by Orion Books Ltd,
Orion House, 5 Upper St Martin's Lane
London, WC2H 9EA
An Hachette Livre UK company

5 7 9 10 8 6 4

A CIP catalogue record for this book is available from the British Library.

ISBN 978-0-7528-8277-2

Typeset by Deltatype Ltd, Birkenhead, Merseyside

Printed and bound in Great Britain by
Clays Ltd, St Ives plc

www.orionbooks.co.uk

All my Australian family –
especially Roy, Linda and Meghan.

BURRACOMBE
BARTON
– The Napiers
TOZERS' FARM
–Ted, Alice & family
VICARAGE
THE CHURCH
Pettifer family
THE BELL INN
–Bernie & Rose
Nethercott
Norman
Tozer
Great Oak
VILLAGE GREEN
Dottie's
Cottage
Mrs
Purdy
Miss
Kemp's House
CHARCOAL BURNER'S
COTTAGE – Luke Ferris
STONE CIRCLE

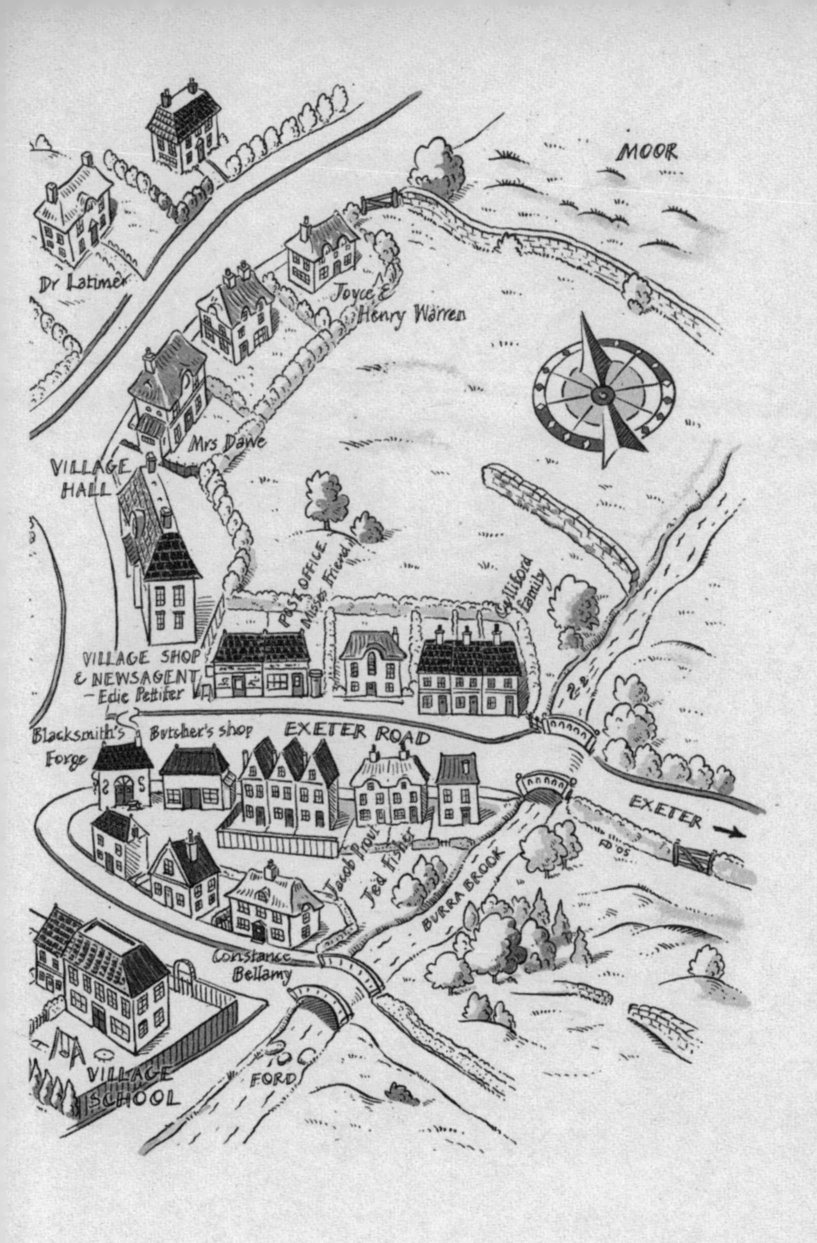
MOOR
Dr Latimer
Joyce & Henry Warren
Mrs Dawe
VILLAGE HALL
POST OFFICE
Misses Friend
Culliford Family
VILLAGE SHOP & NEWSAGENT
– Edie Pettifer
Blacksmith's Forge
Butcher's shop
EXETER ROAD
EXETER
Jacob Prout
Ted Fisher
BURRA BROOK
Constance Bellamy
FORD
VILLAGE SCHOOL

Chapter One

Burracombe, South Devon, 1952

The stranger came to Burracombe on the day the King died.

It was a cold, dry February morning in 1952, with grey skies and no wind. Basil Harvey, the vicar of Burracombe, had just heard the news on the radio and hurried over to the church at once, to find Alice Tozer at the altar, clearing away the flowers from last Sunday's service. Her round, cheerful face beamed as she turned to see him marching up the shadowy aisle, and then, as he came closer, she saw the expression on his face and her smile faded.

'Why, whatever be the matter, Vicar? You look as if you've seen a ghost.'

He stopped at the chancel steps. 'I've just heard the most dreadful news, Alice. I can hardly believe it. The King's died.'

She stared at him. Dead flowers dropped from her hands and scattered themselves over the flagstones. Her mouth worked for a moment or two, and then she said, in a strange, creaking voice, 'Died? The *King*? Are you sure?'

'It was on the wireless. They broke into the programmes. You know how they announce really serious news – "This is London". Grace and I stopped what we were doing at once to listen.' He shook his head. 'I don't quite know what we expected, but it wasn't that.'

'The King dead,' Alice said slowly, and tears spilled from her eyes. 'And with poor young Princess Elizabeth away in

Africa, too. My stars! That means she'm Queen now, don't it! Oh, that poor young lady.'

'I know. I suppose they must have told her already. She'll have to come home straight away. At least she'll have her husband to support her. Well, I'll need to see Ted as soon as possible – the bells must be rung muffled. And there'll be services to arrange.' He turned as they both heard a sound at the back of the church. 'Oh, I'm so sorry. Were you looking for me?'

The woman walking up the aisle looked to be in her early thirties. She was of medium height, rather slight, with a pale, oval face. Her eyes were an almost luminous grey, fringed with thick, black lashes, and her lips were touched with pale pink. She wore a dark green coat, fitted to her slim waist, and a green beret over her chestnut hair.

'I didn't mean to disturb you,' she said hesitantly. She spoke with a Devonshire accent, though not exactly local. 'I was just looking round the church. And then I heard what you were saying. Is it true? Has the King really died?'

'I'm afraid so,' Basil said. He glanced round at Alice again, not wanting to leave her out of the conversation. 'In his sleep, they said. At least we can be thankful that it was peaceful.'

'And he'd been very poorly,' Alice added, lowering her voice to murmur the word, '*Cancer*. And I'll tell you something else, Vicar, now I come to think of it. Me and Ted went into Tavistock last week, to the pictures, and we saw him on the Pathé Pictorial News saying goodbye to the Princess. I said to Ted then, he looked proper grey, and I reckon he knew he'd never see her again. He had such a sad look in his eyes.'

'Well, that's something we shall never know,' Basil said as Alice bent to pick up the flowers that had fallen to the floor. He saw that she was in tears again, and turned back to the stranger. 'Is there anything I can show you? The church is very old – it dates back to Norman times – and we've some interesting features. The font—'

'Oh no,' the woman said hastily. 'I won't bother you now. I just wanted . . .' Her voice faded as she glanced round the dim church. 'Perhaps I'll come back another day. I . . .' Once again, she didn't seem to know how to finish her sentence. 'I'll just go and look outside – there's a bus soon.'

Alice straightened up, her arms filled with dead and dripping stalks, and came down the chancel to where they stood. She stared at the young woman and opened her mouth to speak, but the stranger was already turning away. Basil accompanied her down the aisle.

'I don't want to drive you away. The news has come as rather a shock – as of course it will to everyone. You're very welcome to stay and look around – perhaps say a prayer. And of course you can come back at any time. The door's always open.'

'Thank you.' They stood in the porch, looking out at the village green with its ancient oak tree, the cottages clustered around and the more distant view of meadows rising to the brown, rock-cluttered moors above. 'I wondered—' She broke off again, hesitated, then turned, gave him an uncertain smile and said, 'I think I can hear the bus coming. I'd better go. Goodbye.' And before he could speak again, she was gone, walking quickly down the path to the lychgate and across the green to the bus stop.

Basil watched her go, puzzled and anxious. He knew that the bus wouldn't be along for another five minutes at least and had a strong sense that the visitor was troubled by something. He felt inadequate, as if there ought to have been something he could have done for her. Perhaps if he and Alice hadn't been absorbed by the news of the King's death, she would have confided in him. There must be some reason why she was here in our church, he thought, and for a brief moment he toyed with the idea of following her. Then he shook his head. He could hardly pursue the woman across the green and insist she talk to him. And he might be quite wrong, anyway. He turned to go back into the church.

Alice was at the door, the dead flowers now in a bucket ready to be taken to Jacob Prout's compost heap. She had wiped away her tears, but her eyes were still watering. She followed his glance across the green.

'Who do you think she were, Vicar? Nobody from round here. Sounded as if she come from Plymouth, I'd say.'

'You may be right. She must have come on the bus, anyway. I wonder what she wanted. She hadn't come into the church before I arrived, had she?'

Alice shook her head. 'I did see someone up in the top corner of the churchyard when I arrived, behind the big tomb. It could have been her. As a matter of fact, when I came down the chancel and saw her in a better light, she did remind me of someone, just for a minute, like.' A small frown touched her face. 'But no – 'twas just a trick of the light, that's all.' She looked at Basil and indicated the bucket of flowers. 'What should I be doing about Sunday, Vicar? There's not much about in February. I were going to go down the riverbank and pick some snowdrops, there's always a big patch down there, but would they be right now? Or shouldn't we have no flowers at all, till after the funeral?' Her mouth quivered and her eyes brimmed with tears again. 'I still can't believe it. The King dead! And him such a lovely man – we always listen to his speech on Christmas Day, you know. Remember that one where he said that bit of poetry about the man at the gate of the year? I wrote it down and our Val copied it out in her best writing so we could put it up on the wall. And now he'm gone. It's too soon, Vicar. It's too soon.'

'I know.' Basil laid his hand on her shoulder for a moment. 'We're all going to feel it very much. Well, I think I'll go back to the vicarage and see if I can get in touch with the Bishop. I'll let you know about the flowers as soon as I can, Alice, and you might ask Ted to slip up to the vicarage so that we can decide about the bells. They ought to be rung today, muffled of course, and I think Friday's practice must be cancelled. There'll be a good deal to do, even down here in Devon. Heaven knows what they'll be going through at Sandringham and in London and Windsor! It'll mean a state funeral, you know.'

'And to think that this time last year we were making plans for the Festival of Britain,' she said sadly. 'Whoever would have thought it?'

She carried the dead flowers up to the compost heap in the corner of the churchyard. It was near here that she had seen the stranger, half concealed behind the big family tomb of the Napiers, peering at the headstones. When Alice had thrown the dead flowers on the heap, she paused and then walked round to see what the visitor had been looking at, but the faded lettering gave no clues.

Alice gazed past the church and towards the green. The bus was there now, and she could see the woman climbing aboard. Once again, she was touched by a faint tremor of distant memory, but it was gone before she could catch it, like gossamer on a breeze.

The thought of the King came to her mind again. She felt the ache of grief in her throat, and as she walked back down the churchyard, her eyes were blurred with tears.

By dinnertime the news was all over the village. As usual, it seemed to spread almost on the air. When Dottie Friend, washing glasses and polishing tables ready for lunchtime opening at the Bell Inn, heard it from the landlord, Bernie Nethercott, she immediately went outside to see if anyone was crossing the village green. Jacob Prout was there, sweeping the road and having a look at the ditches to see if they needed clearing, and after he'd shared Dottie's shock, he passed the news on to George Sweet, the village baker, who told Bert

Foster, the butcher, and then Edie Pettifer at the village shop. Edie scurried into the post office to tell Jean and Jessie Friend, and by the time they had all gathered in the road to discuss it, Jacob had reached the blacksmith's forge where Alf Coker came out to stand at his door, wiping his hands on some cotton waste and shaking his big head.

Nobody could quite believe it.

'I know he was poorly,' George Sweet said. 'Had that operation on his lungs, didn't he? But I thought he were getting over it. Reckon his doctors must've thought so, too, or they wouldn't never have let Princess Elizabeth go off to Africa like that. Here, do you suppose they'll be able to find her, out in that jungle?'

'Well, I don't suppose her's camping out with lions and tigers,' Edie Pettifer said sharply. 'Gone to some nice hotel built up in the trees, so I read in the *Daily Express*. I dare say they'll be able to get a message out to her pretty quick.' She took out her handkerchief and wiped her eyes.

All the women had shed tears, and even the men looked stricken. The King – who had never been meant to be King but had been forced into it by his brother's abdication – had been such a stalwart figure all through the war, staying determinedly at Windsor and Buckingham Palace, visiting the most severely bombed areas during the Blitz, seeming to share in all his people's troubles, and he had earned a deep affection in the hearts of his subjects. Like Alice Tozer, everyone had listened to his Christmas broadcasts and drawn strength and comfort from the slightly hesitant voice that had seemed to make him all the more human. They'd felt almost a part of his own family – the pretty, gentle Queen Elizabeth and the two Princesses, Elizabeth and Margaret Rose – and when the governess, 'Crawfie', had published the story of her years with them in *Woman's Weekly*, it had sold out week after week as readers enjoyed the tale of their growing-up: their schoolroom days, their Guide company, the pantomimes they had performed at Windsor. Everyone had celebrated Elizabeth's marriage to Philip Mountbatten and thrilled to the birth of her two children, Charles and Anne.

And now the King was gone and she was Queen. It was hard to take in.

Ted Tozer, who had been out in the fields all morning, heard it from Alice when he came in for his dinner. He saw her red-rimmed eyes and looked from her to his mother, Minnie, sitting in her usual chair by the fire with a handkerchief pressed to her face, and thought at first that something must have happened to one of the family – Val, perhaps, or Jackie. His son, Tom, was all right – he knew that because they'd been together all morning – and Tom's wife, Joanna, was in the kitchen, too, looking equally subdued as she strapped young Robin in his high-chair. He opened his mouth to ask what was wrong, but before he could speak, Alice told him.

Ted sat down heavily in his chair at the table. 'My stars, that's a bad job. He were a good man.'

'Vicar wants to see you about the bells.' Alice set a huge bowl in the middle of the table. 'He says they ought to be rung muffled tonight.'

'So they should, and so they will be.' Ted watched as she ladled meat and vegetables on to the plates. Shock hadn't prevented her from making dumplings as light and fluffy as snowballs, or from boiling a large pan of potatoes to go with the rich golden-brown stew. He helped himself to cabbage and began to eat. 'Us'll need to ring muffled on Sunday, too, and maybe for the funeral. I'd better get word to the ringers.'

'I'll do that,' Joanna offered. 'I'll walk round with Robin this afternoon and call in on everyone. If there's no one at home, I'll drop a note through the door. What time will you be ringing?'

'Better make it half seven, same as on a practice night. And that's another thing, us'll have to put off the practice this week. Wouldn't be fitting.' He laid down his fork suddenly and shook his head, staring down at his plate. 'I dunno – I can't hardly take it in. The King dead! Seems like the end of an era.'

'It is,' Joanna said quietly. 'But it's the beginning of another one.' She looked at the sombre faces round the table. 'A new Elizabethan era.'

At the village school, the two teachers didn't hear the news until the children were either on their way home for their dinner or settling down to the shepherd's pie that Mrs Dawe had made. Basil Harvey came to tell them and sat down in the small classroom to discuss how they should break the news to the children.

'A lot of them will hear it at home,' Miss Kemp observed. 'We'll have to assemble them all in the big schoolroom as soon as they come back and tell the others, or heaven knows what stories they'll be spreading. You know what gruesome imaginations some of them have.' She looked at the vicar. 'Will you stay and have a talk with them?'

'I was going to suggest that myself.' He nodded. 'I expect they'll be upset. And they'll have quite a lot of questions, too. We might make a little service of it – we ought to say a prayer at the very least.'

Stella Simmons, the young assistant teacher, got up and went over to a cupboard, taking out a sheaf of sheet music. 'Perhaps you'd like to have a hymn, too,' she suggested. '"There's a Friend for Little Children", perhaps, or "Around the Throne of God a Band of Glorious Angels Ever Stand". Just to remind them that the King's in Heaven now and we don't need to worry about him.'

'An excellent idea,' Basil approved. 'And singing always seems to relieve the mind. I'm sure that's one of the reasons why we have hymns in church.' They all looked up at the sound of a minor stampede outside. 'There they are now. Let's get them in as quickly as possible.'

Stella went outside to ring the bell and the children rushed chattering into the two schoolrooms. She ushered the little ones into the larger room and had just managed to quieten them down as the headmistress and vicar came through. She then went to the piano in the corner. Miss Kemp took up her position at the big desk, and the children stared at her, their faces taut with anxious excitement.

'Now, some of you have heard the sad news that our beloved King has died,' she began gravely, and one or two of the girls began to cry. 'Of course we're all upset about this – he wasn't a very old man, and although he'd been ill, we all hoped he would get better. I expect you remember saying prayers for him in the church, don't you?' There were a few assenting sniffles. 'Our vicar, Mr Harvey, thought you might like to say a prayer for him now, and for the rest of the Royal Family, who must be so upset at this time. And then he's going to talk to you about the King and about what it means to Christians to die, and then we're going to sing one of your favourite hymns. All bend your heads now and put your hands together like steeples.'

The little service was soon over, and as Basil Harvey had predicted, the children had a number of questions to ask. They accepted the idea that the King was now safe and well in Heaven, but wanted to know about the family he had left behind, and especially about the young Princess who was already Queen and on her way home from Africa. Would she be wearing her crown, Shirley Culliford wanted to know, and looked disappointed but resigned when Miss Kemp explained that she wouldn't have taken it with her. It was always kept at the Tower of London. In any case, the crown was only worn on big state occasions and couldn't be worn at all until after the Coronation. This led to more questions about what happened when a king or queen was crowned, which she and the vicar did their best to answer from their memories of George the Sixth's own Coronation in 1937. Stella, who had been a small girl herself at the time, listened with as much interest as the children and thought how exciting it would be when the new Queen was crowned.

'That won't be for quite a long time yet, though,' Basil finished up. 'It'll probably be sometime next year. There's such a lot to arrange, you see.'

'And I think we've talked about it enough for now,' Miss Kemp said, realising that he must have a dozen other things to do. 'Let's all say thank you to Mr Harvey for coming to talk to us this afternoon, and then we'll go back to our lessons. Except that I don't think we'll have our usual lesson this afternoon,' she added. 'I'll read a chapter or two from *Little Christian's Pilgrimage* to the older children, and perhaps Miss Simmons will find a nice Bible story for the babies.'

The vicar then led them all in a recitation of the Lord's Prayer, and, with the bigger children sitting more quietly now at their desks, Stella took the little ones into their own room next door and did as the headmistress had suggested. All the children loved being read to, although the youngest ones often fell asleep, their heads pillowed on their arms, and nobody was in the mood for ordinary lessons. By the time the bell was rung for the end of the afternoon, they were all much calmer and went out in unaccustomed silence to collect their coats and Wellingtons from the lobby.

'Not that it'll last,' Miss Kemp observed ruefully, watching as they made their way along the village street to their various homes. 'Within a quarter of an hour, they'll be rushing about and making as much noise as ever. But I think the quiet afternoon did them good.'

'It did me good, too,' Stella confessed. 'I was only about six years old when the old King died, and then of course there was all the fuss about the abdication. I never really understood all that then, but we had a book with pictures of the

Coronation and I used to look at the pictures for hours. I always thought he was such a handsome man.'

She said goodbye to the headmistress and walked home through the grey February afternoon to Dottie Friend's cottage, where she lodged. Dottie, who worked for the Napiers and the doctor's wife as well as at the inn, had just taken a tray of scones out of the oven as Stella walked in, and she looked round, her rosy face sad. The kettle was coming to the boil, and while she made tea, Stella buttered some of the scones. They sat on either side of the fire and talked about the only topic of conversation that was in anybody's mind that day.

'The wireless has shut down for three days in mourning,' Dottie said. 'So there's no *Mrs Dale's Diary* this afternoon, and no *Archers* after tea.'

'And no *Children's Hour* at five o'clock!' Stella said. 'The children won't like that. Isn't there anything on at all?'

'Not a thing. Daft, I call it. How are we supposed to know what's going on, with no wireless to tell us? Still, I suppose it's only right and proper that us should show our respect. I mean, it wouldn't seem right to sit laughing at *Take It From Here* or *The Charlie Chester Show*, would it? Not that you and me would do that, we've got more of a sense of what's right, but there's some that haven't got the manners they were born with.' Dottie finished her tea and stretched out a hand to pick up her knitting. 'Oh – do you think I ought to be doing this, maid? I mean, if us can't listen to the wireless, what did we ought to be doing?'

'I don't think knitting a jumper is disrespectful,' Stella said. 'You'd do it if it was someone close to you that had died – someone in the village. It's useful, after all, not just for enjoyment.'

Dottie nodded, and they sat talking quietly, reminding each other of the little things they knew of the King and his family, of the scandal of his brother's abdication and the wonderful way he and his wife had conducted themselves during the war. It seemed almost a relief that there was nothing on the wireless so that they didn't have to decide for themselves if it would be right to listen to their favourite programmes. After a while, Stella cleared away the tea things and worked on her next day's lessons while Dottie got the supper ready, and they both went to bed early.

As she drew the curtains against the dark February night, Stella found the same words in her mind as Joanna Tozer had spoken earlier that day; words that must have been echoed up and down the land.

It was the end of an era. And the beginning of a new one.

Chapter Two

Even after the death of a king, ordinary life must still go on.

Val Tozer and Luke Ferris were thinking about their wedding. It couldn't be just yet – they'd only announced their engagement at Christmas and weren't really planning to marry until the end of the year. But it was nice to dream.

'I really wouldn't mind coming to live in the charcoal-burner's cottage,' Val said as they walked along the lane, hoping to spot some early snowdrops. 'It's cosy enough.'

'Cosy enough for me. I don't think your dad would consider it good enough for his daughter. He's not all that happy about me as it is.' Luke swung his stick at the dead, blackening stalks of a clump of nettles. 'You don't have to pretend, Val. You saw his face when we told the family on Christmas Day.'

'Oh, Dad'll come round,' Val said with a dismissive shrug. 'You know what fathers are like. He'll be just the same when it's our Jackie. And Mum thinks you're the bee's knees – she'll soon bring him round. It's mainly because you're not a farmer.'

'And even worse, I'm an *artist*!' Luke said wryly. 'He just can't believe that's a proper job at all. I don't think he actually thinks I'm a pansy now, but he did look at me a bit sideways at first!'

Val laughed. 'Of course he doesn't think that, you idiot! He likes you, anyway – he's just not sure whether painting pretty pictures is going to keep me in the luxury I'm accustomed to!'

'Which the charcoal-burner's cottage isn't,' Luke said. 'And I'm not sure I'll ever be able to keep you in luxury, anyway, Val. In fact, I've been thinking maybe your dad's right – I ought to get a proper job.'

Val stopped and stared at him. 'What sort of job?'

'Well, it would have to be to do with art – that's what I'm trained for. Teaching, I suppose, or something like that. I might get something in Tavistock, or Plymouth.'

'I wouldn't want to live in Plymouth,' Val said at once, and Luke shook his head.

'Neither would I. But we've got to find somewhere to live, and it's got to be something we can afford. And if I'm going to be teaching, I need to be able to get to the school, which means either living close by or near a bus route. Or within cycling distance.'

'I'm earning—' Val began, but he shook his head again.

'You know you won't be able to go on working for long after we're married – we'll be starting a family as soon as we can, won't we? And that's another reason why we can't live in the cottage,' he added. 'It's certainly no place for a baby.'

Val nodded regretfully. 'I know. But we could live there for a little while – just to start with – couldn't we? It's so romantic.'

'Only if we know for certain there's something better coming along soon,' he said firmly.

They strolled along in silence for a few minutes. It was a cold, grey afternoon with a threat of light snow damping the air. Val was working morning shifts at the hospital in Tavistock, where she was a nurse, and Luke had met her from the bus at the main road, a mile or so away from the village. Val thought about what Luke had been saying.

'I'll go on working for as long as possible after we're married, though. There's no point in staying at home with nothing much to do.'

'So long as it's just day shifts,' Luke said with a grin. 'You don't imagine I'm going to let you work nights, do you?'

Val blushed and laughed. 'No, and I wouldn't want to, either.' They gripped each other's hands tightly for a moment. 'It's a pity we can't live at the farm, like Tom and Joanna. But my room really isn't big enough. And there's Robin as well – he's going to need his own room soon.' She hesitated, then said, 'I've got a feeling Joanna's expecting another baby.'

'Really? Has she said anything?'

'No, but I've noticed one or two things. And she went to see Dr Latimer last week without mentioning it at home. I happened to spot her coming out of his surgery, but she didn't see me so I didn't say anything. She'll tell us in her own time.'

Luke grinned. 'If you saw her, I'm surprised nobody else did. It would have been all over the village by now if they had.'

'Well, it was dark and she had her hood up so probably nobody else would have recognised her. Anyway, back to our own plans . . .'

'I wouldn't really want to live at the farm, anyway,' Luke said. 'I mean, your family are all very nice, but I want us to be on our own. It's different for Tom and Joanna – Tom works on the farm, they'll take over one day. But we're going to have a different sort of life.'

They were coming close to the village now. There were few people about; most of the women would have done their shopping in the morning and be at home now, baking or preparing the family meal, and it was too cold for many strollers. As Luke and Val came round the last bend in the lane the only person in sight was Jacob Prout, who did all the jobs around the village such as clearing ditches, keeping hedges tidy and digging graves. He was raking leaves and other debris out of a culvert and straightened up as he saw them. His rough-haired Jack Russell terrier, Scruff, ran over and sniffed their legs.

'Cold enough for you?'

'Plenty,' Val said, rubbing her arms. She was wearing a thick brown coat, but the wind had seemed to slice through it as they walked down from the road, which crossed the open moorland. It was much more sheltered in the lanes that approached the village, tucked away in its little valley. All the same, the ice covering the puddles and turning mud to stone showed that the temperature was still below freezing.

'Ah, it's a lazy wind today,' Jacob agreed. 'Goes straight through you instead of taking the long way round. It'll be cold for them as have gone to London, queueing up for hours to see the King lying in state.'

'Hilary Napier was saying that her father wanted to go,' Val said. 'She won't let him, though. It's not all that long since he had his heart attack.'

'Asking for trouble, that'd be,' Jacob concurred. 'Mind you, I can understand him wanting it, seeing as he was a colonel and served King and country through the war. ''Tis only patriotic to want to pay his respects.'

'I don't think the King would want anyone to catch pneumonia on his account, though.' Val and Luke made to walk on, then she stopped and turned back. 'I meant to ask you, Jacob – did you notice a strange woman in the village on Wednesday morning?'

'The day the King died? Can't say as I did, maid. Why?'

'Oh, nothing really. She came into the church while Mum was there clearing away the flowers. It was just as the vicar came in to tell her the news. They both got the feeling she was looking for something, or someone, but when they asked her she wouldn't say – just said she'd got to catch the bus and hurried off. Mother said she thought she'd seen her up in the corner of the churchyard just before, looking at the graves.

We wondered if she might be looking for a family grave – someone you'd recognise.'

Jacob shook his head. 'Never saw hide nor hair of her, maid. Mind you, we do get folk poking about now and then, but they'd usually ask the vicar. Happen she didn't like to, when she heard about the King.'

'Probably. Perhaps she'll come back sometime. Only Mum thought there was something familiar about her – she couldn't put her finger on it. As if she might be related to one of the village families.'

Jacob shook his head. 'Dunno who that might be. Us knows most of the families who moved away since the war. Before that, there were one or two emigrated to America or Australia, but I don't suppose it were one of they.'

'No, I don't think so. Mum said she sounded as if she came from Plymouth. Oh well, I expect she'll come back if she really wants to find anything.' Val began to walk on again, with Luke beside her. 'She might just have come out for a bit of an outing.'

'Mm. Odd sort of day to do that, though – at the beginning of February. It would be interesting if she really was looking for a family connection.' Luke had spent some time the previous year helping the young schoolteacher, Stella Simmons, to look for her sister, Muriel, separated from her during the war. 'Pity she didn't say anything to Uncle Basil.'

They parted at the farm gate. Val had asked Luke to come up for tea and some of her mother's rock cakes, but he'd shaken his head and said he wanted to go up to the Standing Stones to catch the last of the chilly afternoon light for the painting he was working on. He'd painted the stones in many of their moods, and this was the most sombre yet, with the grey granite monoliths etched starkly against the pewter sky. He was hoping to catch their mystery and even, with the addition of some subtle shadows, the old tradition that the stones couldn't be counted. Today's conditions were ideal.

He walked up the twisting path through the woods to the cottage where he had come to live the year before, after his slow recovery from the TB that had nearly killed him. If it hadn't been for that, he thought, he would have stayed in London and his godfather, Basil Harvey, would never have suggested his coming to Burracombe. And he would never have met Val Tozer again – the girl he had fallen in love with in Egypt during the war, and never forgotten.

Not that their meeting had been an easy one – there was too much that he hadn't known and that Val hadn't wanted to tell him. But eventually all the secrets had been told. All the tender passion, locked away for so many years, had been allowed to flower again, and their engagement had been announced at Christmas.

It hadn't turned out to be quite the joyful moment that they'd anticipated. Alice and Minnie had been delighted, hugging them both with pleasure, and Joanna had obviously been pleased, while Tom had shaken Luke's hand in congratulation and given his sister an affectionate push. But Ted had taken a moment or two to add his good wishes, and Luke had caught the brief darkening of his face as Val and her mother turned away.

After the dinner of turkey and all the trimmings, followed by a rich Christmas pudding made back in October, the farmer had suggested that he and Luke take a walk outside before it got dark. Tom was doing the milking, along with one of the farmhands, and Alice and Val would see to the hens.

'We'll see to the pigs,' Ted announced. 'And maybe take a turn round some of the fields, see how they ewes are getting on.'

They'd looked at the ewes only that morning, but Luke understood that the outing wasn't really to do with farming matters and he wasn't surprised when, after the pigs had been fed, Ted turned to the matter of the engagement.

'I know you think a lot of our Val,' he began rather

ponderously, 'and she thinks a lot of you, too. But you might have said summat to me before making it an official engagement.'

'I'm sorry if you feel offended, Mr Tozer,' Luke said. 'I think Val considered she was too old to need her father's permission.'

'Well, maybe she is, but it would have been manners all the same. However, 'tisn't that that I wants to talk about. 'Tis only a small matter, after all.' He paused and leaned on a gate, staring into the dusk that was creeping across the meadows. 'I'd like to know what you means to do about supporting her.'

Luke felt his face flush. 'Naturally I want to look after her, Mr Tozer . . .'

'Yes, I dare say you do, but how? That's the question. You can't say you've got a steady job, now, can you? Living from hand to mouth, that's how it seems to me, and what sort of a place is that old shack in the woods to take a decent young woman? Nothing more than a hovel, that be. Ought to have been burned down years ago.'

Luke stared at him, shaken by this outburst. He'd known Ted might find the situation a little difficult, but he'd been unprepared for such strong feelings. As he searched for words, Ted started again.

'Our Val's not had an easy time of it, you know. Should have been married years since, if her young chap hadn't been killed in the war.' He turned his head and Luke saw the glimmer of his eyes. 'You didn't do no fighting yourself, as I understand it.'

'No,' Luke said quietly. 'I was a war artist.'

'War artist!' Ted echoed, although he'd already known that. 'And what's that, when it's at home? Drawing pretty pictures while other boys—'

'No, I'm sorry, Mr Tozer,' Luke said more forcefully. 'The pictures I was drawing weren't pretty at all. They were pictures of what was going on – men fighting, men being killed. And not just men – women and children, too.' He looked at Ted. 'You were in the First World War, weren't you? You know as well as I do that there's nothing pretty about it.'

'All right,' Ted said after a moment. 'Maybe I spoke out of turn there. But I still don't see what use it was drawing pictures instead of getting on with what had to be done.'

Luke sighed. 'I don't really know what use any of it was, Mr Tozer, but we all have to do what we're best at. And it's important to *show* people at home what happens – it's not always easy for them to realise what it was like, without pictures. There were others taking photographs, too, and filming, but sometimes it's not possible to do that – your camera might get damaged, or you might run out of film. It's usually possible to find a pencil and a bit of paper.' He paused, thinking back to some of the situations he'd been in when he'd longed to put down his sketching materials and take part in whatever was going on, when his own life had been in danger yet he had continued to draw the horrors that were before his eyes. 'If I hadn't thought it was important, I wouldn't have done it,' he finished quietly. 'I was trained to fight as well, you know. I could handle a rifle as well as any man.'

'Well, it's all in the past now,' Ted said after another pause, 'and maybe us should leave it there. But it don't answer my question – how be you going to provide for her? Our Val deserves better than a shack in the woods with no running water or proper kitchen. And I don't suppose you'd want to pack into the farmhouse with the rest of us.' He turned his head again, and even though it was almost dark by now, Luke could see the frown on his face. 'Let's put our cards on the table. What sort of an income does your painting bring in?'

Luke hesitated, then said simply, 'It's erratic, Mr Tozer. I can earn quite a good sum from one painting – the exhibition in London last summer brought me in enough to live on for several months. But then I might not sell anything else for quite a while. As my name builds up, things should improve – but it all depends on whether people like my pictures.'

'You'm not likely to get asked to paint portraits and such?'

'Not really. I'm a landscape painter, you see – that's what I enjoy doing and—'

'Now wait a minute,' Ted broke in. 'Who said anything about *enjoyment*? It's earning a living I'm talking about, not playing games.'

'So am I. Don't think I look on painting as a game, Mr Tozer – I don't. I'm as serious about it as you are about farming. I know you may not think it's as useful – and perhaps you're right. But people do like pictures on their walls, and it's what I can *do*. That's what I mean when I say I enjoy it. Just as you must enjoy your farming.'

'Not all the time, I don't,' Ted retorted. 'Not at five o'clock on an icy-cold winter's morning when there's forty cows waiting to be milked. Or when I'm up all night with a difficult calving and then loses the beast anyway. Or sees a field of taters go down with blight. Or any of the other hundred and one things that can go wrong. I'm sorry, Luke, but if you think a farmer's life is all making hay in the sunshine, you got no idea. No idea at all.'

'No,' Luke said with a sigh. 'I don't suppose I have.' There was another short silence, then he said, 'Look, Mr Tozer, I know how you feel about me and what I do. It doesn't seem like work to you at all, and you're worried that Val's going to be spending all her time working to keep me playing games with my time. Looking at it that way, I'd feel exactly the same. And I've got to be honest and tell you that at the moment, my painting won't bring in a living wage – not to support two of us, and maybe a family. So I've decided to look for a job.'

Ted turned his head. 'A job? What sort of a job, then?'

'Anything I can do,' Luke said. 'Something to do with

pictures and painting, if I can find it. Teaching, perhaps. But if not – well, I'm not a bad hand with a saw and a piece of wood. I can turn my hand to a bit of carpentry or joinery, if it comes to it.'

Ted stared at him and then turned back to gaze into the darkened field. 'It's not that I wants you to give up whatever you'm good at,' he said at last, his voice sounding different now. 'I might not be an arty sort, but I can understand when summat's in a man's blood. You'm right, I *am* like that with farming – there might be plenty of times when I wish I had some nice job indoors in the warm, but I'd never really give it up. If it's the same with you—'

'It is,' Luke said. 'I won't ever give up painting, but I can put it to one side if it makes life better for Val. And we won't get married until I can offer her a decent home. I promise you that, Mr Tozer.'

Ted's shoulders moved as he drew in a deep breath. Then he turned back and put out his hand.

'No man could say fairer than that,' he said gruffly. 'And now I reckon us'd better go back indoors, before they sends out a search party. 'Tis Christmas night, and the womenfolk likes a bit of a party. I hope you'm up to joining in a few games, Luke, now you'm one of the family.'

Luke had never told Val exactly what he and Ted had said to each other that afternoon, but he meant to hold firm to his promise not to marry until he could offer her a proper home. Today, as he walked up the twisting path to the cottage, he faced the fact that it wasn't really enough for him to make such a promise – Val expected a say in the matter, too. Gone were the days, as in Ted Tozer's youth, when the man would have made the important decisions in a marriage – that's if he ever did, Luke thought, remembering times when his father had apparently come to a decision already made quietly by his mother – and now women assumed a right at least to consultation. The independence they'd discovered during the war had left them stronger.

Some day soon, Luke thought as he opened the door of the tiny cottage and collected his painting gear, I'll take her to London to meet my own folks. But perhaps not just yet. Not until the King's funeral is over, anyway. I'd like everyone to be feeling happy when they first meet my future wife.

After Val and Luke had gone on, Jacob Prout finished clearing the culvert and gathered the cold, muddy leaves into his wheelbarrow. He wheeled it along the lane and took them just inside the wood, where he had collected a large pile, which were slowly composting down. Then he stowed the barrow in a shed by the bank and went home. He was looking forward to a good meal of Bert Foster's beef sausages with fried onions and mashed potatoes, with a big pot of tea to wash it all down, and maybe a baked apple for afters. You needed something hot and tasty after working outdoors in this weather.

With his hand on his front gate, he paused, frowning. His own cottage looked as immaculate as ever, the garden tidy and ready for spring, the hedges neatly trimmed and the path clear. But the cottage next door, where Jed Fisher lived, was a shambles. Old net curtains, grey with age and grime, sagging at the windows, moss growing on the slate roof, a tangle of weeds in the sour earth, paint peeling off the front door. Inside, Jed had lit a lamp and you could see past the pile of old newspapers on the windowsill (harbouring God knew what vermin) to the battered furniture inside. You could almost smell it.

Jacob turned his eyes away and went up the path to his own front door, stained and varnished to within an inch of its life. He was proud of that door, as he was proud of everything else in his home. He'd learned in the Navy during the First World War how important it was to keep everything spick and span, and he looked after himself and his own cottage as well as he looked after the village. It was a pity Jed had never gone into the Forces, he thought. He'd have learned a bit about what was what. He'd never have gone downhill the way he had.

Inside, Jacob closed the door and switched on the light, driving away the late-afternoon shadows to cast a bright glow on the faded but clean chintz cover on his own old armchair, the round table covered with a green baize cloth, the dresser with his mother's china gleaming on the shelves. His tortoiseshell cat, Flossie, curled up on one of the straight-backed kitchen chairs, raised her head and stretched out a paw as Scruff ran over to sniff at her.

'You've been asleep all day on that cushion, I'll be bound,' he said. 'Reckon I'll be a cat, next time around. Nearest thing to Heaven there be, on this earth. Either that or a swallow and fly off to Africa every winter.'

Flossie gave him a reproachful look at the idea of becoming a bird, and stood up, stretching each leg separately and arching her back before jumping down to walk into the tiny scullery where Jacob kept her saucers. They were all empty and she turned to give him an accusing stare. Scruff went, too, pushing the saucers about with his nose in the hope that some scrap or other might have been forgotten.

'All right,' Jacob said, stooping to open the lower door of the Rayburn and riddle the ashes through. There were just enough embers left to catch on the kindling and sticks that he kept in the basket close by, and, once they were burning well, he'd add a couple of logs. The Rayburn kept the whole cottage snug, and the wood ash was good for the garden. 'You'll get your suppers soon enough.'

Jacob had lived alone ever since his wife, Sarah, had died ten years before. She'd been a few years older than him and it had been a late marriage, so they'd never had children, but they'd been good companions and he had missed her when she'd gone. Now, he was accustomed to living alone again in the cottage where he'd been born and brought up, with just

Flossie and Scruff to keep him company. There were times when he sat quietly, with Flossie on his knee and Scruff at his feet, thinking of days gone by and wondering how it would have been if things had turned out differently, but he wasn't the sort to bemoan the past. Not until the sight of his neighbour Jed reminded him, anyway. Then it took only a word or a look to bring the old bitterness welling up inside him, and he was hard put at times to keep his anger in check. It was funny how it could still boil up, hot and strong as ever, after all this time.

Mostly, though, he could push his thoughts away, and he did this now as he opened the back door to fetch the sausages in from the meat safe outside. Bert's delivery boy had brought them round that morning, and Jacob was pleased to see that they were good thick ones, as big as Alf Coker's fingers. The blacksmith had huge hands, and it was commonly believed that Bert Foster used them as a measure for his sausages. Some people even asked for 'half a pound of Cokers' when they went into the butcher's shop.

Jacob laid the sausages in an old enamel dish, pricked their skins with a skewer and put them in the oven. Then he peeled a few potatoes and set them on the hotplate to boil while he fried an onion to go with them. He made gravy out of the onion juices, with an Oxo cube crumbled in and half a cup of hot water poured over it, and within half an hour his supper was ready. Just before he put it all on a plate, he took the core out of a big cooking apple with his potato peeler, filled the hole with currants and sultanas, and slid that into the oven. He'd make the custard last so that it was hot when the apple was ready.

You didn't have to eat rubbish just because you were on your own, he thought, sitting down at the scrubbed kitchen table while the animals took up their positions on either side of his chair. A man on his own could feed himself as well as any woman. There weren't many weeks when Jacob didn't have a rabbit in his big roasting-pan, stewing gently through the day with an onion and some turnips and carrots beside it, and he always had fish on Fridays, like a Christian should, off the van that came round the villages. He liked a bit of liver, too – pigs' fry was the tastiest, to his mind, especially with a bit of bacon thrown in – and a slice or two of good fatty pork belly was a treat. With his own vegetables, grown in the back garden, Jacob reckoned he lived pretty well.

Not like that Jed Fisher next door, who got his vegetables out of tins if the mess in his back garden was anything to go by, and more than likely lived on bread and jam most of the time. No wonder he was a surly old cuss. You couldn't be cheerful if your stomach wasn't looked after proper.

Jacob turned his thoughts away from his old enemy and reached out to switch on the wireless. Then he remembered that there was nothing on tonight, out of respect for the King, and looked for something else to occupy his thoughts. His eye caught the row of photographs on the mantelpiece.

They were old photographs, most of them – snaps taken of village outings long ago – with a few more recent including one the vicar had taken of the bellringers when they'd won the Burracombe competition last year. There was also one of his parents, taken at their wedding nearly seventy years ago, and another of himself in his naval uniform, when he'd enlisted in 1914.

He stared at it, chewing his sausage and thinking of those days so long ago. Two world wars, there had been since then. Two terrible wars, killing millions of people and changing the whole world. Changing lives everywhere.

Changing his own life.

Chapter Three

After supper, Val took the big torch down from the shelf and announced that she was going up to the Barton to see Hilary Napier.

'That's a good idea, maid,' her mother said. 'I dare say she'll be glad of some company. Not having the wireless makes you wonder how us managed before us had it!'

'Pretty well, from what I remember,' Ted said. He liked the radio as much as anyone, but he spent as much time reading his *Farmer's Weekly* as he did listening and always complained that there wasn't enough about farming. *The Archers*, which was supposed to be a kind of farmers' *Dick Barton*, did give you a bit of information, but it stood to reason it couldn't give much, what with having to have all those stories about Dan and Doris and their family, and that old Walter Gabriel, who set such a bad example and didn't ought to have been in a decent farming programme, to Ted's mind. Not that he wasn't a typical old village character – you only had to look at Jed Fisher to know that every village had one – but you had to remember that town folk listened to the programme as well. Mind you, Walter Gabriel was a lot funnier than Jed Fisher.

'Us could always play a game of cards,' he suggested now, but Alice frowned and shook her head and he recollected the reason why there was no wireless at the moment. 'No, 'twouldn't be fitting, not with the King dead. Got to show proper respect. Reckon I might get that book out, the one I got for Christmas about old Devonshire traditions. Never had time for a proper read of that, I haven't.'

'And me and Mother will get on with that new rug,' Alice said. This was another Christmas present, given by Ted to his wife, and consisted of a half-moon-shaped piece of canvas marked with a pattern of roses, and a set of coloured wools. Alice and Minnie had started it soon after the New Year and it was almost finished. It would look lovely down in front of the fire, they thought.

They settled down for the evening. Jackie was up in her bedroom, writing a letter to Roy Pettifer in Korea, and Tom and Joanna had put Robin to bed and then gone to their own sitting-room. The family got on well, but everyone agreed you had to have your own space as well, to be private. They'd join Ted and Alice in the big, warm kitchen again later on for a bit of supper. Val pulled on her thick coat, wrapped her new purple scarf (knitted for her for Christmas by her grandmother) round her neck and stepped out into the cold, dark night. It wasn't far to the Barton, and she was soon shucking off her Wellington boots on the doormat of the Napiers' kitchen.

'Oh, there you are,' Hilary said, turning, with her hands sticky with bread dough. 'We'll never train you to come to the front door, will we? Leave your boots near the Aga: they'll keep warm for when you go back.'

'That's why I come to the back door,' Val said. 'I'm always too muddy to come in the posh way.'

'Father's in the drawing-room,' Hilary said, going back to her kneading. 'We'll go in and say hello to him in a minute, but we'll have a chinwag out here first. It's Mrs Ellis's night off so I'm doing the chores. He'll be pleased to see you – he needs cheering up, poor dear. And you can help me convince him that it isn't a good idea for a man in his condition to go and queue for hours in the London streets to see the King.'

‘Of course it’s not,’ Val said. ‘I thought Dr Latimer had told him that already.’

‘He has, but you know what Dad’s like. Even a heart attack isn’t enough to convince him he’s not immortal. It scared him at the time, but now he’s feeling better he’s trying to pretend it never happened.’ She set two loaves on the side of the Aga and covered them with a clean tea-towel. ‘It’s all I can do to stop him coming round the estate with me. It wouldn’t be so bad if he’d stay in the Land Rover, but he keeps wanting to get out and look at things. It’s just too cold at the moment.’

‘It must be very hard, when you’ve been used to being active and in charge all your life,’ Val commented as Hilary washed her hands at the sink. ‘Not very easy for you, either, when you’re trying to do his job.’

‘Oh, I dare say we’ll shake down eventually,’ Hilary said, getting a bottle of ginger wine and two glasses out of a cupboard. ‘He’s had nearly six months to get used to the idea, after all. Let’s have a drink here before we go in to him. He’ll probably like a game of cards – pity you didn’t bring Luke with you, we could have had a rubber of bridge.’

‘I’ll bring him another time.’ Val sat down at the big table and waited while Hilary poured out the wine and handed her a glass. ‘Cheers. Actually, there’s something I wanted to ask you.’

‘What’s that, then?’

‘I wondered if you had any cottages coming vacant soon on the estate. Luke and I are going to need somewhere to live, and I can’t think of anywhere in the village. All the farm cottages are tied, and anyway, they’re all occupied, and we can’t live in the charcoal-burner’s cottage. And I really don’t want to move away.’

‘Surely you’re not thinking of that?’ Hilary stared at her friend in dismay. ‘Where would you go?’

‘Well, it would depend where Luke got a job. He’s thinking of trying for an art teacher’s post – he’s well qualified for it, you know. He'd try the Tavistock schools at first, of course, and then Plymouth, but if he couldn't find anything there . . .' She shrugged and left the words hanging as she took a sip of ginger wine.

'He wouldn't go back to London, surely?' Hilary said. 'You wouldn't want to go there, would you?'

'Why not? *You* nearly did! You were really keen, as I remember it.' There was a short silence as both recalled the day of the village outing to the Festival of Britain last May, and their return to find that Gilbert Napier had suffered a heart attack. Hilary had been on the point of leaving Burracombe then, to take up an appointment as an air hostess and share a flat with a friend. She still had moments of regret as she wondered what her life would have been, had she gone on with her plans instead of giving them up and staying at home to take over the management of the family estate. 'Mind you,' Val added, 'I'm glad you didn't!'

'And I feel just the same about you,' Hilary said. 'Except that I think you'd hate living in London. Or even Plymouth.' She sighed. 'Has Luke really got to look for a job? Isn't he earning enough with his painting? I thought he was doing quite well since he had that exhibition.'

'He is, but it's so uncertain, Hil. It's all right for a single man who doesn't need much money – except for paints and canvases and things, which cost a lot – but he couldn't support a wife and family.'

Hilary sipped her drink thoughtfully. 'It's difficult, isn't it? There's nothing at all wrong with being an artist – Luke's got real talent, and he ought to be able to use it – but unless you're lucky and get recognised, you just can't make any money at it. And why *shouldn't* married women be able to work – at least until they start a family? The country was pleased enough to have us during the war.'

'Oh, you know what men are like – it's all to do with their pride. Wanting to be the providers and all that. And despite what we did during the war, most of them still don't really think we can do as good a job as they can. Look at the struggle you had persuading your father that you could run the estate.'

'I know. And in his heart, I believe he'd still rather have Stephen in charge, even though we all know he'd make a mess of it. Dad won't admit that, of course – Stephen's a man and his son, therefore he ought to take over. Never mind that he was never intended to run the estate – that was always going to be Baden's job, as eldest son, and he'd have done it well. But Dad just can't see it that way. Thank goodness Steve's got the sense to see it wouldn't work.'

'How's he getting on in the RAF?' Val asked.

'Oh, he loves it. He's just got promotion. I wouldn't be surprised if he decides to make it his career instead of just doing it as National Service. He thinks he'll be going to Germany soon.' Hilary chewed her lip thoughtfully. 'I'm just thinking . . . There's the estate house we lived in during the war, when the Barton was requisitioned for that children's home. It's always been meant for an estate manager, but since Dad came home and took over it's been rented out. The lease will be coming up sometime this year and I've a feeling the present tenants might not want to renew it. Would that do for you and Luke?'

Val stared at her. 'It would be marvellous! I know the place you mean – up beside the coppice, near the gamekeeper's house. It's a lovely spot.'

'The house might need a bit of attention. I was waiting to see if the Cherrimans wanted to stay before doing any work there. I couldn't evict them, mind,' she added hastily. 'They're friends of Father's and if they want to renew . . .'

'Oh, I understand that. I wouldn't want anyone put out on the street on my account. All the same –' Val put her chin in her hands and looked wistful '– it would be lovely if we could have it. And if not, maybe you might find some other cottage lying about that we could use!'

'Who knows?' Hilary said, laughing. She sipped her ginger wine and rose to her feet. 'Come on, let's take this into the drawing-room. Dad's there all on his own with a bottle of port and you know he's not supposed to have too much of that. I don't want him getting gout on top of his other troubles!'

Val picked up her glass and followed her friend into the drawing-room, with its comfortable, shabby armchairs and sofas, and its roaring fire almost obliterated by the two black Labradors stretched out in front of it. Gilbert Napier, ensconced in his own armchair with *The Times* folded into a pad on his knee so that he could work on the crossword, raised his leonine head.

'And about time, too. I was just thinking of coming out to see if you'd drowned in the washing-up water. Evening, young Val – I suppose Hilary's been keeping you out there gossiping. Never mind her poor old father, left in here all alone with his sorrow.'

'Hello, Mr Napier,' Val said, bending to give him a kiss. Since her help when he had had his heart attack, he had been firmly convinced that she had saved his life and now looked on her almost as another daughter. 'It's sad news about the King, isn't it? You must be very upset.'

'Fine man,' he said gruffly. 'Fine man. Took over a difficult job, even though he was only the second son, and made a better fist of it than his brother ever would have done. Showed his true colours during the war – ought to have had years ahead of him.' He paused, staring into the fire. 'Feel I'm letting him down, not going to pay my respects.'

'He wouldn't have wanted you to make yourself ill,' Val said gently. 'He'd have wanted you to stay here and get your own health back so that you can carry on looking after his countryside. And serving the Queen.'

'Yes,' he said, looking up at her. 'Yes, I think you may be right. Pity nobody else has been able to put it like that. Yes . . .'

There was a short silence, and then he repeated quietly to himself, 'It just shows what a second son can do.'

And the two women looked at each other, knowing that he was no longer thinking of the King.

Chapter Four

Slowly, the country began to look forward to the new Elizabethan era. The new Queen was young and pretty, and had a handsome prince at her side as well as two small children. Her mother now became the Queen Mother, and Mary, the former Queen Mother, was the Dowager Queen Mother. With the state funeral over, attention turned to the future.

'The Coronation won't be until next year,' Basil Harvey said at the next meeting of the Parish Council. 'So we needn't think about that for a while. We can concentrate on this year, instead.'

It was customary, early in the year, to consider the plans for village events until the autumn. Last year, Burracombe had held a pageant in celebration of the Festival of Britain, and a number of other events as well. The bellringers had put on a special competition, there had been a craft exhibition in the village hall, little Shirley Culliford had astonished everyone by her blossoming as Festival Queen, and the games and teas in Ted Tozer's field had been enjoyed by everyone.

'To my mind,' Ted Tozer said now, 'us'd be best to take things a bit quiet this year. Last year was a big effort, right in the middle of harvest and all, and if we'm going to make a splash for the Coronation next year, it don't make no sort of sense to do anything too much this year. Anyway, 'tidden fitting, not with the King still warm in his grave.'

'That won't be the case by summer, though,' Joyce Warren

pointed out. She was the wife of a Tavistock solicitor and had her finger in most of the village pies. 'With all respect, we don't have to be in mourning for the whole year. I'm sure there are lots of people who will want the usual village events – the Summer Fair, the Flower Show and so on.'

'I'm not saying nothing about those,' Ted said. 'They always goes on. I'm just saying, us didn't ought to be breaking our backs over nothing special.'

Miss Kemp, the headmistress of the village school, nodded.

'I'm inclined to agree with Mr Tozer,' she said. 'We're bound to want to do something special next year. I suggest that we confine ourselves to the usual annual events such as those Mrs Warren has already mentioned. Next year's obviously going to be a busy one, and we ought to save our energies for that.'

Joyce Warren looked put out. 'But it does seem a shame not to follow up last year's success. Quite a lot of people came to the village especially for the fair, you know. It brought in a good deal of extra money.'

'And I'm afraid it's money we're going to need,' Basil said apologetically. 'I don't know if any of you have noticed the sounds the church organ's been making just lately?'

The others turned to look at him. His round, cherubic face was pink, and his halo of silver hair seemed to stand out around his head. He glanced down at the papers that lay on the table before him and shuffled them awkwardly.

'It seems all right to me,' George Sweet said dubiously, but since he was well known for being tone-deaf nobody took any notice. Ted, who had a fine baritone voice and would have been in the choir if he weren't already captain of the bellringers, nodded.

'I have, Vicar, now you mention it. I was going to say something to Edie Pettifer about it, as a matter of fact. I wondered if a mouse or summat had got stuck in one of the pipes.'

'I think it's worse than that,' Basil said. 'It's a very old instrument, you know, and probably needs a thorough overhaul. And heaven knows what expense that might involve.'

'Once you starts to look at things like that, you don't know what you might find,' Ted agreed. 'I remember when our thresher went wrong, right in the middle of—'

'Well, never mind that,' Joyce said impatiently. 'It's the organ we seem to be discussing now, not your thresher. Do you really think it needs attention, Vicar? Have you taken advice, for instance?' Her tone made it clear that she didn't think his opinion would carry much weight without the back-up of a professional opinion.

'Not yet,' he admitted. 'I thought I should apprise the Parish Council of it first. The Parochial Church Council has already discussed it, of course. We had a little meeting last night –' he glanced at Ted Tozer, who hadn't been present '– and agreed that it should be brought up here as well.'

'I'm sorry I weren't there, Vicar,' Ted began. 'I had a problem with one of my cows, as young Jackie would have told you when I sent her round with a message.'

'Oh, I know, that's quite understood,' the vicar said hastily. 'I didn't mean to reproach you in any way. I would have let you know before, but I've been busy myself and—'

'Be that as it may,' Joyce interrupted, 'I'm not sure why you think it's a parish matter anyway, Vicar. St Andrew's isn't the only church in the village, after all – there's the Methodist Chapel and the Baptist. I think they'd have something to say if the Summer Fair were only to raise money for the church organ.'

'Don't you think that's a rather narrow point of view?' Charles Latimer suggested mildly. As chairman, he was generally content to let discussions take their course until he felt it time for an intervention. 'We raised quite a substantial amount for the chapel roof not so long ago. This has always been a village where we all pull together, after all.'

'Up to a point, yes,' said Joyce, who had clearly forgotten the chapel roof but didn't want to admit it. 'And I suppose it would be all right to give *some* of the proceeds to the church organ. So long as the rest goes to other village causes.'

'Exactly,' Dr Latimer said, and the others nodded their agreement. 'Just as we've done in the past . . . In any case, there's nothing we can do until the vicar has taken the appropriate advice and knows just how serious the problem is and what will have to be done. As Ted says, once you look into these things, you can find all kinds of problems, and church organs are expensive items. I'm sure everyone in the village, whatever their persuasion, would be willing to contribute. It will probably take us a year or two at least to raise the money.'

'Anyway,' said Bert Foster, speaking for the first time, 'most folk who comes to the fair don't care what the money goes to so long as they has a good time.'

Joyce opened her mouth to say that this was not the point, but Charles Latimer was already moving on to the next item on the agenda – the men's lavatory at the village hall. Since this was a perennial point of discussion and had never yet been satisfactorily resolved, everyone settled back for another ten minutes of tedious argument.

The meeting was over at last and they all filed out into the dark February night. Joyce Warren fell into step beside Miss Kemp.

'Quite a good meeting, don't you think? The Summer Fair as usual and the Flower and Produce Show to look forward to as well as all your usual school events. And I dare say the bellringers will be putting on a competition.' She sighed a little. Living not far from the church, she was well aware of the amount of use the bells received and usually tried to be out of the village on competition days, when the ringing went on all day long. 'What do *you* think about raising money for the church organ, Miss Kemp?'

'I think it's essential,' the head teacher said promptly. 'It's a lovely organ, with a beautiful tone, and Miss Pettifer plays it so well. It would be a tragedy if we lost it.'

'Oh, I quite agree,' Joyce said hastily. 'As a regular churchgoer myself, I'm sure I appreciate the organ as much as anyone else. But I'm not convinced that the villagers will all agree. I know money went towards the chapel roof, but that was something that had to be done to stop the building deteriorating. It would have become an eyesore in no time and affected everybody. I don't know if the chapel people, for instance, will feel the same about a musical instrument they never hear.'

'We'll find out soon enough,' Miss Kemp said peaceably. 'I don't think it's urgent at the moment, anyway, although it would certainly be a good thing to have any repairs done in time for it to be at its best for the Coronation. I think there are vague plans for a music festival as part of the celebrations.'

'*Are* there?' Joyce asked in an outraged tone. '*I've* heard nothing about them! And I thought we weren't supposed to be thinking about next year, just yet.'

'No, we're not,' Miss Kemp said hastily. 'And they're really very vague – I may have got the wrong idea entirely.' In fact, she had been in the vicar's drawing-room only the night before, when she, the vicar and his wife, Charles Latimer and Gilbert Napier had been enjoying a glass of sherry after the meeting of the Parochial Council. Without actually conspiring to keep their ideas secret from the busy WI president, and organiser of both the Bridge Club and the Gardening Club (all in the person of Joyce Warren), there had been a tacit agreement that the less said, the better, at least for the time being. Gilbert Napier, indeed, had gone so far as to say that it would be a good thing if that interfering old busybody could be kept completely out of it.

'She doesn't know a quaver from a roll on the drums,' he'd declared. 'Let her organise the roses and marrows, and keep away from the music.'

'Can I rely on you to help me with some kind of dramatic production with the children for the fair?' Miss Kemp asked now, ruefully discarding her earlier resolution not to let Joyce anywhere near her own plans but realising she had to do something to distract the other woman's attention. 'Last year's pageant was such a success.'

Joyce Warren's voice softened. 'But of course. I shall be delighted. We must get together and discuss what we're to do. I've always had a fancy for putting on some Shakespeare. That lovely scene from *A Midsummer Night's Dream*, for instance, with the fairies . . .'

Miss Kemp opened her mouth to say that she thought Shakespeare might be a little beyond her charges, and then closed it again. 'Actually, that's not a bad idea. Not a bad idea at all. There's a lot of comedy in that, and some nice parts for the boys as well.' Her enthusiasm grew, and as they stopped to go their separate ways, she turned to look into Joyce's face, pale and round in the moonlight. 'Yes, we'll think about it. Thank you, Mrs Warren.'

If it had been less dark, she might have seen the blush of pleasure that suffused the pale face. Joyce Warren wasn't accustomed to enthusiasm for her ideas. Not that she ever allowed any lack of it to dissuade her; she had enough enthusiasm of her own for the rest of the villagers put together.

Still, it was pleasant to hear that note in the headmistress's voice, and the pleasure warmed her all the way home.

The brightest spot on Stella Simmons's horizon these days was the prospect of a visit from her sister, Muriel, whom she was now learning to call Maddy.

'It still seems funny, thinking of her by a different name,' she told Dottie Friend as they sat by the fire one evening. Dottie was knitting a dark blue balaclava for Felix Copley, the young curate, who had acquired an elderly sports car, which he had named Mirabelle and drove with the hood down all the time unless it was actually raining. Dottie had stopped to admire it one day, and he'd told her his grandfather had given it to him for Christmas and he loved it, but his ears got very cold, and Dottie had immediately made up her mind to do something about it.

While Dottie knitted, Stella was working on her lessons for the next day, and Dottie's cat, Alfred, who had feasted on bread soaked in the juice of two leftover pilchards for his tea, was slumbering on the rug like a shaggy black cushion. 'I suppose Madelaine is a more glamorous name than Muriel, but I feel sad that she isn't still called by the name our mother and father chose for her. But she doesn't want to go back to it. She's too used to being Maddy now.'

'It don't really matter what name we call her,' Dottie said comfortably. 'She's a sweet little maid whatever her name be. It'll be good to have her here again for Easter. Not long now.'

'Nearly eight weeks,' Stella said. 'It seems a long time to me! It's that long since Christmas, and that seems ages ago.'

'Spring's on its way, though,' Dottie said, reaching for another ball of wool. 'There's snowdrops out down by the ford – have you seen them? And the primroses'll be along soon after, and the hedges will start to green up a bit, too. And tomorrow's St Valentine's Day, and you know what they say about that.'

'They say a lot of things about St Valentine's Day,' Stella said with a smile, and Dottie laughed.

'You don't have to tell me that, maid! But what I had in mind was the one about birds finding their mates that day. Seen it myself, I have – little bluetits fluttering about, flirting with each other, pretty as you like. And there's a bit of nest-building going on already. I saw a magpie fly over only this morning with a girt big stick in his beak.'

'I hope you said good morning to him, then,' Stella, said, joining in with her own bit of folklore. 'I wouldn't like to think he was one for sorrow.'

Dottie laughed again. 'And how many Valentines d'you reckon will come popping through the door for you?'

'Me? Oh, I shan't get any Valentines,' Stella said at once. 'I've only ever had one and that was in the home – one of the boys sent it for a joke.' She thought a little wistfully of Luke Ferris, whom she'd begun to grow fond of a year ago. 'I don't think many men are interested in country schoolteachers.'

'Now, that's just silly. I know Miss Kemp's never been married, but I don't think it's for want of chances. She were engaged once, so I heard tell, but the chap died in the First World War. That were a cruel time for women, you know – so many of them lost their menfolk, and there just weren't enough to go round when it were all over. But you'm a pretty girl, Stella, and there's plenty of time for you to find a nice young man. I dare say there's more than one in this very village interested in you, only they'm too shy to say so.'

'Well, we won't get very far at that rate,' Stella said with a laugh. 'But honestly, Dottie, I'm quite happy as I am, living here with you and Alfred and getting to know the children and the rest of the village.'

'You've settled in real well.' Dottie nodded. 'And young Maddy turning out to be your sister has helped a lot. Folk are proper fond of her.'

'I know.' Stella gazed into the fire thoughtfully. Finding her sister again after so many years had seemed like a miracle, but she couldn't help realising that those years had had an effect on them both. They had lived such different lives – herself in an orphanage, Maddy adopted by a famous actress – that getting to know each other, once they'd gone through the initial stage of shared reminiscences, had proved more difficult than she'd expected. If only they could have spent more time together . . . but Maddy had gone away with her adopted mother almost as soon as they'd first met again, and had only managed a few days in October and then a week or so after Christmas. It seemed as if Stella's dream of being as close to her as they'd been in childhood was doomed to disappointment.

'It's early days yet,' Dottie said, guessing what was on her mind. 'It takes a long time to catch up on missed years. Why, it even took me a while to settle down again after I'd been in London all those years with Miss Forsyth. It was a bit different living there than down here in Devon, I can tell you. But I know Maddy's as pleased to have you back as you are to have her. All you need is a bit of time together, to catch up.'

'Which is what we don't seem to be able to have,' Stella said. 'A week or two at Christmas and then again at Easter – it's just not long enough to get to know each other. We have to start all over again every time.'

'Well, perhaps her'll come down for longer in the summer, when you have your long holiday. Or you could go away together. I dare say she'd be pleased to have you with her if Miss Forsyth goes abroad again.'

'Miss Forsyth might not be so pleased, though,' Stella observed. Fenella Forsyth was the actress who had adopted Maddy, believing her to be alone in the world, and although she'd been very gracious and welcoming towards Stella, the young schoolteacher had been very aware of the gulf between their worlds and the fact that both felt an equal claim on Maddy's attention.

'It'll all come out in the wash,' Dottie observed, casting off her stitches. 'There, that's done. I'll just sew it up, and maybe you could pop it round to Aggie Madge's on your way to school in the morning. 'Tidden far out of your way. Curate'll be wanting it in this cold weather.'

'All right.' Stella had almost finished her work. 'How about a game of crib when you've done that?'

'That'll be nice, maid.' Dottie sewed industriously for a few minutes and then held up the completed garment. 'That should keep his ears cosy. He's a nice young man, Mr Copley. We've got to look after him.'

Stella smiled. Dottie, who worked as a barmaid as well as helping at the Barton and standing in for Mrs Dawe, the school cook, when she had one of her attacks of bronchitis, seemed to look after most of the village at one time or another. She had often wondered why the plump, comfortable woman had never married; she seemed cut out to be a wife and mother.

Perhaps she was another of those women who had lost a sweetheart in the First World War. There must be so many similarly tragic stories from that time, she thought as she put away her work and fetched the cribbage board and cards. Just as there were, in her own experience, from the Second.

Even now, there was a war raging on the other side of the world, in Korea, and young men like Roy Pettifer fighting it. If only this could be the year when all the conflict might come to an end and the world find peace at last.

Felix Copley was just finishing his breakfast at Aggie Madge's cottage when Stella arrived with the balaclava. He took it out of the paper bag with delight and immediately tried it on.

'That's marvellous! I'll be warm as toast. How do I look?'

'Like a bank robber,' Stella said with a laugh. 'Or Biggles when you've got your goggles on. But I don't suppose that'll matter. You'd better take it off when you visit your parishioners, though.'

He pulled the helmet off and his fair hair stuck out all round his head. Stella smiled at him. The young curate had arrived in Burracombe at more or less the same time as herself and they'd shared a sense of fellow feeling. But Felix had become friendly with Hilary Napier, and Stella had begun to search for her sister, with Luke Ferris's help, so their friendship hadn't progressed. Perhaps now, with Luke engaged to Val Tozer and Hilary occupied with managing the estate, they would find themselves thrown together a little more.

Felix was looking at her oddly. She felt herself colour, and then her blush deepened as he said, 'D'you realise, you must be my Valentine!' He saw her embarrassment and added hastily, 'It's all right, I'm only joking. Only, you know what they say – the first person you see on St Valentine's Day and all that!'

'I didn't think clergymen were supposed to be superstitious,' Stella said, rather more tartly than she'd meant to, but Felix just grinned.

'Is it a superstition when it's applied to a saint? I suppose it is, really – but it's a nice one, isn't it? And I must admit I'd rather it was you than, say, Mrs Warren. Or even Miss Bellamy!' They both laughed, and Stella made a move towards the door.

'I'd better be going. It's nearly time for school.'

'Yes, of course. And thank you for bringing this in.' He picked up the balaclava again. 'Dottie really is a treasure. You're quite comfortable, living in her cottage, are you?'

'Oh yes. She's so kind; she looks after me like a mother.' Stella looked around the living-room, not so very different from Dottie's own. 'You seem snug enough here, too.'

'I am. Aggie's a wonderful landlady. And a very good cook.' He lowered his voice conspiratorially. 'But she can't knit balaclavas!'

Stella laughed again. 'Dottie can knit anything. Jumpers, cardigans, socks, toys – you must have seen her work at church bazaars. In fact, when I first saw her cat, I thought she'd knitted him! He looks exactly like a woolly cushion when he's asleep.' Feeling more at ease now that they were off the subject of Valentines, she opened the door and an icy draught swept in. 'Brr, it's cold out there. I'll shut the door quickly. Goodbye, Felix.'

'Goodbye,' he said. 'And thank you again for bringing the balaclava round for me.'

He moved over to the window and watched Stella step away along the village street. Her dark hair was covered by a scarlet beret, and her blue coat swung round her slim figure. Her hands were encased in warm gloves, exactly the same shade as her hat and probably knitted by Dottie.

He watched until she was out of sight and then returned to the breakfast table. The balaclava lay on the back of the armchair, and he glanced at it once or twice. I must go and thank Dottie properly, he thought. Perhaps later on, around teatime. Stella would be back from school by then . . .

Chapter Five

The stranger came to the village again at the beginning of March.

Once again, she made her way to the church, but this time there was no one there. She opened the door and slipped into the dim interior, moving slowly between the pews, trying to make out the lettering on the tablets that adorned the walls. 'An Excellent Gentleman in All Respects . . .' 'A Virtuous and Faithful Wife, Most Loving and Affectionate Mother to Her Eight Children . . .' 'A Most Beloved Squire . . .' The village seemed to have been filled with illustrious inhabitants, or perhaps it was just that they were the only ones who had memorials erected to them. Or maybe because you only spoke good of the dead, especially on church tablets.

For a few minutes, she explored the church, looking at the worn, faded hassocks and standing at the chancel steps to raise her eyes to the stained-glass window behind the altar. The centre panel depicted the church's patron saint, St Andrew, standing with his cross held before his body. The colours were rich and deep, a blue robe picked out in crimson, with a paler blue sky behind, and the saint's halo shining with golden light as the sun poured through.

The dank chill of February had been replaced, first by blustery March winds and then a softer calm, with no more than a few drifting clouds and a hint of warmth in the pale sunshine. The snowdrops sprinkled along the Devon banks like icing on a cake were already beginning to give way to a golden cloak of primroses and wild daffodils, and birds chased each other from branch to branch. The hedgerows were dripping with yellow catkins, like a shower of golden rain, and there were even a few early lambs in the more sheltered fields.

The woman laid her hand on the ancient stonework as she peered through the squint, through which congregations in the smaller north wing of the church could have seen the Elevation of the Host in bygone days, when the church was Roman Catholic. She looked up at the pulpit, touched the polished wood of the lectern with her fingertips, then moved again to the back of the church to examine the old stone font, plain and uncarved, in which so many babies of the parish had been baptised. Lastly, she sat down in one of the pews.

Basil Harvey found her there when he came in about fifteen minutes later. He saw her at once, her back straight as she gazed towards the east window, and hesitated, not wishing to disturb her contemplation. But as he closed the door softly behind him, she turned and he saw that she was the person who had come to the church the day the King had died. He moved nearer.

'Good morning. We've met before, haven't we? It's good to see you here again.'

She nodded. 'I came about a month ago. I was looking . . .' She paused, as if searching for words. 'I wondered . . .'

'Is there something you want to know?' Basil asked. 'Something about the church? Or the village, perhaps?'

She looked at him, as if wishing he could read her mind. Once again, he was struck by the luminous quality of her grey eyes, fringed by their thick, dark lashes. Her chestnut hair gleamed in the sunlight that filtered through the coloured glass, and her face had a soft, creamy pallor. She wore a light grey coat with a blue scarf tucked into the neck.

'If there's anything I can do . . .' he suggested gently, and saw her chew her lip, as if trying to make up her mind, or perhaps to pluck up courage. Not wanting to press her, he half turned away. 'Shall I leave you in peace for a while? I'll be in the vestry if you need me.'

As he turned, she made a small gesture, quickly withdrawn, as if to ask him to stay. As before, he had a sense that she was troubled in some way, and felt convinced that she had come to the church for a reason and wanted to ask his help. Yet something was holding her back, and he knew that if he made the wrong move he might frighten her away completely. Whatever it was, he must tread delicately.

'You know that you can talk to me in complete confidence,' he said quietly and waited, still half turned.

'It's just—' she began and then caught herself, frowning a little as if inwardly scolding herself. 'It sounds so silly. But I think I might come from here.'

Basil considered her words, several ideas as to what she might mean passing through his mind. He waited for a moment, and she went on, her voice stumbling a little as the words tumbled out, in a hurry now to be spoken.

'I've never *lived* here, I don't mean that. I'd never even *been* here until that day – when the King died. But I think my – my parents came from here. I was wondering if – if I could find out. If anyone would know.'

'It's quite possible,' he said, sitting down beside her. 'What were their names? And when did they move away?'

The woman's eyes fell, and she stared at her hands, clasped together in her lap. She didn't answer for a moment, and then she said, 'Well, that's just it, you see, Vicar. They didn't move away. At least, my mother did. I don't really know whether my father did or not.' She looked up at him again. 'They weren't married, you see.'

'Ah.' He thought for a moment, then asked, 'Do you know his name?'

'No. I don't know who he was. I only know that he had the same initial as me. I found a piece of paper.' She felt in her coat pocket and handed it to him. It was cheap lined writing-paper, yellowing with age, with a few words written on it in the copperplate hand that all children had learned during the early part of the century. It was obviously the end of a letter and was signed 'J'.

'J. That could be any number of names,' Basil said thoughtfully. 'John, James, Jeremy . . . And this is the only clue you have?' She nodded. 'And has your mother never told you any more?'

'My mother never mentioned him at all,' she said. 'I didn't even know I had a different father until a few weeks ago, when she died and I looked through her papers. She married, you see, when I was two years old. I've got two younger sisters – I always thought I was just the eldest of the family. And our father – *their* father – died in the war. So there's nobody to ask at all.'

'I see. And you want to find your real father.' He paused again, wondering how best to deal with the situation. 'You realise he might not want to be found?'

'But I wouldn't actually need to tell him, would I? I'd just like to *know*, that's all. I'd like to see him – to be able to think of him and my mother. Like other people can think of their parents together.'

Basil looked at her. He judged her to be in her early or mid-thirties. There were no rings on her twisting fingers, and she was neatly but plainly dressed. He guessed that the family had not had an easy time and wondered if she might be hoping to find a father who was well off. But she didn't strike him as mercenary.

'Perhaps it would be better if we went across to the vicarage to talk about this,' he suggested. 'That's if you'd like to. It's rather public in the church – anyone might come in. And I have the parish records there as well, if you want to look at them.'

The woman didn't answer immediately. She stared down at

her hands. Then a sound from outside caused her to raise her head again, and she nodded.

'Yes, please. I'd like that – if you've got time.' Uncertainty crept into her eyes. 'You must be very busy – perhaps it would be better if I came back another day.'

'No, not at all.' He didn't want her to go away again, rebuffed for a second time. 'I can always find something to do, of course – what vicar can't? – but I can also always find time for someone who needs my help. That's the most important part of my job.' He smiled at her and got to his feet. 'It's only a few steps across the churchyard, and I wouldn't be surprised if my wife isn't making some coffee at this very moment. I can offer you refreshment, and we'll be quite private in my study.' He held out his hand. 'My name's Basil Harvey, by the way.'

The woman stood up as well and took his hand. Her grave, pale face softened as she smiled back, and a glow lit her luminous grey eyes.

'If you're sure you don't mind, then . . . And my name's Jennifer Tucker. That was my mother's married name – Tucker.'

'I see. Well, it's a pleasure to meet you, Miss Tucker, and I hope I can help you.' He ushered her towards the door and opened it for her. Outside, the sun was flooding the churchyard and the sound of birdsong filled the air. One or two people were crossing the green; Alf Coker was standing at the door of his forge, and he could see Jacob Prout wheeling his barrow towards Constance Bellamy's house.

He hoped that he was not about to uncover a family tragedy, or some old secret best left untold. But that was not for him to judge, he thought a little ruefully. He could only assist Jennifer Tucker with her quest, counsel her if she requested it, and hope that she dealt with her discoveries – if she made any – with wisdom.

He guided her across the churchyard to the gate that led to the vicarage garden.

*

Alice Tozer had just come out of the post office, her shopping-basket over one arm, when she saw the vicar leading his visitor across the churchyard. She paused, visited by a fleeting sense of familiarity, of *déjà vu*, as if the little scene had taken place before. She almost felt, for a moment, as if she knew exactly what would happen next.

Then the two figures were gone, and she shook herself and rubbed her eyes with her free hand. You'm getting fanciful, she told herself. Seeing things. Getting old.

She walked along the lane to the farm track and through the yard. Ted and Tom were both out in the fields somewhere, and Val was at work in Tavistock Hospital. Joanna had taken Robin over the river to Little Burracombe to visit her friend, so only Minnie was at home, preparing the vegetables for their midday meal. She turned as Alice came through the back door, her birdlike eyes bright.

'What's the matter with you, maid? Look as if you've seen a ghost.'

'I feel as if I have.' Alice set her basket on the kitchen table and began to unpack it. She shivered suddenly and said, 'Goose walking over my grave.'

'Why, what's happened?' Minnie dried her hands on a tea-towel, looking concerned, but Alice smiled and shook her head.

'Nothing's happened, Mother. It's just that I saw someone in the churchyard with the vicar and for a minute it took me back—' She stopped, frowning a little. 'The funny thing is, I don't really know *where* it took me back! It was like that feeling you get sometimes, as if it's all happened before, you know? It's gone before you can get hold of it, like a shred of gossamer.'

'Who was it, then?' Minnie tipped some peeled potatoes into a saucepan of water. 'You'll have to lift these over for me, my flower – the pan's too heavy for me.'

'I don't know who it was, that's the funny thing. Not

someone from the village, I can tell you that. But I have seen her before – at least, I think I have.' Alice paused, thinking. 'There was a young woman came into the church the day the King died. She spoke to us then, but she seemed upset – well, us all were – and went straight off to catch the bus. I only saw her back view today, but I think it was the same one.'

'Come to see the vicar, you reckon?' Minnie started to take the outer leaves from a large cabbage. 'Wonder what that be about. But I don't see why it should give you a funny turn, Alice.'

'Neither do I,' Alice said thoughtfully. 'But it was the same feeling as I got the first time I saw her. As if there were something about her – something I ought to know.' She stood staring at the groceries on the table, her brows drawn down, and her lips folded inwards over her teeth. Then she shrugged her shoulders and chided herself again. 'No. There's nothing – nothing I can put my finger on, anyway. Getting fanciful, that's all it is.'

'It's spring,' her mother-in-law said, giving her a nudge. 'Getting your blood up. It gives people all sorts of funny ideas, spring does.'

Alice gave her a dry look. 'Yes, maybe it does. But I'd have thought I was old enough to know better.'

'Go on!' Minnie said. 'You'm not old. You wait till you're eighty-four, like me, then you'll be able to think about getting old. Only *think* about it, mind – I've still got a few years left in me yet, and so have you. Plenty of time for us both to get funny ideas!'

They laughed together, and Alice began to put away the groceries. By the time the water was boiling for the cabbage, they had both forgotten all about the stranger in the churchyard.

Chapter Six

Since calling round to Dottie's cottage to thank her for the balaclava, Felix had dropped in again two or three times, usually late in the afternoon when Stella had come home from school. There was usually a tray of scones or biscuits coming out of the oven just about then, and a pot of tea brewing. Dottie welcomed him with her usual comfortable smile, and the three of them would settle down to tea and a gossip about village affairs.

'Mrs Warren seems to have got plans for the village fair under way already,' Felix observed, spreading a scone with some of Dottie's blackcurrant jam. 'She's a very energetic lady, isn't she?'

'That's one way of putting it,' Dottie replied dryly. 'Busy as a bee, that one is, and got her finger in all the village pies. Still, someone has to do the work, and she don't seem to mind badgering others to pull their weight.'

'Has anything happened about the organ yet?' Stella enquired. 'I saw someone coming out of the church with Mr Harvey the other day – I wondered if it was the person he was getting to examine it and say what was wrong.'

Dottie shook her head. 'No, that were a young woman, at least if you mean the one I saw last week. They went through the churchyard towards the vicarage. Alice Tozer saw her, too.'

'I suppose they might send a woman to look at the organ,'

Felix said doubtfully. 'Women do play church organs quite a lot, after all.'

'I don't see why it shouldn't be a woman,' Stella said. 'Women are perfectly capable of looking at church organs.'

'It could be pretty heavy work—' Felix began, but it was Dottie who interrupted him this time.

'So's rolling out beer barrels, but that don't stop Bernie Nethercott leaving it to me to do round at the Bell. And women did all sorts of men's jobs during the war.'

'All right!' Felix exclaimed, holding up his hands. 'I give in! Of *course* a woman could advise on what needs doing to the church organ, but I don't think anyone's been to look at it yet. I don't know who it was who came to see Mr Harvey last week, but I'm sure that wasn't why she came.'

'Didn't he tell you about her, then?' Dottie asked innocently, and he gave her what she termed an 'old-fashioned' look.

'Now, you know I can't discuss that, Dottie. Anyway, he didn't.' He turned towards Stella. 'What I can discuss is the new film they're showing in Tavistock next week. I wondered if you were thinking of going to see it.'

'I'd like to,' Stella said, 'but it's getting there and back that's the problem. I could catch a bus, but I don't like walking back from the main road in the dark.'

'Well, why don't we go together?' he suggested, and she looked at him in surprise.

'In your car, you mean?'

'Of course. Or we could go on the bus, if you'd rather – so long as you don't mind walking in the dark with me!'

Stella laughed. 'Oh, I think I'd feel safe enough with you. Well – yes – that would be very nice. Thank you. Which evening were you thinking of?'

'What about Thursday?' he asked, and she nodded. 'We'll make it a date, then. We'll sort out a time later on – I'll drop in again one day.' He glanced at Dottie, who was watching them both with a smile on her face. 'That's if it's all right with you, Dottie. I don't want to take advantage of your hospitality.'

'Bless your heart, my handsome, 'tis no trouble to give you a cup of tea and a bite to eat,' she said. 'I know Aggie Madge feeds you proper, but a young chap like you, out and about all the time, needs regular feeding, 'specially in this cold weather. You'm always welcome to pop in here of an afternoon.'

'You've got a heart of gold,' he said. 'But then, so have so many people in Burracombe. This is the friendliest village I've ever known.'

'We're not a bad lot,' Dottie said. 'Most of us, anyway. There's one or two I could mention who could do with a few lessons in manners, but every village has got a few like that. Arthur Culliford, for one – how that poor wife of his puts up with him, I do not know. Not that she's all that much better herself, and those boys of theirs are turning into proper little hooligans. And then there's Jed Fisher, but he's always been a bad-tempered old misery, and his cottage is nothing but a slum.'

'Unfortunately, I can't offer him much comfort,' Felix said regretfully. 'He's Chapel and we can't interfere.'

'It's not comfort he needs!' Dottie retorted. 'It's fumigating!'

The other two laughed, but Felix shook his head as well. 'There must be some reason why he's always miserable. Perhaps he had a bad time in the First World War. Has he always lived alone? Was he ever married?'

Dottie shook her head. 'No girl in her senses would ever have taken Jed Fisher. Though he weren't bad-looking as a young chap, believe it or not. And it weren't his war experiences, neither, not like with some poor fellows who came back with shell-shock and weren't never the same again. Jed Fisher never went to war at all. Got exemption on account of some medical condition, though you'd never have knowed there was anything wrong, while others went off and did his fighting for him. You can see some of their names on the war memorial on the green.' Her voice was suddenly edged with bitterness and Stella remembered how she had wondered if Dottie had been one of those who had lost her sweetheart during that war. 'No, Jed's just that sort and there's nothing anyone can do about it. You can be thankful he'm Methodist, Mr Copley, and no burden of yours.'

Felix smiled. 'I'm sure he's in good hands, anyway, Dottie. The Methodist minister is a good man.' He finished his tea and rose to his feet, stooping slightly under the low ceiling. 'Thank you very much for the tea and scones. I still feel guilty at taking so much of your rations. I'll bring you something in return, next time I come.'

'Go on with you,' the countrywoman said, fetching his coat from where she had hung it behind the door. 'A cup of tea and a scone don't leave the cupboard bare. Mind, you'd think all this rationing would have come to an end by now – who'd have thought us'd still be using coupons nearly seven years after the war finished? At least we'm better favoured out here in the country – we can have a few eggs and a drop of milk and that sort of thing. What it can be like in the towns, I don't hardly like to think.'

Felix departed, promising to call by and make arrangements with Stella for their trip to the cinema the following week, and Dottie began to bustle about clearing away the teacups and making preparations for their supper, smiling to herself as she did so.

Stella gave her a sideways glance. 'What are you laughing at?'

'Oh, nothing. I'm just pleased to see you going out with a young man, that's all.'

'I'm not "going out with a young man"!' Stella exclaimed. 'Not the way you mean, anyway. I'm just going to the pictures with Felix, that's all. It's very kind of him to suggest it, knowing I don't like walking along that road in the dark.'

'If you think that's all it is,' Dottie said, 'you'll believe anything, my dear.'

'Dottie, he's the *curate*.'

'He's a man,' Dottie said. 'A healthy young man. Just because he's a clergyman don't make no difference to that. They're just the same as any other man. Except for Catholics, of course,' she added thoughtfully. 'They're not allowed to be the same. But Mr Copley's not Catholic, he's Church of England, so you don't have to worry about that. And a very nice young chap he is, too,' she added. 'You don't have no call to worry about him not behaving hisself.'

'I'm not,' Stella said with dignity, unpacking her school bag. 'And there's nothing like that in it, nothing at all. We're just going to the pictures together because it's a convenient evening for us both and it's nice to go in company. That's all.'

Dottie's lips twitched, but she said no more. Instead, she went out to the kitchen and began to scrub potatoes. After a little while, she began to sing to herself, and Stella, recognising the tune of 'I'll Take You Home Again, Kathleen', sighed and shook her head.

'And my name's *not* Kathleen!' she called, laughing.

Felix walked back to his lodgings, thinking how pleasant it was to have the evenings drawing out. It was light now until six o'clock; in a few weeks, when the clocks went forward for Summer Time, it would be light until after seven, and from then on the days would lengthen until darkness wasn't falling until after ten.

There could be disadvantages to this, of course. Stella Simmons wouldn't be afraid to walk along the mile of road from the main bus stop to the village and wouldn't need an escort from an evening out at the cinema. But by then, perhaps they would have made a habit of such weekly outings.

Felix had liked the young schoolteacher from their first meeting, soon after they'd both arrived in Burracombe, and they'd met at various village events, but he had been attracted by Hilary Napier, too, and it wasn't until she'd gently turned down his proposal of marriage that he'd really begun to see Stella as a possible companion. He'd also been aware that she and Luke Ferris were spending a lot of time together, although it wasn't until later that he'd realised that Luke's interest lay with Val Tozer.

Being a young clergyman made it difficult to make female friendships. You had to be so careful, especially with parishioners. But Felix liked women's company and wanted someone special in his life. He wanted, eventually, to marry and have the kind of home life that Basil Harvey had, with a wife and family.

Aggie Madge's cottage stood almost opposite the pair occupied by Jed Fisher and Jacob Prout. As Felix came closer, he saw that Jacob was in his front garden, cutting down some bushy twigs.

'They're rather nice,' Felix said, stopping. 'A lovely red colour. Why are you cutting them down? Don't you like them?'

'Won't get no colour next winter if I don't,' Jacob said, snipping another crimson twig off at the base. 'Dogwoods, these be, and you only gets the colour on the young wood. They'll soon grow up again, you don't need to worry about that.' He straightened up and gathered the twigs into a bundle. 'Doctor's wife likes a few of these in a pot in her hallway. I said I'd pass some on to the vicar's wife, too. They makes a pretty decoration.'

'Yes, I've seen them, now you mention it. I thought they were artificial. I'm not much of a gardener, I'm afraid,' Felix said apologetically, catching Jacob's look. 'Mrs Madge asked me to help her last summer, but I pulled up more plants than weeds.'

'Ah, well, there be a secret to that,' Jacob said solemnly. 'Weeds be the ones that are hard to pull out.' He waited a moment while Felix worked this out, then jerked his head towards the fence separating his garden from Jed Fisher's. 'You could do your apprenticeship on that mess next door. Wouldn't matter what you pulled out there, it's all weeds.'

'It does look rather untidy,' Felix agreed, looking at the blackened, soggy mass of last year's foliage. Jacob snorted.

'Untidy! That's all nettles and ground elder and convulsions, and God knows what else – pardon my language, but He'm the only one who does know what's there. Not that weeding would make much difference. Wants a good digging over and all the roots pulling out and a cartload of muck put in before you could grow anything in there. And it used to be a nice little patch, too, full of colour in the summer. Crying shame it is, letting it run wild like that.'

'Well, we can't all be good gardeners like you,' Felix said diplomatically, but Jacob snorted again.

'Us can all keep our own place tidy. 'Tidden much to ask, is it – little bit of ground like this? 'Tis a responsibility to the Good Lord's earth, that's what I say. But there, some folk are nothing more than heathens, and that's the top and bottom of it.'

'I don't think you ought—' Felix was beginning, when the door of the other cottage flew open and Jed Fisher's face appeared, red and angry under his thatch of straggly grey hair.

'What be you two staring at? You been standing there for the past ten minutes looking in at my bit of ground and chewing the fat – what's it all about, eh?'

'Why, nothing, Mr Fisher,' Felix said hastily, taking a step back, but Jacob was made of sterner stuff.

'We'm allowed to look where us likes. It's a free country, or 'twas last time I heard. Not that your rubbishy old garden's anything to look at – nothing but an eyesore, that ain't, and Curate agrees with me, don't you, Mr Copley?'

Felix opened his mouth, but Jed was marching down the path, waving his walking-stick, and he took another step back. 'So you *was* looking at my garden, then? I thought so when I looked out of the winder. They'm talking about my patch of ground, I says to meself. I'm not having that. 'Tis my own business what I does with it, so you get back to your own side of the fence, Jacob Prout, and mind your own. As for you, Curate, you can go back to your church. I'm Chapel, I am, and nothing to do with you.'

'Does the minister know that, then?' Jacob asked. 'I'd bet good money he don't see you inside that building from one year's end to the other.'

'I went in at Christmas, for your information!' Jed retorted. 'And I looks after the graveyard, too, same as you do at the church. Anyway, Chapel folk don't bet,' he added, as an afterthought.

'Don't drink neither, from what I hear,' Jacob said. 'Don't stop you propping up the bar at the Bell, though, do it!' He regarded his neighbour thoughtfully and then said, 'I'll say one thing for you, Jed, you got darn good eyesight.'

The other man looked nonplussed for a moment, then said suspiciously, 'What d'you mean by that?'

'Why, being able to see out through your window,' Jacob replied innocently, glancing towards the grimy panes of glass with their piles of newspapers and oddments on the sills inside. 'I wouldn't have thought you could see anything through that filth. Must have X-ray eyes.'

Jed glared at him, his face reddening and his chest swelling with fury. For a moment, Felix was afraid he was about to strike out with his walking-stick. Then, making a sound rather like a car tyre going down suddenly, he turned on his heel and stamped back to his door. As he went inside, he looked back for one parting shot.

''Tis just your way, Jacob Prout, to make nasty remarks when you'm in the wrong. 'Tis just your way. And it ain't a Christian way, neither – I hope you realises that, Curate. I hope you realises just what sort of a man you got looking after your churchyard and digging graves there. Sooner he digs his own grave, the better for us all, that's what I say!'

The door slammed, and Jacob laughed. 'Silly old fool. Always got to have the last word. Always been the same, ever since he were a little tacker. Never did like no one to get the better of him.'

'You've known him a long time?' Felix said, feeling that he ought to try to mend matters.

'Knowed him since he were a babby in his pram. Grew up together, us did, in these two very cottages. His mum and dad and mine were good friends in those days.'

'And didn't you and Jed get on even then?'

'Oh, ah,' Jacob said, turning away. 'Us got on all right as boys.' His voice was terse, as if he didn't want to pursue the subject, and Felix sighed. He glanced towards Jed's window and, seeing the other man's face peering malevolently at them, decided it was probably better to move away. He didn't want Jed complaining to Mr Harvey that the curate was gossiping about him at his own gate.

'I'd better be getting along,' he said, as Jacob began to snip at the last few twigs. 'Mrs Madge will be getting my supper ready, and I've got Sunday's sermon to prepare. Perhaps we can have another talk, sometime.'

'If it's *him* you wants to talk about, you needn't waste your breath,' Jacob said, obviously still ruffled. 'He ain't worth it. I know you might say that's not a Christian way to talk about him, but I've knowed him for the past sixty years and more, and I can tell you this – when the Good Lord told us to love thy neighbour, he didn't live next door to Jed Fisher. *Nobody* could love that man, and there ain't nothing more to say about it. Nothing.'

He loaded his twigs into his barrow and began to push them up the path, too irritated even to wish Felix goodbye. The curate watched him go and then turned away, rather dispirited, towards the cottage across the lane. He could see smoke drifting up from the chimney. Aggie Madge had lit the fire; the front room where he sat in the evening, working, reading, or listening to the radio, would be warm and cosy. It would be clean and tidy – or as tidy as it ever could be with his papers cluttering the table and his books piled on the shelves. Like Jacob Prout's spotlessly kept cottage, it would feel comfortable and homely.

He wondered what it was like inside Jed Fisher's house. He would probably never know, for Jed was unlikely ever to invite him in, but he had been inside other cottages that were poorly kept and had seen and smelled the dirt and the damp of neglect; of rotting plaster walls, scrappy meals and unwashed clothes and bodies. It was a depressing way to live and something he always found hard to come to terms with. He felt sad that, even in this pretty Dartmoor village, there were people who lived in this way.

With a sigh, he opened the gate to Mrs Madge's garden and walked up the path to her door.

Chapter Seven

Basil Harvey was thinking about villages, too.

Not that this was unusual – most of his time was taken up with thinking about villages, and Burracombe in particular. But his thoughts this evening were taken up with the hidden life of a village – the things that went on behind closed doors. The long-held grudges and the family feuds whose cause had been either forgotten or distorted out of all recognition. The secrets that were perhaps never revealed to anyone else and were taken to the grave.

'It was obviously a very loving letter,' he said to his wife as they sat by the window of their drawing-room, having tea. They didn't often get the chance to have tea quietly together – there would either be a parishioner or two with them or Basil would be at one of the farms or cottages. They were now discussing the woman who had come to Burracombe searching for her father. 'It was the end of it – there were only a few lines at the top of the sheet of paper – but it was so fondly expressed. *"With All my Love, my Dearest Girl, from Your Own J."* Nearly every word had a capital letter – the way they used to write in those days.'

'And that would have been when?' Grace asked, pouring him a second cup of tea. 'You think the woman was in her early thirties?'

'Oh yes – she told me she'd been born in June 1917. So she's now coming up to her thirty-fifth birthday.'

'And she knew nothing about this until her mother died?'

'Not a thing, apparently.' He stirred his tea pensively. They had both given up sugar during the war and never used saccharin, but it still didn't seem to taste the same without being stirred. 'She always believed she was the eldest child of a perfectly ordinary family. The father – her stepfather, as it turns out – was in the Navy and lost at sea during the war. Jennifer Tucker herself was in the Wrens and overseas, so couldn't get back, and by the time she came home, both her younger sisters – half-sisters, really – had married as well and left home, and Jennifer went back to live with her mother. Plymouth was still in ruins, of course, but she managed to get work in a shop, and they rented a small house, somewhere in Devonport. She was never very strong – the mother, I mean – and Jennifer looked after her until she went into hospital a few months ago, and eventually died there.'

'What a sad little story,' Grace said after a moment. 'And what about the two sisters? I suppose they know no more than Jennifer does?'

'No, they're both several years younger. Neither of them lives in Plymouth now, so distance is another problem.'

'So she feels rather alone in the world.'

He nodded. 'I think that's why she wants to find out something about her father. She thinks he may still be alive – he'd probably only be about fifty-five or sixty, after all.'

'But would he be pleased to have a long-lost and unknown daughter turning up on his doorstep?' Grace asked dubiously. 'He's probably got a family of his own by now. He may not even have known there was to be a baby all those years ago. She could cause a lot more problems.'

'I know. I discussed this with her. I think she realises all that, and wouldn't want to impose herself on him – but who knows how she would feel once she'd discovered his name? She might be so desperate to have someone of her own that she'd ignore the consequences and make herself known to him.'

'It's a tricky situation,' Grace said thoughtfully. 'How has it been left?'

'Well, she's asked me to make cautious enquiries, and she says she doesn't mind my discussing it with anyone who might know the truth, or who can be relied on to be discreet. The thing is, she doesn't even know for certain which village the man came from – or if her mother lived there, too. She's given me her birth certificate – the shortened form, showing her date of birth, sex and place of registration, which is Plymouth, so there's no help there. And I've also got her mother's marriage certificate to Arthur Tucker, the man Jennifer believed to have been her own father. This does at least give the name of her mother's father, which is Hannaford, and his job. He was a farm labourer.'

'Hannaford . . . Well, it's a Devon name, but I don't know of any in this area, do you? Not in the village, anyway.'

'No, I don't. I've looked through all our records of baptisms and deaths for the period we might be interested in, and there are none mentioned.'

'So doesn't that mean the mother didn't come from Burracombe after all? What makes Miss Tucker think she did?'

'I don't quite know. Certain references – the occasional mention of childhood games, the school she attended, that kind of thing. The odd local name dropped into a conversation – Cuckoo Wood and the Standing Stones in particular. She's looked at the Ordnance Survey maps in some detail, and although this isn't the only village it could be, from the few clues she has, it does seem to be a possibility. And she says that the first time she came here – back in February – she had a feeling that it was the right one. It felt almost familiar to her.'

'But how could it have done? If she'd never been here before . . . ?'

'We don't know that she hadn't,' he pointed out. 'It's quite possible that her mother brought her here when she was a child. She might have been too young to remember in any detail, yet still have a faint memory of it.'

Grace sighed and shook her head. 'I don't know, Basil. It seems an impossible quest to me. I feel sorry for her – she seems to be a lonely person – but I can't really think that it's going to help her, to search for a father who may not be alive now, or who may have a family of his own and not welcome her. That would only leave her feeling all the more hurt and alone. Is she coming back to see you again?'

'Probably. I suggested she leave it for two or three weeks first.'

'Well, when she does, I think you ought to suggest that she try to make her own life from now on. Looking into the past can turn up all kinds of things that are better left alone.'

'I'm inclined to agree, dear, but I can't make her give up, and if she asks my help, I'm duty-bound to give it to her. And if I'm helpful, she may be more likely to take notice of my counsel if we do find out anything.' He picked up the last of Grace's homemade biscuits. 'I thought I might start by talking to Miss Bellamy. She knows everyone for miles around and she would have been in her twenties at the time Jennifer was born – she might remember something. And I can rely on her not to say anything to anyone else.'

Grace held up the teapot, but he shook his head. 'Well, I can see that you feel you have to help, but I have to say I rather hope it all comes to nothing. If the mother's died only recently, this young woman's probably feeling unhappy and unsettled – in a few months' time, she may have thought it over and decided not to search any further. She might even get married herself. It's a little unusual that she hasn't already.'

'Perhaps there was someone in the war,' Basil said. 'So many young men were killed . . . And I rather gathered that the mother was ill for a long time. Jennifer probably didn't have much chance to meet anyone, what with looking after her and working as well. As you say, that may change now that she hasn't got that responsibility any more.' He got to his feet and stood gazing out through the French windows. 'Look at all those little daffodils! They're like a bright patch of sunshine fallen into the garden. A promise of brighter days to come.' He turned to his wife, his round, pink face smiling a little sadly. 'I'd like to think that there will be brighter days for Jennifer Tucker. I really would like to think that.'

There was certainly a promise of brighter days to come at the Tozers' farm, where Joanna and Tom had just announced that there was indeed a new baby on the way.

'I thought so!' Val exclaimed, laughing and kissing her brother and sister-in-law. 'I didn't say anything, but when you went to see Dr Latimer . . . '

'I wondered, too,' Alice agreed, her face flushed with pleasure. 'I said to Mother – didn't I, Mother? – I wouldn't be at all surprised if our Joanna wasn't expecting again.'

'She did,' Minnie confirmed, nodding from her chair by the range. 'And I said I thought so, too. We've just been waiting for you to give the word so we could start knitting.'

'Honestly!' Joanna said, pretending to be exasperated. 'You can't keep anything a secret round here. It seems as if you all knew even before we did.'

'Well, we'm not farmers for nothing,' Alice remarked. 'And with our Val being a nurse as well . . . Did you hear that, Jackie?' she asked as her younger daughter came through the back door. 'You'm going to be an auntie again.'

'Am I?' Jackie looked at her sister-in-law. 'When?'

'Not until September. Plenty of time for all that knitting,' Joanna replied, giving Minnie a smile. 'And we've still got lots of Robin's things, anyway, so we won't need all that much.'

'But they'm blue!' Minnie said, outraged. 'Supposing it's a girl.'

'That's something we won't know until the day it arrives. We're not going through all that palaver with a wedding-ring again.' At Minnie's insistence, while Joanna was expecting Robin, the women had conducted several experiments with a wedding-ring suspended over her stomach on a length of cotton. If it swung back and forth, the baby would be a girl; if it went in circles, it would be a boy. Or possibly the other way round – they had all differed on which it was meant to be, and since it performed both actions at different times, depending on who was holding it, it didn't seem to matter, anyway. 'We'll dress it in white for the first few weeks and you can knit coloured things then.'

The family continued to discuss the news, with Tom coming in for a good deal of teasing and Ted pretending to be put out that he was to be a grandfather again. 'Making me old before my time,' he grumbled. 'Still, we'll be needing a few more pairs of hands around the place before too long. Maybe then I can look forward to a bit of retirement.'

'Go on, Dad, you'll never retire,' Tom told him. 'You'll be out there in the yard, sticking your oar in, when you're a hundred. We'll have to tie you to your chair to get any peace.'

'I dare say I'll still have me uses,' Ted retorted. 'Look at your grandmother – place'd fall apart if 'twasn't for her keeping us all on our toes.'

They laughed, but they knew there was a grain of truth in his words. Minnie, whose main task now was to prepare the vegetables for the family's dinner, had been a mainstay during the difficult years of two world wars. In the Great War of 1914–18, she had been the one to keep the farm going while Ted and his brother, George, had gone off to war, especially after her husband, William, had been killed in a farm accident. And during the more recent conflict, although Ted had been able to stay at home, when their sons, Tom and Brian, had been called up and their places had been taken by Land Girls – one of them Joanna – it had fallen to Minnie and Alice to help out on the farm and to look after the city girls while they found their feet. Alice had often said that she didn't know how she would have managed without her mother-in-law.

After a while, Val slipped out and made her way across the fields and up through the wood to the charcoal-burner's cottage. She found Luke working on a frame for his latest picture.

'Val! I didn't think you were coming tonight.' He kissed her, then held her away from him for a moment and looked into her eyes quizzically. 'Is anything wrong?'

'No, not wrong at all. In fact, it's lovely. You remember I said I thought Joanna might be expecting again? Well, she is – the baby's due in September. They're thrilled about it, and so are the rest of the family.'

'Including you?' he asked quietly, knowing that the idea of another baby on the way might bring its own small pang to Val's heart.

'Including me. That's all over now, Luke. I'm just looking forward to the future – our future. That's really why I came to see you.' She brushed a few strands of brown hair from her eyes. 'We really do need to find somewhere to live, especially with another baby on the way.'

'It won't need a room of its own straight away, will it?' he asked. 'Or will they need your room for Robin? Has Joanna said anything to you about it?'

'No, of course not. And it'll be a while before they need my room – but they will, eventually. And babies need an awful lot of space for all their stuff. Joanna's still got a lot of Robin's things, of course, but there'll be other things – they'll have to get the cot down from the roof again and the pram and so on. It would be better all round if they had the space.' She looked up at him again. 'I wish we could get married soon. I feel as if we're just treading water at the moment.'

'I know.' He led her over to the fallen log he used as a garden bench, and they sat down, gazing over the rolling meadows towards the sunset. 'But we can't until we find somewhere to live. This place is no good for two. It was only meant for a couple of men working in the woods. It's not much better than camping out.'

'I sometimes think I'd be happy to do that,' Val said moodily, and he laughed and squeezed her waist.

'So would I – you know that. But I don't think your parents would be too pleased about it. And I really don't want to start off on the wrong foot with them. What about that house on the estate that Hilary mentioned? Has anything happened about that?'

Val shook her head. 'The lease is due for renewal in May or June, but nothing's been said about them moving out. And there doesn't appear to be anywhere else. The trouble is, so many of the cottages around here are tied – you have to be working on the land to be allowed to rent them.'

'Oh well,' he said, 'I expect something will turn up.' He glanced down at her hand and played with her fingers. 'I saw an advertisement for a job today.'

'A job!' She turned and looked up into his face. 'A teacher's job, you mean?'

'Well, not exactly. It's a picture-framing business in Plymouth. They're just getting started again in new premises – they were bombed out during the war and have been working in an old garage until now. They're looking for experienced frame-makers.'

'But you're an artist, Luke!'

'I'm also quite good at making frames. I do all my own, after all.'

'I know you do. You're very good at it. But how could you paint if you were working full-time?'

'I could paint at weekends.'

'A weekend painter!' she said. 'That's no good. You need to be free to paint whenever you want to. All day. Or when you see something with just the right light on it. How many times have you dashed out at a moment's notice because the light's just right for some picture you want to paint? How could you do that if you were working in Plymouth? And when would we ever have time to spend together?' she added forlornly.

Luke gripped both her hands. 'That's the important thing, Val. Us being together. I don't care what I do so long as I've got you. At least I'd be working with pictures—'

'Other people's pictures!' she interposed bitterly.

'—and I'd have you to come home to. We'd be together. We'd be married and in our own home. *That*'s what's important to me. We've wasted enough time,' he added quietly. 'After Egypt – well, I thought I'd lost you for good. I didn't think we'd ever see each other again. And then, when I found you were living here, in this very village, it was as if all my dreams had come true. But even then, it was a long time before we'd sorted everything out.' He gripped her hands so tightly she squeaked. 'Sorry. I didn't mean to hurt you.' He stroked her fingers and kissed them, then went on with the same intensity in his voice, 'I don't want to wait any longer, Val, my darling. I want you to be my wife as soon as possible. And if it means working in Plymouth, and only painting at weekends, then so be it. That's what I want.'

Val was silent for a few moments. Then she said, 'But it isn't what *I* want, Luke. I don't think it would be enough for you, either, after a while. You're an *artist*. It's different from me being a nurse – I love it, but I could give it up without any problem. I don't think you could give up painting. It's like – well, it's like asking Dad to give up farming. Only today, he was talking about retiring and Tom said he'd never retire, he'd still be out in the yard, poking his nose in, when he was a hundred years old! And he was right. It's in his blood, just as painting is in your blood.'

'I know which I'd rather give up if it came to a choice between painting and you,' he said, and put his hand beneath her chin so that she was forced to meet his eyes. 'I mean it,

Val. As long as I can earn an honest living, doing something I'd be good at, and paint at least part of the time, being with you is the most important thing in my life. I've known what it's like *not* to be with you, you see. I don't want to go back to that.'

Their glances held for a long moment, and then she said, 'We're not going back to that, Luke. Whatever happens, we're never going back to that.' And she raised both hands to his head and drew him down to her, their lips meeting in a long kiss.

'We'll find somewhere to live,' she whispered. 'We'll find somewhere soon.'

Chapter Eight

Stella was in her classroom, tidying the Nature table, when Felix popped his head round the door a week or so after their outing to the cinema.

'Hello. You look busy.'

'Oh, there's always something to do. They love this corner and bring all kinds of things in. See, we've got some frogspawn from the village pond, and these horse-chestnut buds – stickybuds, the children call them – to watch breaking into leaf, and we're hoping to get some silkworms. Miss Kemp says she always does that, and the children are fascinated by them. They do actually make silk, you know – they wind it round themselves in their cocoons, and then the children can unwind it on to spools and use it for sewing! After the moths have emerged, of course.'

Felix came to stand beside her. 'Perhaps I ought to talk about that instead of what I'd planned. It's a lot easier to understand!' He had taken to calling in at the school on one or two days a month, to talk to the children. It was something the vicar did regularly, and he approved of his curate following his example. Felix had never had much to do with children, other than his older sister's two, but he enjoyed the talks and didn't mind where they led.

Often, they seemed to lead in directions where his own interests lay. At Christmas, the conversations had centred around the Star of Bethlehem, and he had told the children how some people believed that this was a comet, which would appear only very occasionally. This had led to an explanation of comets and what they were, and a description of Halley's comet, which his grandmother had seen in 1910.

'It comes round every seventy-six years,' he said, drawing a diagram on the blackboard of a comet orbiting the Earth. 'It was seen in 1066 just before the Battle of Hastings – we know this because it's shown on the Bayeux Tapestry.' He paused. 'Do you know what that is?'

'Miss Kemp told us about it the other day. Us drew pictures of it,' Micky Coker said, pointing a grubby finger at the gallery around the classroom walls. 'I done King Harold with the arrow sticking out of his eye, see, and Henry Bennetts did a picture of him burning the cakes.'

'But that wasn't Harold,' Felix said, diverted from comets for a moment. 'That was Alfred, and it was a long time before—'

'I knows that,' Micky said in a tone of contempt. 'Henry Bennetts is always getting mixed up between kings. But Miss Kemp said it was a good picture so she'd let him put it up just the same.' From the tone of his voice, it seemed that Micky didn't approve of this departure from accuracy and Felix decided not to pursue the matter.

'Well, anyway, a man called Edmund Halley worked out that this comet came round every seventy-six years, and—'

'And it was called Halley as well, just like him! That's a *coincidence*, that is.' This time, it was Brian Madge who interrupted. 'Miss Kemp told us about coincidences yesterday. It's when two—'

'Yes, that's right, but this wasn't a coincidence,' Felix said, wondering if they would ever get to the end of the story of Halley and his comet. 'They called this comet after Halley because he was the one who found it. He said it would come round again in 1758, and so it did, but unfortunately he died in 1742, so he never knew that his prediction came true. But it's always borne his name, and it's probably the most famous comet there has ever been.'

'Will it come round again?' Jenny Pettifer asked. She was one of the brightest children in the school and had been made head girl last year. After the summer, she and some of the other older children would be going to one of the senior schools in Tavistock. Jenny herself, along with Ernest Coker and Helen Nethercott, had passed the examination for the grammar school.

'Yes, it'll come round again in 1986,' Felix said, and the children drew in their breath. 'So you'll all be lucky enough to see it. How old will you be then?'

There was a babble of noise as the children all worked out their age in that far-off time. 'I'll be forty-five.' 'No, you won't, you'll be forty-four.' 'Forty-*five*. My birthday's in February. Yours ain't till July.' 'All right, then, I'll be forty-five, too. When's it coming?' Aggrieved eyes were turned upon Felix. 'Will it be coming before my birthday?' This caused further agitation as the rest of the children began to wonder if the comet would arrive before or after their own birthdays. Felix raised his hands and called out for quiet, and Miss Kemp, who had been sitting with Stella on chairs at the side of the room, added her voice to his.

'I'm not sure exactly which month the comet will arrive,' he said. 'But it won't just flash through the sky and be gone, all in one night. You'll be able to see it for several weeks.'

'Will you still be alive then, Mr Copley?' asked Shirley Culliford, looking up at him with big grey eyes. Shirley was one of a large family living in a run-down cottage at the end of the village. Her feckless father, Arthur Culliford, scraped a living doing odd jobs and spent as much of it as he could in the pub before his ineffectual wife could get her hands on it and use it for cigarettes or hairdos. As little as possible, it seemed, went on clothes for the children, and most of their food came either from poaching or from payments in kind – a dozen eggs for a morning's hedging, a jug of milk for helping out with the milking.

'I hope I'll still be alive,' Felix said, smiling at her. He had a soft spot for Shirley, who had been chosen as Festival Queen the year before and had unexpectedly blossomed through the honour. She always brushed her hair and washed her face now before coming to school and had started to do the same for her younger sister, Betty. Sometimes they even had quite clean handkerchiefs.

'You'll be ever so old, though,' Betty said doubtfully. 'You'll be nearly a hundred.'

'Well, not quite.' How old did they think he was now? Felix wondered. He glanced at Stella, who was smiling with amusement. 'Not much more than sixty, really.'

'Well, that's old,' Micky Coker said authoritatively. 'My grandad's sixty.'

'So's mine,' came a chorus. 'Mine's sixty-*two*.' They then began to compete with each other. 'Mine's sixty-five.' 'Mine's *seventy*.'

'Yes, well, that's all been very interesting,' Miss Kemp said, rising to her feet. 'I'm sure we'd all like to say a big thank-you to Mr Copley for coming in and telling us about comets and the Star of Bethlehem.' Having reminded them all of the actual purpose of his visit, she raised her hands again for quiet and added, 'We'd all like the curate to come and talk to us again, wouldn't we?' There was a chorus of agreement, and then the head teacher picked up the school bell and rang it to signify that lessons were at an end for the day.

Since then, Felix had found himself giving regular lessons in such subjects as astronomy and other branches of science, though always with an emphasis that it was God who had created these marvels as well as the other wonders of Nature that they could see about them every day. It didn't matter whether it was a star in the sky or a daisy in the field, he told them, they all belonged to God.

'So what are you planning to tell them today?' Stella asked now, as they stood beside the Nature table.

He grinned a little. 'Splitting the atom! A bit more complicated than silk. Although I'm not sure anyone knows exactly how the silkworms make it, so maybe it's not after all.'

'Splitting the atom?' exclaimed Miss Kemp, who had just come into the room. 'Don't you think that's a little advanced for the children? I'm not sure I understand it myself.'

'I'm not sure anyone does,' Felix said cheerfully. 'But doesn't that make it all the more important to help them think about it? It's their world, too, and they'll be the ones to take us even further into the future.'

'We saw something about it on Pathé Pictorial last week,' Stella said. 'I expect some of the children saw it, too, and they might have heard about Mr Churchill announcing that we'd got the atomic bomb a couple of weeks ago. It could be a good idea to see if they've got any questions about it – you know how confused they get if things aren't properly explained.'

'Well, if you think you can do it,' Miss Kemp said. 'I just hope you have better luck than I did over the differences between King Harold and King Alfred!'

Felix grinned, and they went into the large classroom. This time, the subject had been deemed too difficult for the younger children, so Stella kept her class in the smaller room, and while Felix described the principles behind nuclear fission, in the simplest terms he could think of, she let them draw pictures of dinosaurs. This was a perennially popular subject amongst all the children and would prevent any gloating by the older children about their lesson; she just hoped they wouldn't be jealous of the younger ones!

When the afternoon was over, Felix came in to wait for her while she tidied the classroom.

'They do enjoy their painting, don't they?' he observed as she emptied coloured water out of a batch of fishpaste jars and began to wipe the tables. Most of the pictures were too wet to pin on the wall, but Betty Culliford had done quite a good one of an ichthyosaur and another of a plesiosaur. Stella held them up.

'Betty's fascinated by the idea of a little girl only a year or two older than herself finding these fossils in the cliffs at Lyme Regis. In fact, I'm not at all sure that the idea of a *girl* making the discoveries doesn't enthrall her even more than the dinosaurs themselves. Betty suffers rather a lot of teasing by her brothers. She'd probably have been a suffragette if she'd been around during Mrs Pankhurst's time.'

Felix laughed. 'You'd better give them a lesson on women's rights and see what happens. She could be our first woman prime minister.'

'I think that should wait until she gets into Miss Kemp's class,' Stella said. 'I'm only supposed to teach them the three Rs, some Nature, a bit of simple history and geography, and how to say their prayers. Although that's more your department, really.' She gave him a mischievous glance. 'When you can spare time from your science lessons, that is!'

'I *always* teach them their prayers,' he said. 'And science is just a clever way of saying Nature. I'm trying to show them the wonders of the world and how we can use them for good, that's all.'

'And evil,' Stella said, thinking of the atomic bomb. 'I know it won the war for us, but it was horrible, what we did to the Japanese.'

'I know,' Felix agreed more seriously. 'I didn't go into details, of course – even the older children are a bit young for that – but I think they understand that killing on such a scale must be wrong. If the same principles could be used for peace. . . ' He folded his lips and nodded. 'And I'm sure they will be. That's what makes science so wonderful. It can always be used for good.'

Stella finished tidying the classroom and collected her coat from the tiny staffroom. Mrs Purdy had just arrived and was collecting her cleaning materials from the cupboard. She wrapped her crossover pinafore around her thin body, tied a scarf turban-wise round her straggling grey hair and stood for a moment leaning on her mop.

'I hear Jessie Friend's not so well. In bed with her chest again, so Dottie told me.'

'That's right,' Stella said. 'Jean sent Billy round this morning to ask if Dottie would go and see her. Dr Latimer was going in this afternoon, so Mrs Dawe told me when she came to do the dinners.'

Felix nodded. 'And Mr Harvey said he'd pop in as well, just to make sure they had everything they needed.' He smiled. 'The grapevine's been working overtime – expect everyone in the village knows by now.'

'Well, of course they do,' the cleaner said with a touch of indignation. 'Jean and Jessie Friend are important people here, apart from running the post office. Of course us is all interested.' She made a pass or two at the floor with her mop. 'I'll look in myself on my way home – knocked up a batch of scones this afternoon, may as well drop half a dozen in for them while they'm fresh.'

'They'll have more cakes and biscuits than they can eat,' Stella said to Felix as they walked along the lane. 'Dottie never goes to see anyone without a cake in her basket. I hope Jessie's not really ill, though. She's had bronchitis twice already this winter.'

The Friend sisters, who were vaguely related to Dottie in the way that many of the villagers were related to each other without knowing to quite what degree, were identical twins – tiny, birdlike women with halos of snow-white hair and twittering voices. Their younger brother, Billy, lived with them; he was a short, rather tubby man with a flat nose and small mouth. His eyes slanted upwards at the outer corners, and he had been slower than the other children at school, never going on to Tavistock and eventually leaving when he was thirteen. He worked for Bert Foster, the butcher, helping to carry sides of meat and make sausages, and he made deliveries with Bert's horse and cart.

'I hope Billy doesn't get it, too,' Stella said. 'He has a weak chest, you know, and he always takes longer to get over things, for all he likes to boast about how strong he is.'

'I know. People like him don't often live into old age. He's a very sweet-natured person – so are his sisters, of course, but Billy's special. All the villagers seem fond of him.' Felix walked in silence for a moment or two, then added, 'I'll slip into the post office and see how they are.'

'I'll come, too,' Stella said. 'I need some envelopes and stamps anyway. I want to write to Maddy tonight.'

The post office was next door to Aggie Madge's cottage. They went in together, to find Jean Friend behind the counter, working out the postage on a parcel Constance Bellamy was sending to her cousin in America. Her dachshund, Rupert, sat at her feet, taking up most of the floor in the tiny office.

'I suppose we'll be getting stamps with the Queen's head on soon,' Miss Bellamy said, looking at the small portraits of George the Sixth that the postmistress was sticking on to the brown paper. 'If it hadn't been so unexpected, they'd probably have had them ready, but with the King being still a young man . . .'

'I'd like you to come and tell the schoolchildren that,' Felix said, thinking of his talk about Halley's comet. 'They're not at all sure that many of us will survive until sixty!'

Constance snorted. 'I intend to live to at least ninety. Both my parents did, and I shall, too. We're a long-lived family.'

'I don't think I'd want to live that long,' Jean said doubtfully. 'Grandmother was ninety-two when she passed on, and the last few years were misery for her and everyone around her. She was bedridden by the time she was eighty-eight, and I know I shouldn't speak ill of the dead but it's the honest truth, she were a real trial. Poor Mother was up and down stairs all day long, looking after her – 'twas no wonder that her turn came so soon: she were worn out with it all.'

'I shan't be bedridden,' Constance said stoutly. 'Keep myself healthy with plenty of exercise. Don't I, Rupert?' she added, looking down at the dachshund who had stretched himself out to his full length on the floor and was snoring peacefully. She twitched his lead and he opened one eye and looked at her, as if wondering what she wanted him to do. 'Come on, you lazy creature. Get up.'

Rupert staggered reluctantly to his feet, not much taller standing up than when he was lying down, and Constance towed him out of the post office. Felix and Stella grinned at each other and then turned to the little woman behind the counter.

'We were wondering how your sister is,' Stella said. 'We were sorry to hear she's not well.'

'Oh, she's not too bad,' Jean Friend said in her soft voice. 'She caught a cold last week and it went straight to her chest. Doctor's given her some medicine and it's doing her good already.'

'Well, don't let her come back to work too soon,' Felix told her. 'Although I suppose you could do with her help. Is there anyone else who can help you?'

'Not really. You see, it's only Jessie and me who are allowed to do the post office work, and there's not much else apart from the bit of stationery and sweets and so on that we sell. If we were both ill, they'd send someone from Head Office, but I can manage on my own for a few days. And Billy helps with any carrying. He's a good boy.'

The good boy came in at that moment, a smile beaming all over his wide, flat face as he saw Felix and Stella. 'Hello, Mr Copley. Hello, Miss Simmons.' He was always scrupulously polite. 'I'm helping Jean in the shop.'

'So you are.' Felix smiled back at him. 'Could you weigh

me out some toffees, please, Billy? I've got my coupons here.' He handed his ration book across the counter and Jean took it and began to snip out the tiny squares.

'How many do you want, Mr Copley?'

'Oh, the whole week's worth, I think – a quarter of a pound. Two ounces don't get me through an evening!'

They watched as Billy took the big jar down from the shelf, unscrewed its lid and then carefully tilted it over the scales. When enough toffees had dropped in to make the balance equal, he screwed back the lid and returned the jar to the shelf. Then he tipped the sweets on to a square of blue paper, rolled it into a cone and tucked in the end. Finally, with a beaming smile, he handed it over.

'Thank you very much, Billy.' Felix counted out six pennies and put them on the counter. Stella produced her book, too. Normally, both books would have been held by the two landladies, Aggie and Dottie, but they were needed for the purchase of sweets and, like small children spending their pocket money, Stella and Felix were allowed to have them back one afternoon a week.

'Are you having anything, Miss Simmons?' Miss Friend enquired and Stella asked for a tube of Spangles. The brightly striped packet was put into her hand, and she bought her envelopes and stamps as well.

'Is there anything I can do for you and your sister?' Felix asked. 'I expect the vicar's been in already, but if there's anything you need from town, it would be no trouble for me to slip into Tavistock.'

'Bless you, we've got all we need here in the village,' the little postmistress said, smiling at him. ''Tis kind of you to offer, though.'

'Well, just remember the offer's there if you think of anything,' he told her, and they turned to go. As they reached the door, it opened and Jed Fisher came in. He scowled at them both and pushed past.

''Bout time you got yourself a bigger place than this, missus,' he said in a hectoring tone to Jean Friend. 'Not enough room to swing a cat. I wants ten Woodbine.'

Felix, already halfway through the door, stopped and turned back. His face was pale with anger. 'Excuse me, Mr Fisher, but do you really think that's the way to address Miss Friend? Couldn't you at least say please?'

The man stared at him. As usual, he looked scruffy and unkempt, his dark-grey hair greasy on his collarless shirt, and he smelled of old sweat and dirt. His jaw was black with stubble, and his fingernails rimmed with grime. He opened his mouth and Felix caught a whiff of onions and bad breath.

'What's it got to do with you?' Jed demanded belligerently. 'I ain't nothing to do with you. I be a chapel man.'

'And I'm sure the minister would want you to use a little common politeness just as much as I do,' Felix responded quietly. Miss Friend was looking nervous and Stella anxious. 'If you'll just apologise and ask for your cigarettes in a civilised manner, I'm sure she'll be willing to serve you.'

'Her'll serve me anyway. That's what her be here for.'

'She has no obligation—'

'Oh, shut yer mouth!' Jed broke in. 'I ain't got time to stand here all day argufying with pansies like you.' He turned back to the postmistress. 'Ten Woodbine, *please*, if that be good enough for you.'

He threw the money on the counter and the little woman handed him the green packet. He grabbed it without a word and thrust his way past Felix and Stella again, deliberately knocking Felix against the wall as he did so, and slammed the door behind him.

'Well!' Stella exclaimed, staring after him. 'What a horrible man! Are you all right, Miss Friend?'

'Bless you, my dear, I'm all right. I've known Jed Fisher since we were all youngsters together. I don't argue with him.

I just serve him and let him get out as quick as he can. That be the best way with folk like him.'

'Well, I don't think he ought to be allowed to get away with it,' Felix said, still annoyed. 'Didn't anyone teach him manners when he was a child?'

Jean Friend shrugged. 'I'm sure his mother and father tried their best. Good, God-fearing people, they were. And Jed himself wasn't a bad chap when he was a boy, just a bit wild, that's all. It was only when he got older . . . 'Twould have been better if he'd gone for a soldier, like some of the other lads in the village, perhaps, though maybe I shouldn't say that since some of 'em never came home again. But 'twould have taught him a bit of discipline.'

'Why didn't he go?' Stella enquired. 'Was he too young?'

'No, he was just the right age. Went along to the office in Tavistock, if I remember rightly, but they turned him down. Some sort of health problem, though I never heard what 'twas. Flat feet, my dad reckoned. Couldn't have been anything serious because look at him now, hale and hearty – or would be if he looked after himself proper and didn't smoke so much. There was a lot of feeling about it in the village, you know – folk whose own boys had had to go, and maybe got killed or wounded. They didn't like seeing Jed Fisher walking about free as air.'

At that moment, someone else came into the post office and Stella and Felix said goodbye and went outside. They stood for a moment in the street, both looking across at Jed Fisher's cottage and not sure what to do next.

'How about a short walk before going home?' Felix suggested, and they turned and strolled along the lane towards the ford. There had been quite a lot of rain recently and the Burra Brook was flowing briskly, almost covering the stepping-stones. They leaned over the little stone bridge and gazed down at the peaty water, foaming white as it broke over the rocks. Wild daffodils and primroses patterned the mossy banks with gold, and the trees that hung over the water were a silvery drift of soft, furry pussy willow.

'Spring,' Stella said dreamily. 'I think it's my favourite season. And this is my second spring in Burracombe – I can hardly believe I've been here over a year.'

'Do you think you'll stay a long time?' he asked. 'Or will you want to move on – to a bigger school, perhaps?'

'Oh no, I'm not even thinking about moving. Not yet, anyway.' Stella lifted her head and gazed about her. 'I don't think I'll ever want to leave Burracombe, anyway. It's so lovely, and I've made such good friends. And besides, there's Maddy. She lived here as a child. It makes it feel even more like my home.'

'I remember seeing your sister at the pageant last summer,' he remarked. 'She's very pretty, isn't she?' He reverted to their previous topic. 'Still, you might not want to remain an assistant teacher all your life. Don't you think you might want a more senior job – as a headmistress, for instance? You'd have to move away then – it'll be some time before Miss Kemp retires.'

'Listen,' Stella said firmly, 'I've only been here a year or so. This is my first post. I'm still settling in – I don't even want to think about moving on for ages yet.'

'And by that time,' he said, 'you'll probably have found some nice young man to marry you and you won't want to work at all.'

Stella blushed a little. 'Well, that's something we don't know, isn't it?' She gazed pensively down into the water again.

Felix watched her for a moment, then said, 'I thought for a while last year that you and Luke Ferris were very friendly.'

She looked up at once. 'That's all it was! Luke was a good friend – he still is. He helped me try to find Maddy. But it was always Val Tozer he was really fond of – they knew each other during the war, you know.'

'Yes, so I gather.' They were quiet for a minute or two, then he said, 'I really enjoyed our trip to the cinema last week.'

'Yes, so did I. It was lovely, and I enjoyed the drive as well.'

'Shall we do it again? There's quite a good film on this week – we could go on Thursday or Friday, if you like. What do you think?'

Stella turned and smiled up into his eyes. 'I'd like it very much. Friday would be best for me. Thank you.'

'And maybe,' he went on, 'during the Easter holidays, we could go out in Mirabelle for a day, over the moor. Take a picnic. Or will your sister be here then?'

'She'll be here over Easter itself, and for part of the holiday, but I don't know exactly how long for.'

'Well, when you know, we'll see if we can fit in a day to ourselves.' He grinned at her. 'Well away from Burracombe! The trouble with these small places is that everyone knows you, and in my job – yours, too, I suppose – you daren't do anything to cause gossip.'

'Are we likely to do anything to cause gossip?' Stella asked demurely, still gazing down into the stream, and he burst out laughing.

'I don't expect so, but you never know, do you! For one thing, I shan't be wearing my dog-collar – and in these parts, that's as bad as going naked.' He put his hand on her arm and turned her to face him again. 'Not that I'd do anything to embarrass you, Stella, ever,' he said more quietly. 'You can be quite sure of that.'

They stood very still for a moment, their eyes locked. Stella could feel her heart beating fast. Felix was very close. Her lips parted as she drew in a small breath and she saw his glance drop to her mouth.

The silence was broken by a flurry of footsteps and the calling of childish voices. As Felix and Stella moved abruptly apart, half a dozen children appeared round the corner of the lane, chattering like sparrows. They stopped as they saw the two figures on the bridge.

'Coo, look, it's Miss Simmons and Mr Copley. They'm holding hands!' The words were meant to be spoken in a whisper, but the voice of Henry Bennetts, who uttered them, was already beginning to break and they came out in a squeaky croak. The others shushed him, their faces scarlet, and Felix laughed.

'Hello, you lot,' he called cheerfully. 'We've just been playing Pooh sticks. Want to have a game with us?'

The children approached warily. Playing games with the teacher and the curate out of school-time was a new idea and not one they entirely approved of. Stella took pity on them.

'I'm afraid I've got to get back home,' she said briskly, moving away. 'I promised to help Dottie with a frock she's making for Val Tozer, and I've got some letters to write. We'll come out for a Nature walk one day, children, and play the game then, shall we?'

The natural order of things restored, the children looked more at ease and clattered on over the bridge, on their way to round up some cows for Ted Tozer. Stella and Felix looked at each other again.

'Well,' she said a little awkwardly, 'I really had better go. Dottie wants me to put the frock on so that she can make sure the hem's level. It's been nice to have a walk, though.'

'We'll do it again one day,' he said, looking as if he wanted to hold her hand again. 'And you won't forget we're going to the pictures on Friday, will you?'

'No,' Stella said, smiling at him. 'I won't forget.'

She walked along the lane, back to the village street. A robin trilled from a holly bush, and from a taller tree she could hear the liquid song of a blackbird. The wild daffodils and primroses looked even brighter now and the hedges greener. Even the sun seemed more golden as it dipped towards the horizon.

Spring, she thought. The best season of the year. A season of promise.

Chapter Nine

Hilary and Gilbert Napier were also feeling the promise of spring.

'You can let me take over some of the work now,' Gilbert said to his daughter at breakfast. 'I'm perfectly well again. There's no reason why I can't do as much as I ever did.'

'And have another heart attack,' Hilary answered, buttering her toast. 'You know what Charles Latimer said. It was working too hard that caused the first one. If you go back to your old ways, you risk another – and it could be worse.'

'Oh, fiddlesticks. It wasn't as bad as all that. I just got overtired, that's all—'

'Because you were doing too much and working yourself up over Stephen. You must take notice of what Charles says, Father. And I'm managing very well – I enjoy doing it.'

That had been the wrong thing to say. The big, heavy face took on a glowering look. 'So would I enjoy it. I always did enjoy managing the estate. Why take it away from me?'

He sounded like a petulant child, deprived of a toy, Hilary thought. And yet, he had reason to feel aggrieved. The estate was his, after all. It had been his life. And he really did look well – she had no doubt that he *felt* well. You just couldn't see the damaged heart, beating less strongly now.

'Nobody wants to take anything away from you, Dad,' she said more gently. 'We just don't want to risk losing you. And it's not all that long since your attack—'

'It's nearly a year! Whit Monday – that's nine months.'

'Charles wants you to take things easy for a little while longer. Maybe after Easter—'

'I know what it is,' he said suddenly. '*You* don't want to give it up. You've got your head now – you're in control, and you don't want to hand anything back.'

Hilary opened her mouth indignantly, then closed it again. Getting her father excited and upset, Charles Latimer had told her, was as bad as letting him overwork. She'd managed to avoid argument as much as possible until now. She clamped her lips firmly together and tried to think of a less provocative way of refuting his accusation.

'You see,' he said, watching her. 'You can't deny it. You know it's true.'

'I—' Hilary began, and caught herself up once more.

Before she could speak again, he said, 'We're too alike, you and I. Like to be in charge. That's why you did so well in the war, driving generals about. Felt you were in control.'

His fierce eyes met hers and she sighed. Perhaps he was right; perhaps she did like to be in charge of things.

'I don't think I'm trying to hang on to the estate, though, honestly,' she said, trying not to feel a twinge of doubt. 'I just don't want you overdoing things.' She hesitated, not wanting to say anything that would hurt him, then went on carefully, 'Suppose it were Baden who was taking over now, instead of me.' She saw him flinch and went on quickly, 'I'm not trying to upset you, Dad, but just think about it. Would you be so anxious to get back to work if he were in charge? Wouldn't you trust him to manage the estate properly?'

He scowled and she was afraid she had gone too far. All the same, she reminded herself, he had never been averse to bringing his dead son's name into the conversation when it suited him – when he was trying to compel Stephen to taking over, for instance. She saw him look away, out through the window towards the sunlight sloping across the lawn, and then he turned back to her.

'Of course I'd trust Baden if he were in your position now,' he said quietly. 'And he'd trust me, too. He'd discuss things with me – ask my advice, and take it. He wouldn't shut me out.'

Hilary stared at him. 'Is that what you think I've been doing, Dad? Shutting you out?'

'It's what you have been doing,' he answered, and rose to his feet to leave the room. '*You* think about it.'

He walked out, more slowly and heavily than he had done a year ago, but still upright, his big frame still powerful, and closed the door behind him. The dogs got up and padded across the room, but were too late to go through and sat down, facing the door, their thick tails like rudders behind them. One of them looked round, as if to ask to be let out after their master.

Hilary sat quite still, staring towards the garden. Beyond the trees at the far end of the lawn, she could see the rise of ground towards Dartmoor. A sheen of gold lay on the gorse, lit by the March sunlight. A cluster of ponies moved slowly across the grass, nibbling it to a fine sward.

Is he right? she wondered. Have I really shut him out? Only a few moments ago, she had likened him to a child whose toy had been taken away; now she saw herself suddenly as the bigger child, the bully who had snatched it. Surely that couldn't be true! She had acted in his best interests – setting aside her own plans to leave Burracombe to make a new life for herself, taking over the management of the estate so that her brother, Stephen, could follow his own career in the RAF, keeping the house and its lands in the family when her father was taken ill . . . Had it really been so selfish of her?

She got up, leaving her coffee unfinished, and opened the door. The dogs were through it immediately, their claws scrabbling on the wooden floor of the hall as they scuttled to find their master. The front door stood open, letting in the cool March air, and they raced outside and disappeared round the corner. Probably he'd gone round to the stables, Hilary thought. That was the first place he'd gone when he was allowed outside again after his heart attack, the place where he seemed to find most comfort. She half turned, meaning to follow him, then paused, aware that she was too shaken herself to be able to offer comfort to her father – not even sure she could offer reassurance. She needed time to come to terms with this unsettling view of herself.

Jackie Tozer came out of the kitchen carrying a tray to collect the breakfast things. She had been working at the Barton since leaving school, but Hilary thought she was capable of something better than domestic service and had been trying to persuade her to take training for some sort of career – cooking, or hotel work, perhaps. Jackie was a bright girl, and since her boyfriend, Roy Pettifer, had been called up for his National Service and sent to Korea, she'd seemed rather at a loose end.

'Is there anything wrong, Miss Napier?' Jackie asked, seeing Hilary hesitating in the doorway. 'I saw Mr Napier go by the window just now. He's all right, isn't he?'

'Yes, I think so.' Hilary came back into the hall, still feeling troubled. 'He's just fed up with not being able to do much.'

'I expect he is, poor man.' Jackie paused, the tray held against her hip. 'I remember when Dad had pleurisy one winter, he were like a bear with a sore head because he couldn't go out on the yard. It's worst when they're on the mend, you know,' she went on, sounding like her grandmother, Minnie. 'They start to feel a bit stronger and they just want to be *doing*. Especially when they've been used to being outside. It don't seem right to them to be stuck indoors all the time.'

'That's exactly right,' Hilary said, amused to find herself having this discussion with her eighteen-year-old housemaid. 'What did your mother do about it?'

'She got our Tom to sort it out. Doctor said Dad could go

out for a bit every day so long as he was wrapped up proper, and Tom asked him to help him out with a few jobs round the place – feeding the calves, things like that, mostly in the sheds and barns so he wasn't out in the cold in all weathers. He made out he couldn't manage without Dad, see. Mind you, I reckon Dad knew what he was up to, but he never said nothing, and he gradually stopped outside a bit longer until he were back working as usual. But it made him feel he could still be a bit of use while he couldn't do too much.'

'Yes, I see,' Hilary said thoughtfully. 'But I've already done that. There was all that work my father did for the pageant last year – sorting out those papers and photographs for the history display. That kept him busy for quite a while. And Dr Latimer absolutely forbade him to do any outside work during the winter. But now, with spring coming, he's getting restless, and I really don't want to ask too much of him.'

'I thought he was going to make a book of all them papers,' Jackie said. 'Lots of folk'd be interested in that.'

'Yes, he did talk about it.' But Hilary knew that even this wouldn't be enough to satisfy her father. It was the estate he wanted. It was control.

And I don't want to give it up, she thought as Jackie went into the breakfast room. I'm afraid that if I let him start doing even the smallest things, he'll gradually take over again, as Ted Tozer did with the farm. Except that the Tozers were happy with the situation – and Hilary wasn't. Ted and Tom worked well together, but she wasn't at all convinced that she and her father could.

I really am selfish, she thought miserably, going upstairs to get ready for the day's work. I'm like a dog in the manger, snapping at Dad whenever he tries to get too close. And I have the nerve to tell myself I'm trying to make things easier for him, when what I'm really doing is making them worse.

Yet if he took over the estate again, Hilary would be back where she started, running the house. Her one bid for freedom, which she had been just about to make when he had his heart attack, had had to be abandoned. She could never make it again. She could never leave him now and risk causing another attack.

I've made this my career, she thought, staring from her bedroom window at the meadows and farmland that ran up to the moor. And I enjoy it. I want to go on doing it. But it's still Dad's property, and somehow I've got to learn to share it with him. We've both got to learn.

She moved to her dressing table and looked at the photograph that stood in its frame beside the mirror. It was a family photograph, taken before her mother had died – the five of them together; her parents, her elder brother, Baden, herself and Stephen, the youngest. Even at that age, Baden looked like his father – the same strong build, the same thick mane of hair over strong brows, the same fierce, uncompromising stare.

I'm not like that, she thought. I'm not like Father at all. And yet . . . Maybe he was right. Maybe she did like to feel in control. But did that really mean she was stopping him from getting properly better?

The thought came as an unpleasant shock.

Dottie had finished Val Tozer's frock, and Val came to collect it one afternoon after she had finished her shift at Tavistock Hospital. She tried it on and admired herself in the long mirror that had been taken off an old wardrobe door. Dottie and Stella looked on approvingly.

'It looks proper handsome on you,' Dottie said with satisfaction. 'That green suits your colouring.'

'You're a good dressmaker, Dottie,' Val said, twisting round to examine the back view. 'I'd never get anything to fit as well as this in a shop.'

'Oh, shop clothes!' Dottie said scornfully. 'All the same, they be. You can tell in a minute where they come from, and the quality's not there these days. Better off with a nice piece of fabric and a good Butterworth pattern.' She narrowed her eyes as she considered her workmanship. 'I'm still not happy about that back seam . . .'

'It's perfect, Dottie. I'm not letting you change a stitch.' Val began to take the dress off and Dottie laughed.

'Well, if you say so. Now, my flower, when be you going to let me make your wedding-dress? Set the date yet, have you?'

Val made a face as she pulled on her old skirt and jumper. 'We can't until we know where we're going to live, and there doesn't seem to be anywhere around here. Luke's talking about getting a job in Plymouth. Well, between ourselves, he's actually applied for one. He's waiting for an answer now.'

Dottie and Stella stared at her.

'In *Plymouth*?' Dottie said at last, as if it were somewhere on the moon. 'But do that mean you'd be leaving Burracombe?'

'Not unless we've got to. He could go on the bus. But if we can't find anywhere to live in the village . . . ' She shrugged.

'Oh, Val,' Dottie said in the same tone, 'do you think you'd really like that? All them streets – and no fields for miles and miles. And all them strangers everywhere.'

'I don't know why you're talking like that,' Val said with some amusement. 'You lived in London long enough.'

'Only because I had to, and we weren't in London all the time. Miss Forsyth took me on tour with her. Anyway, that was different. It were my job.'

'Well, being married to Luke will be my job,' Val said. 'I might even get work in the hospital – Freedom Fields, perhaps.'

Dottie shook her head dubiously. 'I thought the two of you were settled here. He always seemed so happy in the village.' She looked at Stella. 'When he used to come round here of an afternoon for tea, or go off with you for walks on a Sunday after a bit of dinner, I was sure he'd want to stay.'

Stella blushed and glanced sideways at Val, embarrassed by the reference to the time when she and Luke had spent a lot of time together. But Val was folding the new dress and laying it in her basket and didn't seem to have noticed. Stella felt a small pang of envy for the other girl. She'd obviously had sadness in her life – she'd lost her fiancé in the war and had grieved for him for years, so Dottie had said – but now she'd found happiness with Luke, and there was a serenity about her that Stella longed for in her own life. A certainty that as long as she was with Luke, nothing else mattered too much.

'When's Maddy coming again?' Val enquired.

'Easter. Not long now.' It still seemed strange to Stella that people in Burracombe knew her own sister better than she did. 'I can't wait to see her again.'

'They'm in Paris now,' Dottie said. 'Miss Forsyth spends a lot of time there. She's very popular in France – speaks the language like a native, and she's got a lovely voice. Sings like an angel, she do.'

'But is Maddy going to spend the rest of her life going about with her?' Val asked. 'Doesn't she want a career of her own? Although I suppose she'll be getting married before long. She must meet all kinds of interesting people, travelling about like that. I don't suppose she'll ever want to settle in Burracombe.'

'No,' Stella said, feeling suddenly miserable. 'I don't suppose she will.'

Dottie glanced at her sharply, and after Val had gone, she said, 'You don't want to worry too much about your sister, maid. I know she'm enjoying her life now, but she always seemed to me to be a little homebird at heart. I don't think her'll ever want to settle down abroad permanent.'

'But Val's right. She must meet all kinds of people. And she's so lovely to look at – there must be men falling in love with her all the time. I should hate to think that she'd stay abroad and hardly ever come back. I've missed her so much, all these years.'

'I know, flower,' Dottie said softly. 'But I still think her heart's here in Burracombe. And if it turns out different, well, there's nothing us can do about it. And you'd want her to be happy, wouldn't you?'

'Yes, of course I would. I'm being selfish, Dottie. It should be enough for me to know that she's alive and well and that she's been so happy all this time. And a lot of that is because of you!'

She hugged the plump little body and gave the round cheek a kiss. Dottie stayed still for a moment or two and then moved away. Her face was pink, and her voice shook a little as she said, 'Well, that's as may be. I only did what anyone would have done for the poor little mite. Now, let's get all this clutter out of the way and you can get on with your school work while I thinks about supper. I got a nice piece of lamb's liver from Bert Foster this morning – how do you fancy that with a bit of bacon and an onion and some mashed potatoes?'

'Lovely,' Stella said, starting to pick up scraps of coloured fabric from the rag rug in front of the fire. 'Oh, Dottie, look at Alfred! He's made a bed for himself out of your sewing.'

'Alfred!' Dottie exclaimed, picking the big cat up unceremoniously and dumping him on the floor. 'You bad cat! I shan't let you in again, if you don't behave. My stars, if you sits on Val Tozer's wedding-dress and leaves black hairs all over it, nobody'll never trust me again to make their clothes. And that'll mean no more fish-head suppers for you, my boy!'

Alfred sat on the rug, his fur tousled, blinking indignantly. Then he got up and stalked out of the room, his thick tail held erect and offence in every line of his body. The two women laughed.

'He's a star turn, that one,' Dottie said. 'Mind you, it's my fault, really. I ought to know what he'm like by this time. And he's been good company while I've been by meself. You can't beat an animal for company when you'm on your own.'

She went out to the kitchen, and Stella settled down with her preparations for the next day's lessons. She thought briefly of her sister, possibly marrying and living abroad, and of Val Tozer, ready to go anywhere with Luke, and wondered how she herself would end up.

Married, with a family of her own? Or alone, like Dottie, with just a cat or a dog for company?

Chapter Ten

'I think I've made an enemy of Jed Fisher,' Felix said ruefully. He was in the vestry with Basil Harvey slotting numbered cards into the hymn board for the next day's service. Normally, one of the churchwardens would have done this, but Ernie Crocker was busy on Ted Tozer's farm, and George Sweet had been kept busy baking for a wedding in Little Burracombe. 'He was so rude to poor little Miss Friend when I was in the post office the other day, and I couldn't help being sharp with him. This morning, when I met him in the village, I said good morning, but he just looked the other way.' He hesitated, then said, 'He *spat*.'

'At you?' Basil asked, but Felix shook his head.

'Not directly at me, no. He'd turned his head away by then. But it was meant for me, all the same.'

'He's an unpleasant person,' Basil said thoughtfully. 'And not one of our parishioners. All the same . . .'

'. . . it's not a good idea to have bad blood between us,' Felix finished. 'I know. I'm sorry.'

Basil sighed. 'It's not your fault. If it hadn't happened then, it would have done some other time. He sets out to create it, I'm afraid, and it's hard to resist. However determined you are not to fall into the traps he sets, a time will come when he's just too clever for you. He seems to take a perverse sort of pleasure in it.'

'So in the end, nobody likes him,' Felix said. 'Poor man.'

'I know. Even though it's by his own doing, it's still rather sad.' Basil finished sorting out the notes for his sermon and laid them on the rickety wooden table. He placed a large pebble on them to stop them blowing away in the draught that came through the open doorway. 'It's difficult to imagine what it must be like to be such a person – what it's like inside his head. And his heart.' He shook his own head, and the sunlight slanting through the narrow window gleamed on his halo of silver hair. 'Very lonely, I should think.'

'Does he get any help from the Chapel? Any comfort, I mean?' Felix went through to the church to hang up the board. He glanced around before coming back, taking his own comfort from the stone walls, the sturdy round pillars, the barrel-shaped roof. Lozenges of brilliant, jewel-coloured light lay flung on the stone-flagged floor from the east window, and the altarcloth glowed deep purple. He went back into the vestry. 'The minister must know him pretty well.'

'As well as anyone, I imagine. But I don't think Jed goes through the door very often. He looks after the graveyard – in a fashion.' Basil walked to the door and looked out at his own churchyard, immaculately kept by Jacob Prout. 'And he knows a good many Bible texts, learned in his childhood at Sunday school, I've no doubt. He's not above quoting them at you if it suits him. But I don't think religion figures very large in his life these days.'

'What about his family? Does he have any?'

'Not that I know of. He lived with his parents until they died some years ago. I don't think there were any brothers or sisters, and there don't seem to be any other Fishers hereabouts, or any other relatives at all.' He sighed. 'If there are, they don't have anything to do with Jed – and quite honestly, who could blame them?'

'And never married, I suppose.'

'I've never heard of a wife, but of course I've only been in the village twenty years or so. But don't take it too much to heart, Felix. There's someone like Jed in almost every community, and we can't win every heart and soul.'

'I certainly don't seem to have won this one!' Felix said wryly, and Basil slapped him on the shoulder.

'Think of those hearts you *have* won, Felix. The young schoolmistress's for a start, or so I've heard.'

Felix's fair skin flushed. 'I don't know about that. We've just been out a few times, that's all – to the cinema, or for a walk. Nothing more.'

'Well, perhaps not. But she's an attractive young woman, Felix – you need to keep your head. She also strikes me as being rather innocent, especially with her upbringing. And she *is* a parishioner.'

'It's all right,' Felix said soberly. 'I'm not going to do anything foolish. She's safe with me.'

'And are you safe with her?' Basil asked, and the young curate laughed.

'That's something we'll have to wait to find out! Honestly, Mr Harvey, you don't need to worry. We're friends, that's all. If it turns into something else, I'll let you know. But I won't do anything to cause gossip in the village.'

'I'm sure you won't. Just remember that in a village, you don't actually have to *do* anything at all to cause gossip. It causes itself! It's usually kindly gossip, and we don't need to worry about that, but in our position . . .'

'I know,' Felix said. 'My father's a vicar, and my grandfather's a bishop, so I've grown up with it. I'll be careful – but I've got to be allowed to have friends. Even girlfriends.'

'Of course you have,' Basil said as he looked round the vestry to see that everything was tidy. They went out into the churchyard together. Primroses clustered at the foot of the stone wall surrounding the graves, and the blue saucers of periwinkles brightened the tumble of green leaves that spilled over one corner. 'After all, you'll be wanting to marry one day, so of course you must be allowed to make friends. But it's not an easy path to tread.'

'A nice one, all the same,' Felix said with a grin, and they both laughed.

'I think,' Basil said to his wife at lunch, 'that I ought to make a few enquiries about Miss Tucker. She's written to me again, asking if I've made any progress, and I'm rather ashamed that I haven't tried harder.'

'You were going to ask Miss Bellamy if she knew anything,' Grace said, serving him a fillet of haddock. The fish van had been round that morning and half the village would be eating fish of some kind for their main meal. She spooned out some mashed potato as well and brightened the plate with a helping of broccoli and some sliced carrots.

Basil took some parsley sauce. 'Yes, I think that's a good place to start. She knows everyone for miles around, and she won't gossip. I think my enquiries should be discreet.'

'Certainly they should.' Grace served herself, and they began to eat. 'It's sad to think of someone so lonely that they have to search for relatives who may not even be here any more. She has sisters, doesn't she?'

'Half-sisters, yes. But there's still a need to find out about where her mother and father came from. A gap in her history. She seems to have grown up believing that Tucker was her father and that they were a Plymouth family, and suddenly she's found herself with a completely different background, and possibly relatives she's never known about. Relatives who would in all probability have known her mother. She might even find her real father.'

'Which might not be such a good thing,' Grace observed. 'But we've been through all this before, and it's not for us to judge. I think you're right, Basil – you ought to make some enquiries. Go and see Miss Bellamy this afternoon.'

Basil agreed, and set out as soon as they had finished lunch.

The clear skies of the morning had clouded over, and a spiteful wind had sprung up, rattling the still bare branches of the trees and cutting through the gateways of the fields. He walked past the village hall, the shop and Alf Coker's forge to Constance Bellamy's house opposite the school. The children were still in the playground, making the most of their freedom before afternoon lessons started, and they waved and called out to him.

'Be you coming to see us, Vicar?'

'Not today,' he answered, pausing by the fence. They clustered round, voices babbling eagerly as they vied to tell him their latest news.

'My cousin's got a new babby!' Henry said importantly, then added in less exultant tones, "Tis only a girl, though.'

'What's the matter with girls?' demanded Brenda Pellow, who lived on a farm at Little Burracombe. 'Us had a new calf in the night and it's a heifer. My dad says heifers is much better than bull calves, and heifers is girls!'

'*Are* girls,' Basil murmured, and they stared at him blankly. 'Heifers *are* girls.'

'Well, I knows that,' Brenda said. 'That's just what I said.' The children looked at each other with resignation at the obtuseness of grown-ups, but before the discussion could continue, the headmistress came into the playground to ring the school bell and they ran to line up and file into school. Basil caught Miss Kemp's eye and she came over to him.

'Do you think we'll ever get them to understand the difference between *is* and *are*?' he asked. 'I know you try, but it never seems to sink in.'

'Oh, I think they do understand it,' she said. 'They just don't think it's worth bothering about. They hear their parents and other adults using the local dialect, and everyone seems to manage perfectly well, so why bother to change? And in some ways, I sympathise with them – after all, it is the old way of speaking. Remnants of an earlier language. Who are we to say it's wrong?' She gave him a mischievous look, then added, 'But don't let anyone else know I said that. It's far too radical for a head teacher!'

Basil smiled, and as she turned away to follow the children into the school, he crossed the road to the Grey House, where Constance Bellamy lived. It was larger than the cottages that stood near it, set back a little from the road and surrounded by a sprawling garden in which Constance spent a good deal of her time. As well as lawns, there were shrubs and a number of trees, and Basil was surprised at the colour that greeted him as he came through the gate. Several large camellia bushes were smothered with a variety of red, pink and white blooms, an early cherry tree was a froth of blushing-pink blossom, and the ground beneath the trees was covered with the nodding cup-like flowers of white and purple hellebores, while the grassy Devon banks were spattered with primroses. Even the lawns were a carpet of gold and white crocuses, with the chequered heads of fritillaries swaying above them in a mosaic of colour.

An old wooden wheelbarrow was standing on the path, half filled with twigs and dead stalks, and as he pushed open the gate Constance herself came round the corner of the house, wearing a baggy tweed skirt that sagged halfway to her ankles, muddy Wellingtons and a baggy brown jumper with threads pulled out. Her black-and-tan dachshund was following her and he stopped and barked when he saw Basil.

'Oh, hello, Basil. Quiet, Rupert!' She dumped another armful of foliage into the barrow and started to push it across to the far corner of the garden. 'I'll just get rid of this.' As she tipped the barrow up, the dachshund came over and sniffed Basil's shoes. 'Leave the vicar alone, you bad dog. You know him well enough. It's more out of duty than anything else,' she added, leaving the barrow upturned over the heap and brushing her hands together as she came back. 'Anyone who comes through the gate must have the statutory couple of barks. After that, he shuts up. Coming in for a cup of tea?'

'Well, I've only just had lunch,' he said, following her round the cottage to the back door. 'But I'd like to—'

'Lunch? Good heavens, is it that time already? I lose all sense of time when I'm out in the garden,' she added, pushing open the back door and leaning on the jamb while she trod on the heel of one boot and pulled it off. The second one dumped beside the first, she led the way through an untidy area, not much more than a corridor, with coats hung on one side and shelves along the other, laden with bags of dog biscuits, chicken feed, gardening tools and other paraphernalia. Two or three steps at the end led into another small hallway with doors to left and right, and Basil followed his hostess to the left, into a large kitchen with an Aga taking up much of one wall. Rupert pushed past his legs and flung himself down on an old rug.

'Trust a dog to pinch the best spot,' Constance remarked, leaning over him to slide a big kettle on to the hotplate, where it immediately began to sing. She took the lid off a fat brown teapot and peered in, then carried it over to a bin in the corner and tipped out the tea leaves. 'Find yourself somewhere to sit, Basil.'

The vicar looked around. There was a big table in the middle of the kitchen, with chairs around it, and a battered sofa at the end of the room, occupied by a large ginger cat, which had evidently been woken by their arrival and had raised its head and fixed the newcomer with a suspicious stare. Basil decided not to disturb it further – he had tried to stroke it once, and had to go to Charles Latimer afterwards with a badly swollen hand – and took one of the chairs at the table. Constance shifted a heap of papers with one hand and dumped a cup of tea in front of him with the other.

'I'll have a cheese sandwich in a minute,' she said. 'Do you know, a cheese sandwich with some watercress will give you all the nourishment you need. You could live on that. Better still with some Marmite,' she added.

Basil, who had loathed Marmite ever since he was a small boy and his older sister had encouraged him to spread it thickly on his toast in the belief that it was chocolate, shuddered slightly. He shook his head at the sugar bowl Constance proffered, but stirred his tea anyway. She sat opposite him and gave him a sharp look. The cat, evidently deciding that the vicar wasn't worth bothering about, put his head down again and went back to sleep.

'Well, what did you want to see me about? Not to talk about the weather or cheese sandwiches, I can tell. There's something on your mind.'

Once again, Basil marvelled at the old lady's perception. He'd hardly said a word, yet she knew that this wasn't purely a social call. He stared thoughtfully at his tea, trying to arrange his thoughts, then said, 'I need your help, Constance. Well, to be specific, I need your memory. You see, a young woman has come to see me recently – well, not *so* young, perhaps, in her mid-thirties—'

'*That*'s young!' Miss Bellamy interrupted. 'Anyone under fifty's young to me these days.'

'To me as well,' Basil said with a smile. 'Anyway, this young woman is searching for her family. For her parents, to be exact. She thinks they came from Burracombe.'

'She *thinks*? What happened to them, then? Were they killed in the war?' She thought for a minute. 'No, it couldn't be that, could it? If she's in her thirties now, she'd have been a young woman when the war broke out. Did they die when she was very young?'

'No. At least, her mother didn't – she died only a few months ago.' Basil recounted the story Jennifer Tucker had told him. 'So, you see, she doesn't really know for certain that it was Burracombe her mother came from, and she knows nothing at all about her father. He might have been a

Plymouth man, or come from anywhere in the country. He might not even have been English,' he added with sudden realisation.

'Didn't you say she had a letter? That was written in English, wasn't it?'

'Yes, although that doesn't mean he couldn't have been foreign.' Basil tried to remember the wording of the few phrases at the end of the letter. 'No, I don't think he was foreign. It *felt* English somehow. But he still needn't have been local.'

'She did think her mother had come from here, though?' Constance asked, and he nodded. 'So that's where we need to start looking. And she would have been born – when? Around the time of the Great War?'

'In 1917.' The vicar looked at her. 'Do you remember anything from that time? A young woman, unmarried but expecting a baby? Or leaving home on some pretext? There would surely have been some scandal.'

'There certainly would. It would have been the talk of the village. But I wasn't here then, Basil. I was a VAD nurse in Malta. By the time I came home after the war, everyone was too busy trying to get back on their feet again to worry about telling me old news. And no sooner was the Armistice signed than we had that 'flu epidemic. I went to help out in Plymouth. It took us a long time to settle down, and the world was never the same again. People were trying to look forward, not back – not that they had much to look forward to, what with the General Strike and the Depression and then another war coming.'

'No, I can see that,' he said thoughtfully. 'So you remember nothing that might help?'

'Sorry, I can't.' She sipped her tea, her weathered face, walnut-brown even in March, screwed up in concentration. 'There must be plenty of people here who would, though. Anyone over fifty would be the right age – probably know the girl well, might even know the man involved. You could ask anyone.'

'I was asked to make *discreet* enquiries,' Basil said mildly, and she laughed.

'Yes, see your point. Need to be careful who you approach or it'll be all over the village by teatime.'

'That's why I came to you first. Whom do you think I should ask next?'

She thought for a moment. 'What about Alice Tozer? She's the right age, and her mother might know even more. They won't spread gossip.'

'You're right. I need to go and see Ted soon about the Easter bellringing. Perhaps I'll ask them then, if the rest of the family aren't around. Not that I wouldn't trust them all just as much,' he added hastily, 'but somehow, once you start to talk about things like this, they seem to spread through the air, with no need of human assistance. I really don't want poor Miss Tucker to find herself a subject of general interest next time she comes to Burracombe.'

'And yet, if she does find anything out, she's bound to become one,' Constance pointed out. 'You can't have long-lost relatives turning up and people not notice. Look at young Maddy Forsyth and her sister. That caused plenty of excitement when they found each other.'

'Nice excitement, though,' he said. 'Everyone was so pleased for them, having known Maddy since she was a child and Stella being such a popular teacher.' He thought for a moment. 'I see what you mean, though. One of the village men suddenly discovering he has a daughter he knew nothing about might not be such a pleasant surprise.'

'If you ask me,' Constance said in her forthright voice, 'she'd be better off forgetting all about it. She might find out things she'd rather not know. Why did the mother have to go to Plymouth, for instance? Did the man refuse to stand by her? He might not be at all pleased by this. He might even refuse to acknowledge her. I don't see how this Miss Tucker can hope to prove anything, anyway.' She shook her head. 'No, I'm sorry, but I think some things are best forgotten. Let sleeping dogs lie.'

They both looked down at Rupert, stretched out on the rug, and Basil, who knew that the dachshund had an uncertain temper and could suddenly decide to nip unwary ankles, couldn't help agreeing. 'But I can't stop this young woman making her enquiries,' he said. 'And if she asks my help, I don't see how I can refuse it.'

'No, don't suppose you can. But you might put in the odd word – a little bit of guidance here and there. Anyway, I'm afraid I can't help you. I'll give it some thought, though,' she added as Basil put his cup back on the saucer. 'See if I can call anything to mind – any scrap of conversation when I came home, any young girls not being around the village, that sort of thing.' She furrowed her brow so that her wrinkled face looked as if it might crumple into pieces. 'But I can't say anything strikes me at the moment.'

'Oh well.' Basil stood up, one eye on the dachshund, the other on the cat. Both opened an eye at his movement and either could have been ready to spring. He edged towards the door. 'I'll try the Tozers. If anyone is likely to remember, I should think it would be them. But you know, I don't think the answer lies in Burracombe at all. I can find no mention of any Hannafords in the church records.'

'They might have been Chapel people,' Constance said thoughtfully. 'But if she came to you, that doesn't seem likely.'

'She was definitely brought up as Church of England.' He nodded. 'But it could have been in any of the villages hereabouts – Little Burracombe, or Meavy, perhaps, or Walkhampton. Or even the other side of Tavistock – Peter Tavy or Mary Tavy. It could have been anywhere.' He reached the door unmolested. 'Well, all I can do is try, and if I don't find anything, that'll be an end of it, as far as we're concerned. I don't mind telling you, Miss Bellamy, that would be a relief to me. I'm very much inclined to agree with you – some stones are best left unturned.'

Constance Bellamy saw him to the door and began to pull on her boots again. He looked at her.

'You never had your sandwich.'

'So I didn't,' she said. She turned her head to see the time on the clock that hung on the wall of the inner hallway. 'Bit late for it now. It'll be teatime before we know where we are, and I've got a few jobs I want to do outside before the sun goes down. At least the evenings are drawing out a bit now, and the clocks'll be going forward in a week or two.' She hauled on an old waistcoat that looked as if it had once belonged to a man. 'Not that it really makes any difference to the amount of daylight we get! It just means that people make better use of what we do have, for a while at any rate.'

Basil knew that Constance was up with the sun at any time of year. She worked like a beaver in her garden, though she kept a large part of it wild, to encourage birds, and could always be relied upon to find something for the church decorations. She had a vegetable patch, too, and was an enthusiastic member of the village Gardening Club – even though it had been started by her arch-enemy Joyce Warren. This year, they were to hold the Flower and Produce Show in June, when everything would be at its peak.

'Well, don't forget to eat entirely,' Basil said as he departed, and she gave a snort of laughter.

'Not much chance of that! Rupert and Tibby will remind me when it's suppertime. And then there's the hens as well.' As if on cue, three brown chickens came stepping round the side of the house. 'Got too many other mouths to feed to forget my own.' She picked up a pair of secateurs from the old wooden bench just outside the door and waved them at him. 'Nice to see you, Basil. And good luck with your search – I just hope turning over these old stones doesn't bring out too many worms.'

He smiled and waved to her from the gate, then set off back along the lane, his brow furrowed in thought. Constance was right – this investigation might not produce the results Jennifer Tucker wanted. But it was not for him to tell the young woman to abandon her search, and he knew from the wistful way in which she talked that if she didn't find out who her father was, the mystery would haunt her all her life. Perhaps it really was better to know, even if the knowledge itself brought more sadness.

All I can do, he thought as he waved to the children, out in the playground again, is help her in whatever way she asks, and be there in case she needs something more.

Chapter Eleven

Minnie Tozer was sitting in the garden by the kitchen door, cutting the purple heads off some stalks of sprouting broccoli while her daughter-in-law, Alice, planted out pea seedlings. She had been growing them in a cold frame in a corner of the kitchen garden, but the weather had turned so mild that she'd decided it was safe now to put them in the ground.

'I won't do the broad beans, though,' she observed as she knelt on the grassy path. 'You know what Ted's like, always puts them in himself on Good Friday. He says that be the proper day to plant them.'

'And so 'tis,' Minnie said. 'Just coming up to full moon, see? Plants always do better if you put them in near the full moon. It draws up the water – just like the tides.'

'Well, I think these little chaps will do all right,' Alice said, straightening up and dusting off the front of her skirt. She looked down at the row of seedlings and gave a little nod of satisfaction. ''Tis nice and sheltered here, and I've got they old cloches handy in case there's a frost. I'll just get the can and water them in.'

She fetched the galvanised watering-can and sprinkled water over the plants. She had already furnished them with twiggy sticks, gleaned from the hedge Jacob Prout had been cutting in the lane, and as she sat down next to Minnie both women looked forward to the day when the first peas would be harvested. 'A nice leg of lamb and some new potatoes and spring greens,' Minnie said. 'Go down a treat, that will. With some rhubarb and custard for afters.'

Alice laughed. 'You'll never stop enjoying your food, will you, Mother!'

'When you stop enjoying your food, you might as well go,' Minnie said. 'Not much else to live for, when you'm my age.'

'Don't talk so mazed! You've got years ahead of you yet, and there's plenty to look forward to. Joanna's new baby, our Val's wedding – though heaven knows when that'll be, at the rate they'm going. They've still not found anywhere to live.'

'Nor likely to,' Minnie observed. 'All the farm cottages for miles around be spoken for, and some of the ones that were took over in the war haven't been given back yet. And there's city folk still living in some of 'em – look at the Cherrimans, over in that estate house. Val said Hilary told her the lease would be coming up for renewal soon, but it seems as if they might want to stay on.'

'You'd think they'd want to go back to Plymouth, where they came from, wouldn't you?' Alice said.

'I don't see why,' Minnie argued. 'I mean, who in their senses'd want to go back to a city that was bombed to bits and still isn't properly rebuilt?' 'Tis like a bombsite still, Plymouth is – I wouldn't want to go back, not when I had a place like that estate house to live in.'

'It's not theirs, though, is it? That makes a difference. And their house in Plymouth's a lovely one, from what I've heard. Big place, down in Mannamead, with a good garden. It were took over for offices or summat for the Government during the war. But you'd think they'd have given it back by now, wouldn't you?'

'Maybe the Cherrimans don't want it back. They know when they'm well off – must be getting a good rent for it, and they can stop out here in the country. Still, it don't seem fair, not when there's proper country folk like our Val needing somewhere to settle down and raise a family. And didn't her say young Luke's thinking about getting a job in Plymouth? Us don't want them moving down there, Alice.'

'No,' Alice agreed. 'Us don't. But I don't know what us can do about it, Mother, I really don't.' She got to her feet. 'I'll put the kettle on for a cup of tea, then I'll get on with a bit more gardening before it turns cold. There's a heap of weeding wants doing in that front flowerbed; the seeds must have been waiting all winter, and now they'm sprouting up like I don't know what.'

She went indoors, and Minnie turned her face to the sun and closed her eyes. Whatever she might say about getting old, there was still plenty to enjoy in life apart from good food. The family, the life of the village, the sunshine and the song of the birds. Her mind drifted back to her younger days, when it had seemed impossible to believe that she would ever be an old woman. Queen Victoria had been on the throne then, and life had been slower. Wars were fought in far-off places such as Africa, and the village had been full of young people and families, none of whom ever ventured far. Even a trip to Plymouth was only undertaken by the more adventurous, and Minnie knew many people who lived out their entire lives without going any further than to Tavistock Goosey Fair.

It hadn't been all good, of course. There was plenty of poverty and families, like the Cullifords today, who filled their tumbledown cottages with children, many of whom died young. But most of the cottagers had enough garden to grow a few vegetables, as Alice was still doing today, and there were enough rabbits in the fields to be able to snare one for the pot now and then. Looking back, it seemed a good enough life, and Minnie felt thankful that she'd had her youth then, and not known of the terrible wars that were to come.

It would be a shame if Val and Luke were to be forced to move to Plymouth, away from the family and from the peace and good fresh air of the countryside.

*

As it happened, Hilary had gone out that very day to see the Cherrimans. The estate house was some distance away, and although you could reach it via several field paths and a pleasant walk through a beech wood, she drove round by the road in the Land Rover and went up the long, narrow track to park in the gravelled forecourt. She parked next to the smart, silver-grey Austin Somerset already standing there, stopped the engine and sat for a few moments, looking at the house her family had lived in during the war.

It was nearly as old as the Barton itself, and had been built originally to house the head forester. Over time, many of the trees had been felled and the head gamekeeper had been put there instead. At some point, the squire – probably Hilary's grandfather – had decided that the gamekeeper, being a single man at that time, didn't need so much space and had moved him to the smaller house known now as Keeper's Cottage, leaving this one free for someone he considered more deserving. A succession of farm managers, Napier relatives who needed housing and various other tenants had followed, and the house had somehow lost its 'tied' status, so that now it could be let to anyone, not just agricultural workers.

The Cherrimans had come at the end of the war. When Plymouth was suffering its Blitz and the Government was requisitioning houses for its offices, Arnold Cherriman, who had been Gilbert Napier's friend since their schooldays and had become an eye specialist, had moved out of the house in Mannamead, where he had his own surgery, and taken a house in Tavistock. After hostilities ceased, the owners had returned, and as his own house was still under Government control, he had had to find somewhere else to live. It was then that the Napiers were about to return to the Barton, which had been occupied by a children's home, and Gilbert had offered the estate house to the Cherrimans.

It was like a game of 'musical houses', Hilary thought. But it really was time that it came to an end, and she wondered why the Cherrimans had stayed so long, and whether, when the lease ran out, they would be wanting to go back to Plymouth. It would certainly be the answer to Val and Luke's problems if they did.

Arnold Cherriman was waiting for her at the front door. He was a tall, broad-shouldered man with black hair combed smoothly back from his high forehead and dark, rather intimidating eyebrows. Hilary climbed down from the Land Rover and walked across the gravel to greet him. The front of the house had trellis fixed to its walls, which she knew would be covered in pink roses during the summer. Evelyn Cherriman was a keen gardener and had worked hard in the patch of ground surrounding the house, turning it from a practical vegetable patch to a blaze of colour. There were still vegetables and soft fruits hidden away behind the house, but flowering shrubs were Evelyn's joy, and here at the edge of the woods she had created a small arboretum of camellias, azaleas and even one or two magnolias. The camellias were already covered with glowing pink and scarlet blooms, their petals unfurling like roses.

She isn't going to want to leave this, Hilary thought with a sinking heart. She's put too much of herself into it.

Arnold reached out to shake her hand. 'Good afternoon, Hilary. Nice to see you. Father not with you?'

'No, he generally rests in the afternoon.' Hilary didn't tell him that she hadn't actually mentioned this visit to her father, knowing that he would immediately take over the discussion and she would be left to make pleasant but fruitless conversation with Evelyn Cherriman. Moreover, if the Cherrimans wanted to renew the lease, her father would agree at once and Val's hopes would be dashed.

She pushed away the guilt that she couldn't help feeling, and followed Arnold Cherriman indoors, aware that he was probably disinclined to talk business with her, but determined to do so anyway. She had grown accustomed to being greeted with suspicion, but she'd found that it could usually be dispelled by a firm manner and obvious knowledge of estate business. The tenant farmers all knew her, anyway, and although some of them seemed to find it difficult to accept that she was now a grown woman and in charge, they were slowly coming round to the idea.

Arnold Cherriman wasn't a tenant farmer, though. He was an educated man, accustomed to doing business with other men, and almost certainly believed that a woman's place was in the home.

Evelyn Cherriman came out of the sitting-room. She was a slender woman with brown hair drawn back from her face and rolled loosely on her neck. She had rather pale blue eyes behind glasses with tortoiseshell rims and a soft, almost whispering voice.

'Hilary, how nice to see you. I've made tea.' Hilary followed her into the room, which looked out to the front of the house. A fire burned in the grate, with a sofa and two armchairs drawn up around it, and a low table was laid with a china teapot and a plate of buttered scones. Arnold Cherriman took one of the armchairs by the fire, and Hilary and her hostess sat on the sofa.

'How do you like your tea?'

'Milk and no sugar, thank you.' Saccharin tablets were offered as well, but Hilary shook her head. 'I've always preferred it unsweetened.' She accepted a scone, wondering how to introduce the subject of the lease. The Cherrimans must know why she was here, but they seemed to be determined to treat it as a social visit. 'You've made this room very comfortable,' she said, looking round at the newly papered walls and the pretty curtains.

'Oh, we're very happy here,' Evelyn said at once. 'It's a delightful little house.'

Hilary seized on the word. 'It is, isn't it? But it must seem rather small after your house in Plymouth. I remember coming to see you there before the war – it seemed almost as big as the Barton.'

Arnold laughed a little patronisingly. 'Not quite up to that standard, I'm afraid. But yes, it's a good size. Room for me to have my surgery and offices there.'

'But you do still have your practice in Plymouth, don't you?'

'Certainly. It was a little inconvenient when we had to live in Tavistock, but there was no scope there so I had to keep it on. And of course the Eye Infirmary is in Plymouth, too. I used to go in by train.' He looked proudly out of the window, where his highly polished Austin stood beside Hilary's rather muddy Land Rover. 'Don't need to do that now. I can be in Plymouth within half an hour.'

Hilary turned to his wife. 'Don't you find it rather lonely out here, though, Mrs Cherriman? Especially if you have no transport of your own.'

Evelyn's hands fluttered a little and she glanced quickly at her husband, then away again. 'I have my garden—'

'Yes, you've done wonderfully with that. It was nothing much at all while we were here, though Mother did grow quite a lot of vegetables. Your camellias are a picture.'

'Well, the larger ones were here before we came,' Evelyn admitted. 'But I did put in some more. I love flowering shrubs, don't you?'

Hilary nodded. 'We're lucky to have the right soil for things like camellias and azaleas. I expect you had a nice garden in Plymouth, too, didn't you?'

Evelyn looked wistful. 'It was lovely. I spent a lot of my time there. I had a gardener, too, of course, and a boy who came in to help with the heavy work, but I did all the design and a lot of the planting. I often wonder . . .' Her voice trailed away, and Hilary spoke quickly, seeing that Arnold was beginning to look impatient and afraid that he was about to change the subject.

'Have you seen it since the war? Do you know how it's being looked after?'

'I don't suppose it's being looked after at all,' Evelyn said sadly. 'It's still Government offices, you know.' Her voice brightening a little, she looked at her husband and said, 'But there's a chance we may be able to move back soon, isn't there?' She turned back to Hilary. 'Arnold had a letter only the other day – they'll be moving out sometime this year and we can have the house back. I'll be able to see it then. It'll need a lot of work, I know, but . . .' She was clearly looking forward to it and Hilary's spirits rose.

Arnold Cherriman, however, was not looking so pleased. 'I'm afraid Evelyn's jumping the gun a little,' he said to Hilary, and frowned at his wife. 'I've already told you, my dear, it won't be as easy as that. We have no idea what condition the house is in – it's been used as offices for years now, it'll be quite unfit to live in. It'll need complete renovation before we can even think of moving back. And I'm not at all sure that I want to. It might be better to sell.'

'*Sell?*' Evelyn repeated faintly, and Hilary realised that this was the first she had heard of it. 'But Arnold—'

He shook his head at her, the black brows drawn heavily over his eyes, and lifted one hand, palm outwards, so that she fell silent. Hilary waited, biting her lip, her heart sinking. At last, having apparently considered his words carefully, he turned to her and spoke again, making it very clear that not only was his wife not included in the discussion but he would have preferred it if Hilary hadn't been either.

'I've been thinking this over very carefully, and of course I'll need to talk to your father as soon as I come to a decision. But you might be kind enough to tell him, my dear, that we shall almost certainly be renewing the lease on this house. Obviously, we shall be looking to move back to the city at some point, but whether we renovate the old house and go back there or look for somewhere different has yet to be decided. I've been thinking of building something new, and that would take some time. There's position to be considered, architects and so on – I needn't trouble you with all that now, but you'll realise that it can't be done in a moment.' He paused, ignoring his wife, who was clearly completely taken aback by all this, and suddenly produced a charming smile. 'But you don't want to be worrying your head over all this. You didn't come to talk about such tedious subjects as leases, I'm sure. Have another of these delicious scones, my dear – Evelyn, pour Hilary some more tea – and then you must look at the garden. It's my wife's pride and joy and there's a surprising amount of colour, even at this time of year. It's going to be a big wrench for her to leave it when we eventually do go, I know.'

Dazed and feeling as if she'd been neatly manoeuvred into a corner, Hilary took the scone he offered and gave her hostess a sympathetic smile as she poured the tea. After a few more moments, and before she had time to gather her thoughts, Arnold Cherriman rose to his feet and declared that he must be off.

'One or two patients to see. The working man's job is never done!' He waggled his palm to show that she shouldn't get up, and leaned down to shake her hand. 'Very pleasant to see you again, Hilary. Give my regards to your father and tell him I'll be glad to see him at any time. We can discuss things more fully then. Evelyn, don't forget to show Hilary that new magnolia you planted last year, and remember we've got the chairman of the Rotary Club coming to dinner on Wednesday.' He dropped a kiss on his wife's hair and was at the door before either of the women could speak. 'Goodbye, then.'

Hilary drew in a deep breath. She stole a look at the other woman and saw that she was looking distressed and embarrassed. It wouldn't be fair to say anything more, Hilary thought, even though she was screaming inside and wanted nothing more than to pick up the pretty china teapot and throw it at the door her host had gone through. Her host? He was her *tenant*, for heaven's sake! It was for her to say whether or not he could take on the lease of the house again, yet somehow he'd ridden roughshod over her, treating her as if she were the supplicant. While making it perfectly clear that he didn't consider her an appropriate person to negotiate, he would have no hesitation in telling her father that she'd agreed to their staying on. He'd patronised her, talked over her and outmanoeuvred her, and she was furious.

There was no use in taking it out on his wife, however, and Hilary had heard enough to know that Evelyn wanted nothing more than to return to her own home and garden. She could be an ally, even if not a very strong one. At any rate, she was the only one Hilary had at the moment.

She finished the scone and drained her cup, grateful for the soothing heat of the tea. Then she wiped her lips with the dainty lawn napkin she had been given, and said, 'Let's go and look at the garden, Mrs Cherriman. You can tell me about the one you had in Plymouth as well. Perhaps I could take you to have a look at it sometime. I'm sure the people there wouldn't mind.'

Evelyn gazed at her. Her eyes were suddenly moist and Hilary felt guilty again, at using this pleasant, rather mousy little woman for her own ends. But not entirely mine, she thought. Mrs Cherriman really did want to go back. If Hilary could help her to do that, while at the same time securing this house for Val and Luke, who could possibly object?

Apart from Arnold Cherriman, that is.

Chapter Twelve

'He more or less told me to go away and play with my dolls,' Hilary told Val indignantly as they sat in the Barton kitchen with a bottle of sherry between them. 'He practically said I wasn't to worry my pretty little head about it! Honestly, I could have thrown the teapot at him. I would have done, if it had been my own old brown one instead of Evelyn Cherriman's rather nice Wedgwood bone china.'

Val smiled, but her smile faded quickly and she sighed. 'Oh well, thanks for trying anyway, Hil. It looks as if we'll just have to start thinking about Plymouth.'

'I hate the thought of you going to live in Plymouth,' Hilary said morosely. 'Especially when we've got that dear little house that would be just right for you and Luke. And the thing is, I know Mrs Cherriman would like to move back to Plymouth. She's longing to get back to her own garden.'

'I thought you said she'd done a lot with this garden, though,' Val said doubtfully. 'Are you sure she'd want to leave it?'

'I'm sure she'd be quite sorry to leave it, but she'll be more pleased to have her own garden again. And I think she misses being in the town – she's not really a country person. She must be awfully lonely out here. There's not another house within half a mile. Have a drop more of this.' She poured some more sherry into Val's glass.

'Maybe she'll be able to persuade her husband to move back, then.'

'I don't think so,' Hilary said grimly. 'Arnold Cherriman doesn't strike me as the sort of person who could be persuaded to do anything.'

The two women sat in silence for a few moments, then Val said with an obvious determination to look on the bright side, 'Still, you did say he's talking of looking for somewhere else to live. Or even building a new house.'

'And how long will that take? You know what it's like in Plymouth now. All that rebuilding – the entire city centre was flattened during the war, and they're only just getting to grips with it now. They need shops, new streets and thousands of houses. Every builder in Plymouth will be employed for years to come – getting a house built of the sort Arnold Cherriman would want is going to be almost impossible.' Hilary drew in a breath of exasperation. 'I don't know why he can't be satisfed with the house he's got! It wouldn't take nearly as long to renovate it. Using it as offices can't have done it that much damage.'

'Well, we can't force him to go back if he doesn't want to,' Val said. 'Unless you refuse to renew the lease. And you can't really do that, can you, since he and your father are friends.'

'It would give Dad another heart attack,' Hilary agreed. 'But it makes me so cross, Val. *I'm* running the estate now, yet men like Arnold Cherriman just don't seem to believe I'm capable of it. You should have seen the way he looked at me, and heard his voice! I might have been three years old.' She thumped the bottle on the table, gripping its neck so tightly that her knuckles turned white.

'Well, don't strangle the poor thing,' Val remarked mildly. 'It's not Mr Cherriman's neck you've got there. Honestly, Hilary, you don't need to get so worked up – it's not the end of the world. Something will turn up, and even if it doesn't and we have to go to Plymouth, I dare say we'll still be able to mount the odd expedition back to Burracombe.'

Hilary stared at her, then relaxed. She grinned reluctantly and let go of the bottle.

'Sorry. I just get so fed up with it. And you're right, it doesn't really matter. It's finding you somewhere to live that's important, not how pompous old fools like Arnold Cherriman treat me.'

'The rest of the tenants accept you, don't they?' Val asked. 'And the other people you have to deal with?'

'Most of them, I suppose. A lot of them still think I'm only *helping* Father – that I report everything back to him and take his advice, like a messenger, and that when he's better we'll go back to the way things were before.' Hilary sighed and looked down at the table, tracing a pattern with her forefinger on the wood. 'Sometimes I think Dad thinks that, too. And maybe he's right. Maybe I *am* just a temporary substitute.'

'Of course you're not!' Val reached across to touch her friend's hand. 'Surely that's all been agreed. He knows he can't ever do all the things he used to do. He knows you're perfectly capable of running things.'

'He also knows that *he's* capable of running quite a lot,' Hilary said. 'I know I'm being selfish – trying to take it all over for myself. But I'm so afraid that if I let him start to take control again, I'll be back here in the kitchen—' she waved her hand '—and my one chance to make something of my life will be gone for ever.' She thought for a moment. 'Well, not for ever. Just until he has another heart attack and kills himself. And I don't want that to happen, Val.'

'Of course you don't.' Val regarded her friend with sympathy. Her own problems seemed small when set beside Hilary's. She had Luke, and although they had nowhere to live just yet and didn't know whether their future lay in Burracombe or Plymouth – or somewhere else entirely – she did at least know they had a future together. Hilary's life, centred round her father and the estate, seemed bleak in comparison. It's a shame she lost her fiancé in the war, Val thought. And a shame she's never found anyone else to love.

'Stop worrying about Luke and me,' she said. 'You've got enough on your plate without trying to find a home for us. We'll find somewhere eventually. And if all else fails, I *will* go and live with him in the charcoal-burner's cottage. It's not that bad.'

Hilary laughed, although her laughter sounded a little wobbly. 'I suppose you could always build on another room or two.' She looked at the sherry bottle. 'I'd better not have any more of this. I've got to have a clear head in the morning – the accountant's coming and we're going to go over last year's figures. It's coming up to the end of the tax year, and I need to get everything right or I'll have yet another man telling me not to worry my pretty little head over it!'

'I've got to go, too.' Val stood up and then reached over and patted Hilary's shoulder. 'Don't let them get you down, Hil. You're proving you can do it. They wouldn't be getting so worried otherwise. That's what all this is about, you know – they're scared women are going to take over the world. We showed them during the war that we could do all their jobs just as well as they could and they're terrified!'

'Arnold Cherriman didn't look very terrified,' Hilary said ruefully. 'He wound me right round his little finger. And I'll tell you something else, Val – he's a bully. That poor little wife of his is scared stiff of him.'

'Well, that's a shame, but there's nothing much we can do about it.' Val pulled on her green tweed jacket. 'Just don't let him bully you.'

She grinned at Hilary and let herself out of the back door. The evening was drawing in now, the sun gone and dusk creeping over the meadows like a soft brown fuzz. From the hedges came a busy twittering as the birds settled down for the night, and she heard the first soft hoot of an owl. Val walked down the drive and along the lane to the track leading to the farm and paused for a moment, her hand on the gate, looking up into the velvet sky.

I really don't want to leave here, she thought. I was away long enough during the war to learn to appreciate all that we have in Burracombe, and I want to make it my home for ever. But if Luke and I can't find anywhere to live, we'll have to leave.

She had lost Luke once, years ago. She didn't intend to lose him again.

Basil was already in the kitchen of the Tozers' farm when Val arrived home. He'd come round after supper, knowing that Ted would be there and the family settling down for the evening. Alice and Joanna were just clearing away the dishes when he knocked on the back door, and Jackie let him in.

'Jackie, how nice to see you, my dear. How are you these days? And how's that boyfriend of yours? Any news of him coming home from Korea yet?'

Jackie blushed and shook her head. 'Doesn't seem like it, Mr Harvey. But he's not really my boyfriend, you know. We stopped being serious when – well, before he went away. I just write to him as a friend now, that's all.'

'Ah, I see. Very sensible.' He wiped his feet on the doormat and came into the kitchen, pulling off his woolly gloves. They were the ones that Minnie had knitted him as a Christmas present and he'd been careful to wear them this evening, just as he always tried to wear the various gloves, mittens and scarves his parishioners had given him whenever he visited their houses. Sometimes he got it wrong and had to endure quizzical glances and queries as to whether the gifts had fitted or been the wrong colour (not very likely, since they were invariably black, dark blue or grey), but on the whole he thought the donors were satisfied that their gifts were appreciated. He looked around the big kitchen and thought for the hundredth time how warm and cosy it seemed.

'I hope it's not inconvenient, my calling round now,' he said apologetically. 'You weren't planning to listen to anything on the radio, were you? I looked in the *Radio Times* to make sure *Take It From Here* or *PC 49* weren't on.'

Alice laughed. 'Bless you, Vicar, 'twouldn't matter if they were. Us have always got time for our friends. Now, I dare say you wants to talk to Ted about Easter bellringing, is that it? I'll give him a call. He's just popped outside for a minute.' She indicated the wheel-back chair by the range. 'Sit you down, flower.'

Basil sat down opposite Minnie. Joanna had taken Robin upstairs to put him to bed, and Jackie had disappeared as well. Tom was evidently out in the barn; probably he and Ted were busy with lambing. Basil half turned, meaning to tell Alice not to bother her husband now, he would come back later, but she had already gone.

''Tis all right,' Minnie said comfortably. 'Ted won't mind coming back in. He's owed a rest, anyway, been travelling ever since six o'clock milking this morning, he has, and only sat down for his meals. Tom can look after things outside for a bit.'

Basil knew that 'travelling' simply meant that Ted had been busy, not that he'd been away from the farm. The first time he'd heard this expression, he'd enquired innocently where the person had been, expecting to be told Plymouth, Exeter or even London, only to be met with a blank stare. It had been his first introduction to the local dialect, and he sometimes felt he was still learning.

'And how be you, Vicar?' Minnie asked. She was busy knitting something in fine, white wool, and Basil wondered if Joanna was expecting another baby. Nothing had been said officially yet, but he'd heard one or two speculative murmurs around the village, and young Tom had had an air of suppressed pride and excitement about him lately. Minnie's knitting seemed to confirm it, and when she caught him looking, she smiled and said, 'That's right, Vicar. Us got another little one on the way. 'Tisn't common knowledge yet, but I dare say there's a few keeping watch on our Joanna's shape. You can't keep news like that secret for long in Burracombe.'

'You can't keep anything secret for long in Burracombe,' Basil said, thinking of Jennifer Tucker. Surely if her parents really had come from this village, someone would know. Minnie herself was one of the most likely ones – she would have been almost fifty in 1917 and would surely have been aware of any scandal. Alice herself would have been about seventeen or eighteen, and Ted only a few years older. But Ted had been away during the First World War, in the Army, and might have missed any goings-on in the village.

Basil realised that his thoughts had led him away from the kitchen and from Minnie and her news. Belatedly, he congratulated her on being about to become a great-grandmother again. 'I expect they'd like a girl this time.'

'I don't think they'll mind, so long as it's healthy,' Minnie replied. 'Mind you, most folk like to have their pigeon pair. Then it don't matter so much what the next one is, though I thinks meself that two of each is the best family. Everyone gets a brother and a sister that way.'

'Goodness me, you *are* in a hurry!' Basil said, laughing. 'This is only Joanna and Tom's second – it'll be quite a while before they think about a third and fourth.'

Minnie wagged one of her knitting-needles at him. 'That's for the Good Lord to decide,' she said severely. 'If He wants our Tom and Joanna to have a big quiverful, then that's what they'll have. Still, maybe we'm looking ahead a bit there. We've got to get our Val settled next. She don't have too much time ahead of her for starting a family.'

The door opened before they could say any more, and Ted and Alice came in, bringing a gust of March night air with them. Since dusk, the warmth that the sun had brought had disappeared and a thin, cold wind had sprung up. Ted closed the door quickly, and shucked off his boots on the mat.

'Evening, Vicar. Turning cold out there again.'

'It is, Ted. You're busy, I dare say. Everything going well?'

'Mustn't grumble.' Ted came over to the range, rubbing his hands and holding them out to the glowing fire. 'Got a few twin lambs coming along. Lost a couple last night, but that's always the way of it. What can I do for you, now? Easter bellringing, is it?'

'That's right.' Basil glanced up at the ceiling. It was criss-crossed with dark oak beams, and from each one hung a row of handbells, their leather straps as highly polished as a pair of undertaker's shoes and their metal gleaming. 'I was wondering if we might bring these little fellows into the service this year, for a change. I often think they're not used enough, except at Christmas.'

Ted looked up, too. The handbells had come down through his family and he'd collected more over the years. Nearly every church had their own set, some well used and others packed away in their cases and hardly ever touched, and occasionally a privately owned set was sold by a family who had no use for them. Ted's father had been an enthusiastic handbell-ringer, making up his own changes for them to ring, and Minnie had arranged the notation for several carols. During the war, when the church bells couldn't be rung, Ted had kept interest going by having a handbell practice one evening a week.

''Twould be nice to use 'em a bit more,' he admitted. 'It seems fitting at Christmas, somehow, but I don't see why us couldn't do summat with 'em the rest of the year. What was it you were thinking of, Vicar?'

'Well, not Christmas carols, of course. Do you have any other music?' He glanced at Minnie, who had laid down her knitting and was looking interested. 'I know you're a talented musician, Mrs Tozer – could you do some arrangements for us?'

'My stars, Vicar, that be laying it on a bit thick,' Minnie exclaimed, laughing. ''Tis a few years since I put me hand to anything like that. Isn't there no one else could do it?'

'I really don't think there is. You're the one who understands the bells, you see. And you used to play the church organ, so I know you're a musician – why, you still play that harmonium you've got in your parlour, don't you?'

'Yes, she does,' Alice said quickly, before Minnie could deny it. 'We often has a bit of a sing-song of a Sunday evening – starts off with a few hymns, of course, and then goes on to some of the old tunes – and Mother plays as well as ever. There are all sorts of tunes we could play on the bells, if she did the notes for us.' She looked at her mother-in-law. 'What about "All On the April Evening"? That's a lovely tune, and just right for Easter.'

'Well, I might be able to do it,' Minnie said, her sparkling eyes belying any reluctance in her voice. ''Twould be nice to hear it on the bells, I can't say it wouldn't.' She nodded her head. 'I'll think about it.'

'That's very good of you, Mrs Tozer,' Basil said warmly, knowing that this was virtually a 'yes'. 'And perhaps one or two hymns. I thought "All Things Bright and Beautiful" might be appropriate, and perhaps "Jesus Lives!" But I'll leave it to you to decide what would sound best on handbells.' He turned back to Ted. 'The band's ready for the normal ringing, I expect? Early, for eight o'clock Communion, and then again for matins? And there'll be no ringing during Holy Week, of course.'

'No, Palm Sunday'll be the last time the bells is heard until Easter Day,' Ted confirmed. ''Tis always a quiet week, then.' He didn't mention his plan to plant broad beans on Good Friday. 'Let's hope for a nice spring day and a good attendance in church, eh, Vicar?'

Basil agreed a little self-consciously, aware that the collection on Easter Day was, by tradition, his to keep. He then glanced at the three Tozers and cleared his throat.

'Now that we're here together, with nobody else around, there's another matter I wanted to discuss with you. It's a little delicate, and I know you won't mention it to anyone else, but I think you might be the best ones to help. You see—'

The door opened and Val came in. The three heads, which had bent nearer to the vicar as he began to make his interesting statement, turned in some frustration and she looked at them with surprise.

'Whatever's going on? You look like conspirators! Not planning to rob a bank, are you?'

'Don't be silly,' Alice said with a touch of asperity. 'We've just been having a talk about the handbells, that's all. Vicar wants 'em used in the Easter service this year. And how are things over at the Barton?'

'Oh, all right.' Val took off her coat and hung it with the others on the row of hooks inside the door. 'Hilary's a bit fed up. She went over to see the Cherrimans today and Mr Cherriman treated her like a kid. And they don't look as if they're going to move out of the house in a hurry, either.' She came over to the fire. 'It's getting really cold out there. I wouldn't be surprised if we get a frost tonight.'

'My peas!' Alice jumped up. 'I meant to cover 'em up . . . I'd better do it now, while I'm thinking of it. I'm sorry, Vicar,' she added, turning to Basil. 'If you don't mind waiting a bit, I'll make you a cup of cocoa before you goes. But if I don't do this now, I'll forget and then we'll have nothing to go with our roast lamb.'

'No, I'd better be going,' he said, standing up. 'I promised Grace I wouldn't be late, and I've got another call to make first.' He nodded towards Minnie and Ted. 'I'll look forward to hearing what you do with the handbell music. I think it will make a delightful addition to our Easter Day service. Now, I really must be on my way – Grace will think I've absconded with the offertory box!'

He pulled on his coat and gloves, gave them all a little wave and went out of the door that Ted was holding open for him. Alice, who was still looking for the old net curtains she used to cover her plants when a frost threatened, looked after him thoughtfully.

'I wonder what it was he wanted to talk to us about,' she mused. 'Something *delicate*, he said. Whatever do you think it could be? I wondered if it might be about old Jem Squires, over at Little Burracombe. 'Tis his funeral on Monday.'

'I shouldn't have thought so,' Ted said, shaking his head. 'That's not much to do with us, although I'll be going along, of course. Old Jem was a good old boy, and a fine bellringer in his day.' He shrugged. 'No, if 'twas anything important Vicar wanted to say, he'll get round to it again sometime. And there can't be anything going on in the village that one of us don't know about. One way or another, all the news gets to the Tozers sooner or later.'

Alice nodded. But as she found her curtains and went out to the kitchen garden to tuck up her peas, she was still looking thoughtful. Whatever it was, the vicar had obviously not wanted to discuss it once Val had arrived. What could be so 'delicate' that it couldn't be mentioned in front of her?

As Ted had said, however, if it were at all important, the vicar would find some other opportunity to broach the subject. Alice, her curiosity now aroused, just hoped he wouldn't take too long.

Chapter Thirteen

Basil's next call was at the village inn, where Bernie Nethercott presided behind the bar, helped by his wife and, on busy nights, Dottie Friend. It wasn't so much that the vicar wanted a drink – although he wasn't at all averse to the odd pint and often joined the villagers in a game of darts or dominoes – but he knew that Jacob Prout was likely to be there at this time, and it was Jacob that Basil wanted to talk to.

'It's about Jem Squires's funeral,' he said, finding the odd-job man sitting in his favourite corner nursing his own pewter tankard, kept specially for him on a hook over the bar. 'The vicar over at Little Burracombe is ill with bronchitis so I'll be taking the service, and now I've heard that their gravedigger's had an accident and broken a rib. Do you think you'd be able to dig the grave for them?'

Jacob took a swallow of his beer and nodded. 'Reckon so. I could make a start on Friday, get young Billy Friend to give me a hand, and if us don't finish it, then us can have another crack on Saturday. I dare say they'll be ringing the bells, too, seeing as old Jem were a ringer.'

'I believe so. Will you be going to the funeral, too?'

'Oh, ah, Ted's already had a word with us about that. Us'll all be going along, and tower captain's said us can ring a special peal for him after the burial. Give him a proper send-off, like. Why, when you comes to think of it, he must have rung those bells for Queen Victoria herself, God bless her.'

'So he must. Just think of all the changes he must have

witnessed.' Both men were silent for a few moments, their minds roaming back through almost a century of history. 'Aeroplanes, cars – why, there probably weren't even bicycles when he was a boy.'

'Just about coming in, I reckon,' Jacob said. 'He told I once, he saw a couple of penny-farthings at Tavistock Goosey Fair when he were a young chap. Two young chaps rode 'em all the way out from Plymouth. Cars didn't come in till after the turn of the century, though – and it were a while even then before one were seen in Burracombe. I reckon Jem must've been well over forty before he saw one with his own eyes.'

Basil shook his head wonderingly. 'And now there are cars everywhere, and jet aircraft flying across the sky. So much change in just one lifetime. And what will happen next, I wonder. People are even talking about going to the moon.'

Jacob gave a scornful grunt. 'That'll never happen, not in my lifetime nor yours, Vicar. Stands to reason, don't it? I mean, how many millions of miles is it? And you can't even go to London without wanting more petrol, so they tell me. No, there'll never be anyone going to the moon – that's just for far-fetched stories in boys' comics, like that *Eagle* they all reads now.' He took another long swallow of his ale. 'Reckon I'd better go over to Little Burracombe tomorrow and have a look at where they wants this grave dug. The ground's going to be pretty hard, with all this frost we been having lately. Better sharpen up my old mattock.' He looked down into his tankard. 'Can I get you another pint, Vicar?'

'No, no, let me get this. I only want a half, anyway – have to be going soon.' Basil went back to the bar. A few more men had come in, and he saw his godson, Luke, among them, and then Jed Fisher. Basil nodded to them both and went back to his seat beside Jacob. After a few minutes, Luke came over and joined them on the settle.

'Jed's in a nasty mood tonight,' he murmured. 'Got a bee in

his bonnet about incomers. Apparently, he went over to the Cherrimans in the estate house to look for some work and they gave him a flea in his ear.'

'So they should,' Jacob said indignantly. 'He ought to know I does their gardening for them. He'd no right to go there, pestering.'

'I suppose he has a right to ask,' Basil said mildly. 'And he doesn't get as much work around the village as you do, Jacob.'

'And why's that?' the old man demanded. 'It's because he don't do as good a job, that's why! Scamps his work and leaves it all at odds, always has done. He only gets chapel work because his old dad did their graveyard for them and the minister's got a kind heart. *Too* kind, if you asks me.' He snorted.

'We all have to live,' Basil began, but Jacob's indignation was taking a hold on him now, especially when he saw Jed coming towards them, his own tankard in his hand.

'I knows that, Vicar. I knows the Good Lord put us all on this earth for a purpose. We all got our place, human beings, cows and sheep, dogs and cats, the lot of us. But that don't stop some of us being vermin, all the same!' He raised his eyes and stared defiantly at the man who now stood opposite him.

'I suppose you means me,' Jed exclaimed angrily. 'That's slander, that is!'

'I never said a word about you. Not a single word. I was talking about everything being for a purpose, even rats. If you thought I meant you, maybe that's because you—'

'Gentlemen, gentlemen,' Basil interposed hurriedly. 'I'm sure there's no need for this. Jacob, sit down again, and Jed, why don't you join us here for a while? We were just talking about old Jem Squires. It's his funeral on Monday.'

'I knows that. I knowed old Jem, too, and his sister. Good friends to me, they was.' He glowered at Jacob, who bristled at Basil's side. 'Better than some others I could mention. I won't join you, Vicar, thanks all the same. No offence, but I don't like the company you keeps.' He turned and made his way to the other side of the room.

Basil sighed. 'I wish you and Jed could get along better, Jacob. It makes it so difficult for you both, living next door to each other. Have you always been such enemies?'

Jacob scowled into his beer. ''Tis too far back to mend matters now, Vicar, and best not talked about. Jed and me'll never get on, and that's all there is to it. Now, what about a game of darts before you goes?'

Basil shook his head. 'I'm afraid I'll have to be going now. Perhaps Luke will give you a game – although he's better at dominoes.' He half feared that in Jacob's present mood, one of the darts might go astray, even as far as the corner where Jed was sitting now. He rose to his feet and laid his hand on Luke's shoulder for a moment. 'Good to see you, my boy. Bring Val over to the vicarage for supper one evening. You'll be wanting to make arrangements for your wedding before long.'

'Got to find somewhere to live first,' Luke said ruefully. 'Val's beginning to get a bit downhearted, I think. But somewhere will turn up, eventually.'

'And don't you worry about old Jem's grave,' Jacob said. 'I'll see that's done proper. Be a pleasure to me, that will, doing something for Jem. Last of the family, he was. There be no more Squireses now, over at Little Burracombe.'

Basil left the warmth of the inn and walked back to the vicarage. The sky was thick with stars, shining down on the dark streets of the village, and the only lights were those that glowed behind curtained windows. He felt in sombre, reflective mood, saddened by the bitter enmity between the two old men, and still humbled by the long stretch of memories that had died with Jem Squires. He would probably have known Jennifer Tucker's family, if they really did come from round here, he thought suddenly. People like him and Minnie Tozer had lived all their lives in this small corner of the country, and seen so many changes, yet their main interest had been the doings of their own families and neighbours.

He'd meant to ask Ted, Alice and Minnie if they had known of a young woman forced to leave the village through her pregnancy during the First World War, but Val had interrupted them and the moment had passed. I must do it soon, he thought. Minnie herself is over eighty, and although she seems hale enough, you never know when the Lord might decide her time is up. I really must do something about it soon.

He opened the front door of the vicarage, still thinking of all the changes that had taken place during the lifetime that had just ended. Not even bicycles on the road when Jem Squires was born – and now look at the world. And yet people were much the same. They still took more interest in their families and neighbours than in anything else. Look at Jennifer Tucker, searching for the father she had never known.

He felt suddenly ashamed. It's important to her, he thought, and I haven't tried hard enough. I'll go and see Minnie again.

Stella Simmons, too, was thinking about family matters.

'I just can't wait to see Muriel again,' she said to Dottie, as she enjoyed a cup of tea after school the next afternoon. 'Sorry – I mean Maddy. I suppose I'll get used to it eventually.'

'When is she coming, maid?' Dottie asked. She was making pastry at the kitchen table, her strong fingers rubbing the fat and flour together so that the mixture was as fine as tiny breadcrumbs. 'Easter, isn't it?'

'The week before, on the Wednesday before – the ninth. We break up on Friday, so that'll be just right. And she's staying two whole weeks! Isn't that lovely, Dottie? – we'll really have time to get to know each other.'

Dottie made a hollow in the middle of the mixture and poured cold water into it. She began to stir, gently drawing the dry flour and fat into the liquid until it became a stiff lump. 'I've been wondering where she means to stay. Usually, when she comes down with Miss Forsyth, they stop up at the Barton, with the Napiers, but when she's on her own she comes to me. And then, of course, she has your room. Well, 'twas hers when she lived here, so naturally—'

'Of course it was. Do you know, I hadn't really thought about it.' Stella looked at her in dismay. 'I suppose because they stayed at the Barton last time . . . It would be much nicer if she could be here, though.'

'It would,' Dottie said, sprinkling flour on the board and turning the lump on to it. 'But there's not room for another bed in that room, and you can't sleep in that single one together for two weeks, 'twouldn't be comfortable. And mine's not much better, or I'd say have that. But it's something us ought to be thinking about.'

'You're right. I can't think why it never occurred to me before.'

Stella looked around the living-room, which did duty as part of the kitchen as well. It was furnished with a couple of armchairs, the table where Dottie was working and where they ate their meals, and some kitchen chairs. There was a small footstool made of woven seagrass and Dottie's sewing-box, which was also a footstool, and in one corner, near the window, stood her treadle sewing-machine.

'I suppose there's room here to put a mattress on the floor, or a camp bed if we could borrow one,' she said doubtfully. 'I could sleep down here then and Mur— *Maddy* could have my bed.'

'If the worst comes to the worst, that's what us'll do,' Dottie declared, rolling the pastry out with her wooden rolling-pin. 'Better if I sleep down here, though, then Maddy can have my bed and you can stop where you are. It's handier for me coming in late from the pub, too – I'd only be disturbing you if 'twas you down here.'

'Oh no, we can't turn you out of your bed!' Stella exclaimed, horrified. 'I'm sure Maddy wouldn't want that. There, I did it,' she added with a pleased smile. 'Called her Maddy, I mean.'

'You'll soon get used to it once she'm here again,' Dottie said comfortably. She folded the strip of pastry into thirds and rolled it out again, gently so as not to push the air out. 'I wonder if there's anyone else nearby might let her have a bed. There's the Bell, of course – Bernie's always talking about letting rooms for a bit more income, only I don't know if he'd be able to get it ready in time. And a pub's not really the place for a young lady like Maddy. Not saying anything against it, mind, a better village inn than the Bell you'd go a long day's march to find, but it don't seem right for a young lady on her own.'

'No, I wouldn't want her staying at the pub.' Stella watched as Dottie fetched an enamel pie dish from the scullery. It was already filled with the blushing pink stems of chopped rhubarb, sprinkled with sugar and scattered with a few pieces of chopped crystallised ginger. 'Is that for our supper?'

'It is, and there's some nice clotted cream to go with it, made from the top of our own milk.' Dottie laid the pastry over the rhubarb, where it settled into a knobbly blanket, and cut round the overlapping edges, crimping them together in a pattern with the back of her knife. She gathered the scraps into another lump, rolled it out and cut it into strips, which she twisted into ropes and laid across the top of the pie. Then she dipped her pastry-brush into a cup of beaten egg and stroked it swiftly across. 'There,' she said, opening the oven door and sliding the dish inside. 'A feast for a king, though I says so meself. You can't beat the first rhubarb pie of the season. A real treat, that is.'

Stella agreed. Although she'd been living with Dottie for over a year now, she still hadn't got used to the meals Dottie seemed to make out of almost nothing. The rhubarb had been grown in their own garden, forced under galvanised buckets with holes in the top; the cream had been made from the milk of Ted Tozer's cows, simmered in a bowl on top of the range until it formed a thick crust; and the butter had been made by Nathan Pettifer's wife, Iris. Only the flour had come from a shop in Tavistock, and a few years ago even that could have been obtained from the mill, just along the valley.

Maddy had been so lucky to live with Dottie during those last years of the war, she thought. Her own years in the children's home, kind though the staff had been, seemed bleak in comparison. All the same, she was glad it had been that way round – she could never have felt completely happy, even if living in complete luxury, while she had no idea where her little sister was.

All those years lost to us both, she thought wistfully. But it was no good mourning them now. The main thing was that she and Muriel – *Maddy* – had found each other and would soon have a whole fortnight with nothing to do but get to know each other again.

We must find her somewhere really nice to stay, she thought. Somewhere close by, if she can't be here in the cottage with Dottie and me. I don't want her even as far away as the Barton.

'But it's simple,' Felix said when he and Stella went for a walk the next evening. They were following the brook through the woods, picking their way along a narrow footpath that wound between moss-covered rocks and gorse bushes yellow with flowers. 'Aggie's got another room. She lets it to visitors in the summer sometimes. Maddy could stay there and be just across the road from you.'

Stella paused and looked at him. 'I never thought of that.

But would it be all right, do you think – her and you staying in the same house? You know how people gossip.'

Felix burst out laughing. 'Oh, come on, Stella – she's your sister! Everyone must know by now that we – well, that we're friends. They couldn't possibly find anything to gossip about in Maddy staying at Aggie's. Why, there was quite often a single woman staying there last summer. Don't you remember the birdwatcher lady, with her binoculars and boots and haversack?'

Stella smiled. 'Yes, I do, but she was about sixty-five and looked like a tortoise. That's a bit different from Maddy, who's only just over twenty and looks like a film star.'

'I hope you're not suggesting that I wouldn't behave like a perfect gentleman,' Felix said, pretending to be offended, and she laughed and took his arm.

'Of course not. But not everyone knows you as well as I do. And some people can be quite spiteful.'

'How sad,' he said more seriously, 'that you should know that already. I hope it's not from personal experience.'

Stella hesitated. 'Children can be very cruel, you know. The children's home where I lived had all kinds of children in it, most of us orphans, so you'd think we'd have some sympathy for each other, but there were still some who could make some very unpleasant remarks about you and your parents. And outside, in the local school, children who had ordinary home lives seemed to think there was something peculiar about us – almost as if we weren't quite right in the head. It was better at college, but it wasn't really until I came to Burracombe that I began to feel normal.'

He stared at her. 'Stella, that's dreadful. I had no idea.'

'I don't talk about it much,' she said with a shrug. 'It's all behind me now, and I feel as if I've come home. Especially now that I've found Maddy and know she lived here, too, as a little girl.' She gazed about her, at the tall chestnut trees with their rough bark and the leaves just beginning to come out, at the green, furry humps of the moss-covered rocks, at the tumbling waters of the brook. 'I don't think I'll ever want to leave Burracombe,' she said softly.

Felix took her hand. 'Never? Even if you found a better job, say, in another place? Or – or fell in love and got married?'

Stella gave him a quick glance and then looked away again. 'I don't know. I can't say how I'd feel then, can I? We talked about this before, remember? I still don't think I'd want to move to another job.' She glanced at him again and then went on, a faint blush touching her skin, 'And if I ever did get married, it might be to someone in Burracombe.'

There was a short silence. They were standing very still, and the only sounds were the babble of the water and the singing of the birds as they went to their roosts. The setting sun was spreading a haze of apricot across the sky, laced with a delicate pattern of filigree branches. The air was as soft as silk against their faces.

Felix laid his hand on her cheek and turned her head gently so that she was looking up at him. His dark blue eyes were very intent and she felt her colour rise again, warming her cheeks. Her heart quickened.

'You're a lovely girl, Stella,' he said quietly. 'I hope you do fall in love.' And he bent his head and touched his lips against hers.

Chapter Fourteen

There was a good turn-out for Jem Squires's funeral. The rivalry between the two villages didn't mean that there wasn't plenty of friendship as well, and on Monday afternoon, a steady stream of people from Burracombe itself could be seen taking the path down the valley to cross the old wooden footbridge and climb the track on the other side to the smaller village. Once, both had been mining villages and there were still several remains to be seen – the old engine house of Wheal Freda, with its chimney pointing like a stark finger towards the sky from the broken ground, the fences around the adits that led down to the abandoned lead and copper mines, the tumbled walls of a few buildings where miners had once scoured a living from the harshness of the moor. There had been a large community in Little Burracombe then, with several inns and cottages, and both a church and chapel, but now much of it was gone and there was just one inn, a handful of cottages, one or two larger houses and some more scattered farms and dwellings in hidden combes and valleys.

Both church and chapel still retained their congregations, however, and before going to the church for the funeral, Basil called at the vicarage. Mrs Berry, the vicar's wife, showed him up to the bedroom where her husband was sitting up in bed, propped up by several pillows and looking frail.

John Berry was growing old now, and Basil suspected that when he finally gave up, the living would be merged with his own, and his parish enlarged. He shook the thin, bony hand and sat down beside the bed.

'Sorry you're not feeling well, John. But you're in the best place – there's a nasty chill in the air today. I just hope the mourners won't all go down with colds as well.'

'There'll be plenty of them,' John Berry said, his voice wheezy. 'Jem was well known and well liked in the parish. I'm sorry I can't take his funeral.'

Basil nodded. 'I'm sure you'll be missed,' he said. 'But I'll do my best.' He looked at John's grey face. He seemed very tired and fragile, and Basil hoped that there wouldn't be another funeral in Little Burracombe in the near future. They talked quietly for a few minutes and then shared a short prayer before Basil rose to take his leave.

'I'll come again when it's over,' he promised, holding his friend's hand. 'And I know you'll be with us in your thoughts.'

The old man nodded weakly. Each breath he took rattled in his chest, and as Basil went down the stairs, he felt anxious. He found Mrs Berry waiting for him in the hall.

'What does the doctor say?'

The vicar's wife lifted one shoulder. She was as old as her husband, and looked nearly as frail. Why ever hadn't they retired long ago? Basil wondered. But he knew the answer. Like many clergymen, John Berry had never been able to buy a home of his own, and once he gave up working, he would have to leave the vicarage. There were houses available for people in his position, but they usually meant moving away from the community where you had spent so many years and had so many friends, and for a couple like the Berrys, who had no family of their own, such a move would mean a lonely old age.

'He says if John gets any worse, he'll have to go to hospital. And if he does that . . .' She left the sentence unfinished, but again Basil knew what she was thinking. If John went into hospital now, he would probably never come home again. They would both rather he stayed at home, and either get better or die in his own bed.

And then what would happen to this poor old lady, who had given so much to the community and would be left quite alone?

With a heavy heart, Basil left the house and walked round to the church. There were already a few mourners there, their black clothes making them look like dark birds of sorrow amongst the gravestones, and as Basil stood at the door, welcoming them quietly, he saw the hearse approach. It had taken the long way round the village, passing every point of which Jem Squires might have had fond memories – the cottage where he had been born, the school where he had learned to read and write, the old mines where his grandfathers had worked, the farm where his father had tended the tough moorland sheep and cattle after the mines had closed during the 1870s. Jem had been a boy then, and had often talked of the hardship this had brought to the area, with families breaking up as the younger men were forced to leave the area and look for work elsewhere. Like the Cornish tin miners, many of them had gone to the Americas or Australia and lost communication perhaps for ever.

As the hearse came to a stop, the mourners made their way into the little church. The bells were already ringing, their clappers muffled so that only every other round sounded clearly, the others soft and sad. The bearers – all friends of the old man – carried his coffin slowly up the path, and Basil preceded it into the church, while the chief mourners – Jem's nephew and his wife, their family and two or three more distant cousins – came after it. There was just one bunch of flowers on the coffin: a posy of spring flowers gathered that morning from Jem's own garden.

As Basil came to the chancel steps and turned to face the

congregation, he saw a last mourner slip quietly into the church and take a place in the pew at the very back.

It was Jennifer Tucker.

'I saw it in the newspaper,' she said afterwards. 'Jeremiah Squires. And since the name began with "J" . . .'

'My dear, I owe you an apology,' Basil said. 'I've begun to make enquiries, but I haven't got very far. And it never occurred to me that old Jem might have anything to do with you – he'd have been nearly sixty when you were born.'

'It doesn't mean he couldn't have been the one, though, does it?' she said. She had waited after the service and they'd arranged to meet in the churchyard, after everyone had gone. Basil had made a brief visit to Jem's nephew's house, where the mourners were being given sherry and sandwiches, and had then come back to find her wandering among the gravestones. They sat on an old bench in a sheltered spot and talked. Over in the far corner, a mound of fresh earth spread with a few flowers showed where Jem had been laid to rest. Basil saw Jennifer Tucker looking at it. 'Men of sixty have become fathers before now.'

'That's true,' he admitted. 'But even so . . . I can't believe that Jem . . .' He thought for a few moments, then looked at her seriously. 'I know this is really none of my business, Miss Tucker, but do you really want to go on with this? You might find out things you'd really rather not know. You might even upset other people.'

Jennifer Tucker was silent for a while. He watched her anxiously, noting the delicacy of her profile and the warm chestnut of her hair against the pale, oval face. She closed her smoke-grey eyes and he saw the thick, dark lashes lying on the creamy skin and wondered again why she had never married.

At last she said, 'I've thought of that, too – that it might be painful to find out the truth. And I don't want to cause any trouble – if it looks like that, I'll stop. At least, I think I will.'

She turned her head and gave him a rueful smile. 'I can't know for sure. I feel so driven, you see – driven to find out something about my family, about *myself*. I thought I knew, until my mother died, and now I feel as if I've lost her in more ways than just by her dying. I feel as if I didn't even know her – not fully. And until I find my father, I *can't* know her.' She shrugged. 'Maybe I'll never find him. I may be looking in the wrong place, or he may be dead.' Her eyes went to the mound of fresh earth. 'But there might still be people who knew him – and who knew my mother. There might still be people who can fill in the gaps.' She paused again. 'I suppose I just want to find my family. People of my own.'

'But you have a family,' Basil said kindly. 'You have sisters.'

'Half-sisters. And the other half – well, that's nothing to do with me. The funny thing is, they don't seem to want to know any more about our mother. They'll be interested if I find anything out, but it's not the same for them as it is for me, because they have their father's family. I feel I have no one.'

'And has there never been anyone else?' he asked. 'You've never married?'

Jennifer sighed. 'It's a familiar enough story. We were engaged during the war, but he never came home. I've never felt the same for anyone else.'

'So what would you like to do now?' Basil asked. 'As you saw at the funeral, Jem's only close relative was a nephew, and he's in his seventies. All the others have died or moved away. If you make enquiries now, you'll have to rely on gossip, and ancient gossip at that. Jem was a well-respected man, and a very old man, too.'

'And if I start to ask questions, when he's no longer alive to answer them, I'll be besmirching his reputation,' she said. 'I can see that. Well, it probably wasn't him, anyway – as you say, he would have been quite old to have fathered a baby. Especially an illegitimate one.'

'I've never heard that he had a reputation in that area,' Basil said delicately. 'He was married years ago, and widowed in his fifties. After that, he lived with his sister, who died a year or two ago. I suppose it's possible that in the early years of his widowhood . . .' He sighed. 'I really think it's something we'll never know for sure. It might be better to look for people who knew your mother – they might know something.'

'Yes, I think you're right. And you've found out nothing?'

'No.' He told her about his conversation with Constance Bellamy. 'As she says, life was very uncertain in those last months of the Great War, and then with the 'flu epidemic and the upheavals of the 1920s – there was so much change going on, even in Burracombe. I'm sure there would have been gossip at the time, but whether anyone still remembers it . . .' He glanced up as a figure came round the corner of the church. 'Here comes Ted Tozer. He's one of the farmers in Burracombe itself – he came over to ring the bells for the funeral, with the Burracombe team. He would be the right age to ask, and he's utterly trustworthy.' He stood up and hailed the sturdy figure. 'Ted! That was a fine peal you rang.'

'Well, 'twas the least us could do for old Jem.' Ted came up to them and looked at the woman standing beside the vicar. 'Be you a relative, miss?'

'No. I thought I might have known him – or his family – but now I'm not so sure.' She hesitated, glancing at the vicar, and Basil said, 'Miss Tucker thinks she might have relatives in the area, Ted. I wondered if you or Alice might be able to help her. I was going to suggest she might come and see you at some time.'

'No time like the present,' Ted said cheerfully. 'Look, I be going home now and I know my Alice'll have the kettle on the hob and a few scones or something in the oven – why not walk back with me and have a chat? 'Tis no distance over the Clam.'

'The Clam?' she asked, and Basil smiled.

'It's the word for the footbridge over the river. Ted's right, it's only about ten minutes' walk that way, and you can catch the bus back to Plymouth in the village, as you know. I'd come with you, but I promised to go and see John Berry – the vicar here – before I go home. He's in a poor way,' he added to Ted. 'I was shocked when I saw him earlier.'

Ted nodded soberly. 'Always suffered with his chest, he has, and he's not getting any younger. Well, 'tis the same road for us all, and not always an easy one. I reckon old Jem had the best of it. Hale and hearty up to the last week or two, and then just drifted away. A good end to a good life.'

They stood for a moment or two in respectful memory of the man whose funeral they had just attended, and then gave each other a nod, Basil turning towards the vicarage and Ted setting off down the path towards the river, with Jennifer Tucker following him.

The church of Little Burracombe cast its shadow on the graveyard surrounding it, and the mound of fresh earth faded into the deep shade of the tower itself as old Jem Squires settled down into his last long rest.

Alice and Minnie were in the kitchen as usual, waiting for *Mrs Dale's Diary* to start with its signature tune of harp music and the pleasant, slightly anxious tones of the doctor's wife whose family doings were recounted each day on the radio. The fact that, unlike the farming programme *The Archers*, it depicted a life that was quite different from their own only added to their enjoyment. Joanna often listened to it, too, but Val was indifferent, and Jackie openly scornful.

Minnie was working on the tunes the vicar had asked her to arrange for the handbells. Spread all over the kitchen table, she had sheet music for the hymns he had suggested and a large pad of paper for writing down the notes of the handbells. Each one had its note embossed on its leather strap, and Minnie was writing the notes in columns so that several bells could be chimed together to create a chord. Sometimes only one bell would sound, its clear note striking a different sound amongst the harmonies, and this too was indicated in the columns. Once Minnie had finished the arrangements, Joanna, who had the best handwriting, would put them all on to large pieces of card and the handbell team would stand in front of it, striking their bells as the conductor pointed at the columns.

'We can use these old changes as well,' she said. 'My William did these years ago. Pretty little tunes they be, too. It'll be good to hear they again.'

Alice came and looked over her shoulder. The changes were in a small, yellowing notebook, written in a copperplate hand that was fading with age. She took the book, unhooked the small, wooden-headed hammer that could be used to strike the handbells, and picked out some of the changes on the bells hanging from the beams overhead.

'That's really pretty. I think us ought to do some of them as well. Is that what they call scientific ringing?'

Minnie shook her head. 'I don't think so. That's what they do on tower bells up-country. Makes a terrible noise, it do, all the bells clashing against each other all the time instead of changing decently one at a time. My William wouldn't have no truck with that.' She went on with her notation, carefully drawing straight lines with her ruler so that the columns of figures would stay in their place. 'I think while our Joanna's doing this, she might as well make some new cards for the Christmas carols and the tunes us've already got. Be nice to have them all new and fresh now we'm getting the team together again.'

Mrs Dale's Diary had just begun when Ted opened the kitchen door. As soon as she saw that he was ushering in a visitor, Alice turned off the radio and moved the kettle on to the hotplate. She came forward, holding out her hand in welcome.

'This is Miss Tucker, Alice,' Ted said. 'This is my wife, and this is my mother. She lives with us – keeps us all in order. I met Miss Tucker over at the funeral,' he added to Alice.

'Oh, I see,' Alice said. 'A relative of old Jem, are you?'

Jennifer shook her head. 'I don't think so. I don't really know – that's why I came today. I've been telling Mr Tozer—' she glanced at Ted '—I've been looking for relatives I think might have lived in the area. I came a few weeks ago and talked to the vicar, and he was wondering if you might be able to help me.'

Alice looked at her, frowning slightly. 'I've seen you before, haven't I? Didn't you come to the church once?' She moved back to the stove and poured hot water into the teapot, swilling it round and tipping it into the sink before going back to make the tea. 'I know when it was! 'Twas the day the dear King died. I was clearing out the flowers when the vicar came to tell me, and you were there then. That's it, isn't it?'

'You're right.' Jennifer sat down in the seat indicated by Ted. 'It didn't seem the right time to ask questions then, so I just went away again, but I came back to see Mr Harvey and we had a long talk. And then we met again at Mr Squires's funeral. I'd seen it was today in the paper, and I wondered . . . But I don't think it was him.'

'I'm sorry, maid,' Alice said, leaving the tea to stand for a few minutes while she got an extra cup and saucer from the dresser and brought a plate of fresh scones from the larder. 'I don't understand what you'm saying. You don't think *what* was him? And who d'you mean by "him"?'

'Sorry. I'm not making any sense, am I? The trouble is, I don't really know what does make sense.' Jennifer looked round at them all. 'The vicar says I can trust you not to talk about it if I tell you.'

'And so you can,' Alice said. She poured milk and tea into the cups and brought them to the table, where Minnie had swept all her papers into a pile. 'If you asks us not to talk about it, we won't. But you don't have to tell us if you don't want to,' she added. 'Every family has its secrets and there's no reason why you should tell us yours.'

Jennifer smiled. 'Thank you, Mrs Tozer. But I won't get very far if I don't tell someone, and Mr Harvey thinks you might be the best people. He's talked to Miss Bellamy, but she was away during the war and doesn't know anything—'

'No, that's not right,' Ted broke in. 'I don't know why he should say that – Constance Bellamy hasn't been out of the village for years, except for the odd week when her goes to stay with a cousin somewhere up north – Bristol, or Gloucester, or some such place. And she was certainly here during the war, because—'

'No,' Jennifer said, 'I don't mean the last war. I mean the first one – the 1914–18 war. She was in Malta then, as a nurse.'

'That's right,' Minnie said. She had been gazing at Jennifer in silence until that moment. 'What they called a VAD, she were. But why be you asking about that time, Miss Tucker? What are you trying to find out?'

Jennifer looked at their faces, puzzled yet kindly, and took a deep breath. Alice pushed her cup of tea a little nearer. She split and buttered a warm scone and put it on a plate at Jennifer's elbow. Sudden tears swam in the grey eyes.

'I'm trying to find my family,' she said. 'I don't even know if there's anyone left now, and I don't know for sure that they came from Burracombe. But I *feel* that they did. I feel as if this is somehow my home – the place where my mother and father grew up. There must be someone who knew them. There must be *someone* who knew that I was going to be born.'

Briefly, she told them the story of her mother's life in Plymouth, the stepfather she had believed to be her own father and the sisters who now seemed to have stepped away from her. As her voice broke and she put her hand to her eyes, Alice came over and put an arm round the young woman's shoulder.

'There, my bird, don't you upset yourself. We all understand how you must feel. And if there's anything we can do, we'll do it. Now, dry your eyes and have a sip of that tea while it's hot, and tell us if there's anything you know. Anything at all. For one thing, is there any names that might help?'

'Yes,' Jennifer said, doing as she was told. The hot tea warmed her chilled body, and she cradled the cup in her palms and closed her eyes. 'I know my mother's name. It was Hannaford. But the vicar says he can't find any record in the church papers of any Hannafords at all.'

'No more he would,' Minnie said unexpectedly. 'They were chapel folk.'

Jennifer stared at her. 'Chapel? But my mother was Church of England – she had me christened at St Budeaux—'

'So her might have done,' Minnie said. 'But her was Chapel when her lived here.' She turned to Alice. 'You must remember the Hannafords, over to Whinberry Cross. You knew young Susan. Disappeared off to Plymouth when she were about eighteen years old.' She tilted her head towards Jennifer. 'And now, us knows why!' To Jennifer herself, she added, 'I knowed it the minute you walked in. Like seeing a ghost, it were.'

Alice turned her eyes first to her mother-in-law and then to Jennifer. 'You mean you think this is Susan Hannaford's child? But how could you know, Mother? She don't look a bit like Susan.'

'No, she don't,' Minnie agreed. 'But she'm the spitten image of her grandmother. And I ought to know – Liza Lilliman were my best friend when us were girls, right up to when she wed Abraham Hannaford. And afterwards, too, whenever the poor soul were allowed off the farm.' She turned back to Jennifer. 'I know who your mother was, my maid, and I got a good idea who your father was, too. And I reckon you'd better stop here for supper, because us has got a lot to talk about.'

Chapter Fifteen

'Liza Lilliman come from t'other side of Tavistock,' Minnie said as they sat round the kitchen table.

They had eaten shepherd's pie and carrots, followed by a bottle of plums Alice had taken from her store cupboard and a bowl of junket, and now the dishes had been cleared away and Joanna and Val were tackling the washing-up while the others talked, a large brown pot of tea on the table in front of them.

'Over Horndon way, that's where her lived. So of course us didn't know each other as little uns, but us both went into service together up at the Barton, for old General Napier. Took to each other straight away, us did. She were a nice little body, and it were a proper shame when she wed Abraham Hannaford.'

'Why? What was he like?' Val asked, hovering nearby with a pie dish and tea-cloth in her hands.

'He were a bully,' Minnie said tersely. 'A lot older than her for a start – he'd been wed before and his first wife died, of overwork and misery, I dare say – and he just wanted a strong young woman to do the work around the farm and give him children. Oh, he were smooth enough when it come to courting – good-looking man, in his way – and poor Liza was proper taken in by him. Like a fly walking into a spider's web, she were, and by the time she realised what he was really like, 'twas too late. She were out there on that farm, miles from anywhere, nobody nearby to know what was going on, and the only time she were allowed out was on Sunday to go to

Chapel. Hardly saw her after that. I saw the baby, of course – little Susan – but she were just as downtrodden as her mother. Well, you'll remember that yourself,' she added, turning to Alice. 'You knowed her well enough.'

'I remember her at school,' Alice said. 'Her father used to bring her in on the trap. But she was such a quiet girl, none of us really knew her very well, and she was never allowed to stay after school, to go to tea with anyone, and she never came on picnics or the Whit Monday outings. He was always there after school, waiting for her, and she had to go straight home.'

'But what about after she left school?' Val came and sat down at the table. 'Didn't you have village dances and things like that? Wasn't she allowed to come to any of those?'

'Yes, she did, whenever she could. There wasn't no village hall then, that was built as a memorial after the Great War, but Dad used to let us use the big barn when it was empty. I got quite friendly with her then. She told me once she used to slip out when her father was busy in the barn of an evening, or reading – he used to read the Bible a lot, so she said, not that you'd know it from the way he carried on – and one of the farmhands would give her a lift into the village. And that was where she met . . .' Alice drew in a sharp breath and stared at Jennifer, her eyes growing large and her mouth opening wide. She put up her hand to cover her lips. 'But that don't mean anything. It couldn't have been him. It could have been any of the boys there – she were a pretty girl, they were all after her, and there was plenty to give her a lift home again. It *couldn't* have been him!'

The others stared at her. Jennifer was pale and tense, the rest of them leaning forward. At last, as Alice sat gazing at them, clearly picturing scenes from years ago in her head, Val burst out, 'Who are you talking about, Mum? Is it someone we know? Someone still living in the village? Come on – you can't leave us like this! You've got to tell us!'

Ted slapped his hand on the table.

'Now just you wait a minute, our Val! This isn't some party game, you know. It's people's lives we'm talking about. *This* young lady's life in particular.' He laid his hand on Jennifer's arm. ''Tis for her to say if she wants us to go on talking about it between ourselves. 'Tis for her to say if your mother mentions any names, and who she mentions them to. Us can't know the truth of it, anyway, and bringing names into this without knowing that could cause a lot of trouble.'

Val bit her lip and sat back in her chair, abashed, and Joanna, who was standing behind her, put a hand on her shoulder. There was a short pause, and then Ted turned to Jennifer Tucker.

'Well, what do you think, maid? Would you rather go in the parlour with my mother and Alice here, and talk it over quiet together? Nobody'll bother you, if that's what you wants. None of us'll talk out of turn, anyway – you needn't worry about that.'

'No, I know you won't, Mr Tozer.' She thought for a moment or two, then looked round the ring of faces. 'I think I'd rather stay here, actually. You've all been so kind – I feel almost as if you're part of my own family, especially now I know you knew my mother.' She looked at Minnie. 'And if you were my grandmother's best friend – it seems to bring them both so close. I want to hear as much as you can tell me about them. But – but I would like to find out who my father was as well, if there's any chance.'

'Well, as to that,' Alice said slowly, 'I don't know if we'll ever know, not without going and asking straight out. And that's not an easy thing to do, is it? We don't know what the chap I'm thinking about might say. We don't know for *certain* you're his daughter, you see. All I know is, he was sweet on Susan. He might be proper upset to think that there were somebody else she thought more of than him. And I don't see as that would do anyone any good.'

There was another silence. Then Jennifer said, 'Tell me

about my mother. What happened to her? When did she leave the village – and why? Or at least, why did people *think* she left?'

Alice frowned at the table, and Val reached out and lifted the big brown teapot to refill their cups. They waited while Alice got her thoughts into order.

'I'm just trying to cast my mind back,' she said slowly. 'I know I said I was friendly with Susan, but I didn't know her all that well – none of us did, even though we'd been at school with her and all that. But when we all come to leave school, she didn't go into service or nothing, like her mother did, she just stopped at home on the farm. There weren't no more children, you see, and her mother always seemed a bit frail and poorly—'

'Anyone would be, married to that old termagant,' Minnie said grimly.

'—but I always liked her,' Alice went on. 'She were a sweet little soul, for all she grew up in such a miserable household. Like a flower, she were. Must have been a real comfort to her poor mother.'

'I'm glad she was,' Jennifer said quietly, and they remembered that this was her own mother that Alice was talking about. Her mother, her grandmother and her grandfather. Val wondered suddenly what it was like to discover that your own grandfather had been a bully and a tyrant at home.

'And the boys liked her, too,' Alice said, a little apologetically. 'I don't mean she were a flirt or nothing. Well—' she glanced with a trace of a smile at Ted '—no more than the rest of us! She didn't encourage them. But she were sweet and pretty, 'twould have been a wonder if they *hadn't* gathered round her like bees round a honeypot. And there were always a few wanting to see her home.'

'And was there one in particular?' Jennifer asked. 'One she seemed to like better than all the rest?'

Alice flicked a look at her and seemed to debate with herself for a moment. Then she went on, firmly, 'I'll tell you about Susan first. Then us'll think about that. Well, 'twas wartime soon enough – the First War, this was, that they called the Great War and was supposed to make England a land fit for heroes to live in. The war to end all wars – only we all knows what happened to *that* idea! And a lot of the young men went off to fight, those that could be spared from the farms, and a lot that couldn't. You went yourself.' She looked at Ted again. 'In the Army, you were, and never said a word about it all once you come back.'

'Nor ever want to, neither,' Ted said sombrely. 'It were a bad time, and those of us who came home safe and sound just wanted to get back to our ordinary lives and forget it ever happened.'

Alice touched his hand. 'The women went, too, some of 'em – like Miss Bellamy, who volunteered as a nurse and went to Malta. And some went into the towns and cities to take over the men's jobs there, and some stopped on the farms to do that work, and some even come out *from* the cities, like our Joanna in the last lot. It were a proper musical chairs. Anyway, top and bottom of it was that you hardly knew where anyone was, and goodness knows what happened in all the muddle. And a lot of the young men never come home – you can see their names on the war memorial down on the green – and some of the women didn't neither. And us'd hardly got ourselves shaken down and sorted out when it all started all over again.' She shook her head.

'And my mother?' Jennifer asked. 'She went away from the village, didn't she? But was it because of me, or because of the war?' She stared at Alice and then at Minnie. 'Perhaps it wasn't someone from Burracombe at all. Perhaps it was someone she met in Plymouth.' She glanced round the table in sudden dismay. 'If that's what happened, I'll *never* be able to find him!'

'No,' Minnie said before Alice could speak again. 'It didn't happen like that. You see, me and your grandmother, poor Liza, we still managed to have a word now and then, when they came into the village of a Sunday for Chapel, and other times, too. I used to walk out to the farm sometimes when I thought Abraham might have gone to market in Tavistock. She told me how her Susan were fond of a boy in the village. She hoped that in time Abraham might see his way to letting the maid get married. She'd get away from the farm then, see, and have a proper life. 'Twas all poor Liza wanted by that time – she'd given up hopes of any decent life for herself.'

'Poor Grandma,' Jennifer said softly, her eyes filled with tears.

'Then the war started,' Minnie went on. 'The boy went away – joined the Navy. Poor Susan were heartbroken, and so was Liza.' She paused.

'Didn't he ever come home?' Val asked. 'Is his name one of those on the memorial?'

'It couldn't be,' Jennifer objected. 'I wasn't born until 1917. He *must* have come home again. Unless he was killed later on,' she added.

'No, maid, he weren't killed. He were one of the lucky ones – he got through the war, though it took him hard, like it did a lot of the poor souls. He come home on leave once or twice, wounded, and that's when him and Susan started seeing each other again.'

'He used to write to her, mind,' Alice put in. 'And she wrote back, but of course he couldn't ever send the letters to Whinberry. He sent 'em to me, as a matter of fact, and I used to pass them on.'

'Mum!' Val exclaimed. 'Why, that's really romantic!' She caught her father's eye and subsided again.

Alice sighed. 'I suppose 'twas, when you come to think about it, but it didn't seem so then. It just seemed to be the only way . . . Anyway, 'twasn't long after he come home that time that Susan went off. Took a job in one of the hotels in

Plymouth, so us was told, and the next thing us heard was that her'd caught that pesky 'flu and died.'

Jennifer gasped and Minnie turned to her quickly. ''Twasn't true, though, maid. Liza told me on her deathbed, but she made me promise not to tell anyone else, except for Alice here.'

'That's right,' Alice confirmed. 'I was that upset to think of poor Susan sick and dying all by herself in Plymouth. I used to think if only I'd known about it, I could have gone and found her and brought her back here. But us didn't know where she was, and by the time I knew the truth it was too late.'

'In the family way, she was, poor little flower,' Minnie said, 'and sent off the farm in disgrace. 'Twas Abraham who put the story about, and threatened his wife with all sorts if she ever let out the truth. She couldn't live with the secret, though. It killed her. Went downhill from that very day, her did, and died herself eighteen months later. Crying out for her Susan till the last, she was, and crying for the poor little babby as well.'

All the women were in tears as she finished her tale, and even Ted's eyes were moist. There was a silence, and then, while they fumbled for handkerchiefs and blew their noses, he cleared his throat and turned to the young woman who was sitting with Val's arms about her, tears streaming down her cheeks.

'It's a sad story,' he said gruffly, 'but I reckon you knew there'd be sorrow in it when you first decided to come looking. Now, what you got to make up your mind about is this: do you want Alice here to tell you the rest of it, and who the young feller was, or do you want to let it rest? Once you knows, there's no going back, and until she tells us who it might be, us don't know what trouble might be heaping up. And come to that,' he added, 'us still won't know for certain.

It could still have been some other chap, took advantage of her, like. You got to remember that as well.'

'I know,' Jennifer said quietly. 'But whatever happened, at least I know there was someone who really loved her. I'd like to know who that was – whether I'm his child or not.' She turned back to Alice and gave her a steady look. 'Who was it, Mrs Tozer? Who was the man who loved my mother?'

Once again, the faces round the table were tense, all watching the two women who knew the secret of this stranger's birth. Without taking her eyes from her mother's face, Val laid her hand on Jennifer's, pressing it gently in reassurance.

Alice and Minnie looked at each other and Minnie gave a tiny nod. Even then, it took a moment or two for Alice to find the words, but at last she spoke and a soft breath of relief sounded in the room.

'All right,' she said. 'I'll tell you. The man who was sweet on your mother, and had to leave her to go to war – the man I think must be your father – was Jacob Prout.'

Chapter Sixteen

The silence this time was stunned. The family stared at her and then at Minnie. Then Val said in shocked, unbelieving tones, '*Jacob Prout?* Do you really mean it?'

'Would your mother say so if she didn't?' Ted demanded, but his voice was rough with amazement. He looked from Val to his wife and mother in turn. 'Old *Jacob*?'

'Not so very old,' Minnie retorted. 'Only in his sixties – not that much older than you, Ted Tozer. And he was young enough back in 1914 or so, and proper handsome, too. There was more young girls than Susan Hannaford taking a shine to him, I can tell you.'

Jennifer reached down and picked up her shabby handbag. They watched as she took out a brown envelope and looked at the faded snaps and scrap of paper she laid on the table.

'Is that him?'

Minnie reached across and picked up one of the yellowing photographs. She fumbled for her glasses and rested them on her nose, then peered at the young sailor in the picture. For a moment, she seemed undecided, then she nodded slowly.

'That's Jacob Prout all right, as a young man. And look at those rocks – they'm up by the Standing Stones. That's where all the courting couples go, in Burracombe,' she added to Jennifer. 'I reckon this must've been took just before he went away the first time.'

She passed it to Alice, who stared at it as Ted leaned over her shoulder. They both nodded their agreement, too.

'I'd forgotten he ever looked like that,' Alice said a little ruefully. 'But you're right, Mother, 'tis Jacob. It just shows how we all change over the years . . . And what's this?' she added as Jennifer handed her the fragment of writing-paper. 'A bit of a letter?'

'It's the only piece I've got. It was with the photographs – I think she must have kept it because of what it said.' Jennifer's voice was shaking and Val patted her arm comfortingly. 'It's signed "J". And if you say that's Jacob Prout in the photograph, that must be him, mustn't it! He *must* be my father!'

'It do look a bit like it,' Ted agreed, although his voice was still cautious. 'But it's still not really proof, is it?'

'But surely,' Val began 'if Mum and Grandma both know that Jacob and Susan were courting, and Jennifer's got this photo and this bit of letter – surely that's proof enough. They were in love – they wanted to get married. Who else could it have been?' She stopped abruptly, then stood up and said, 'I'll make some more tea,' and went over to the sink, standing with her back to them.

Alice glanced at her curiously, but Minnie was speaking again. 'There's some funny things happen in wartime, maid – any other time, come to that – and there's many a slip 'twixt cup and lip. It do look as if the babby could have been Jacob's, but if 'twas, why didn't he marry the maid? He'm a decent sort of chap, he'd have stood by her. Even if he were away at the time, he'd have done the right thing when he come home again.' She shook her head and looked at the photograph again. 'Seems to me there's more to this than meets the eye.'

'Well, there's only one person who can answer those questions,' Ted observed. 'And that's Jacob himself. And that's a tricky sort of a question to ask, you got to admit that. If 'twasn't him, he might be mortally offended or upset – and whether it was or wasn't, it could open up all sorts of old wounds.'

They sat in silence for a few minutes. Val made a fresh pot of tea and came back to the table with it. Alice glanced at her and thought she looked upset, though what about she had no idea. All the same, it triggered a memory in her mind – a remark she'd once made, either to Minnie or Ted, about how Val had never seemed quite the same since she'd come home from Egypt during the war. But that was years ago now, and it had been understandable. Val had lost her own fiancé at that time. Perhaps all this had reminded her of her own grief.

'I don't know what to do,' Jennifer said at last. 'It seems so cruel, to find the man I think must have been my father and yet not see him and talk to him. I can see that it might upset him to be reminded of it all – but mightn't he be pleased to find he's got a daughter? What sort of man is he? Is he married? Does he have any other family?' She paused, and then added in a small voice, 'Other children?'

The family looked at each other. Joanna, who had said nothing until now, asked, 'How would you feel about that? Would you like to find some more brothers and sisters?'

'I don't know—' Jennifer began, but Alice spoke quickly.

'No, maid, you don't have to even think about that, because Jacob never had no family. He did get wed in the end, mind – married Sarah Foster, over from Walkhampton. Widow, she were, lost her first in an accident with the thresher, nasty business, took her a long time to get over it. She didn't have any children, and by the time she and Jacob got wed 'twere too late so Jacob never had none neither. Not as far as anyone knew, anyway,' she added, looking at Jennifer.

'And Sarah died a good few years back now,' Minnie supplied. 'Don't think they were together much more than ten years, all told. Jacob's lived on his own ever since, in the cottage he was born in.'

'He must be lonely,' Jennifer said, her eyes filling with tears. 'And the way you talk about him – you like him, don't you? He's a nice man?'

'Oh, everyone likes old Jacob,' Val said. 'The village wouldn't be the same without him.'

'It wouldn't be as tidy, that's for sure,' Alice said. 'Keeps the whole place looking pretty, Jacob do. Trims the hedges, clears out the ditches, looks after the churchyard, does a few gardens – there's nothing Jacob can't turn his hand to. And always got a smile and a cheery word, too. Not like that surly old crosspatch that lives next door to him.'

'Oh well, him and Jed have been at loggerheads for years,' Ted said. 'Not just him, neither – Jed's at loggerheads with everyone in the village.'

'Never mind him,' Val said. 'The point is, is Jennifer going to tell Jacob she thinks he might be her father? How do you think he's going to feel about it?'

They all sighed and looked at each other again.

'I dunno how he's going to feel,' Ted said at last. 'I dunno how I'd feel meself. Not that it's ever going to happen,' he added quickly. 'There ain't been nothing like that here. But in Jacob's shoes – well, I don't know, and that's the truth. And when you comes down to it, it isn't for us to decide, is it?' He nodded towards Jennifer. ''Tis none of our business after all, maid. 'Tis your decision.'

'I know.' She gazed down at the photograph. 'I just can't decide what's right.' She looked up at them again, her eyes shadowed. 'And there's another thing. He probably thinks my mother died then, just as you did. If her parents put that story about in the village, he'd have heard it, too. He must have been broken-hearted!'

Alice stared at her, shocked. 'So he was, the poor dear soul. It took him a long time to get over it – that's why he never married for such a long time. Oh, what a wicked thing for them to do! Not so much poor Liza, because Abraham treated her so bad she'd have been frightened to tell anyone the truth – though it must have been a sore trouble to her, having to pretend her own child was dead – but that Abraham, he was a wicked man, there's no two ways about it, and I hope he's paying for it now, wherever he is.' Her tone left no doubt as to where *she* thought Abraham was now. She turned to Ted. 'This makes it all the worse, don't it? I mean, think how poor Jacob's going to feel when he knows his Susan was alive all that time, not twenty miles away, and had his babby and all. It's going to bring it all back to him.'

They sat in silence for a time, thinking over the problem, and then Alice turned to Jennifer again.

'Why not ask the vicar? You've already talked to him, after all, and I'm sure he'd be willing to help. He knows Jacob well, and he'll never say anything to anyone else.'

'I think that's the best idea,' Ted agreed, and the others nodded. 'Mr Harvey's a funny little chap sometimes, always worrying about being late and that, but he'm a good man and got a wise head on his shoulders when it comes to serious matters. He's the best one to talk to about this.'

Jennifer nodded. 'Yes, I'll do that. He's been very nice to me, and it was him suggested I should come here. I ought to go and tell him what you've told me.' She gathered the scraps of paper together and put them back into their envelope, looking wistfully at the photograph as she did so. 'I wish I could see him, though – my father, I mean. Even if I didn't say anything . . . It would be nice just to see what he looks like – just to *look* at him and think "he's my father".'

'Well, you could,' Val said. 'He's round the village all the time. You've only got to walk round the lanes and you'll bump into him somewhere. You could even stop and talk to him.'

'I don't know,' Jennifer said. 'It would be a bit like spying. I don't think I ought to do that – not until I've talked to Mr Harvey again, anyway.' She put the envelope back into her handbag and smiled round at them. Her eyes were bright with tears. 'Thank you, all of you. You've been a real help. I'll get in touch with Mr Harvey again. But now I ought to be thinking about going back to Plymouth. The last bus goes soon.'

'That's right, maid.' Alice stood up and fetched Jennifer's coat from the hook by the door. 'Now, you come and see us again, whatever you decide to do, won't you? And let us know how you get on – that's if you want to,' she added hastily. 'Like Ted says, it's none of our business, really. But you'm Susan's maid, when all's said and done, and us'd like to know how you go on.'

'I will,' Jennifer said, smiling at them a little waveringly. 'I'll come and see you again.' She looked around the big, warm kitchen with the family sitting at the table, the brown teapot in the middle and a big jug of fresh milk beside it. 'I feel as if I've found a family already,' she said. 'I feel as if Burracombe's my home.'

There was very seldom a day when Val and Luke didn't manage to meet at some point. After Jennifer Tucker had left the farm, Val put on her coat and said she was just going to walk up to the charcoal-burner's cottage to see him for an hour or so. 'Don't wait up,' she said to her mother. 'Luke'll see me home.'

'Well, don't you be too late, mind.' Alice said. 'You've got an early start in the morning and it's been a funny sort of evening. Given us a lot to think about.'

'I won't be late,' Val said, and walked out into the cool night air. Joanna and Tom had gone to their own room, and she sensed that her parents and grandmother weren't sorry to be left on their own to discuss Jennifer's story. There were more old memories there than they had divulged, she thought, and a lot for them to talk about and come to terms with.

Who would have thought that old Jacob Prout might have a daughter! And born out of wedlock, too. Val thought of the sturdy, upright man who worked so hard around the village and was held in such high regard and tried to imagine him as a young man, leaving his home village and going to sea and to war. She thought of the girl he'd left behind. She too had known the aching loneliness of being parted from the one she loved, and the terrible grief of losing him. And there was something else that she and Susan Hannaford had in common . . .

'I felt as if I could share in what she was going through,' she said to Luke as they sat on his old settee in front of the smouldering log fire. 'I felt as if I were Susan herself – having to leave home in disgrace, turned away by her family. It could so easily have been me.'

'Your family would never have treated you like that,' he said, tightening his arm about her shoulder.

'I don't know. Girls did get turned out into the snow with their little white bundles. I knew a girl it happened to and her family have never spoken to her again.'

Luke drew her closer. 'Val, all this must have brought back that time when you—'

'Yes, it did,' she said quietly. 'I honestly don't know what I'd have done if things hadn't turned out the way they did. Not that I was *glad* to lose the baby – he was our baby, and I've grieved for him ever since. I think I always will.'

'There'll be other babies,' he said, and she nodded.

'I know. But never that one. Never that little boy. Oh, *Luke* . . .' She turned and buried her face against the soft wool of his pullover. He wrapped both arms around her and held her close, rocking her gently, his heart aching as he thought of that time, years ago, when he and Val had first fallen in love. It had been an impossible, forbidden love then, but its power had been too great for them, and the hurt it had caused had kept them apart for a long time. Now, at last, they were together, and he felt a sudden urgent desire to make sure that nothing should ever again come between them. He thought of the promise he had made to Ted Tozer on Christmas afternoon, and suddenly it didn't seem so important any more. It was what Val wanted that was imperative to him now.

'Darling,' he said, when her tears had eased, 'don't let's wait any longer to get married. Let's do it as soon as possible, and if we haven't got anywhere in Burracombe to live, we'll go to Plymouth and find somewhere there. I'm tired of having you go back to the farm every night. I'm tired of being engaged. I want to be married!'

She raised her head and looked at him. Her cheeks were wet and her eyes brimming, but her mouth broke into a trembling smile. She tried to speak but a hiccuping sob shook her, and she gasped and felt for a hanky. At last, she said, 'Luke, do you mean it? Do you really want to get married soon?'

'Well, of course I do!' he exclaimed, laughing. 'I'd get married tomorrow if it was possible. But since it isn't, let's see just how soon we can do it. An Easter wedding, perhaps – how about that?'

'Oh, Luke, yes!' she cried, hugging him to her. 'But we won't go to Plymouth – not yet. We'll stay here, in this cottage. I know it's too small and it's cold and draughty, but summer's coming and we needn't be indoors all that much. We'll have months to find somewhere to live before winter comes. And we'll have all that time to enjoy being married.'

'I'm going to enjoy being married for a very long time,' he said, taking her face in his hands and looking deep into her eyes. 'I'm going to enjoy it for the rest of my life.'

Chapter Seventeen

Aggie Madge said she would be delighted to have Stella's sister staying in her cottage.

'I remember her as a little maid,' she said when Felix asked her. 'Proper little ray of sunshine, she were. Everyone loved little Maddy, and Dottie looked after her like a mother.'

'And you don't think there'll be any problem with her staying here – since I'm here as well?' Felix asked, wondering how to put the question delicately.

Aggie stared at him. 'Why should there be a problem? You don't use the spare room for anything.'

'I didn't mean that. I meant . . . well, with me being a single man and—'

'But you'm the *curate*!' Aggie exclaimed. ''Tisn't like you'm an *ordinary* young man, now is it!'

Felix thought that in some respects he was very ordinary indeed, but this wasn't the moment to explain that to Aggie. He hoped the rest of the village would take the same view as her. He was looking forward to having Stella's sister staying in the cottage. For one thing, she was a very pretty girl, and for another, it meant that he would see more of Stella herself.

Felix had begun to feel very fond of Stella, and having the little sports car had helped a lot. Taking her to the cinema had become the highlight of his week, and they'd discovered similar tastes in films, music and even books. Both loved the stories written by Daphne du Maurier, though Felix's favourite was *Jamaica Inn*, whereas Stella liked *Rebecca* best.

It had become an accepted fact that they would spend at least some of their spare time together, and now that the evenings were getting lighter, Felix had plans for runs out across the moor in the little car, and walks in some of the spots that were less accessible by bus or on foot.

He'd been thinking of kissing her for a while before he actually plucked up the courage to do so – and then it wasn't pre-meditated at all, just a spontaneous gesture because she was so pretty and he felt so sorry for the sadness in her life, and because they'd been talking about Burracombe and whether either of them might ever move away; because he'd known, suddenly, that he didn't want to leave the village, and he didn't want Stella to leave either.

Stella's lips had been soft and tasted faintly sweet, as if touched with honey. They'd trembled a little under his, and he'd realised that this was her first real kiss. He'd ended it gently and held her for a moment before turning to begin the walk home.

I must go very carefully with Stella, he'd thought. She's sweet and innocent, and she's been hurt enough already – I mustn't do anything to hurt her more. I must be very, very sure . . .

'Now then,' Aggie was saying. 'I'll have to think how to make young Maddy comfortable. She'm used to something better than an old cob cottage these days, what with living in London and Paris and all them places. My stars, I expect her'll be used to having her own bathroom and everything!' She gazed at Felix in dismay. 'She'll have forgotten what it's like down here, with the bath having to be brought in from the back yard every Friday night and everyone using the same water!'

'I hadn't thought of that.' Felix himself had found this to be quite an embarrassing procedure when he'd first arrived in Burracombe. Some of the larger houses, like the vicarage and the doctor's house and the Warrens', had their own bathrooms, but most of the cottages were still reliant on tin baths hung, like Aggie's, on a nail outside and hauled in once or twice a week to be filled with kettles of hot water. It wasn't all that long ago, so he'd been told, that some of the cottages hadn't even had their own water supply and had had to fetch supplies from a standpipe or the old well at the far end of the village. Felix and Aggie didn't exactly take turns with the bath, sharing the water as many families did, but since this meant that there wasn't enough hot water for two baths in the same evening, it was still quite a procedure bringing it in two nights a week. With Maddy here, it would mean another night – perhaps more.

'She probably wants a bath every day,' Aggie went on, anxiously. 'A lot of they posh people do, you know. Sometimes twice!'

Felix rubbed his hand over his fair hair, tousling it into a mass of curls. 'You're right, Aggie. I hadn't even considered it. We'd better ask Stella what she thinks. I suppose she could have a jug of hot water in her room every day – you've got that old washstand set, haven't you?'

Aggie thought for a minute. The set Felix meant had been her grandmother's and stood on the washstand in the spare bedroom, almost as if it were ready for use, but Aggie couldn't remember the last time it had been put to its proper purpose. There was a large china washbasin and a big, heavy jug, both patterned with full-blown roses, and there was a soap-dish and a saucer for a flannel or sponge.

'You could have a proper all-over wash in that,' she agreed. 'And it'd be no trouble for me to take up the hot water every morning, so long as she don't mind not having a real bath. It's just as clean, anyway, to my mind. Cleaner, really – you're not laying there in all your dirt, are you?'

'I'll ask Stella,' he said. 'After all, Maddy must know what it's like in these old cottages. She lived at Dottie's for long enough.'

Aggie shook her head, still looking doubtful, and he tried to reassure her.

'She'll be perfectly comfortable here, Aggie. The bedroom's very pretty, and if the bed's as comfortable as mine, she'll never want to get out of it. And your cooking is marvellous.'

'Her won't be having much of that, though,' Aggie said. 'Her'll be having her dinners over at Dottie's with her sister.'

'Well, she'll be having breakfast here, and you know what they say – you should breakfast like a king, lunch like a lord and dine like a pauper. Your breakfasts are fit for any king, Aggie.'

'They might be too heavy for her. Maddy's more like a little princess.'

'Aggie, for goodness' sake! Stop worrying. She'll be perfectly comfortable here. Anyway, we haven't asked her yet – she might want to stay at the Barton after all. That's where she's been before, isn't it?'

'Yes, because Miss Forsyth was a friend of Hilary's mother. But she'm coming on her own this time, to see her sister. I'm sure her'd rather be in the village.'

'I'm sure she would, too,' Felix said firmly. 'And I'm sure this is the best place for her – just across the road, as near to Stella as she could possibly be. Between us, we'll make her as comfortable as any princess could wish. Honestly, Aggie, she'll be as happy as can be staying here.'

'And I'll be happy to have her,' Aggie said, cheering up at last. 'You can tell Miss Simmons that. It'll be a real pleasure to have little Maddy staying here.'

Getting married at Easter seemed less easy than Val and Luke expected.

'But that's only just over two weeks away!' Alice exclaimed, outraged. She was decorating a simnel cake and stopped in the middle of rolling out marzipan balls to stare at her daughter. 'You've not even had the banns called yet. You've got to have at least three weeks, and that's nowhere near long enough to get a wedding arranged proper.' She gave Val a close look. 'There isn't no *reason* for this sudden hurry, I hope, is there?'

'No, of course there isn't,' Val said indignantly. 'It's just that Luke and I are tired of waiting—'

'You only got engaged at Christmas. In my day, engagements lasted a good two years. More, sometimes, while people saved up and the bride got her bottom drawer filled up. I haven't noticed you doing anything about yours, Valerie.'

Alice so rarely used her daughter's full name that Val knew she was seriously disturbed. Lamely, she said, 'Well, we've all been busy knitting for Joanna's new baby . . .'

'Then maybe you shouldn't have been,' Alice said smartly. 'If you were so keen to get married all in a hurry, you should have been thinking about that! There's plenty of time till Joanna has her babby.'

'Mum,' Val said, feeling as if she were a child again, asking for more sweets, 'Luke and I are over twenty-one. I'm almost *thirty*, for goodness' sake! We just don't want to wait any longer.'

Alice looked at her daughter and her face softened. 'Yes, I can understand that. I'm sorry, Val. You've waited a long time for happiness to come to you. But I'd really like you to have a proper wedding – all in white, with bridesmaids and all, and a proper reception with your dad making a speech. I've been looking forward to it for so many years, and if you wants to get married all in a rush, there just won't be time. Don't you want that yourself? Don't every girl want a lovely wedding? A day to remember and look back on?'

Val sighed. She looked at the mantelpiece where a framed photograph of Ted and Alice on their wedding day stood in a brass frame. Her mother never allowed anyone but herself to polish that frame, and Val had seen her fingers lingering over it as she did so. The happy couple looked, in fact, anything but happy, both standing so stiff and formal, Alice in a cream-coloured lace dress, and Ted in the suit he had worn again only a day or so ago for Jem Squires's funeral. But Val knew that they must have been happy inside – warm and excited, filled with joy and anticipation of the life ahead.

That's how I want to feel, she thought.

'You'll enjoy it all so much more if you've done it right,' Alice went on, more coaxingly now. She began to place the marzipan balls around the edge of the cake. 'I know there's a lot of preparation, a lot of sewing and planning, and maybe a few little arguments along the way. Weddings are always like that. But it all turns out right in the end, and it's like everything else in life – you gets out of it what you puts in. That's what makes things worthwhile.' She was silent for a moment, and then she said, 'There's your dad to think of, too. You know he's got his own opinion about Luke – not that he don't like him, mind, it's his job your dad can't seem to understand. Painting pictures for a living – it just don't seem to be proper work, to him.'

'Luke works very hard,' Val said indignantly. 'He's done a lot of training at art college, and he's had exhibitions of his work – think of those pictures he showed in London last year. And he could get a good job as a teacher if he wanted to.'

'Well, your dad might think a bit more of him if he did,' Alice said. She saw the look on Val's face and added hastily, 'Not that he don't like him – I've already said that. And he's agreed he won't say no more about it. You're of age and you love each other, and it's your business. But if you goes on with this idea of getting married all in a hurry – well, he's bound to be upset. And that's not a good way to start off, now is it?'

'I suppose not,' Val said unwillingly. 'Though it's not my fault if he takes that attitude . . .'

'It's your fault if you don't take it into account, though. You can do what you like in this world, Val, but you has to take the consequences. And hurting other people without good reason – if there ever *is* a good reason for hurting someone that loves you and only wants what's best for you – always has consequences. You just think about that before you makes any decisions. In any case,' Alice added, reverting to her first argument, 'you can't get married at Easter because you haven't had the banns called, and that's all there is to it.'

Val thought of saying that they could get a special licence, but decided against it. There was no point in prolonging the argument and she had a feeling that her mother had already won, anyway. She folded her lips tightly and stared at the kitchen table, and after a moment or two, Alice came round and put her arm across Val's shoulders.

'Don't look so miserable, maid. Nobody wants to stop you and Luke from being happy together. We just wants it done proper. Can't you think again – put it off till the summer, perhaps? A June wedding's always nice.'

'I don't know,' Val said miserably. 'I'll think about it. I'll talk to Luke.'

'You do that,' Alice said, satisfied. 'He's a good chap – he'll understand, I'm sure. After all, what's two or three months? Give us all time to get things ready, that will. We wants to give you a day to remember all your lives, don't we.' She straightened up, looking at her cake with satisfaction. 'Now, I'll just put this away in the larder and then I'll make a pot of tea. Your gran will be coming down from her rest soon, and the men'll be in from the fields. I made some flapjacks this morning; they're in that tin if you wouldn't mind getting them out.' She bustled about the kitchen, filling the kettle and setting the big teapot by the hob to warm up, and Val got up, too, and did as she was told. The flapjacks, made of oats and butter and golden syrup, were a rich toffee-brown and smelled delicious, but somehow she had no appetite and when she had put them on the table she turned towards the door.

'I won't stop for a cup of tea, if you don't mind, Mum. I don't feel much like talking, anyway. I think I'll go for a walk.'

'All right, maid.' Alice was busy with the kettle and didn't look round, but once the door had closed behind her daughter, she moved to the window and stood for a moment, watching Val trudge dispiritedly across the yard and out to the track.

It's a shame she's got to wait, she thought, but it's the best thing, really. People never quite forget or forgive a wedding that's not arranged right, and I don't want these two starting off on the wrong foot.

It was something in the story Jennifer Tucker had told them that had set Val off like this, she thought, with a small, puzzled frown. I saw her face then, while she was listening. There was something in that story that upset her, but I don't know what it was.

Still, there were bound to be things in your children's lives that you didn't know – things you never would know. And once Val was safely married to Luke, and everyone happy about it, perhaps whatever it was could be put in the past and not upset her any more.

The kettle began to sing, and Alice heard the voices of the men coming across the yard at the same moment as sounds from above announced that Minnie was on her way down from her afternoon rest. She turned back to her duties, wondering if mothers ever stopped worrying about their children.

'I suppose it was a bit optimistic,' Luke said as they climbed the hill to the Standing Stones half an hour later. Val had found him putting the finishing touches to a painting of a patch of snowdrops they had found along the riverbank a few weeks ago, glowing like pearls in a pool of sunlight. 'I'd thought about the banns, too. I was going to come and see you and suggest we went and had a talk with Uncle Basil about it.'

'We could always get a special licence,' Val argued, unwilling to let go of her dream. 'You can get married in three days, then, can't you?'

'I don't really know. But we don't want to do that, do we?' They reached the grassy plateau where the big, granite Standing Stones formed their ancient circle, and stopped. Luke took her in his arms. 'Val, there really isn't that much hurry. I know we're tired of waiting, all we want to do is get married and live happily ever after – but not in a way that will upset a lot of other people, especially when they're the people we love. Your mother will be terribly disappointed if you don't have the wedding she wants for you, and so will your father. And they're not the only ones—'

'But it isn't their wedding!' Val broke in, angry tears forming in her eyes. 'It's ours! And we should be able to have what we want. We're not just doing it to please other people.'

'No, of course not, and nobody expects us to,' Luke said, not entirely certain that this was true. 'But I thought it was what we wanted – a traditional wedding, with a church service and you in a long white dress, and the bells ringing and everything. And there's no nicer place than Burracombe to have it.' He drew her across to one of the stones, and they sat down on the short, springy turf, leaning their backs against the sun-warmed granite. 'Tell me the truth, Val. Is that what you want? Or have you just been going along with it because you thought I wanted it?'

Val frowned and stared down at her hands. She picked at the turf, tearing out small lumps and piling them up beside her. Then she said, 'Do you know, I've never even thought about it until now. I just took it for granted, I suppose. It's what you *do*, isn't it? I mean, I'd want to be married in the church, of course I would, with all our friends and family around. I don't want something that looks like a hole and corner affair. But it doesn't have to be like that, does it? It can be simple and quiet without being second-rate.'

'Of course it can. It can be whatever you want.' He took her hand and stroked it, rubbing his thumb over her engagement ring. 'But if we're going to have our friends and family there, it's not going to be small, is it? It's going to be over half the village. And there's my family, too. We'll probably fill the church.'

'Oh dear,' she said dismally. 'It's impossible, isn't it? We can't arrange anything like that in a couple of weeks.'

'Not even in a couple of months,' he said. 'I think your mother's right, you know. We're going to have to wait till the summer at least.'

Val nodded, her lips pressed together in resignation. Then she turned her head to look at him and said, 'There's something else I've realised.'

'What's that, sweetheart?'

'This white dress,' she said hesitantly. 'I don't think – it seems wrong to me, to wear that. It's like telling a lie.'

'Oh, *Val*—'

'Well, it is, isn't it! It's a symbol of purity – it's supposed to show that the bride's a virgin. And I'm not.' She turned her head away again and he saw the glitter of a tear on her cheek. 'It's worse than that. I've been a mother.'

'Val—'

'I know he didn't live,' she said tonelessly. 'He wasn't even big enough to be born. But he existed just the same, and I can't go up the aisle in our own church wearing a white dress and pretending it never happened. I just can't!'

Chapter Eighteen

Maddy arrived on the Wednesday before Easter, and Stella met her from the train at Tavistock. She had brought an array of suitcases and Stella looked at them in some dismay as the guard helped pile them on the platform.

'I'm not sure we can get all these in Felix's car. He's waiting outside.'

'Isn't there a taxi?' Maddy asked, looking around the quiet station.

'Well, there are taxis down in the square. I could ask Felix to go down and get one. But I can easily go back by bus, if you can get yourself and all your cases into his car.' She looked doubtfully at the luggage. 'You're staying with him, anyway.'

'Staying with Felix?' Maddy said in surprise. 'Isn't he that rather nice-looking young curate I met at Christmas?'

'Yes, that's right. He lodges just over the lane from me, at Aggie Madge's – you remember her, don't you? She's got a spare room you can have, and you'll have breakfast there but your other meals with me and Dottie. I hope that's all right?' Stella asked anxiously. 'You wouldn't rather be at the Barton, would you?'

'No thanks. We used to stay there when Fenella came down, but that was because she and Mrs Napier were friends. I was always rather scared of Mr Napier and I don't know Hilary or Stephen all that well. I thought I'd be staying at Dottie's, with you.'

'That would have been best, but there just isn't room. Dottie would have moved out of her room, but I didn't think you'd want her to do that. And you'll only be just across the road.' Stella turned as Felix came on to the platform, looking enquiringly at them. 'Oh, there you are. We were just trying to decide what to do. Maddy's got quite a lot of luggage.'

'So you have.' He regarded the pile of suitcases. 'Well, why don't I just cram all that stuff into Mirabelle and take it home, and then come back for you? You can have a cup of tea in Goode's or Perraton's or go for a walk in the Meadows. Show Maddy round a few of her old haunts.'

'That would be nice,' Maddy said. 'Not that I knew Tavistock all that well in those days. We only came here occasionally. But wouldn't that be an awful bore for you?' She gave Felix a bewitching smile and he blinked.

'No, of course it wouldn't. It'd be a pleasure.' Looking slightly dazed, he bent to heft some of the cases into his arms and carried them out of the station. Stella picked up the remaining case, Maddy swung her handbag on to her shoulder, and the two girls followed to find him stacking the cases into the sports car.

'There,' he said, squeezing the last one into the dicky seat. 'Just room. However did you manage on the way down, Maddy?'

'Oh, there are always porters about,' she said vaguely, glancing around the deserted station yard. 'Well, usually. And people are terribly kind and helpful, I always find.'

'I'm sure you do,' Felix said, with a glance at her delicately featured face, framed in soft, pale curls, and the curving lips. 'I should think people fall over themselves to help you.'

Maddy laughed. 'Well, I wouldn't say that. It's Fenella they really want to help. But there was a kind man on the train who put the cases in the rack for me and helped me get them down again. Anyway, never mind that now. Are you really sure you don't mind, Felix?'

'I don't mind at all. I wouldn't have been able to get both of you in the car, anyway – Stella was talking about going back on the bus, but I didn't think you'd want her to do that.'

'I don't mind going on the bus with Stella,' Maddy said at once, but he shook his head.

'Definitely not. You can use the bus other days if you want to, but not today. I'm your chauffeur.' He swung himself into the driving seat. 'I'll meet you in the square in about an hour.'

The little car roared out of the station yard and left silence behind. A moment or so later a pickup lorry came grinding up the hill, and two burly men jumped out with shovels and began to fill it with coal from the huge pile at the end of the yard. Stella took Maddy's arm.

'Come on. We'll go over the bridge and down the steps into the town. It's easier than walking all the way round.'

'I remember this,' Maddy said as they emerged in the main street. To their left and right were rows of shops, with several entrances to the Pannier Market across the road and the tall granite tower of the church dominating the end of the street. There were two or three cafés, and since Maddy declared herself to be dying of thirst, they made for one of these and settled themselves at a table with a pot of tea and a plate of scones.

'We'd better not eat or drink too much,' Stella said, pouring tea. 'Dottie's putting on an enormous spread in your honour. She's looking forward so much to seeing you.'

'I'm looking forward to seeing her again, too,' Maddy said, spreading a scone with jam and clotted cream. 'She was a mother to me. Not like our *real* mother, of course, but you know how warm and kind Dottie is. She really took me to her heart and looked after me.'

'I know.' Stella could hear that her voice sounded wistful. 'You were very lucky, Muriel.' She caught herself up quickly. 'Sorry, I mean Maddy, of course. I've been trying but I still forget sometimes, especially when I think of when we were little.'

'It's all right. I've almost forgotten being Muriel now, because nobody else knows me by that name. I don't mind you using it, though. It makes it rather special.'

The two sisters smiled at each other, then drank their tea, and Maddy began to talk about her recent stay in Paris, where Fenella Forsyth had her own apartment. Stella wanted to ask more questions about her childhood in Burracombe, and in the children's home she had lived in before the actress had adopted her, but she realised that Maddy needed more time, and perhaps this crowded café wasn't the place. There'll be time enough in the next two weeks, she thought, more time than we had at Christmas, when there were so many people about and so much to do. We'll be able to go for long walks together and talk till all hours, just the two of us.

There would be Felix, too, some of the time, she thought with a thrill of warmth touching her heart. Felix, Maddy and me. That's all I want.

Easter Day was fine and sunny, with just a hint of a warm spring breeze to freshen the air. After the sobriety of Good Friday, with all the shops shut and the village feeling more like a Sunday, it was good to wake to a cheerful breakfast of eggs boiled in onion skins or food colouring and walk along lanes sprinkled with primroses and violets to find the church bright with sunlight and spring flowers, and hear the music of the bells welcoming them in with extra joy in their tone.

As usual on Easter Day, the nave was filled with people, all in their best clothes, and there was a feeling of happiness and renewed growth in the air. It was, Stella thought as she sat in her pew gazing up at the jewelled colours of the east window, the beginning of a process that would come to fruition with the Harvest Festival – the start of the most productive part of the year, when seeds were planted, when birds laid their eggs, when lambs were born and trees began to blossom.

And it was the start of a new stage in her own life, too. There was Maddy, who had arrived a few days ago and was sitting beside her now, and there was Felix, coming in with the vicar at the head of the little procession of choirboys and men as the congregation rose to sing the Easter hymn: 'Jesus lives! No longer now, Can thy terrors, death appal us . . .'

Nothing, Stella thought, can 'appal' me now. I've got everything I want. And she watched the sunlight gleam on Felix's corn-gold head, and then turned her own head slightly to see the same rays catch the almost silvery blonde of her sister's soft curls, and wondered how it had come about that her life should have changed, in such a short time, from the loneliness of her years at the children's home to the fulfilment and happiness she had found in Burracombe.

It's this village, she thought. It's such a happy place. It's like a miracle, living here, as if nothing can ever go wrong. It's a magic place.

Near them sat the Tozers, with Ted stiff and smart in his best suit, Alice wearing a pale green costume she had made herself, Minnie in her best feathered hat, Jackie looking bored, and Val and Luke together looking a little wistful. In the front pew were Hilary Napier and her father and, behind them, the Cherrimans, who were so seldom seen in the village that some members of the congregation weren't sure who they were. Constance Bellamy, whose accustomed pew they had taken, had been forced to move back and when she stood up for the hymns her stocky back was stiff with indignation.

As the service progressed, the ringers got up from their seats and made their way self-consciously to the chancel steps, where they formed a semi-circle round Minnie, who was holding up the cards with the bell notations carefully written up by Joanna. The silvery notes made a dainty contrast to the deeper tones of the church bells themselves as they went into the old changes, and then to the more familiar tunes of 'All in the April Evening' and 'All Things Bright and Beautiful', finishing with the stirring chords of 'Jerusalem'. As they ended their recital and returned to their seats, there was a small sigh of approval from the congregation, and if it had been the custom to clap in church, there would have been a burst of applause. Instead, people turned and smiled at each other.

'That was really nice,' Maddy said afterwards as they made their way back to Dottie's for dinner. Felix had been invited as well, and afterwards he was taking the two girls out for the afternoon in Mirabelle. 'They couldn't ring the big bells when I was here, of course, because it was during the war, but Mr Tozer did get the handbells out at Christmas for carols. It was a lovely idea to have them in church today.'

'I wonder if he'd come to the school and teach the children to ring them,' Stella said thoughtfully. 'We could have them as part of our concerts. I'll mention it to Miss Kemp as soon as school starts.'

Dottie had roasted a leg of lamb, boned and stuffed with pork sausagemeat and dried apricots. To go with it, they had new potatoes, carrots and spring cabbage, and for pudding she had made a lemon sponge soufflé, which had magically separated itself into two layers, the top one of feather-light sponge and the bottom of creamy lemon sauce. Afterwards, she made a big pot of tea and they lay in their armchairs or on the sofa, declaring themselves too full to move.

'I shall never need to eat again,' Maddy said. 'I've missed your cooking, Dottie.'

'Go on with you,' Dottie said, looking pleased. 'After all that lovely cooking you get in Paris?'

'It's not the same as yours. Mind you, they do have scrumptious *pâtisseries*. But it's only just starting to come back after the war. They've had rationing, too, you know.' She sighed and stretched her arms above her head. 'Actually, their peasant cooking – the sort they do in the country – is more like yours. *Proper* food – vegetables and things like pigeons and goose and that sort of thing. And they don't waste a single thing – it all gets eaten, one way or another.'

'And when did you ever eat peasant food?' Dottie asked, picking up her knitting. She had begun making things for the Summer Fair and was working on a pale-blue baby's cardigan. 'You and Miss Fenella spend all your time in the city, don't you?'

'No, we go to the country quite a lot. We stay in a château in the Dordogne. As a matter of fact, that's where we're going to live.' A small frown touched her face. 'At least, it's where Fenella's going to live. She's getting married.'

Dottie dropped her knitting. 'Getting married? Miss Fenella? After all these years? I can't believe it.'

Maddy nodded her head. 'Yes, she is. He's a French aristocrat, or he would have been if they hadn't had the Revolution. He owns the château itself, and acres and acres of land, and I don't know how many villages. He's terribly rich.'

'I should think he must be.' Dottie picked up her knitting again. 'Well, fancy Miss Fenella getting married again. I never thought she would.'

'Has she been married before, then?' Stella enquired. 'I never knew that.'

Dottie pursed her lips and nodded. 'When she were a little slip of thing, just twenty-one years old. Had her head turned by an actor in the London theatre – didn't have nobody to advise her, you see, and went and got married without knowing a thing. He was twice her age and a drinker. Drank hisself to death in two years and left poor Miss Fenella alone, a widow at twenty-three. Not that it wasn't a good thing, when you look at it all ways up,' Dottie added, joining on a fresh ball of wool. 'She were well rid of him. But 'twas a hard time for her, all the same.'

'Oh, poor Miss Forsyth,' Stella exclaimed. 'But why didn't she have anyone to advise her, Dottie? Was she an orphan, like Maddy and me?'

'Not exactly, but as good as. Told me the whole story, her did, one day. I'd been working for her as her dresser for a few months then and we got on as well as if we were sisters. It were her dad, you see. Wouldn't countenance the idea of her being an actress, and when her wouldn't give up the idea, he just turned her out of the house. Told her never to go back. 'Twas no wonder her turned to an older man for comfort.' Dottie shook her head. 'Changed his tune after she became a success, but Miss Fenella wasn't having any. She kept in touch with her mother up to the day the old lady died, but she never saw her father again. And after that dratted husband of hers died, she swore she'd never marry again, neither.'

'And so she thought she'd never have any children,' Maddy said. 'That's why she adopted me.'

They sat in silence for a few minutes, thinking over the story and trying to imagine the tragedy and pain that lay behind the words. Then Dottie said, 'And now she'm getting wed again! Well, she ought to be old enough not to make a mistake this time round.'

'Oh, I don't think it's a mistake this time,' Maddy said. 'She really loves him and he thinks the world of her.' But there was a faint note of desolation in her voice and Stella glanced at her.

'What will you do?' she asked quietly. 'Are you going to live in France with them?'

'I don't know,' Maddy said. 'I don't know what I'm going to do.'

After a while, the three of them crammed themselves into the sports car and set off across the moor. Despite Dottie's protests, they had done the washing-up first and left the kitchen clean and shining. They had to be back for Felix to take part in evensong, but apart from that the afternoon was theirs and they felt as free as birds as the little car climbed valiantly up the steep hills and dropped into the hidden valleys of the moor.

'This is Dartmeet,' Felix announced, stopping by a narrow bridge over the flashing river. 'It's where the east and west tributaries of the River Dart come together. There's the old packhorse bridge, see? And there's a nice tearoom, too – we could come back here for tea if you like.'

'I'd like to walk along the river,' Stella said, and they parked the car and set off along the narrow footpath.

'Do you really not know what you want to do, Maddy?' Stella asked after a few minutes. 'Don't you want to stay with Miss Forsyth?'

Maddy, walking just behind, between Stella and Felix, shrugged. She was wearing a flowered dress and a light-blue cardigan, and her fair hair bounced on her shoulders as she moved. 'I don't know what I want to do. It's been lovely until now, travelling about with Fenella – it was exciting and fun when she was still on the stage, and now that she's left it, we've had a good time just visiting all her friends and seeing Europe. She knew it so well before the war, you see, and she's enjoyed showing me France and Italy and Switzerland. And I've enjoyed seeing it all. But now – well, she's not going to need me for company any more, is she? And I feel I ought to be living my own life – earning a living, like you. Only, I'm not trained for anything, and I don't know what I'd be good at. I might not be good at anything.'

Once again, Stella heard the faint note of melancholy in her sister's voice and felt an urge to reassure her. 'Of course you must be good at things. Look at all you've done – the places you've seen. Much more than I have. There must be heaps of jobs you could do.'

'Like what?' Maddy asked. 'I don't think I could teach, and I'd be hopeless as a nurse. I could work in a shop, I suppose.'

'You'd make a jolly good secretary,' Felix said, turning his head. 'You must have lots of experience in arranging things for Miss Forsyth.'

'Yes, I suppose so.' Maddy still sounded doubtful. 'I looked after her diary and did all the travel and that kind of thing. I did learn typing and shorthand at the finishing school I went to, but I've never worked in an office, and I don't know really what else secretaries do.'

'Well, it depends whose secretary they are,' Felix said. 'The thing is, would you like that sort of work?'

'I don't know. I might.' Her voice was so dispirited that they both stopped at once and Maddy walked into Felix and almost knocked him into the river. Stella grabbed them both and the three of them clutched each other, laughing. 'Oh, don't let's bother about all that now,' Maddy exclaimed, resting her head against Felix's shoulder as he steadied her. 'This is a holiday – let's just enjoy ourselves. How far do you want to walk, Stella? I was hoping we could go to Widecombe.'

They turned and walked back to the car, the brief discussion over. As they soared up the steep hill out of the valley, Maddy's spirits seemed to recover, and Stella, taking her turn in the dicky seat, smiled at the sight of the two blond heads so close together. She had no qualms about her sister's ability to find work, if she needed it. But would she actually need it? Fenella Forsyth had looked after her so well until now, adopting her as a daughter and never allowing her to want for anything, that it was difficult to believe that Maddy would ever really need to work for her living. It seemed almost wrong that she should have to – she was so pretty, so enchanting, so different from the plain little Muriel she had once been, that it seemed unnatural to imagine her teaching a class of unruly schoolchildren or serving in a shop. Even sitting at a typewriter . . .

Even if she does have to work, Stella thought, it won't be

for long. Someone will marry her and look after her for the rest of her life. I just hope he's someone who treats her as she ought to be treated.

Chapter Nineteen

'It's this morning Miss Tucker's coming to see me again,' Basil said to his wife at breakfast a few days after Easter. 'I think she's found out quite a lot from the Tozers. Alice wouldn't tell me anything of course, she said she'd leave it to the young woman herself, but it's obvious they know something.'

'Well, if anyone would know, the Tozers would,' Grace said, opening a new pot of homemade marmalade. 'That's if the parents actually did come from Burracombe.'

'I think they must have, or she wouldn't be coming to see me.' Basil folded his newspaper. 'I just hope it won't lead to trouble for anyone. It isn't always a good idea to dig up the past.'

'It's only natural for her to want to know the truth about her parents, though. It's not exactly the distant past, is it?'

'No – it might be better if it were.' Basil dipped a spoon into the marmalade and frowned. 'I believe in the truth as much as any man of my calling, my dear, but I still can't help feeling that some truths are best left untold. But it isn't for me to say what's best in this case. It's Miss Tucker's life we're talking about, and it must be her decision. I'm sure God will guide her.'

'I'm sure He will,' Grace said, smiling. 'And I can't help admitting that I'm very curious to know more myself. Are you ever going to take any marmalade out of that pot, Basil, or are you just going to stir it for a while?'

'Oh – I'm sorry, dear.' He hastily removed the spoon and dropped a dollop of marmalade on the side of his plate. 'Yes, I'm curious, too. But we really ought to set our curiosity aside, Grace. Miss Tucker may have decided to look no further into the matter. She may decide never to say who she believes her father is, and if that's her decision, I shan't question it. Curiosity is a human emotion, my dear – not a godly one.'

His wife smiled again. It might be human, but it was a very healthy emotion, and as long as you kept other people's secrets and never betrayed their confidences, there was no harm in it. It was what kept you interested in your fellow human beings, and that was the most important thing of all.

Grace could understand her husband's reservations, though. A secret like this might be better never told.

'*Jacob Prout?*' Basil stared at his visitor, too astonished even to close his mouth. '*Jacob Prout* is your father?'

'I believe he is, yes.' Jennifer sat in his study, a cup of coffee on the small table beside her. Basil was opposite her, in his armchair beside the fireplace. The fire was unlit, the room warmed by April sunshine, and through the open window they could hear a robin singing. Basil glanced round, then got up hastily and closed the window.

'Jacob comes and helps in the garden sometimes,' he explained. 'He might easily pass at any minute and hear what we're saying . . . My dear Miss Tucker, are you sure about this? I can hardly believe it. *Jacob Prout . . . ?*' He shook his head and sat down again.

'That's what Mr and Mrs Tozer think,' Jennifer said. 'They knew my mother, you see, and old Mrs Tozer knew my grandmother. They were close friends.' She recounted the story of her grandmother's marriage to the bullying Abraham Hannaford. 'They used to see my mother and Jacob together. She came into the village for dances, when she could get away, and she and Jacob . . .' She raised her eyes to Basil's. 'We don't know for certain, of course. But it really does seem as if he must have been my father. He wrote to her all the time he was away, and then he came back for a while in 1916, when he was wounded. Susan was expecting me when she left the village – when her father turned her out. It *must* have been him.'

'It certainly seems likely,' Basil said slowly. 'And of course I didn't know Jacob then – I didn't come to the village until a good many years after that. But still . . .' He shook his head again. 'Who would have thought it? Who would have dreamed of such a thing?'

'It isn't all that unusual,' Jennifer said defensively. 'People do have babies without being married. I'm sure they *would* have been married, if it hadn't been for the war.'

'Yes, I'm sure they would,' Basil hastened to reassure her. 'I'm not speaking against Jacob, my dear, or your poor mother. It must have all been very difficult for them, especially if she was having such an unhappy time at home.'

'He was a bully,' Jennifer said flatly. 'My grandfather, I mean. He might have been a chapelgoer and read the Bible every night, but he was a bully just the same. He used to beat my grandmother, so old Mrs Tozer says, and probably my mother as well.' She glanced down at her arms and pushed up the sleeve of her cardigan to stare at the faint blue lines beneath the pale skin. 'And this is his blood in my veins. Do you know how that makes me feel?' She leaned forward. 'I need to know who else there was in my life,' she said. 'I need to know who my father was, and to know he was someone good.'

'Jacob is certainly that,' Basil said seriously. 'A very good man – the salt of the earth. But do you really think it matters so much whose blood you have, my dear? It's how you were brought up that's really important, and anyone can see that your mother—'

'Oh, she was a wonderful mother. And my stepfather, too – he was always kind to me, he never treated me any differently from my sisters. But –' she looked at her arm again '– I still need to know about my real father. I'm sorry, Mr Harvey, but I really do need to know.' She pulled down her sleeve and sat back, looking at him almost with a touch of defiance, as if she were presenting him with a challenge.

There was a brief silence. Basil returned her gaze and then picked up his coffee cup. He drank, then put it down again and said, 'Yes. I can see that you do, and of course it must be your own decision. But may I ask what you intend to do next? It's not just curiosity on my part –' he remembered his conversation with Grace and almost blushed '– but Jacob is not only one of my parishioners, he's also a churchwarden and looks after the churchyard. He works closely with me. And while acknowledging that this is really a matter between the two of you, if there's anything concerning his spiritual welfare . . .' He stopped and sighed. 'I haven't the right even to ask you this. It's entirely your business and his. If Jacob wants to confide in me himself, then of course he may. But if not . . .'

Jennifer fiddled with her own cup. 'But I've made it your business, too,' she said at last. 'I came and asked you to help me. And the Tozers as well – I've already involved you all. Are you asking me not to tell him, when you all know already?'

'We don't know,' he corrected her gently. 'Not for certain, anyway . . .' He sighed. 'I think what you are saying is that it isn't fair for so many of us to know – or suspect – while he remains in ignorance. Is that right?'

'Yes, it is,' Jennifer said slowly. 'You were all so surprised, you see. You'd never thought that there might be anything like this in his past. So it's changed the way you think of him. It doesn't seem fair that he shouldn't know that.'

'I hope it won't make any difference to the way I treat him—' Basil began, but she shook her head.

'I don't see how you can help it. You know something he doesn't. Things aren't the same between you any more – they can't be.' She paused, then added, 'I know, because things aren't the same between me and my half-sisters. I'm not saying they've changed in any bad, or hurtful, way, but they're different. It'll be like that with you and Jacob. You and the Tozers know something that he doesn't, and it's something important.'

Basil sat for a few moments staring into the fireplace, filled now with fir-cones for the summer. He gazed at them thoughtfully and at last turned his head and looked back at the woman sitting opposite him.

'You're right,' he said. 'You're quite right. But it still doesn't mean he should be told. Perhaps we should just accept that we know this – or think we know it – and try to adjust. You see, I think it might hurt him very much to know that your mother – his sweetheart – was in such trouble and that he didn't even know about it. And remember that he did, eventually, marry and his marriage seems to have been happy. And your mother, too, seems to have made a good life for herself and for you. After all, she could have contacted him herself, couldn't she? Have you ever wondered why she didn't – before she married?'

'I thought it was probably because he was still away. Or because she knew that everyone had been told she was dead. Her father must have made it impossible for her to come back.'

'Yes, it could have been difficult.' Basil sighed. 'How can we know, so long after the event? But mightn't it still be better just to let things lie? Might you not be able to put this knowledge you have into its own compartment and go on to make your own life? So far, nobody has been hurt by this knowledge, and—'

'Except for me,' she said quietly, and he inclined his head.

'Yes, I'm sorry. Except for you. And I'm afraid it is you

who have to make the decision – whether to go on carrying your secret or whether to approach Jacob. And if you do that, we just don't know what will happen next.'

'He might be pleased,' she said. 'He might be happy to have a daughter. He's never had any other children.' Once again, the challenge leaped into her eyes. 'I'm not a young woman, Mr Harvey, but I'm still young enough to have my own children. He could have grandchildren as well. Wouldn't that make him happy?'

'Yes,' Basil said. 'I'm sure it would.'

They sat silent for a while, then she put her cup back on the table and made to rise. Basil stood up quickly and held out his hand, and she took it in hers.

'Thank you, Mr Harvey,' she said simply. 'Thank you very much. You've given me quite a lot to think about. And I promise I won't do anything in a hurry.' She looked him in the eye. 'I'll promise you something else as well. Whatever I decide to do, I'll let you know first. And if I do tell my father – Jacob – I'll tell him that you know. I don't want anyone else having secrets they can't share.'

Basil nodded, but he still looked doubtful. 'He might prefer to think that I didn't know.'

'But you do,' she said. 'And once we start telling the truth, we're not going to stop. It will all have to come out into the open – every bit of it.'

Basil saw her to the door. As she went out and walked down the path, he caught sight of Jacob himself approaching along the lane. His heart in his mouth, he waited for them to meet, wondering if Jennifer would realise who the man was and whether she would be able to resist speaking to him.

They met at the gateway. Jennifer paused and Jacob stood back a little to let her pass. She said something to him and he touched his cap and dipped his head slightly. Then she walked on past and he came up the path to the door where Basil was still standing.

'Nice-looking little body,' Jacob commented as he came within earshot. 'Haven't seen her around the village before. Visitor, was she?'

'Yes,' Basil said, finding his voice. 'A sort of visitor. She just came to ask me something.' Already, he was realising the truth of Jennifer's words, that the knowledge he had been given was forming a barrier between them. He summoned up all his determination to overcome it, but Jacob's next words almost destroyed his resolve.

'Put me in mind of someone,' the gravedigger said, pushing back his cap to scratch his head. 'Can't quite put me finger on it, though. Maybe she's got family living hereabouts.'

'Yes,' Basil said faintly, 'maybe she has.'

Stella and Maddy met Jennifer Tucker, too, as they were strolling towards the bus stop. They had decided to spend the day in Plymouth, looking at the new buildings and going up to the Hoe.

'There was almost nothing left, you know,' Maddy told Stella. 'The Blitz was over before I came here, of course, and we never went to Plymouth – there wasn't much to go for by then – but Dottie told me about it. She said the flames were so bright when it was burning that you could read a newspaper by their light, all the way out here in Burracombe.'

'I've seen pictures of it,' Stella said. 'Dottie kept a lot of newspapers, and someone put them all into a book. It's like Portsmouth was, when we were little.' They were both silent for a moment, remembering the times their own home had been bombed and that final catastrophic raid when their mother and baby brother had been killed. 'Thank goodness it's all over. I hope we never have a war like that again.'

They came to the bus shelter and looked with friendly interest at the woman already waiting. She smiled back a little shyly and said, 'Going to do some shopping?'

'We're just going for a look round, really,' Stella said. 'My sister used to live here when she was little, but I've only been in the village for just over a year. I haven't been to Plymouth very often.'

'I want to see Dingle's,' Maddy said. 'Dottie told me what a lovely shop it was before the war, and I want to see what it's like now the new one's been opened.'

'That's where I work!' Jennifer exclaimed. 'It *is* a lovely shop – it's really big and open, and there are all sorts of things on sale. I work on the ladies' fashions floor. I'm a senior sales assistant, but I hope to be a buyer.' She looked at Maddy's slender figure and blonde hair. 'Are you a model?'

'Good gracious, no!' Maddy laughed. 'Whatever makes you ask that?'

'With your looks, you could be,' Jennifer said, and Maddy blushed and laughed again. Before she could say any more, they heard the sound of the little country bus trundling along the lane and prepared to climb aboard. The two sisters sat behind Jennifer so that they could continue their conversation.

'Do you mind me asking something?' Jennifer said after a few minutes. She looked at Maddy. 'Your sister said you lived here when you were little. Were you evacuated here?'

'Yes, I was with a children's home – Stella and I lost our parents in the war and we were separated. I was lucky – I was adopted, but my new mother had to be away and couldn't look after me herself, so she left me with Dottie Friend, a village woman that she knew. And Stella lodges with Dottie now, and we found each other again last year!'

'You mean you lost touch completely?'

'That's right,' Stella said. 'I started to try to find Maddy when I came here. It was the first chance I had, you see. But it was pure coincidence that I actually came to the place where she'd been living. Like a miracle,' she added, squeezing her sister's arm. 'You don't know how wonderful it is to find someone you've been looking for all your life.'

'No, I don't,' Jennifer said slowly, gazing at them. 'But I can imagine it . . .' She turned suddenly and stared out of the window.

A little startled by her abruptness, the two sisters glanced at each other and Maddy raised her eyebrows. Stella shrugged and was about to make a remark about the scenery when the older woman twisted round to speak to them again.

'So you're living in the village again now – both of you?'

'No, only me,' Stella said. 'I'm teaching at the village school. Maddy lives in France most of the time.'

'In France?'

'It's where my adopted mother lives,' Maddy explained. 'But I'm not sure I'm going to stay there much longer. Now that I've found Stella again, it would be nice to come back – especially as she lives in Burracombe. It's the place I always think of as home, you see.'

'Yes,' Jennifer said. 'It seems the sort of place where you could really feel at home.'

'Do you know it well?' Stella enquired, thinking that it was their turn to ask a few questions. 'Have you got family in the village?'

To her surprise, the stranger's face coloured and she looked for a moment as if she didn't know how to answer. Then she said, 'My mother used to bring me here when I was a little girl. I don't remember it well, but I've never really forgotten it. I think she had relatives.' Once again she stopped, as if she had said too much, and turned away. Then she looked back and said, 'You know how it's been since the war – people lost touch with each other. Everyone was so busy trying to get back to normal and make new lives for themselves.'

Stella nodded. 'I didn't think I'd ever find my sister again. And we still don't know if we've got any other relatives. I don't suppose we ever will.'

For the rest of the journey they chatted about other things. Maddy was eager to know about the rebuilding of Plymouth after the devastating damage of the war, and Jennifer described the new stores that were being built and the long, straight roads that had taken the place of the narrow streets that had been there before.

'The King himself came to open Royal Parade,' she said. 'I was there – I saw him almost as close as I am to you now. It's a shame he died so young. As a matter of fact, I was in Burracombe the day he died – I was in the church when the vicar came in to tell Mrs Tozer.'

'You know the Tozers, then?' Stella asked, and Jennifer bit her lip, as if once again she'd given herself away.

'Only a bit, just to say hello to. I saw Princess Elizabeth, too, once. She makes a lovely Queen, doesn't she? I'd love to go to London and see the Coronation procession. A lot of people are saying it's going to be on television, but hardly anyone's got it, so I don't see what use that will be.'

'I expect a lot of people will get sets especially to see it,' Maddy said. 'I would.'

By the time they arrived in Plymouth, they felt they were old friends. They got off the bus in Royal Parade, with Jennifer pointing out the big Dingle's store to them and making them promise to come and see her in ladies' fashions next time they came. As they parted, she stood for a few minutes watching them stroll away, arm in arm and chattering like a pair of budgerigars.

She heard Stella's voice in her head: '*You don't know how wonderful it is to find someone you've been looking for all your life . . .*'

Jennifer hadn't been looking for her father all her life. She hadn't even known about him until recently. But that didn't mean he hadn't known about her. It didn't mean he hadn't been carrying his own secret through all these years.

Perhaps *he* had been looking for *her* – or at least missing her – all his life.

Chapter Twenty

The next morning, Stella woke up with a cold. It was the sort of cold that leaps upon you suddenly, rather than creeping up over a few days, so that when she opened her eyes they were already streaming, her throat felt as if it were on fire, and her head was thumping as if half the infant class were banging their tambourines beside her pillow.

'My stars, you look a bit under the weather,' Dottie said, coming in with a cup of tea. Stella had told her time and time again that she didn't have to do this, but Dottie took no notice and this morning Stella was grateful for it. 'You've got that nasty cold that's been going round the village. Mrs Warren had it last week. She couldn't come to the Parish Council meeting and we got through everything in half the usual time.'

'I feel terrible,' Stella said miserably. 'Felix was going to take me and Maddy to Becky Falls today, but I really don't think I can go. Anyway, I don't want to pass it on to them.'

'Do you want me to slip over the road and tell them?' Dottie enquired. 'I'll pop across first and then bring you a bit of breakfast, shall I? I dare say you'll be better by the weekend – you could go then.'

'No, Felix is going to be busy all weekend. He's taking a wedding at Little Burracombe on Saturday and he's going to Exeter to see the Bishop on Monday. Tell them to go without me. It's such a lovely day, and it would be a shame not to make the most of it. It'll probably be raining again by the weekend.'

Dottie nodded and went out, leaving Stella to sip her tea and snuggle back beneath the bedclothes. After a while, she reappeared with a breakfast tray.

'I've been over to see them. Maddy wanted to come and see how you were, but I wouldn't let her. No sense in you catching it, too, maid, I told her, and she knows if she catches a cold it goes straight to her chest.'

'So are they going to go out?' Stella asked, sitting up and wondering how much she would be able to eat of the breakfast Dottie had brought her. 'That looks lovely, Dottie, but I really don't think I've got much appetite.'

'You can manage some Weetabix and a boiled egg,' Dottie said firmly, settling the tray across Stella's lap. 'And there's some nice honey from Iris Tozer's bees, which she keeps up in the corner of the churchyard, to go on that toast. Good for colds, honey is. Feed a cold and starve a fever, that's what I was always told. You've got to keep up your strength when you'm poorly. Now, my blossom, you take your time and eat it all up. You aren't going anywhere else today, not if I've got anything to do with it.'

Stella didn't want to go anywhere else. She ate as much as she could and then put the tray down on the floor and lay down again, feeling exhausted. Outside, she could hear the usual sounds of village life – the clip-clop of horses' hooves as the baker's cart or the milkman went along the road, the cheerful voices calling to each other as the men went to work in the fields and the women came to do their shopping. She heard the church bells chime the hour and the bleating protests of a flock of sheep being driven from one field to another. And she heard laughter coming from almost beneath her window and realised it was her sister and Felix, setting out for their day across the moor. A moment or two later, she heard the sound of the car starting up and roaring out of the village. For a moment or two after that, it seemed as if everything fell silent. It was as if Felix and Maddy had taken all the life of Burracombe with them.

Feeling miserable and bereft, Stella pulled the bedclothes up over her head. I'm being stupid, she told herself crossly. I'm sorry for myself because I've got a cold and I'm missing a day out with my two favourite people. I should be pleased they're enjoying themselves. I *am* pleased.

Tears filled her eyes and she sat up and found a handkerchief to blow her nose. Then she lay down and tried to go back to sleep and not think about Maddy and Felix, together in the little sports car, enjoying their day out together.

'It's such a shame poor Stella's got a cold,' Maddy said, snuggling down beside Felix in the front seat. 'Just when we've got time to spend together and really get to know each other – it doesn't seem fair.'

'You and I'll have to get to know each other instead,' Felix said. 'I'm disappointed, too, but at least Stella and I see each other quite a lot. You'll be going away again soon – back to France, I suppose.'

'I suppose so.' But her voice was unenthusiastic and Felix glanced sideways at her.

'Don't you want to go back?'

'I don't know. It's all different, now that Fenella's getting married. I like Raoul, of course, and I'm really happy for them both, and they both say I'm welcome to stay with them – there's room enough in the château, after all! – but I just don't know what I'd do with myself. Up till now, since I left school, I've been Fenella's main companion. I've looked after her and made sure everything happened properly for her – where she was supposed to go, what she was supposed to do. I've made all our travelling arrangements and that sort of thing. But she'll be living a different sort of life now, and

Raoul has his own people to take care of all those arrangements. There won't be anything for me to do.'

'You could just enjoy yourself,' Felix suggested, slowing to avoid a Dartmoor pony that had decided to amble across the road in front of them. 'I should imagine they'll be having an interesting sort of life.'

Maddy made a face. 'Interesting for people like them, I suppose. Lots of socialising and parties and so on for Fenella. And Raoul has his estates to look after.' She turned her face up to his, regarding his profile as he concentrated on his driving. 'But there's nothing for me to do. I want to feel useful, and I don't think I shall any more.'

'Where will you live, if you don't stay in France?' he asked. 'Would you come back to Burracombe?'

'How could I? I'd need to earn a living somehow. Oh, I'm sure Fenella would want to give me an allowance, and she might find me somewhere to live – a flat or something in London. And I suppose if I said I'd rather stay in Burracombe, she'd help me do that. But I'd still want something to *do*. I can't just spend the rest of my life being a butterfly. Anyway, I'm tired of being kept and looked after. I want to be independent.'

'You'll probably get married,' he said. 'A lovely girl like you isn't going to stay single for long.'

'That's what Fenella and Raoul say. Stella said something like it, too, the other day. But suppose I don't, Felix? Suppose I just never meet anyone I want to marry? Anyway, not all girls get married. Some have careers. Stella and I met a woman on the bus yesterday, she's a senior sales assistant in Dingle's, and she's hoping to become a fashion buyer. She really seems to like it. Maybe I could do something like that. I don't want to get married just so that I don't have to work for my living, Felix.'

They drove in silence for a while, passing the grim buildings of Dartmoor Prison at Princetown and a working party of convicts labouring close to the road. Maddy shuddered and pulled her jacket closer around her.

'Cold?' Felix asked. 'I could put the hood up.'

'No, I love to feel the air. It was just seeing those poor men and thinking of that horrible prison. Imagine spending years and years of your life in a place like that.'

'They probably deserve it,' Felix pointed out. 'They're criminals – maybe even murderers.'

'I know, but it's still horrible to think of. Whatever awful things they've done, they're still human beings. They can still feel desperately miserable.'

'A lot of people would think that was the least of their punishment.' He glanced down at her. 'You're very soft-hearted, aren't you?'

'I suppose so. It's probably because I've been so lucky in my own life. Except for the first few years, I mean – being bombed out and losing my parents and baby brother, and then Stella, none of that was lucky. But afterwards, when Fenella found me and adopted me – well, ever since then I've been very lucky indeed. I've had an easy life – much easier than Stella has.' She thought for a moment or two, then added in a slightly surprised tone, 'And yet, she's the one with a career. She's the one who's got a purpose in her life.'

From Princetown, they drove through a maze of steep, narrow lanes to Widecombe and stopped for coffee at a teashop opposite the church. Its tall tower soared into the air, looming over the little green and the huddle of cottages. Felix and Maddy walked about for a while, and he told her about the famous fair held here every September.

'You wouldn't know the place then. There are gipsies telling fortunes, wags telling jokes, town criers ringing their handbells, children dancing round the maypole, sheep and cattle and ponies for sale – but you must know all about it,' he added. 'Surely you came here when you lived in Burra-combe?'

'No, they couldn't hold it during the war. Maybe I could come this year, though.' She looked up at him with shining eyes. 'We could come together! And Stella, too, of course.'

'Yes,' he said. 'Of course.' And they turned and went back to the car, to continue their journey to the famous waterfalls a few miles away at Manaton.

'It was a lovely day,' Maddy told Stella later, peeping in through the bedroom door. Dottie had told her that Stella seemed a bit better now, and so long as she didn't go right into the room, she shouldn't catch the cold, which seemed to be one of those that came suddenly and went just as fast. 'Manaton is so pretty, and the falls were beautiful. And we went to Haytor as well and climbed right up on the rocks – the view from there is wonderful. You can see as far as Exmoor and even to the sea! And there are lambs everywhere now, and Felix says the ponies will be having their foals soon.' She smiled at the thought. 'It's so nice to be back in the country. London and Paris and Rome are all very exciting, but there's nowhere quite like Burracombe!'

'I'm glad you had a good time,' Stella said, trying not to sound wistful.

'Oh, I did! Felix is such good company, isn't he? And he knows just how to look after a girl. He made sure I wasn't cold in the car, and he found a lovely spot to have our picnic by a little stream, and then we had tea at Badger's Holt, like we did when you were with us, and I had junket as well as those special scones they make.' She glanced a little enquiringly at her sister. 'You're very lucky, you know.'

'Lucky? Why?'

'Well, having a nice young man like Felix.' There was still a slight questioning note in her voice, and Stella felt the hot colour sweep into her cheeks.

'Felix isn't my "young man"! We're just friends, that's all.'

'Oh. I thought – oh, never mind. Sorry.' But Maddy didn't

sound sorry; in fact, she sounded rather pleased and Stella felt suddenly depressed. She felt for her handkerchief and blew her nose.

'You'd better go downstairs. I really don't want you to catch this, especially as you'll be going back to France at the end of the week. And I'm feeling a bit tired again.'

'You look a bit feverish to me,' Maddy said anxiously. 'All pink and flushed. I'll ask Dottie to come up and have another look at you in case you've got 'flu or something.'

She disappeared and Stella heard her voice downstairs. A few moments later, Dottie came up and peered at her in concern.

'Are you feeling worse, my flower? I wonder if I should ask Dr Latimer to look in.'

'No, don't do that. I'm all right – it's just a cold. I'll be better in the morning, when I've had a good sleep.'

'Well, we'll see.' Dottie didn't sound convinced. 'If you'm no better then, I'll pop into the surgery.' She plumped up Stella's pillows and smoothed her coverlet. 'Seems like Maddy had a lovely day out with Felix. Shame you couldn't go with them.'

'Yes. I'm glad she enjoyed it, though.' Stella lay down again, still feeling depressed. It's just because I'm not well, she told herself. I really am glad Maddy had a nice day. It's silly to feel left out, when I know they'd have liked to have me with them.

But that was the wrong way round, wasn't it? It shouldn't be *her* going with Maddy and Felix. It should be Maddy coming out with Felix and Stella.

Somehow the balance between the three of them had changed, and Stella wasn't at all sure that she liked it.

Chapter Twenty-One

Miss Kemp had not forgotten the plan she and Joyce Warren had discussed for a dramatic production to be put on by the schoolchildren at the Summer Fair, and she and Stella had agreed that a scene from *A Midsummer Night's Dream* could be quite a good idea. As soon as the summer term began, she decided it was time to start planning.

'We'd better have all the children together in my room,' she said to Stella. 'I'll explain the story to them first. I'm sure they're going to enjoy it.'

Stella, who had never understood Shakespeare when she was a child and wasn't sure of all of it now, nodded a little doubtfully. Still, the play was all about country people and woods, which were familiar to the children, and a lot of the smaller girls firmly believed in fairies, so that was a good start. After those who went home for their dinners had returned, and those who stayed had helped clear the tables, she shepherded her infant class into the larger room and they all settled down to hear the story of *A Midsummer Night's Dream*.

'I knows Shakespeare,' Henry Bennetts announced confidently. 'My dad took me to see it at the pictures. There's this Prince, see, that comes home from school and finds his dad's dead. His dad was King, see, so the Prince thinks he'll be King, like Princess Elizabeth was Queen when our King died, only he's not because his mum's been and got married again and so there's another King. And then the old King comes back to life as a ghost, and—'

'You can't do that,' Micky Coker interrupted. 'You can only be a ghost if you'm dead. If you comes back to life, you must be alive again, so—'

'Well, he'm a ghost, then,' Henry said, determined not to be deflected. 'And he tells 'Amlet that he didn't die natural, he was murdered through having poison poured in his ear—'

'In his *ear*? Why didn't they make him drink it?'

'He was asleep, so they couldn't.'

'They could have waited till he woke up. They could have put the poison in his cup of tea. My mum says she'm going to put poison in my dad's tea if—'

'Micky!' Stella broke in, dismayed. 'I'm sure she doesn't say that.'

'Well, 'tis only a joke,' he admitted. 'But they could have done that, couldn't they, miss?'

'Well, they didn't,' Henry said, beginning to sound irritated. 'They poured it in his ear, and Shakespeare said so, so it must be right. Anyway, then 'Amlet – that's the Prince, 'Amlet – decides to kill the new King, see, and there's this soppy girl who keeps following him about saying she loves him, so he pushes her in the river and drowns her—'

'I'm sure he doesn't do that,' Stella exclaimed. 'Ophelia drowns *herself*—' She caught the huge, horrified eyes of one of the smaller girls and stopped. 'Perhaps we'd better forget *Hamlet* now and think about—'

'But it be a good story, miss,' Henry said, outraged. 'There's skulls in it and people fighting with swords, and in the end everyone dies. I wanted to go and see it again, but my dad said, no, we was going to the football instead.'

'Please, miss,' said Katy, the smallest Culliford girl. 'I don't want to die. Can't us do *Goldilocks and the Three Bears* instead? They done it at Horrabridge last Christmas and it were ever so good. They didn't have proper bears, mind,' she added. 'Just people dressed up with heads on.'

'I wouldn't mind being a bear,' Micky volunteered, but

before an argument could break out between the girls as to who should be Goldilocks, Miss Kemp came in and rang the bell for silence and the children subsided.

'Now, children, you all know what this is about,' the headmistress began. 'We're going to do a short piece from one of the plays written by William Shakespeare, who was a very famous playwright—'

'That's a man that writes plays,' Henry explained in a loud whisper to Katy Culliford, who was sitting next to him. 'I've seen it at the pictures, it's all about—'

'—and this play is called *A Midsummer Night's Dream*,' Miss Kemp went on, fixing Henry with a reproving eye. 'The part we're going to do is set in a big forest—'

'Like Cuckoo Wood?' Jane Pettifer asked, and Miss Kemp nodded.

'Like Cuckoo Wood, only much bigger. In the forest there is a band of fairies, with a king called Oberon and a queen called Titania.' At the mention of a king and queen, Henry, who had been looking mystified up to this point, nodded with satisfaction. 'There's also a little group of craftsmen – a carpenter, a weaver, a tinker, a tailor—'

'Like in *Tinker, Tailor, Soldier, Sailor*,' Jane supplied helpfully, and Miss Kemp nodded again but held up her hand to indicate that she would rather there were no more interruptions.

'—a joiner and a bellows-mender. They're rehearsing a play to perform at a very important wedding. There's also a rather mischievous servant called Puck, who has been sent into the forest by Oberon to find a magic flower. The juice of this magic flower could be squeezed over someone's eyes when they're asleep so that when they wake up they will fall in love with the first person they see.' Miss Kemp paused for dramatic effect, which was ruined by Henry's indignant tones.

'No, miss, that's not right. It's poison that you pour in

their ears so that when they wake up they'm dead! I saw it at the pictures.'

The headmistress stared at him for a moment, baffled, but decided to continue. 'Please be quiet, Henry. I don't know what you saw at the cinema, but it couldn't have been this play. Nobody wakes up dead.' She continued. 'In fact, when Titania, the Queen of the Fairies, does wake up, the first person she sees is the weaver and she falls in love with him. But Puck has been up to mischief again and has given him the head of an ass – that's a donkey, Katy – and as he doesn't realise that he now looks like a donkey and doesn't know anything about the love potion, he thinks the Fairy Queen really has fallen in love with him, and there's a great muddle. But in the end everything is sorted out and the right people get married to each other and Puck comes on to tell the audience he's sorry for all the trouble he's caused and asks them to imagine it was all just a dream.'

She stopped and the children gazed at her in silence. Then Henry, obviously still smarting with indignation, said, 'That's not what I saw at the pictures! There was a ghost in it and a skull and lots of fighting. With proper swords. And a prince called 'Amlet. And everyone got killed. And it *were* Shakespeare, because it said so in the title. I reckon this play you've been telling us about is by a different Shakespeare. And 'tisn't anywhere near as good, neither. This is just soppy.'

'That's right,' Micky agreed. 'I wouldn't mind being in something with swords and skellingtons and things. But I'm not being a fairy. Fairies is girls' stuff.'

'*I'd* like to be a fairy,' Shirley Culliford said. 'I could be the Fairy Queen, couldn't I, miss? I'll still have a bit of time left over from being Festival Queen last year, won't I?'

'No, you won't,' one of the other girls argued. 'There'll be a new Queen by then, won't there, miss?'

'Can't us do *Goldilocks and the Three Bears*?' Katy Culliford asked plaintively. 'Micky Coker says he'll be a bear.'

It looked as if another argument was about to break out; several, in fact, as the girls continued to debate the question of who should be Fairy Queen and the boys began at least two heated discussions about sword fights, skeletons and bears' heads. Miss Kemp rang the bell again and called for silence, and eventually order was restored.

'I think the film Henry saw must have been *Hamlet*,' she said firmly. 'It was certainly by William Shakespeare, and many people think it was his best play, but the play we're doing, which was also by William Shakespeare, is called *A Midsummer Night's Dream*. And if Micky really wants to wear an animal's head, he can play Bottom.'

There was a horrified gasp from the children, who then instantly dissolved into giggles. Micky turned scarlet and Miss Kemp closed her eyes for a moment.

'There is nothing funny about the name Bottom,' she said, raising her voice above the smothered laughter. 'It's the name of the weaver whose head is turned into a donkey's and who falls in love with the Fairy Queen. All the craftsmen have funny names, just like they do in – in –' inspiration struck her '– in pantomimes. In fact, this story is very much like a pantomime. And one of the other craftsmen plays a lion, so nobody need think they're going to look silly or soppy—'

'Well, if it's just a pantomime, why can't us do a proper one, then?' Micky demanded, still crimson in the face. 'I'd rather be a bear than a stupid donkey with a rude name.'

'Us could do *Cinderella*,' Jane Pettifer suggested. 'There's some nice frocks in that, too.'

'Or *Dick Whittington*,' someone else called out. 'I could bring our cat, only I don't think he'd like wearing them boots.'

'I saw *Babes in the Wood*, once, there was robbers in it, and—'

'Why can't us do the one with skellingtons and ghosts?'

came Henry's disappointed voice. 'It were ever so good, and I got a wooden sword with proper silver paint on its blade—'

'Because it's not a pantomime!' Miss Kemp snapped, and then, recalling that they weren't planning to do a pantomime, anyway, added hastily, 'We're doing *A Midsummer Night's Dream* and that's all there is to it.' She inserted a note of encouragement into her voice. 'You'll enjoy it once we start. The boys can play the craftsmen and the girls can be the fairies, so there's something for everyone. Except for Oberon, of course, he'll have to be played by a boy. But I'm sure one of you would make a very good King.'

There was a long silence. The children stared up at their teachers and then looked at each other. They had all heard that tone in Miss Kemp's voice before and knew that there was no point in further argument. They heaved deep sighs and folded their lips in resignation.

Micky had the last word.

'Well, if us got to do it, I suppose us got to do it. But you'll have to change the name of that donkey, miss. I'm not going to be called Bottom, not for nobody.' He looked up at her with pleading eyes. 'Couldn't I be a bear instead, like in *Goldilocks*?'

Maddy had gone back to France after her visit to Burracombe, promising to come again soon. Felix had driven her and Stella to Tavistock to catch the train, and afterwards he took Stella for a cup of tea at Goode's, on the corner opposite Creber's grocery shop.

'I'm going to miss her dreadfully,' Stella said, wiping her eyes. 'Oh, I'm sorry about this, Felix – I didn't mean to be a cry-baby. But we were apart for such a long time, and I didn't know if I'd ever see her again. It makes it harder to part from her now.'

'I know. But I'm sure you're going to see lots of her in the future. I know she's got to go back to France now, for Miss

Forsyth's wedding and everything, but it seems pretty likely that she'll come to live in England once that's over. Maybe even in Burracombe!' he added with a smile.

'That would be lovely, but I don't really see how she could do that, unless—' Stella stopped suddenly and spooned sugar into her tea, stirring busily. Felix cocked an eyebrow at her.

'Unless what?'

'Well, unless she found somewhere to live, for a start. She couldn't lodge with Aggie for ever. And what would she do with her time? I know she talks about getting a job, but she doesn't seem to know what kind of job she wants to do. And she's not used to the quiet country life any more – she's spent the last few years in big cities with really sophisticated people. She'd be bored to death in a few weeks.'

'Do you really think so?' Felix asked. 'Maybe it's the sophisticated people, as you call them, who really bore her. Anyway, there might be an alternative to her getting a job. She could get married.'

'Who could she find to marry in Burracombe?' Stella demanded, and then looked up and caught his eye. Immediately, she felt the hot colour rise into her cheeks. She looked down again at once, furious with herself and trying to ignore the twinge of pain in her heart. I might have known this would happen, she thought miserably. All the breakfasts they had together, the evenings when Maddy went back to Aggie's, that day out they had at Becky Falls. Maddy's so lovely, how could I expect Felix *not* to fall in love with her? And Felix is so kind and funny and good-looking . . . I wish I'd gone over to Aggie's and let Maddy have my room at Dottie's cottage.

'Well, it doesn't have to be someone in Burracombe itself,' Felix said after a moment. 'Once she was here, she'd meet all sorts of people. In Tavistock, for instance, or one of the other villages. You'd like to have her living nearby, wouldn't you?'

'Of course I would. And I'd be very happy for her to marry someone nice. It's all I want, really – for her to be happy.'

Stella paused, then said, 'You know, when we were little, I always used to look after her. She was my little sister, and I always felt I had to be grown-up and take care of her – especially after our mother died and we were evacuated. And then, when we were separated and I didn't know where she was or who was looking after her – or even if *anyone* was taking proper care of her – I used to cry myself to sleep, worrying about her. It was horrible, not knowing where she was. Sometimes I even thought she must be dead.' Her voice broke a little. 'And then, last year, when I found her again, it was like a miracle. All I want now is for her to be happy, and safe, and for me to know about it.'

Felix said nothing for a moment. Then he put both his hands across the table and folded them around hers. She looked up at him, startled, and he said quietly, 'But you need to be happy, too, Stella. You can't live all your life through your sister.'

'I'm not. I've got my teaching, and Burracombe. I've made my home there. I love it. I don't need anything else to make me happy.'

'Don't you?' he asked seriously. 'Don't you remember telling me one day that you'd like to fall in love? Don't you think you'd like to get married one day?'

Stella met his eyes, then looked away quickly. 'No,' she said. 'No, I don't. I'll be perfectly happy to be like Miss Kemp and teach in the village school all my life. I honestly can't think of anything nicer – and if Maddy's happy, too, I shall have everything I want. Everything!'

Chapter Twenty-Two

'So have you got any further with your wedding plans?' Hilary enquired, handing Val a cup of tea. They were sitting on the terrace at the back of the house, looking out towards the sweeping moors. The hillsides were a blaze of golden gorse, and the garden was full of birds. Gilbert Napier's two black Labradors were lying as if exhausted on the flagstones, their paws twitching as they dreamed, and the old tabby cat was curled up at the edge of one of the flowerbeds.

Val took the cup and set it on the low wicker table. 'We have and we haven't. We're definitely getting married this summer, but we haven't actually set a date yet. And we still haven't got any forrader with finding somewhere to live.' She sighed. 'Luke's still talking about getting a job. It's such a shame – he's got a wonderful talent, but he says he just can't sell enough to keep a wife and family. And even if I keep on working for a while after we're married, I'd still have to give up once the family starts. And we do want a family.'

'Of course you do. And I'm sorry I haven't been able to help over the estate house. I really don't know why Arnold Cherriman is so set on staying there. He's still talking about building somewhere new in Plymouth, but I don't know if he actually means it. I know his wife loves the garden, but I got the impression she'd rather go back to her old one.'

'Never mind. Something will turn up,' Val said, not sounding as if she really believed it. 'In the end, I suppose we'll have to live wherever Luke gets a job. And that'll probably be in Plymouth.'

'Well, it's not so far away,' Hilary said encouragingly. 'He could go on the bus if you did find somewhere local. Even if you had to go to Plymouth to start with . . .'

'I know. It's not as if he's talking about going to London.' Val sat staring pensively at the plate of biscuits Hilary had placed on the table. 'We're lucky, really, I know that. It's just that – well, I thought once we'd decided to get married, everything would fall into place. But it hasn't.'

Hilary laughed ruefully. 'It hardly ever does. Are you going to have one of those biscuits, Val, or are you trying to hypnotise them? They're very good – Mrs Ellis made them yesterday.'

'Oh yes – thanks.' Val took one and nibbled it absent-mindedly. There was a small frown between her brows, and Hilary looked at her thoughtfully.

'Is there anything else the matter? Your dad's not still worried about Luke, is he?'

'Mm?' Val looked up. 'No, not really. He'd be happier if Luke got what he calls a "proper job", so at least someone will be pleased when he's a wage-slave. No, it's not that.'

'So what is it?' Hilary asked gently. 'Unless you'd rather not tell me, of course.'

Val chewed her top lip and sighed. 'I might as well. Some of it, anyway. Hil, d'you think I'm too old to wear white?'

Hilary blinked, taken by surprise by the sudden question. 'Too old? No, I don't think so. Why, do *you* think you're too old?'

'I don't really know. I'm almost thirty, after all. It's quite old to be getting married at all, and the thought of a long white dress – well, it seems a bit inappropriate, somehow. I just wondered what other people might think.'

'Does that matter?'

'It would be nice to say no, it doesn't matter at all,' Val said wryly. 'But you know what it's like in a village, Hil. Things do matter an awful lot to some people. I don't care about the spiteful old gossips who have nothing to do with me or Luke, but I do care about the people who are important to me. Like Mum and Dad and the rest of the family, and friends like you.'

'Well, it's not going to upset me to see you in a long white dress, and it wouldn't whatever age you were,' Hilary said roundly. 'I can't see why it should. As far as I can see, it's how *you* feel about it that matters. Would you rather wear a colour?'

'No, that would make me look like a bridesmaid – people would be looking for the bride! But I wondered about a costume. A nice smart jacket and skirt, in a light colour, that I could wear for best afterwards. A pale blue, perhaps. What do you think?'

'I suppose that would be all right,' Hilary said slowly. 'But don't you think some people might feel they'd been done out of seeing a bride in all her virginal glory? It's the white dress that makes a wedding special, isn't it?'

Val put down her cup abruptly, rattling it in its saucer. 'Is it? Is that what you really think? The dress is the most important thing?'

'No, of course not. I didn't mean that at all. I just meant that a lot of people think the white dress is something special. It *means* something. It isn't the most important part of it, though – that's the bride and groom. You and Luke . . .' Hilary looked at her friend again, and then said, 'Val, what's the matter? Why are you so upset?'

'I'm not upset. It's all right, Hil, I know what you mean. I'm just being silly – all this uncertainty's getting on my nerves a bit. Sorry.' Val's voice was tense. 'Is there any more tea in that pot?'

'Yes. Pass me your cup.' Hilary gave her friend another

curious glance. 'Are you sure there's not something else the matter? If there's anything I can do—'

'No, there's not. There's nothing anyone can do.' Val caught Hilary's look and added hastily, 'There's nothing that *needs* doing. Honestly. I'm just a bit fed up, that's all, and I don't have any right to be. I'm getting married to the man I love, and that's all that matters. Let's talk about something else. How's your father these days?'

Hilary pulled a comical face. 'Just the same as he always is – wanting to do too much. He thinks that because he feels all right, he can go back to doing everything he did before. All he wants is to get back to managing the estate. I keep telling him that was what caused his heart attack in the first place and he'll be risking another, but he can't see it. I just wish he'd let me get on with it. I wish he'd *trust* me.'

'I don't think it's that he doesn't trust you,' Val said thoughtfully, glad to have the conversation moved from her own concerns. 'He just can't let go. It must be difficult for him, you know. One minute he was in charge, with the reins firmly in his own hands, and the next it was as though they'd been snatched away from him. And now that he feels he could drive again, he can't get them back. It must be horribly frustrating.'

'Yes, I expect it is, but that's something he's got to get used to, isn't it? Charles has told him he mustn't go back to working as hard as he did before. And part of it was the fact that he used to worry so much about what was going to happen to all this.' She waved her hand at the landscape stretching before them. 'All that fuss over Stephen not wanting to take over. He doesn't need to worry about that any more. He knows I can do it instead.'

'He might think you won't want to do it for ever, though,' Val said. 'Suppose you got married?'

Hilary shrugged. 'I might marry someone who'd be happy to stay here with me. Still, I can see what you mean. But the latest bee he's got in his bonnet is if I *don't* get married. If neither I nor Stephen can produce an heir who'll want to take it over—'

'Oh, for goodness' sake!' Val exclaimed. 'He's worrying about what's going to happen for the next fifty years or more! Honestly, Hil, we could all drive ourselves into the grave if we did that.'

'I know. But you try telling Dad that.'

They were silent for a few moments. Eventually, Val said thoughtfully, 'D'you think if you let him take over some of the work – enough to occupy him for a few hours a day – it would help? Being frustrated isn't going to make him any better – it could do just as much damage as working too hard. You don't really have to do it all yourself, do you?'

'It's what he used to do,' Hilary said obstinately.

'And it's what made him ill.'

'Oh, come on, Val – *I'm* not going to have a heart attack!'

'No, I don't suppose you are. But then, he didn't think he was going to, either. And we're trying to think of a way to help him, aren't we?' Val stood up and brushed down her skirt. 'I'd better be going. I promised to help cook supper tonight and Luke's coming round so I've got to make a good job of it – don't want him backing out now! Thanks for the tea, Hil, and tell Mrs Ellis her biscuits are scrummy and I want the recipe.'

Hilary laughed and got up to walk round to the front of the house with her friend. 'I don't expect she'll give it to you. She keeps her best recipes a secret. I'm sorry about the house, Val. But I'll keep my eyes and ears open. Something will turn up in the end.'

'Hope so.' Val gave her a quick hug and then walked off down the drive. Hilary stood watching her for a few minutes, her face thoughtful. Despite her friend's protestations, she was sure that there was something else worrying Val, something she wasn't prepared to talk about. But then, Val had always played some of her cards close to her chest. Deep though their friendship had grown since those days when they'd been in Egypt together, Hilary had always been aware that there were areas of Val's life that she simply didn't discuss. Not that this present worry could be anything to do with that, she thought, going back to collect the tea tray and take it indoors. Egypt was years ago, during the war. That water had flowed under the bridge long ago.

Her mind turned to their discussion about her father. It was true that Gilbert seemed to be fully recovered from the frightening heart attack he'd had last year, but Hilary was acutely aware of the danger of another one. It was this fear that kept her from letting him take on more of the burdens of the estate work. At least, that was what she told herself.

She wondered if Val was right, and that frustration at not being able to do more might be even more harmful. Could it be true that she just didn't want to let the responsibility go, now that she'd been given it? Was she being selfish?

It was an uncomfortable thought.

As she walked away from the Barton, her hands thrust deep into her jacket pockets, Val's mind returned to the question of the white dress. And it wasn't only that which concerned her. Even more important was the whole matter of whether she should be married in church at all.

The Tozers would not have called themselves a particularly religious family, but they were regular churchgoers and believed in the ethics that they had been taught. The children were baptised as a matter of course and attended confirmation classes when they reached the age of fourteen. Once confirmed, they went to Holy Communion once a month, at least until they were adult. It was true that Tom didn't go so often, and Joanna, who had been brought up differently, only went at Christmas and Easter and a few other occasions, but the whole family was in church for either matins or evensong, with Ted and Tom present half an hour earlier to ring the bells.

St Andrew's wasn't a 'high church', but there were certain rules that were understood. One was that the bride wore white to show that she was a virgin. If you didn't, you were more or less lying. And if you'd been married before and divorced – though that was so rare that nobody could remember it happening in Burracombe – you couldn't get married again in church, at least until your former spouse had died.

So what, Val wondered, was the position of someone like her? How could she put on a white dress and walk up the aisle, as if she were a young girl, innocent and untouched? She would be lying to everyone there. She would be lying to God – except that He already knew . . .

I don't know what to do, she thought miserably. And there's no one I can talk to. Luke's got enough to worry about, what with having to find a job when he ought to be using his talents as an artist, and Mum would be dreadfully upset. And nobody else knows about what happened in Egypt – not even Hilary. There are only the girls who were on the ship with me when I lost little Johnny, and they're scattered all over the country now.

She paused for a moment, leaning on a gate and gazing at a flock of sheep. The lambs had begun their usual teatime games, racing from one end of the field to the other and leaping on and off rocks. One was standing on its mother's back, bleating triumphantly, a sight that usually made Val chuckle, but there was no laughter in her heart this afternoon. Instead, hot tears prickled her eyes and for a moment she almost wished that Luke had never come back.

Shocked by the thought and angry with herself for thinking it, she brushed her hand across her eyes and looked up. The church tower was directly in her view, serene and grey against the tender blue of the sky, and she knew at once who she must talk to.

I'll tell him everything, she decided, pushing herself away from the gate. If he says I mustn't get married in church, then I won't. And if I have to tell everyone the truth, I'll do that, too. I may lose a lot of friends, but I won't lose those who truly love me, and even if my family are upset, I'm sure they won't desert me. But I can't start my new life with Luke with a lie. I just can't.

'It's not just that I need to know my father,' Jennifer said to Basil as she sat once again in his study. They had been talking for some time and had drunk two cups of tea each. 'He may need to know me. Well, not *need*, exactly, since as far as we know he doesn't even know I exist. But if he did know, wouldn't he want to meet me? Wouldn't he want us to have at least some time together, especially as we've missed so much? And we can't be really sure that he doesn't know I exist. He may have known my mother was expecting a baby. In fact, I think he must have done – surely she would have written and told him.'

'It's certainly a possibility,' Basil said slowly. 'What I can't understand is why nobody else seems to know if she did. Minnie Tozer knew Susan was pregnant, and Alice was told later. Were they the only ones? There must have been gossip. Why didn't all that come to Jacob's ears when he came back from the war? Or was it all such a turbulent time that some things just disappeared from people's minds?' He rubbed a hand over his fuzz of silver hair. 'People may have felt sorry for the girl, of course. By all accounts, Abraham was a very strict father—'

'He was a bully,' Jennifer said tersely. 'I should think everyone knew that.'

'Yes. You're probably right.' Basil sighed. 'Not that that helps us to decide what to do now.' He shook his head at himself. 'I'm sorry. As I said last time we met, it's your decision, not mine. I can only tell you what seems right to me, but I could be quite wrong and you have to make up your own mind.'

'But you're not really sure yourself what's the right thing to do, are you?' she asked.

'No, I'm not. And it doesn't really help that I know Jacob so well. Or thought I did . . .' He heaved another deep sigh. 'I suppose when all's said and done, it's truth that matters. People should know their true place in the world. If Jacob is a father – your father – he has a right to know it. And I think you're right – he would be pleased to know.'

Jennifer blushed, and he thought again what a pretty woman she was. Not in the first flush of youth, yet attractive, with a warmth in her face when she wasn't looking anxious. Perhaps knowing her true father would take that anxiety away, and that shadow of loneliness he could detect at times in the grey eyes. It was strange, he reflected, how important a blood relationship was. Jennifer had had a stepfather who loved her, and half-sisters she had grown up with on equal terms. Yet she still hankered after her real roots. And having searched so hard, and come so close, who was he to advise her against taking that final step?

'I'll go and see him,' she said decisively, and stood up. 'I'll go now – this afternoon.' She smiled a little ruefully. 'I feel that if I go back to Plymouth now, I'll lose my nerve!'

'Very well, my dear,' he said, getting to his feet as well. 'I wish you luck. And happiness, too. Jacob's a fine man. I don't know what Burracombe would do without him.' He held out his hand. 'Thank you for taking me into your confidence. I hope all goes well. And if you feel you need to come and see me again – or want to let me know how you get on – the vicarage door is always open to you. You're welcome at any time.'

'Thank you,' she said, taking his hand. He looked at her face and saw that the anxiety had fallen completely away. She looked young and happy and excited. 'You've been a real help. I'll come and see you again, and tell you all about it.'

He saw her to the door, warmed by her happiness, yet still feeling a twinge of anxiety for both her and Jacob. She seemed so sure that she was doing the right thing, that Jacob would take her instantly to his heart and that the lost years could be somehow regained. But Basil's experience told him that this wasn't always so easy. Sometimes things did just fall into place, but sometimes the jigsaw was just too difficult.

As he stood at the door, watching her walk out through the gate into the lane, his wife came to stand beside him.

'Has she made up her mind?' Grace asked, and he nodded.

'She's going to see Jacob now. I hope it won't be too much of a shock for the poor man. You know, even if he did realise that Susan was expecting his baby, he probably thinks they both died, just as the Tozers did. Seeing her now, without any warning, could be like meeting a ghost.'

'You think she should have written, or asked you to talk to him first?'

Basil turned away from the door, shaking his head. 'I really don't know, Grace. Without being able to see into the future, how can we know if any of our actions are for the best or not? We can only do what seems to be right at the time. That's what Jennifer Tucker is doing now, and I only hope she really is right. After all, it may be a shock to Jacob, but it must, surely, be a pleasant one. And there's no other wife or children involved. I don't see what trouble can come of it, do you?'

He went back to his study to finish the work he had been doing when Jennifer had arrived. But before he could gather his thoughts, Grace was at the door again and he found Jennifer's problem driven out of his head by another one, even closer to home.

'Val Tozer's here to see you,' Grace said. 'She says she needs to talk to you urgently.'

He stood up at once, beaming a welcome, but his smile faded when he saw her face. 'Why, Val, whatever's the matter? I thought you were coming to tell me the date for your wedding.'

'I'm not sure there's going to be a wedding,' Val said, and burst into tears.

Chapter Twenty-Three

Basil came swiftly across the room and put his hands on her shoulders, guiding her to the armchair so recently vacated by Jennifer Tucker. He pressed her into it and then took the chair opposite, wishing the fire was laid instead of being piled with fir-cones so that he could put a match to it. The afternoon had been warm, but distressed people always seemed to feel the cold.

'Would you like some tea?' he asked. 'Grace would willingly—'

Val shook her head at once. 'No, no, I've just had some at Hilary's. I came straight here. I've decided I must talk to you.' She looked suddenly doubtful. 'You're not too busy, are you?'

'My dear, I'm never too busy to talk to any of my parishioners. Especially when it's you, and you seem to be in such distress. Tell me what's happened. Have you and Luke quarrelled?'

'No. No, it's nothing like that. It's just that—' She began to cry again. 'I don't know how to tell you!'

'Val, please. Surely it can't be that bad.' A number of possibilities flashed through his mind, but he discarded them all. 'I've heard most things in my time as a vicar,' he said gently. 'People think clergymen are easily shocked, but really we're not. We wouldn't last very long in the job if we were.'

Val mopped her face and looked up at him, her eyes still brimming. 'I suppose you've come across lots of girls who have been silly enough to get into trouble before they were married, then.'

'Getting into trouble' was the phrase most used to mean pregnancy. Basil looked at her in some surprise.

'Is that what's happened to you? Well, it's not the end of the world. You're planning to marry soon, anyway – we can arrange it more quickly, if that's what you want.' He frowned, remembering Val's words when she had first come into the room. 'Luke *is* the father, I take it?'

'No!' she cried, and then added hastily, 'Nobody's the father! I mean, there isn't a baby – not now.' She sobbed into her handkerchief while Basil waited, disturbed and anxious. Luke was his godson and, although the boy had had his wild moments, working as a war artist and then contracting tuberculosis seemed to have subdued him, though there could still be a wicked gleam in his eye at times. Basil was extremely fond of him, and of Val, whom he had known ever since she was a young girl.

'Try to tell me all about it,' he said quietly. 'Take your time – there's no hurry. And I think I will ask Grace for some tea, but I'll fetch it myself. I won't be long.'

He got up and slipped quietly from the room, leaving Val by herself. In the kitchen, his wife looked at him enquiringly, but he shook his head and filled the kettle. Grace immediately began to set cups and saucers on a tray and put a few biscuits on a plate.

'Don't bring it in,' he said. 'Just knock on the door and I'll come and take it. Val's in rather a state, I'm afraid.'

By the time he returned to the study, Val had managed to stop crying and was more composed. She gave him a small, rueful smile as he came in and said, 'I'm sorry, Mr Harvey. I didn't mean that to happen.'

'It's quite all right, my dear. It often happens when someone's been bottling up a problem. You have to get the tears out first. Now, Grace is going to bring us some tea in a moment – you don't have to drink it, but you do need to replace those tears! Can you tell me what it is that's upsetting you so much? It's to do with the wedding, isn't it?'

'Yes.' She looked down at the sodden handkerchief she was twisting between her fingers. 'It's nothing that's happened now – I mean, recently. It – it goes back rather a long way.' She raised her eyes again. 'It goes all the way back to the war, when I was in Egypt.'

'Ah.' Basil nodded slightly. 'Egypt. And Luke was there, too, wasn't he?'

'Yes.' She stopped as Grace knocked softly on the door. Basil got up and collected the tray, bringing it over to the table and pouring milk and tea into the two cups. He returned to his own chair and waited again.

'We got to know each other,' Val said tonelessly. 'I was engaged then, to Eddie, but it had been so long since I'd seen him. And there were dances and things. You had to go to them, there wasn't much else to do, and we needed . . . I was a nurse, you see. We really did need to have time to forget – time just to enjoy. Oh, it sounds so selfish!'

'It's not selfish at all,' Basil said. 'You needed the recreation. You couldn't have done your job without it. And I know just how difficult that job must have been at times.'

'Yes. We saw some terrible injuries. It was very hard – they were so young. So when we went to the dances, we sort of let ourselves go a bit. And when I met Luke, we fell in love.' She looked at the vicar as if expecting condemnation, but he merely nodded. After a moment, she went on. 'I never meant to be unfaithful to Eddie. I loved him. But he was so far away, and – well, I *was* unfaithful. Luke never tried to force me or anything,' she added quickly. 'It was my fault as much as his. And I think we really must have loved each other, because we do now, don't we? It wasn't just – you know.'

'I know.' He waited again and then said, 'And what happened then?'

'We had to part – I told him we must. I came back to England. But on the way, I found—' Her voice broke again. 'I found I was expecting a baby.'

There was another silence. Val's eyes were dry now as she stared at the fir-cones piled in the grate. Basil said nothing. He knew she would finish telling her story now, and he was beginning to have an idea as to why she had come to him.

'I lost it,' she said at last. 'I had a miscarriage. It was a perfectly natural one. The baby was very tiny, but I knew it was a boy. I called him John.' She turned back to the vicar. 'We buried him at sea.'

'Did you tell anyone?' Basil asked after a moment. He had told Val he couldn't be shocked, but he had felt his heart quiver as she spoke the words so baldly. It was her pain he was feeling, he thought, the pain that had haunted her all these years. A pain that she had, he guessed, borne all alone.

'No. The girls with me knew – three or four close friends. That's all. I hadn't started to show much, you see, so no one else guessed. And it was so early in the pregnancy that he wouldn't have been counted as a person – not officially. I counted him, though,' she added in a lower tone.

'Of course.' He let the silence continue for a moment and then asked, 'Did Luke know?'

'No. Not then. We'd parted, you see. I'd told him it was over – I was going back to Eddie. I was going to marry him. That was before I knew about the baby, of course. But then Eddie was killed. And I never saw or heard from Luke again until he came to Burracombe. I didn't know his address, and I wouldn't have tried to get in touch with him, anyway. I felt so guilty – even when we did meet again, I could hardly bear to look at him. It was a long time before I could bring myself to admit that I still loved him.'

'And does he know now? About the baby?'

'Oh yes. I told him everything in the end.'

Her throat was dry and she sipped her tea. Basil, too,

picked up his cup, although he felt as if he'd been drinking tea all afternoon. At last he asked, 'So what are you worried about now? I can see that this story is still haunting you – which is only natural, and I'm afraid it will probably do so to some extent all your life – but why do you say that you and Luke may not marry after all? Is it causing him problems? Should I be talking to him as well?'

'No! No, he doesn't even know I'm worried about it. And we *are* going to get married – there's no question of that. It's just that –' she looked at him with piteous eyes '– I don't know if we should get married in church.'

'Ah,' he said, understanding breaking through at last. 'I *see*.'

'Do you?' she asked. 'It's not just the dress – although that was the first thing I thought about. Wearing white, I mean, when I'm not a – a virgin. It's everything else as well. It feels like telling lies. Nobody else knows anything about it. I feel as if I should tell them. But if I did – well, I just don't know what would happen. They'd be so hurt. Mum and Dad and Grandma especially. Everyone else might be just disgusted,' she added forlornly.

'And do you think that would be better than leaving them in ignorance?' he enquired gently. 'Leaving aside those who might be, as you say, disgusted – and I'm sure your real friends and family won't be – let's think about those who might be hurt or disappointed. Your parents, and the rest of your family, for instance. Is it really necessary to hurt them in this way? What happened, happened years ago, in another time and another place. War does strange things to people, and it isn't fair to yourself to judge your actions as though it were peacetime. And you and Luke must have been truly in love. You're marrying now.'

'But I was unfaithful to Eddie.'

'Yes, you were. But isn't that between Eddie and yourself? You weren't married to him—'

‘I was engaged.’

‘Engagements can be broken,’ he said. ‘The reasons are nobody else’s business but the couple’s involved. You’d made no vows in church, and we don’t know for certain that you would actually have married him, had he lived. I’m not excusing you,’ he added, when Val began to protest again, ‘but I want you to think carefully about why you are punishing yourself like this. Is it really about Eddie, or is it about the baby?’ He paused, while Val stared at him, her face first crimson, then deathly pale. ‘Do you feel it was your fault the baby miscarried?’

‘I didn’t do anything to cause it!’ she burst out. ‘I really didn’t!’

‘But you must have wished it hadn’t been conceived. Don’t be ashamed of that, Val. Any girl would feel the same in your position. Do you, perhaps, feel that you brought it about just by wishing it would happen?’

Val stared at him. Her eyes were like black pools in her white face. He wondered uneasily if he had gone too far, and when the tears burst forth again, he reached out and caught her by the arms, his hands gentle but firm. She sank forward, crying, and he held her, rocking her a little. I’m not good at this, he thought anxiously. I’ve said all the wrong things. I’ve made matters worse.

‘Val,’ he said, when the storm seemed to be passing, ‘these wounds can sometimes take a very long time to heal. Perhaps you buried the pain and are only now having to suffer it properly. You need to grieve for your baby. You have a *right* to that grief.’

‘I don’t have a right to anything,’ she said dully. ‘It’s all working out so well for me, and I don’t deserve it.’

‘That isn’t true. You do deserve it. Yes, you made a mistake and you did wrong, but you did no more than thousands – millions – of other women have done down the ages. And I think you've atoned for it. What I *don't* think you're entitled to do is pass on your pain to other people. That's what you'll be doing if you tell your parents what happened. You won't get rid of your own pain but you'll give it to others. You'll increase it, and what is the point of doing that? What good is it going to do?'

'But marrying in church—'

'It's not a lie,' he said firmly. 'You made no vows. Remember the marriage service requires you to "forsake all others". It doesn't say that there mustn't have *been* any others. We *are* supposed to be a forgiving church,' he added. 'And you don't have to be married in white. Why not choose a cream dress, for instance? It's not pure white, if that's what's worrying you, but it's near enough for people not to wonder.'

'Do you really think that would be all right?' she asked doubtfully.

'I'd be perfectly happy with it myself. It would suit your colouring, too.'

Val smiled a little at the idea of Basil Harvey as a fashion adviser, and he beamed at her. 'There's that's better. Quite honestly, my dear, I don't mind what colour you wear, so long as you feel comfortable with it. I think a rich, creamy colour would be admirable. Or, if you still feel uncomfortable, a very pale silvery grey. I once married a bride wearing that colour and it looked most attractive.'

'And you don't think I ought to tell my parents about Luke and me and the baby?'

'I can't see any purpose in it at all. What's the point of hurting people with knowledge they don't need? They love you as you are, Val, and whatever has happened to you in the past is part of what has made you what you are. I dare say there are quite a few other things you've never mentioned to them!' He smiled at her and she laughed a little chokily. 'And you have no intention of doing so, either – yet none of them would cause the pain that this could. You don't feel you're lying by not telling them everything you've ever done, do you?'

'No,' she admitted.

'Then why should you feel it about this? You know, we often feel that telling such truths might ease our consciences, but why should we be eased at the expense of others' peace of mind? I've always thought that was rather a selfish way to go about things.' He leaned forward a little. 'What happened was between you and Luke and Eddie – nobody else. What God will have to say about it is a different matter, and I can't speak for Him. I can only try my best to do His work on earth.'

Val sat quietly for a few moments, then she looked up at him. To his relief, he saw that some of the strain had gone from her face and there was a new clarity in her eyes. She nodded slowly and began to get up.

'Thank you very much, Mr Harvey. You've given me a lot to think about, but I can see things a bit more clearly now. I'd better go. I've taken up too much of your time.'

'You haven't at all,' he said, taking one of her hands in both of his. 'It's what my time is for. I hope I've been able to help. The main thing to remember is that once words have been spoken they can't be taken back. Always wait until you're quite sure, and remember that they're often better left unspoken.'

'Yes. Thank you.' She turned to go and he released her hand.

'Come and see me again if you want to talk any more.'

'I will.' The colour had returned to her face, and she smiled at him. 'Perhaps the next time I come, it really will be to set the date of the wedding!'

He saw her to the door and then went back to the kitchen. Grace was peeling vegetables for their evening meal. He went to stand beside her and leaned his head on her shoulder.

'I feel utterly exhausted,' he said. 'I just hope I've said the right things to both those young women.'

'You need a cup of tea!' Grace said, and went to put the kettle on again.

Chapter Twenty-Four

Jacob was working in his front garden when Jennifer arrived. He gave her a friendly look as she stopped by the gate, and straightened up for a moment. Scruff, stretched out on the path, gave a wuff and ran over to sniff her hand.

'I've seen you before,' he remarked. 'Come to live hereabouts, have you?'

Jennifer shook her head. Her heart was beating quickly and she felt a sudden twinge of apprehension. Suppose he didn't want his old memories revived? Suppose he didn't welcome the news that he had a daughter? But she knew that if she left it and went home now, she would only have to come back and try again. She took a deep breath. 'I've been looking for relatives. I think my mother came from this village.'

'Did her, now?' He looked at her consideringly. 'Who would she have been, then? I been living here all my life – maybe I knowed her.'

Before Jennifer could say any more, the door of the next cottage opened and Jed Fisher came out, carrying a long-handled spade. The look he gave Jennifer was as unfriendly as Jacob's had been pleasant.

'More incomers?' he said unwelcomingly. 'Village is full of 'em these days – there's that young woman teacher, hardly old enough to be out of school herself, that idle good-for-nothing what calls hisself an artist and those stuck-up city folk that Squire's let have Woodman's Cottage. Now here's another of 'em, looking to buy up a place where decent village folk ought to be living.' He glowered at Jennifer again. 'Well, mine ain't for sale, I can tell you that for nothing. I'm not going out of here till I goes feet first.'

'And that might be sooner than you reckon, Jed Fisher,' Jacob retorted, his face reddening. 'I can hear you coughing your lungs up every morning through the walls. You want to stop smoking all they fags, you do. They'm doing you no good.'

'S'pose you thinks I ought to smoke a pipe like you do,' Jed said, taking a packet of Woodbines from his pocket and sticking one between his lips. He struck a match and held it up defiantly. 'Fags don't do nobody no harm. I only coughs *before* I has one, not after.' He lit up, drew in a deep breath and coughed.

Jacob gave him a look of contempt. 'Anyway, that ain't no way to treat visitors.' He turned back to Jennifer. 'You don't want to take no notice of this old misery, miss. Most of us in Burracombe got better manners.'

'It's all right,' Jennifer said, rather taken aback by the animosity between the two men. It seemed to sully the idyllic picture she had had of the village, but she supposed that every community had their less appealing characters and their squabbles and feuds. She looked uncomfortably at Jacob, wondering how to broach the subject now that Jed was present. He might well have known her mother, too, she realised, but she certainly didn't feel like discussing the matter with him.

'The vicar told me that you look after the churchyard,' she said. 'I've been looking at some of the graves there. I suppose you'd know everyone who was buried there over the past twenty or thirty years.'

'I can go back further than that,' he said with pride. 'My old dad was the gravedigger, too. Between us, us buried almost everyone in the parish over the past hunnerd years.

Except for Chapel folk, of course,' he added, glancing at Jed. 'They has their own burial ground.'

'An' I looks after that,' Jed said belligerently, as if someone were about to argue with him. 'An' that's what I oughter be doing now, not standing here chewing the fat with all and sundry.' He gave them a look as if to imply that they were keeping him from his work. 'I'll be on me way, if you don't mind.'

'Us don't mind at all,' Jacob retorted. 'Us never asked you to stop in the first place.'

It looked for a minute as if Jed would start a fresh round of abuse, but after a moment's hesitation, he shrugged, spat into the hedge and shouldered the spade he had leaned against the wall. With one last unfavourable glance at Jennifer, he marched away along the lane.

'Good riddance,' Jacob muttered, and then gave Jennifer a wry look of apology. 'I'm sorry about that, maid. He brings out the worst in me, Jed Fisher does, and always has done, ever since we was young fellers, though we got on well enough as tackers. Born within a day or so of each other, we were, and lived in these two same cottages, side by side, since we was babbies, and somehow we got to put up with each other till we dies. But that's no worry of yours.' He looked at her thoughtfully. 'Did you say you got family round here?'

'It seems so.' She hesitated. 'As a matter of fact, it was Mr Harvey who suggested I come and talk to you.' She held out her hand. 'My name's Jennifer – Jennifer Tucker. You are Mr Prout, aren't you? Jacob Prout?'

'I am,' he said slowly, taking her hand. 'I dare say he sent you to me because I been in the village so long – except for a few years when I was away in the Great War. So what is it you wants to know, maid? You said you reckoned your mother come from round here. What was her name?'

Jennifer glanced along the lane. There was nobody about, but she didn't want to be interrupted again. Diffidently, she said, 'I wonder if we could go indoors? It might take a little while . . . '

Jacob looked surprised, then opened the gate and stood aside for her to pass. Her heart hammering again, Jennifer walked past him, then paused at the front door. Jacob pushed it open for her, then bent to take off his boots and followed her in his socks.

'Straight in, maid, and sit you down in the armchair. Push the cat off if her's on it – that's the way.' He came in after her, his feet now encased in brown slippers, and took a chair at the table, leaning his arm on it as he surveyed her. 'Now, what's this all about? I can see there's a bit more to it than just looking for an old gravestone.'

'Yes, there is.' Jennifer stopped again. All the way out here on the bus, she had been rehearsing various ways of introducing the subject, and had decided that it would be best to approach it cautiously, in a roundabout way, so as not to give him too much of a shock. But as she looked at the lined, weatherbeaten face and the direct blue eyes, her carefully prepared speeches fled from her mind and all she could think of was that this was the man her mother had loved, and that she ought to have been living with him her whole life. With tears suddenly choking her throat, she blurted, 'I think you're my father!'

There was a long silence. Jennifer looked down at her lap and then felt in her bag for a handkerchief. She pressed it to her face, blotting the tears from her eyes, and blew her nose. When she raised her eyes again, Jacob was staring at her, his face rigid with shock.

'I'm sorry,' she said. 'I didn't mean to come out with it like that. I meant to be a bit more tactful.'

'Your *father*?' he said at last. 'Why, maid, whatever makes you think that?'

'Because my mother was Susan Hannaford. And Mrs Tozer remembers that you and she were friends. The old Mrs

Tozer was very friendly with my grandmother, and Alice Tozer was about the same age as my mother, Susan. I'm sorry,' she said, thinking suddenly that he might object to his private business being discussed with others. 'I had to try to find out somehow, and I went to the vicar and he suggested I should ask the Tozers. You see, I couldn't find out anything about my mother at first. He had no records, because her family were Chapel, and—'

'But Susan died,' he said, as if he hadn't heard any of this. 'Her died years ago – while I was away in the war. When I come home, 'twas all over. And the babby died, too, so I were told.'

'No,' Jennifer said. 'We didn't die, either of us. My grandfather turned her out and she went to Plymouth. He told her she was never to come back to Burracombe again. And he spread the story that she'd died. He made my grandmother say so, too.'

She looked anxiously at Jacob. His face was white, his eyes almost black. He shook his head slowly and brushed back his hair with a trembling hand, and stared at her again.

'I thought she were dead. All these years – I thought she were dead . . .'

Jennifer got up. 'Can I make some tea? I've given you a shock – I'm sorry. Perhaps I should have written, or asked the vicar to tell you. But I wanted so much to find my father – and when I found out that it was you . . .' She went out to the kitchen and filled the kettle, shaking almost as much as Jacob as she looked around the small, tidy kitchen for the tea and teapot. Both were easily found, and she took two cups and saucers from the dresser, opened the larder door and took the milk from the cold slab on the deep windowsill, and made the tea. By the time she carried it in, Jacob had moved to the other armchair and was sitting with his head bent, staring at the rag rug. Scruff was at his feet, staring up with anxious eyes, and Flossie, the tortoiseshell cat, had climbed on to his lap. He was stroking her absently, as if he barely knew she was there.

'I remember now,' he said as Jennifer put the cup beside him. 'You come round the day the King died. You were asking about graves and such then. You been here a time or two since, I reckon.'

'Yes, I have. I wasn't sure to begin with that it was Burracombe, you see. I looked at other villages as well – I thought for a while it might be Meavy, since there's a green and an oak tree there, too. Or maybe Walkhampton . . . But I always felt it must be Burracombe, because it seemed familiar. My mother brought me here once, when I was very small, and I felt I could remember it.'

'Susan come to Burracombe?' he asked. 'Why did her do that?'

'I don't know. Perhaps it was when her own mother died. I don't remember much about it,' Jennifer said apologetically.

'I never knew,' he said, quietly and regretfully. 'I never knew she'd been here. If I'd just been working in the lane that day, I'd have seed her. I'd have seed you both.' He stared at the mantelpiece. 'I'd have thought she were a ghost.' He turned back to Jennifer, his eyes filled with pain. 'Why didn't her never come to see me? Why didn't her never even write?'

'I don't know,' Jennifer said helplessly. 'She – she did get married, after I was born. Perhaps that's why.'

'Got *married*?' His brows came together and he shook his head again. 'Well, I dare say 'twas the best thing for her. And for you, too, I hope. Treated you well, did he? Looked after you both proper?'

'Oh yes,' Jennifer said. 'He was a good husband and father. They – they had two more daughters. My half-sisters.'

'Two more liddle uns,' he said, almost to himself. 'My Susan. And all these years I've thought . . .' His voice faded away.

'Drink some tea,' Jennifer said gently. 'It's been a shock for you.'

Obediently, Jacob picked up his cup and drank. Jennifer had put in two spoonfuls of sugar, not knowing whether he took it but believing it was good for shock. He put the cup down again without comment and met her eyes.

'Tell me about Susan. Tell me what sort of a life she's had.' A sudden hope leaped into his face. 'Will she come out and see me, d'you reckon? What about her man? Is he still living?'

'No, he died in the war.' Jennifer hesitated, realising that she'd handled this badly and now had to deal him another blow. 'She – she married again, but it was a bad choice and he left and went to London – we've never heard from him again. And I'm afraid my mother died, too, a few months ago. That's why I came to look for you – I didn't know anything about all this until I found my birth certificate.' She stopped and added, 'I'm very sorry. I ought to have told you differently.'

His head drooped again, and his shoulders sagged. Jennifer looked at him with pity. He'd come out to work peacefully in his garden for an hour or two, and now his life had been changed for ever. She didn't know whether he welcomed the news that he had a daughter or not. He was too caught up in his memories of Susan, in the sudden revival of a life he had thought long gone and, more painful still, the resurgence of his loss.

She remembered that he had asked her a question and began, haltingly, to answer him, telling him about her mother, her stepfather and half-sisters and the life they had lived in Plymouth. 'I think she was happy enough,' she said uncertainly. 'I mean, she and my father – my *step*father – got along, they were very fond of each other, and we were a happy family. We didn't have much money, but who does these days? And the war was hard, too – we used to go out to Clearbrook on the bus every night and find somewhere to sleep while Plymouth was being bombed. Hundreds of people did the same. Local people took in as many as they could, or farmers would let you sleep in their barns if there was room, but lots of people just camped on the moor, or even huddled up against the walls and banks.'

'Ah,' he said, and nodded. 'They came out here as well. Maybe your mother's folk would have taken you in, but they were dead by then. Old Abraham's got a lot to answer for,' he burst out. 'Him and his Bible-thumping ways!'

'Once the bombing was over, it wasn't too bad,' she said. 'Our part of Plymouth wasn't flattened like so much of it was. I lived with my mother after I came home. Both my sisters are married, with families.'

'And didn't you never marry, then?' he asked, looking at her as if seeing her for the first time. 'You know, I can see a likeness there now. Not to Susan – I can't see nothing of her in you. But there's a look of her mother, poor soul. Downtrodden, she were, and my Susan was going a fair way to being the same. That's why I wanted to get her away from there and marry her, give her a proper life.' He sighed and looked away again. 'We were proper sweethearts, me and your mother. And I reckon if all had gone the way it should, we'd have stayed sweethearts all our lives.'

'I know,' Jennifer said quietly. 'That's why I wanted so much to come and find you. Because you're my proper father, and if you and my mother can't be together, then at least we can have something of what we all ought to have had all these years.' She slipped out of her chair and knelt on the rug before him, taking his hands in hers and looking up into his face. 'I know you haven't any other children. There's no other family at all, is there? So I hope you'll be pleased that you've got a daughter after all. I hope you'll be pleased to have me as part of your life.'

There was a long silence. Jacob looked into her eyes. She waited, her heart thumping again, for his reply, and was just about to assure him that he didn't have to answer at once, that he could have time to take in all this sudden news, when he drew in a deep breath and spoke at last.

'I'm glad she had a good life,' he said slowly, in a gruff, aching voice. 'I'm glad my Susan found a good man to take care of her and give her more children. I'm glad you took the trouble to look for your real father, and come and told me about it all.' He stopped, and she waited, understanding that he was having difficulty in finding his words. 'But I'm afraid you'm wrong, maid. Susan and me never went that far, you see.' He took another deep breath. 'I'm sorry, maid. The plain truth is, I'm *not* your father.' His eyes were filled with tears. 'I only wish I were . . .'

Chapter Twenty-Five

Ted Tozer was walking his fields when he saw Luke coming towards him. He waved cheerfully, pleased to see the younger man. Since their talk at Christmas, they'd developed a respectful understanding of each other, and Ted was pleased now that Luke was to be part of the family. He'd even been talking of getting a job, and it seemed as if there might be something for him in Tavistock.

'Nice afternoon,' he called. 'I suppose you'm looking for a pretty picture to paint.'

'Partly,' Luke said, drawing closer. 'It's not just that, though. I want to talk to you, Mr Tozer.'

They stopped, facing each other about two feet apart. Something in the young artist's bearing struck Ted as being different; he couldn't put his finger on it, but it made him wary. He waited a moment, watching the long, mobile face, and then said, 'All right, then. Out with it. I can see you've got summat to say.'

Luke drew in a deep breath. 'Yes, I have. It's about what we talked about at Christmas – about Val and me.' He looked Ted straight in the eye. 'I'm going to have to take back that promise I made, Mr Tozer. We don't want to wait any longer to get married. We could do it at Easter, but we want to set a proper date. We thought we'd make it the end of July.'

'July!' Ted stared at him, holding back his immediate response. It was his way to consider first and get his thoughts into order before making any answer. 'That's pretty soon, isn't it?'

'Yes, it is, but we've both had enough of waiting.' Luke took another breath. 'I don't know if you realise how unhappy Val's been—'

'I know she've been a bit under the weather.' His glance sharpened and he asked the inevitable question. 'There's no *reason*, I hope—'

'No! At least, not the one you mean.' Luke took half a step nearer. 'Look, Mr Tozer, I know what I promised you and I meant it. But I didn't really have the right to make that promise – not on Val's behalf. We want to be equal partners in our marriage. I can't make decisions that she doesn't agree with – and she doesn't agree with that one.'

'So you'm putting the blame on her—'

'*No!* It's not a question of blame. It's simply a question of wanting to be together, husband and wife. Somehow, in the next few weeks, I'll find a job that will support us both. But we're not waiting until then to fix our wedding.' He paused, then added, 'I'd wait for ever to marry your daughter, Mr Tozer, if that was the way it had to be. But I don't like seeing her unhappy. I don't like seeing her in tears when all we need to do is walk up the aisle and say "I do".'

'And is that how she's been?' Ted asked slowly. 'In tears?'

'Yes, it is. And I'm not prepared to see it again.' Luke gave him one of his straight looks. 'I'm going to be responsible for Val now, Mr Tozer, not you. If you don't want to take any part in this wedding, then we'll both be sorry, but we're going ahead all the same. And I'm not asking you to pay—'

'Now, you can stop that sort of talk straight away,' Ted broke in. 'Not pay for my own daughter's wedding? What do you take me for, a skinflint? Of course I'll pay for it! It's me privilege and me right. Why, if I didn't give our Val a decent wedding, my Alice would never speak to me again.'

'And you won't object if we set the date for the end of

July?' Luke asked. 'We really don't want to wait any longer than that, Mr Tozer.'

Ted said nothing for a moment. Then he lifted his shoulders and said, 'If that's what you both wants, then I reckon us got to go along with it. To tell you the truth, boy, I *have* noticed the maid looking peaky just lately, and I'm as sorry about it as you. Maybe I was wrong to ask you to make that promise.' He put out his hand and Luke, hardly daring to believe what was happening, took it in his. 'And there's one thing about it – us'll be able to do away with all this "Mr Tozer" nonsense. You can call me Father, like young Joanna does, or Ted if you've a mind. I'll be glad to look on you as a son, and that's the honest truth.'

Luke looked into the weatherbeaten face and saw a smile lurking amongst the seams and wrinkles. He grinned and shook the farmer's hand. 'Thanks, Mr Tozer. Ted. Thanks very much. And I'll make you another promise here and now – one I really do mean to keep. I'll take every possible care of your daughter. I'll do all I can to make her happy.'

'Can't say fairer than that,' Ted said gruffly. 'Now, I got my crops to see to, and you got your picture to paint, so us'd better get on with it. Us can leave the women to organise this wedding, I reckon. That's what *they'm* good at!'

'*What sayest thou, bully Bottom?*' Henry Bennetts demanded in loud, angry tones, and Micky Coker turned to Stella in indignation.

'I'm not a bully, am I, miss? Anyway, that's not the bit we'm supposed to be doing.'

'No, it's not.' The performance had been shortened so much that by now it was a mere snippet. 'We decided to start later in the scene, Henry, don't you remember? And "bully" didn't mean the same then as it does now – it was more like "fine fellow". A term of encouragement.'

The children stared at her doubtfully. She took Henry's

book from him and turned over the pages. 'There, that's where we're starting now. Flute, Quince, Starveling and Bottom are in the wood, where they've been rehearsing the play they want to perform at the grand dinner, when Puck comes across them. He stays to watch and when Bottom leaves the scene, he goes after him. The others carry on and when Puck and Bottom come back, Bottom has an ass's head. The others are frightened and run away. We'll start from where Bottom leaves the stage – from "*But hark*". Say that, Micky, and then just move aside as if you've left the stage – remember, they're in a wood so you'd probably go behind a tree.' The children giggled and she gave them a stern look. 'Micky?'

Micky, who was beginning to fancy himself as an actor, cupped one hand over his ear and said, '*But hark, a voice! Stay thou but here awhile, And by and by I will to thee appear.*'

'Now it's your turn, Flute,' Stella said. '*Must I speak now?*'

'No, miss,' said Brian Madge, who was playing Flute. 'It's me that says that.'

'Yes, I know, Brian. Go ahead and say it.' She smiled encouragingly.

'*Must I speak now?*' Brian enquired.

There was a long silence.

'Quince?' Stella prompted Henry. 'You have to answer him – see? *Ay, marry, must you . . .*'

'I don't understand that bit, miss. Nobody's said nothing about getting married before.'

'Nobody's said *anything*,' Stella said automatically. 'That's because it doesn't mean "marry" like we mean it today. It means – ' she racked her brains for an explanation '– it means "yes, you have to".' At least, I think that's what it means, she thought. 'You see, what Quince is saying is that Bottom has heard a noise and gone to see what was making it, and will be back in a minute.'

Henry looked at his script and nodded. He planted his feet

wide apart and declaimed, in a hectoring voice: '*Ay, marry, must you; for you must understand he goes but to see a noise that he heard, and is to come again.*'

'Now, Brian, you have to say what Flute is supposed to say in the play. *Most radiant Pyramus, most lily-white of hue . . .*' It's like wading through treacle, she thought as, after another long hesitation, Brian read the speech in a wooden monotone quite unlike his normal lively tones. Henry followed with another tirade, ending with '*Your cue is past; it is "never tire".*'

'I don't see why he got to shout at me like that,' Brian said.

'Well, he could tone it down a bit, perhaps,' Stella agreed. 'But what he's saying is that Flute has said it all wrong. He's said Ninny's tomb instead of Ninus's tomb and he's also saying that Pyramus ought to have entered by now.'

'We haven't got no one for Pyramus,' Henry objected.

'Yes, we have. Bottom is playing Pyramus and he ought to have come in when Flute says 'never tire'. Flute, say your words next. You're repeating the words you said before, you see, so that Pyramus – Bottom – will come in on cue.'

Brian gave her a doubtful look and repeated, in the same monotone as before, '*O – As true as truest horse, that yet would never tire.*'

'Puck and Bottom come in now,' Stella said. 'And remember, everyone, that Bottom has the ass's head on now and you must all look very frightened. You think it's a monster, or maybe a ghost.'

Micky and Shirley Culliford, who was playing Puck, marched in from the side of the space that had been cleared for a stage, and the others struck poses of extreme fear and horror. Well, at least they can do that, Stella thought. She waited for Micky to speak.

'*If I were fair, Thisby, I were only thine*,' he remarked, quite clearly without the least idea of what it meant.

'*O monster! O strange!*' Brian Madge said expressionlessly. '*We are haunted. Pray, master—*'

'No, that's not how it ought to be said!' Henry Bennetts exclaimed, almost beside himself with frustration. 'It's just like what I seen at the pictures. When 'Amlet saw the ghost he was proper frightened, and he were a *prince*, with a sword and everything. Old Brian looks more scared than that if he sees a spider!'

'I don't!' Brian retorted, showing signs of life at last. 'I'm not scared of spiders, Henry Bennetts, and if you says that again I'll knock your block off—'

'*Brian!*' Stella exclaimed. 'How dare you talk like that in my class! Now, say sorry, both of you, and let's get back to what we're supposed to be doing.' She waited while the two boys glowered and shifted their feet and finally muttered a grudging apology. 'Now, you all looked very frightened when Micky came in, but you do have to sound frightened as well. And the word's "monstrous", Brian, not "monster". Try it again. Remember, you are looking at something very strange indeed – a man with a donkey's head. You'd be frightened if you came across that in Cuckoo Wood, wouldn't you?'

'Yes, but I wouldn't hang about saying a lot of stupid Shakespeare,' Brian said, still smarting from Henry's accusation. 'I'd go and get my dad.'

'Well, they did things differently in those days,' Stella said, wondering why Miss Kemp had ever thought this was a good idea. 'Come on now, try it again, and then you all scream and run out. And then we'll stop rehearsing for today and try again tomorrow.'

The promise of release seemed to energise the children's performance and even Brian's voice took on a faint quiver of expression. As soon as he finished his speech – '*Fly, masters! Help!*' – the others joined in with piercing shrieks and everyone made for the door.

'Very good,' Stella called before they managed to get it open. 'All right, you can all go home now. Take your words with you and all try to learn them. We'll need to go on to the next part tomorrow. What's the matter, Shirley?'

'I never got a chance to say my words,' the little girl said tearfully. 'I been practising all day, and you never give me a chance. It was all them boys.'

'I'm sorry.' From the corner of her eye, Stella caught a glimpse of a figure outside the door and knew it was Felix. 'Say them to me now. Start with "*I'll follow you . . .*".'

Shirley, whose family was one of the poorest in the village and had never shown any ability until being made Festival Queen last year, stood very straight. She was dressed, as usual, in a frock that had seen better days, with stains that hadn't washed out and tears that had been clumsily mended, but since her appointment she'd always made an effort to come to school with a clean face, and her fair hair shone. She fixed her large grey eyes on Stella's face and recited Puck's speech.

I'll follow you, I'll lead you about a round,
Through bog, through bush, through brake, through brier:
Sometimes a horse I'll be, sometimes a hound,
A hog, a headless bear, sometimes a fire:
And neigh, and bark, and grunt, and roar, and burn,
Like horse, hound, hog, bear, fire, at every turn.

There was a short silence. Stella was aware of Felix, coming to stand just inside the door. Shirley looked at her anxiously and said, 'Was that all right, miss?'

'It was very good,' Stella said, clearing her throat. 'You spoke it beautifully, Shirley. Do you understand what Puck is saying?'

'Oh yes, miss. He's saying that he'll pretend to be all sorts of different animals and lead them into the bogs. Like we has on the moor. Pixie-led, we calls it. I reckon that Shakespeare must have been to Dartmoor, don't you, or how would he know about all that?'

'Well, Shakespeare might have been to Devon – who knows?' Stella said, struck by this idea. 'But I think the idea of pixies leading people astray happens all over England. Anyway, the main thing is that you understand it and you've learned it beautifully. Well done. Now you'd better go home.' She watched as the little girl scurried away and then smiled at Felix. 'I suppose you've been lurking there for ages.'

He nodded, grinning. 'I heard most of the rehearsal. I was aching with laughter at those boys. How on earth are you going to lick them into shape?'

'I'll call in reinforcements,' she threatened. 'If you've got time to eavesdrop, you've got time to help. Mind you, it all seems worthwhile when a child like Shirley turns out to be such a natural. Who would have thought it this time last year, when she and the rest of the Cullifords were always at the back of the class and nobody thought they'd ever amount to anything? It just shows, you shouldn't judge children by their parents. I wonder what other talents lie hidden in that family?'

'Well, if anyone can bring them out, you can,' Felix said, smiling. 'Now, are you coming for a walk? Dottie caught me as I walked past the cottage and said I've got to come to tea at five, so we've got over an hour. Time to go all the way up to the Standing Stones.'

'All right. Just let me clear up a bit here first.' Together, they replaced the chairs and tables that had been moved to make acting space, and Stella gathered up a few scraps of paper and pencil stubs that had been left lying about. Mrs Purdy could be heard outside, rattling her bucket and mops, and would be displeased if the room was left untidy. She was at the door as Stella closed the lid of her desk.

'Oh, hello, Curate. I didn't know as you were in here. I see someone been sick in the lobby again.'

'It was Betty Culliford,' Stella said. 'I cleared it up as best I could, but the smell never quite goes away. I'm always afraid it's going to affect the others as well.'

'It would if they thought they could get away with it,' the cleaner said. ''Tis all right, Miss Simmons, I'll put down some Dettol. You get out in the fresh air now. Lovely afternoon, it is. I been doing a bit in the garden, them weeds shoot up like rockets the minute you turns your back at this time of year.'

Stella and Felix said goodbye to her and left the school, turning right to walk beside the brook until crossing a cattle grid on to the open moor. From there, it was a steady climb to the stone circle that stood on the hill above the village. They reached the top, panting a little, and leaned against the tall granite slabs.

'It's a lovely view from here,' Stella remarked. 'It's not all that high, yet you can see for miles. Look at the sea glinting in Plymouth Sound. And the chimney on top of Kit Hill, right down in Cornwall. You can even see the china clay dumps near St Austell.'

'Let's sit down for a few minutes,' Felix suggested. 'I've brought a couple of apples. They're the last ones, I'm afraid, until the new ones come along.'

'They look like it, too,' Stella, said, inspecting the wrinkled red skins. 'I'm amazed they've kept so long.'

'So were Aggie and I. She found half a dozen at the back of her shed yesterday – they'd been pushed behind some seed trays and forgotten. But they're all right – just!'

They sat together on the short, springy turf, munching. Then Felix said, 'Have you heard from Maddy lately?'

'I had a letter yesterday. She's awfully busy at the moment – the wedding's next week, you know, and she's been helping with the arrangements. I don't know what she'll do after that; she'll feel rather lost without so much to do.'

'I should think she'd be glad of a holiday. I suppose Miss Forsyth and her new husband will be going away somewhere.'

'Yes, they're going to America for a few weeks. I think there'll be quite a lot for Maddy to do after that – sorting out the château, that kind of thing – but I don't know what her plans are then. I'd like her to come here again, of course, but she hasn't said anything about that.'

'Well, I'm sure Aggie would always be pleased to put her up. And I'd be delighted – I really enjoyed having Maddy around during the Easter holidays.'

'Yes,' Stella said quietly. 'I know.'

Felix glanced at her, but she was looking down at some strands of grass she was plaiting between her fingers. He hesitated, and then said, 'There's something I want to tell you, Stella.'

'Mm?'

He waited, but she didn't look up. He bit his lip, frowned a little, and then reached out, gently removing the grass from her hand. As she looked up at him, a trace of panic flickering in her eyes, the sound of voices on the slope below them made him drop his hand and look away with a small sigh of frustration.

'Well, look who's here!' cried a cheerful voice, and Val Tozer and Luke Ferris came into view over the crest of the hill. 'No, don't move – we'll plonk ourselves down beside you.' Val dropped to the grass beside Stella and leaned back against the stone. 'Phew, that climb doesn't get any easier, does it! Hope we're not interrupting anything,' she added, rather belatedly.

'Of course you're not,' Felix said. 'Stella and I had just come up the other way, from the school. It's too nice an afternoon to be indoors. How are you two getting on? Haven't seen you for a while.'

Val made a face. 'No, I seem to have been working all hours

and Luke's trying to get as much painting done as he can. We're spring-cleaning the cottage, too.'

Stella looked at her. There had been a time when Val had been rather cool towards her, but now that she was engaged to Luke she was friendliness itself. 'Any special reason?' she asked.

'Well, it is spring,' Luke began, but Val laughed and interrupted him.

'Oh, let's tell them! You can be the first to know,' she said, smiling all over her face at Stella and Felix. 'We've set the date for our wedding! It's to be the last Saturday in July. We've just been to see Mr Harvey to make sure he can do it that day, and he says yes! It gives us nearly three months to get ready, which Mum seems to think is the least possible time, and if we can't find anywhere else to live by then, we're going to stay in the cottage.'

'July! Oh, that's lovely,' Stella cried, giving Val a hug. Luke leaned across and she kissed his cheek. 'I'm so pleased. I hope you can find somewhere else to live, though. The cottage is a bit small for two, especially when winter comes.'

'Oh, we're bound to find something by then,' Val said gaily. 'And if we don't, we'll just have to move somewhere else.' She seemed to Stella to have shed ten years. The last few times they'd met, Val had seemed anxious and weighed down, but all that had gone. That's what the prospect of getting married to someone you love does for you, Stella thought.

'Move? Where to?'

'Wherever we can find work and a place to live,' Luke said firmly. 'I've been looking for a job. There's a teaching post advertised in Tavistock that I'm going to apply for – it would give me time to paint in the holidays. If I don't get that, I've been offered work at a picture-framer's in Plymouth. I know what you think,' he said as Val began to speak, 'but we've been through all this before, and it'll be better all round if I can support my wife and family. Living in a shack in the woods and being fed by half the village is all very well for a single man, but it won't do once we're married. We have to face up to it.'

'I'm going to go on working for a while,' Val said to Stella. 'He's doing so well with his painting – look at that exhibition he had last year. I'm sure it won't take long before someone recognises his talent.'

'Well, you have to decide that for yourselves,' Felix said. He was still trying not to show his irritation at being interrupted. 'And I think we'll have to leave you to it for now – Dottie's expecting us for tea at five and we mustn't keep her waiting.'

'Goodness me, no,' Luke agreed. 'If I know Dottie, she'll be taking something delicious out of the oven as you walk through the door. You go on down. Val and I will stay here and enjoy the sunshine.' He lay back on the grass and Stella saw his hand move to stroke Val's waist. 'I'm sure we'll be able to amuse ourselves.'

Stella and Felix set off down the hill in silence. After a few minutes, Stella said, 'They seem very happy, don't they? And it'll be exciting to have a wedding in the village. A summer wedding, too. It's really romantic.'

Felix nodded. He seemed lost in thought, as if he were considering something in his mind. Stella stole a glance at him and saw the expression on his face, and her heart sank. He said he was going to tell me something, she thought. Something about him and Maddy. And she knew, quite suddenly, that she didn't want to hear it – not now. Not on this bright, sunny afternoon, with the sound of Val and Luke's happy voices still ringing in her ears.

'Let's hurry,' she said, quickening her pace. 'Luke's right – Dottie will have been baking something special. And there are one or two things I need to do before tea.'

She walked ahead of him down the narrow path through the old wood, but as they passed the charcoal-burner's cottage where Luke and Val were going to make their home, she slowed down and cast it a wistful glance. Felix saw her expression and the thoughtful look in his eyes deepened. He followed Stella the rest of the way back to the cottage in silence, and although he gave every appearance of enjoying the sandwiches and sponge cake Dottie had prepared, he seemed abstracted, as if his mind were miles away. By half past six he was gone, and the two women were left alone.

'Is anything the matter with the curate?' Dottie asked as they washed up together. 'He didn't seem at all like his usual self.'

'I don't know,' Stella said, although she had a strong suspicion that she did. 'He was quite cheerful earlier on this afternoon.'

'Oh well,' Dottie said after a moment or two. 'I dare say he has his own worries, like the rest of us. Let's hope it's nothing too serious.'

'Yes,' Stella said rather sadly. 'Let's hope so.'

Chapter Twenty-Six

'Don't you ever just sit and admire your garden?' the vicar asked Constance Bellamy. He had been passing her gate when he noticed her wheelbarrow parked in the middle of the front path, and paused to say hello.

Constance, who had discarded her baggy tweed skirt in favour of a drooping cotton one, and her woolly jumper for a man's shirt, straightened up from a flowerbed, a small weeding-fork in her hand.

'Afternoon, Basil. Of course I do. I come out here every day with a cup of tea and settle myself down on that bench over there. But it's only two minutes before I notice something that needs doing – a weed that's popped up overnight, or a shrub that's getting a bit straggly – and I think I'll just see to that before it gets worse, and the next time I think about my tea, it's gone three o'clock and the children are coming out of school. And then I think I might as well carry on for another half an hour before I make myself another one.'

'And I suppose you forget about that one as well,' he said. 'Grace is just the same. I tell her the weeds are God's contribution to the garden, but she doesn't seem to think much of His abilities. Says it's no wonder He had to get Adam in to help Him! But I must say, your garden is looking a picture, Constance. You ought to open it to the public.'

The old woman looked around her at the banks of azaleas, now in full bloom, and the borders, bright with lupins like a colourful army on the march, and spotted with scarlet poppies and red-hot pokers. Geraniums were beginning to flower, too, and on the path lay several trays of bedding plants, which Basil guessed she had been hardening off in her greenhouse and were now ready to be planted out. Once in the ground, cared for by their green-fingered grower, they would leap into action and add to the colour that blazed all around them.

'Do you know, I've been thinking about that,' Constance said. 'Not just my garden, but some of the others in the village. Charge people sixpence or so to go round them and put the money to the Organ Fund.'

'It's an idea,' Basil said. 'I haven't done much about that yet, but we're going to have to think about it. We'll need all sorts of fund-raising efforts, I'm afraid – the renovations are bound to cost a lot.'

'Well, it's something to think about for next year. We could put on some teas in the village hall as well. Mind you, we'd have to be careful whose gardens we chose – some of the best ones are Methodists! They might not be too keen to support the church organ.'

'I'm sure they must need funds as well,' Basil said thoughtfully. 'The village hall itself, too – that needs quite a bit of refurbishment. I don't see why we can't all pull together and split the profits. I'll suggest it at the next meeting, and I'll have a chat with Mr Doidge, the Methodist minister, as well.'

'You might have a chat about Jed Fisher, while you're at it,' Constance observed, bending to pull out a dandelion that seemed to have sprung up even as they spoke. 'That man's getting worse, you know. More bad-tempered and abusive than ever, but it's my opinion he's ill. Sometimes when I hear him coughing, I think he's going to turn himself completely inside out.'

'I know. You can't help feeling sorry for him, unpleasant though he is. I don't know that Arthur Doidge will be able to do much about it, though. Jed looks after their graveyard, after a fashion, but I don't think he ventures in through the door very often. And nobody can force him to see the doctor.'

'We've still got to do our best to look after the old curmudgeon, though,' Constance said. 'Good job Jacob Prout's not like that. It's funny how two men who grew up together and have lived next door to each other all their lives can be so different, isn't it? D'you know, I heard them arguing the other day, at it hammer and tongs they were, and all over nothing at all. They seem to enjoy picking fights with each other.'

'I don't know that Jacob does,' Basil said. 'I'm a bit worried about him, to tell you the truth. He's seemed rather down this past week.' He hesitated, wondering whether to confide in Constance about Jennifer Tucker's belief that Jacob was her father, and then decided that he mustn't. Constance would certainly not pass it on, but neither should he. He looked around the garden again and reverted to their original subject. 'I'll certainly think about your idea of opening several of the village gardens to the public. I'm sure it would attract a lot of visitors – people love seeing what lies behind the hedges! I've often thought a postman's job must be pleasant from that point of view – they have free entry to every garden in the area and can watch their progress right through the year!'

Constance laughed. 'And never have to pull a single weed. I'll consider that, if I decide I need a job. Well, nice to see you, Basil. Tell Grace I've got some bedding plants for her, sowed far too many seeds, as usual. I'll walk round to the vicarage later on with a few.'

Basil went on his way, cheered by the little chat and the colourful garden. The idea of opening other gardens to give people the same pleasure was a good one, he thought. The Latimers' garden was lovely, and so was Joyce Warren's. He wondered if Gilbert Napier could be persuaded to allow visitors to walk in the Barton grounds. And there were probably others he didn't know about. He made a mental note to discuss it with Grace and then bring it up at the next meeting of the Parochial Church Council.

Somewhat reluctantly, he turned his mind to his anxiety about Jacob Prout. The village handyman was definitely upset about something, and Basil was sure it must be to do with Jennifer Tucker. Had Jacob found her news unwelcome? He must have been upset to realise that his sweetheart had been living just a few miles away all those years, married to another man – did he feel betrayed? Whatever the reason, it must have been a shock to discover the truth, and Basil desperately wanted to help him.

I can't broach the subject, though, he thought, strolling along the lane deep in contemplation. I'll have to wait for Jacob himself to bring it up – if he ever does. It was one of the frustrations of Basil's job that people often came to him with their problems but seldom came to tell him when they had been resolved!

'Hello, Uncle Basil. Where are you off to? You look as if you've got the cares of the world on your shoulders.'

Basil looked up, startled, and saw Luke Ferris leaning on the drystone wall and laughing at him. He smiled back, shrugging away his sober thoughts like a dog shaking water from its coat.

'Hello there, Luke. No, just contemplating life in general. I've been into Constance Bellamy's garden. It's a real picture. What a wonderful woman she is, always busy. She does tapestry as well, you know, when she can't get into the garden.'

'I know, I've seen some of her work.' Luke eased himself away from the wall and fell into step beside his godfather. 'I can't tell you how pleased I am that Val and I have got the wedding fixed. I'm taking her up to London at the weekend to meet the family. She's met Ma and Pa, of course, but some of the others are gathering, too, apparently, to give us a belated engagement party. Hope it doesn't put her off marrying me when she sees what a zoo the family is.'

'I don't suppose it will. Val's a tough young woman.' As he said the words, Basil remembered her distress when she'd come to see him a few weeks ago, and wondered if they were really true. 'And she's too fond of you, for some inexplicable reason, to let a mere family change her mind. I think you're going to be very happy together, Luke.'

'So do I. It's like a miracle, finding her again.' Luke hesitated. 'I know she told you about Egypt.'

'Yes. A difficult time for you both, but especially for her. I'm glad it's turned out well in the end.'

'I sometimes feel a bit guilty that her fiancé died and sort of made way for me,' Luke confessed. 'I'm sure she would have married him, you know.'

'We can't know that. She might have felt very differently when she met him again – especially after all that had happened.' They were both silent for a few moments, and then Basil went on more briskly, 'Anyway, it's all in the past now. It's the future you have to think of – and the present as well, of course. Enjoy the one and plan for the other, that's the way I believe we should live.'

Luke laughed and clapped him on the shoulder. 'You can always be relied on for good advice, Uncle Basil! I'll walk back through the village with you – I'm on my way to do a painting of the pool down by the Clam. There was a kingfisher there the other day, and a dipper on the rocks.'

They walked together as far as the green. The great oak tree was in full leaf now, shading the grass with its ancient canopy, and there were a couple of girls in riding gear by the horse trough letting their ponies have a drink. Luke waved his hand and sauntered off in the direction of the river, and Basil went through the lychgate into the churchyard.

Jacob Prout was there, clipping the yew trees. Basil

hesitated, and then as Jacob looked round and saw him, walked over to say hello.

'Is everything all right, Jacob?' he enquired when they had discussed the yew trees, the state of the gravestones and the great-tit's nest Jacob had found in a hole in the stone wall. 'You're keeping well, I hope, are you?'

'Me? 'Course I am. You knows me, Vicar, one cold a year and that's my lot. It's living in the fresh air that does it, and looking after meself proper.'

'That's good. Only I've been a bit worried about you lately. You don't seem quite your usual self.' Having given Jacob the opportunity to say what was worrying him if he wanted to, Basil changed the subject. 'I've just been looking at Miss Bellamy's garden. She does a wonderful job there, doesn't she?'

'She does that, right enough. Mind you, her old mother were just the same, out in the garden in all weathers, she were, and what her didn't know about plants wasn't worth knowing.' There was a short silence, and Basil began to turn away, murmuring something about the church. As he did so, Jacob took a sudden deep breath as if he were diving into a swimming-pool, and said, 'Before you goes, Vicar – if you got a minute, I'd be glad of a word, private like.'

'Of course, Jacob,' Basil said. 'Shall we sit on the bench by the door, in the sunshine? I don't think anyone's likely to overhear us there. Or would you rather go across to the vicarage?'

'No, out in the air's good enough for me.' He wiped the blades of his shears on a piece of rag he drew from his pocket, and they walked over to the bench. There was a good view of the path from the lychgate there and nobody could come upon them unawares. They sat down together and Basil gave the old man an enquiring glance.

'You'm right when you say I haven't been meself lately,' Jacob began after a few moments during which he seemed to be gathering his thoughts. 'I've had summat to think about, that's what it is. Had to turn it over in me mind and sort of find me way through it, if you understands my meaning. I couldn't talk about it till I'd done that.'

'I understand,' Basil said gently. 'Take your time, Jacob.'

''Tis about that Miss Tucker,' he said abruptly. 'I know her talked to you about me.'

'Yes, she did. She came to me for help and then advice. It wasn't easy to know what to say to her, to be honest.'

'No, I don't suppose 'twere. She went to Alice Tozer, too, and old Minnie. By the time she got round to me, her'd got the whole story worked out in her mind.'

'Yes, I think she had.' Basil wondered if Jacob were offended that so many others seemed to know the story before he had done. Yet it was only through talking to them that Jennifer had discovered it. He waited while Jacob seemed to consider his next words.

'Only trouble was,' the old gravedigger said at last, 'that her got it wrong.' He slid his eyes round to Basil's. 'You dunno what I be talking about, do you, Vicar? You dunno what I mean.'

'Well, no, I don't, Jacob. In fact, I'm thoroughly confused. Are you saying that she wasn't Susan Hannaford's daughter after all? But surely—'

'Oh no,' Jacob said. 'Her's Susan's maid, all right. That part's true enough. But she ain't mine.' His voice was low, and the next words even lower as he stared at the earth beneath their feet and repeated in a gruff, almost heartbroken voice, 'She ain't my daughter, Vicar. I only wish she was.'

There was a long silence. Basil looked at the dejected figure beside him, then turned his eyes away. The old man's sorrow was so apparent that it seemed an intrusion to witness it. Nor could he understand what he had just been told. He remembered that at the start of Jennifer Tucker's enquiries, he had warned her that the story might not be as simple as she thought. But she had seemed so sure – the Tozers themselves had seemed so sure – that it must be Jacob. He rubbed his forehead and then the back of his neck, trying to find the right words to speak next.

'Do you want to tell me about it, Jacob?' he asked at last, in a quiet voice.

Jacob nodded slowly. 'Reckon I better had, Vicar. Reckon I got to tell someone or I'll burst, what with it going round and round in me head all the time. And you're the one that knows most about it – you and the Tozers, anyway.' He thought for a moment. 'Reckon I might go and talk to them as well. Alice was a good friend to my Susan and old Mrs Tozer used to go and see her poor mother, too, whenever her had a chance.'

'It is true that you and Susan were sweethearts, then?' Basil asked, feeling his way.

'Oh, that's true enough. Knew each other right through school, us did, and I always had a fancy for her. I used to look after her in the playground, you know, just keep an eye out and make sure none of the others picked on her – you know what devils some little tackers can be. She were such a quiet, pretty little maid, and as she got older she just got prettier, to my mind. Once us all left school, I didn't see so much of her. Her family were chapel so we didn't even get the chance of running into each other in the churchyard of a Sunday. But then we started going to the village hops and dances in old man Tozer's barn and she used to slip down to them whenever she could get away. And we used to meet up on the moor and go for walks. And if it hadn't been for that bloody war – excuse my language, Vicar – I reckon we'd have got wed, never mind what old Abraham thought about it.'

'And you're quite sure that Jennifer isn't your daughter?' Basil asked. 'There's no possible chance. Alice Tozer did seem to think that you might have been home at the right time—'

'Oh, I was home all right! Home with a broken leg!' Jacob

gave a short, bitter laugh. 'They sent me back for Mother to look after, and the minute I could walk again I was back to the trenches. I only saw my Susan twice in that time – once when her come to the house to see me, when her father were away at market, and once the day before I went away again, when I met her in Tavistock with her mother. We weren't on our own for more than five minutes either time. And anyway,' he added with bitter regret, 'we never did nothing in that way. I had more respect for her. And I tell you what, Vicar,' he burst out, 'I wish now I hadn't, and if that's wicked of me to say so and goes against God's law, well, I can't help it. It's the way I feel!'

Basil felt his heart go out to the old man, robbed of his sweetheart and not even able to take comfort in the child that should have been his. At the same time, he thought of Val Tozer, who had also borne her lover's child, tiny and unformed though it had been, and suffered her own regrets. He said, 'But if you weren't the father, Jacob, then who was? I suppose we'll never know.'

'Oh, I knows that all right,' Jacob said in a tone of deep disgust. 'I knew she were in the family way, you see, Vicar. It were just after I went back – that's why Alice Tozer and her mother thought it were me. But it weren't. It were that other bastard – excuse my language again, Vicar, but there's times when no other words will do. Always had his eye on her, he did, even though she wouldn't even give him time of day. And I reckon when he saw me out of the way again and saw my Susan all upset, he saw his chance and took advantage of her. Oh, he could charm the birds off the trees in those days, though you'd never think it now, and I dare say he made up to her and offered her a shoulder to cry on, and my poor maid didn't see no harm in taking a bit of comfort. And no more *should* she!' he burst out again, as if Basil had denied it. 'Chapel folk, his family were, same as the Hannafords. She *should* have been able to trust him, now shouldn't she!'

'Certainly she should,' Basil murmured. An idea was beginning to take shape in his mind, an idea that was almost too horrifying to contemplate, and as he asked the next question he almost hoped that Jacob would refuse to answer. But it had to be asked, and it had to be answered. 'So who was it, Jacob? And – before you name names – can you be absolutely sure, without any possible doubt, that you're right?'

'I'm right. There's no doubt about it, none at all. My Susan wrote and told me all about it. Blamed herself, she did, poor little maid, though no one else would have blamed her, except for that bully of a father of hers. And there weren't nothing I could do about it. Not a blind bloody thing.' He didn't apologise for his language this time. For a moment or two, he stared at the earth path, his jaw clenched and his face set in hard, bitter lines, and then he turned and looked Basil full in the face.

'It were Jed Fisher. That's who it was. Jed Fisher is Jennifer's father.'

'Jed Fisher?' There was a long silence. At last, Basil found his voice. Even though he had begun to suspect it, hearing the words spoken still came as a shock. He stared at Jacob's face, recognising the despair and misery in the other man's eyes, and felt again a powerful compassion. 'But . . . are you absolutely sure?' It was a weak response, he knew. Jacob had already made it clear that he was sure. Yet he could think of nothing else to say, and was once again painfully aware of his own inadequacy.

'I know it for a fact,' Jacob said, returning his gaze to the path. 'I told you, my Susan wrote and told me what he done. All smarm and charm, he were, making out he were my best friend and I'd asked him to keep an eye on her, and then taking advantage of her – filthy bugger!' His voice trembled at the thought of what had happened all those years ago, and Basil marvelled that he had managed to keep it to himself all that time. No wonder he and Jed have always been such enemies, he thought. How could they have gone on living next door to each other with something like this between them?

'Anyway, 'twasn't long before her knowed her was in the family way. I tell you, Vicar, I near enough deserted then to come home to her, but 'twouldn't have done no good. Another bloke in our unit did that one day – turned tail in the middle of all the fighting – and our officer pulled out his gun and shot him. Shot him dead, and us others weren't even allowed to go and get his body. Wouldn't have done my Susan no good for that to happen to me, and anyway, we were in the middle of France somewhere, I don't even know how I'd have got home. And by the time I did –' he seemed to dredge a huge sigh up from somewhere deep within his body '– it was all over. Or at least, that's the story her father put round the village. Said her'd gone off to Plymouth to go into service there, and then caught that 'flu and died of it. And when I went up to the farm one day and asked her mother, she said the same thing. I told her I knew about the babby, of course, and she told me that'd died as well. Wouldn't even say whether 'twas a girl or a boy. And that was the end of it.' Another deep, quivering sigh. 'Or so I thought, until Jennifer Tucker come to my door a week or so back. And now – well, I dunno what to think. It seems like everything's been turned upside down and I don't know how to put it back in its place.' He turned a face full of distress to the vicar and said, 'The worst of it is, I keep thinking she must have waited for me to go and fetch her. She must have thought I didn't want no more to do with her. That's why she went and got married to someone else.'

He fell silent at last, the words that had been spilling from him coming to a sad, despondent end. Basil sat silent beside him, surprised after a moment or two to find his hand on

Jacob's knee. He patted it awkwardly and removed it, and said, 'Have you ever had this out with Jed?'

'Well, what do you think, Vicar? Of course I have. Knocked on his door the minute I got back and found out what had happened – or what I *thought* had happened. His mother come out and saw me and said Jed was away from home, working on some farm up Chagford way. I got it out of her where he was and went off straight away and found him. I told him Susan had told me everything and then I knocked him down. Then I stood him up and knocked him down again.' Basil saw that he was rubbing his knuckles, as if the memory of the force of his blows was still there. 'I reckon I'd have killed him, too, if farmer hadn't come and separated us. He sent us both on our way – threatened us with the law if us didn't go quiet – and us both come home then. There weren't no more I could do about it, so us just went back to ordinary life.' He saw the astonishment on Basil's face. 'Well, what else could us do? Times were hard. There hadn't been the bombing in that war that us had last time – not down this way, anyway – but there'd been thousands of young men lost, *millions* of 'em, and there was work to do. There weren't time for argufying over things that couldn't ever be put right. I never spoke to him more'n I had to and he never spoke to me neither. It was only later, when his mum and dad had died, that he started to go downhill, and that was when he started to shoot his mouth off at me. And I give as good as I got, I don't mind admitting that, and don't see why not, neither. I had more to complain of than he ever had, Vicar, and you can't say nothing any different.'

'No, perhaps not.' Basil sighed and rubbed his face again, still wondering how to deal with the situation. A thirty-five-year-old tragedy had come suddenly to life in this village that, with all its small feuds and fusses, had seemed on the whole to be stable and well balanced. Briefly, he wondered how many worms lay hidden under other stones, and then returned his mind to Jacob's troubles. All this might have happened thirty-five years ago, but the consequences were making themselves felt now, and he was here to help and guide this bewildered man, and the woman who might have been his daughter – but wasn't.

'I can see that this has brought back a lot of painful memories,' he began. 'And some bitter regrets as well. Can you tell me what you would have done if you *had* found Susan – and her baby? How would you have felt about that?'

'Why, I'd have married her, of course.' Jacob sounded astonished that the question could even be asked. 'There's no two ways about it. She were my girl.'

'But what about the baby?' He waited a moment. '*Jed's* baby?'

Jacob, who had seemed to be about to say something more, checked himself. He put his fingers to his forehead and pushed them up through his grey hair. 'I'd like to say I'd have taken her on as well,' he said at last, in a heavy tone. 'But I don't honestly know. She were Susan's babby, and that ought to have been good enough for me – but if every time I looked at her face I had to think of Jed Fisher, I dunno as I could have put up with it.' He scowled at the gravestones all about them, stones that dated from two or three centuries ago and marked graves that might have been dug by his own ancestors. 'I'd like to say I'd have taken her,' he repeated. 'I'm pretty sure I would have done. It was Susan that mattered, when all's said and done, and the babby was as much hers as his. I reckon I could have come to think as much of her as I did of me own, though I dunno how we'd have got on if us had gone on living next door to Jed Fisher.'

'And now?' Basil asked. 'How do you feel about her now?'

This time, Jacob turned again and looked him straight in the eye. 'I'll be honest with you, Vicar. I'll be honest, because there ain't no sense in being nothing else. When that young woman come to my door and told me she thought I was her father, I wanted to believe her. I knew it couldn't be true, but I wanted it to be. She's a nice young woman, and don't seem to have a scrap of likeness to *him*, and in a funny sort of way I felt as if I already knew her. She don't look much like Susan, neither, but there's a lot of her poor old gran in her, and I suppose I warmed to her because of that.' He fell silent for a moment. 'It was one of the hardest things I ever did in the whole of my life, to tell her that she wasn't mine. And even then, I couldn't bring meself to tell her the whole truth.' His eyes reddened and brimmed with tears, the tears he should have shed thirty-five years ago. 'I couldn't bring meself to tell her she was Jed Fisher's maid. It would have been like handing my Susan over to him all over again, like I felt I did when I went back to the trenches and left her on her own. I just couldn't do it.'

He dragged a large red handkerchief out of his pocket and buried his face in it. Basil waited, his heart filled with pity, and after a few moments he asked his final question.

'And now? What do you think you must do now, Jacob?'

The old man seemed to shrink into his heavy work clothes. He looked ten years older. He heaved a sigh so deep that it seemed to come all the way up from his boots, and said in a dispirited, hopeless sort of voice, 'Well, I got to tell her, haven't I? I got to tell her the truth.' He shook his head and then looked at Basil again. 'Why is it that a devil like Jed Fisher can do that sort of thing, Vicar? Where's the fairness in it? He had my Susan, and now he's going to have my daughter as well – or her that ought to have been my daughter. Because she *felt* like mine, even when I knew she couldn't be.' He shook his head again. 'I don't understand it, Vicar, and that's the truth.'

'I don't understand it myself, Jacob,' Basil said honestly. 'It's a tangle. But I don't think you should despair. There's still a strong link between you and Jennifer. You were the one that Susan loved. She isn't going to forget that. And I think she may need you in the months ahead. It may not be easy for her, when she knows the truth.'

'Easy!' Jacob said with a short bark of laughter. 'It ain't going to be easy for *any* of us.'

Chapter Twenty-Seven

'I think it's a lovely choice,' Dottie said, gazing with satisfaction at the yards of lace swathed over her kitchen table. She draped some of it over Val's bare arm, admiring the effect. ''Tis as fine as gossamer. You'm lucky to find such beautiful stuff for your wedding-dress.'

'I know.' Val stroked the delicate fabric. 'And I never would have if it hadn't been for Stella thinking to ask Maddy if she knew of anywhere to get it. Imagine me, having a wedding-dress made of French lace!'

'Not that we can't make good stuff in England, too,' Dottie said at once. 'Right here in Devon – think of Honiton lace. They use that for royal weddings, you know. Why, one of my own great-great-aunts helped make the lace for Queen Victoria's wedding-veil. But this is handsome, there's no denying that.'

'And you think the colour's all right?' Val enquired a little anxiously.

Dottie nodded vigorously. 'I do. It's such a pale bluey-grey it looks almost silver. It suits you, and it's a bit different. After all, you'm not a young girl and white can be a cruel colour to wear. Now, what sort of pattern have you got? You ought to have it fitted to your waist, princess-style, and maybe with a little bolero jacket. Or draped sleeves, like bats' wings.' She held the material up against Val's body, her head on one side as she considered.

The back door opened and Stella came in, already talking.

'Honestly, Dottie, I can't think what possessed Miss Kemp to agree to do *A Midsummer Night's Dream*. It's more like a midsummer night's nightmare! Oh, hello, Val. Is that the material for the wedding-dress? Oh, how *lovely*!'

'D'you like it?' Val asked a little shyly. She watched as Stella touched the lace with gentle fingertips. 'It's beautiful, isn't it? Maddy's been so kind, taking the trouble to find it and have it sent over.'

'I think she enjoyed it. She's coming over herself soon.' Stella was still looking at the cobwebby fabric. 'It's so unusual, too. You'll look gorgeous, Val.' The two young women smiled at each other. 'I can see life is going to be all lace for the next few weeks, while Dottie's working on this!'

'You won't tell anyone else, will you?' Val said, suddenly anxious. 'Luke mustn't hear about it. It's got to be a complete surprise for him.'

'I won't say a word. And we'll have to make sure he doesn't come calling unexpectedly.' Stella looked at the lace again. 'What's going underneath?'

Val held up a roll of satin, exactly the same shade of silver-blue as the lace.

'Oh yes, that'll look lovely. How many bridesmaids are you having? Is Dottie making their dresses, too?'

'Three. Our Jackie and two little ones – my cousin's little girls, June and Patsy. They're only a year apart and look like twins, with curly fair hair and the most enormous blue eyes. They're wearing sky-blue. I've got a bit here . . . ' Val fished around and found a scrap of taffeta, which she held against the satin and lace. It made the pale colour look even filmier, and Stella nodded.

'It's going to be lovely. All of it. I'll have to get something new. Oh!' She put her hand to her mouth. 'Listen to me! I don't even know if I'm invited!'

'Well, you'll have to be now!' Val laughed, and then as Stella began to protest, 'It's all right – I was going to ask you, really I was. In fact, I think we're going to have to ask almost all the village. With one or two exceptions, perhaps,' she added almost under her breath.

'That Jed Fisher for a start,' said Dottie, never one to mince her words. 'You wouldn't want him like a skeleton at the feast.'

'Well, no. And he really is beginning to look more like a skeleton every day,' Val said. 'I saw him this morning. His skin looks really yellow. I don't think he's at all well.'

''Tis all they fags he smokes,' Dottie said. 'Always got one stuck in his mouth. I reckon if he smokes one a day, he smokes fifty or sixty – must be one of Jessie Friend's best customers. Stands to reason it can't do your chest no good. Jacob says he can hear him through the walls of a morning, coughing so bad he wonders he don't bring his lungs up.'

'I can't help feeling sorry for him,' Stella said thoughtfully. 'I know he can be very unpleasant, but he has a miserable life. Nobody seems to like him.'

'And that's nobody's fault but his own,' Dottie said. 'Now, Val, let's have a look at they patterns and decide what you want, a little bolero jacket or those long draped sleeves. I can do either, it's no trouble, and 'tis your day so you must have whatever you want.'

Val produced a sheet of paper with various styles drawn on it and they bent their heads over it, holding up swathes of fabric and letting it fall this way and that as they tried to decide which looked best. Stella left them to it and went up to her bedroom. She had her own problems with the costumes for the play, and had been busy for the past fortnight gradually building up an ass's head with papier mâché.

As she added another layer of scraps of newspaper and flour-and-water paste to her model, she gazed out of the window and thought about her sister. Now that Fenella Forsyth's wedding was over, Maddy would soon be coming back to England, and Stella wondered what her plans were.

The last time she had been here, she'd seemed unsettled and uncertain about her future. She didn't want to stay in France with Fenella and her new husband, but she was anxious that she had no qualifications for a job. Not that there was any real need for her to work – Fenella had promised her a good allowance – but although Maddy had grown up as a privileged young woman, her childhood had been that of an ordinary little girl in an ordinary family: first in a pleasant house in one of Portsmouth's quiet streets, then in the small, neglected two-up, two-down terraced house that they'd been allocated after their own home had been bombed. Stella still grimaced when she thought of the state of that house when they'd first moved in, with no electricity and gas lamps only downstairs, and the smell of cats everywhere. But their mother had scrubbed and cleaned and made a home of it, and they'd been happy enough until the night when that, too, had been bombed and the two girls left motherless.

After that, they'd lived in a country village not unlike Burracombe, billeted at the vicarage with Tim and Keith Budd from a few houses away, and life had been more settled – until their father had been lost at sea, and they were separated from each other and swept up into a world of orphanages.

Even after Maddy had been found and adopted by Miss Forsyth, she had been brought to live with Dottie in this very cottage – once again, the life of an ordinary child, where grown-ups had to work for their living. It wasn't until she left school that she began to travel and live in smart hotels. It was no wonder that now that phase of her life was over, she was unsure what direction to take.

'I feel a bit like a ship at sea, with no rudder,' she'd told Stella and Felix one evening before she'd gone back to France. 'Once Fenella's wedding is over, I'll have nothing to do but go around in circles. Up till now, I've always felt useful – now, I won't be any use to anyone.'

'Of course you will!' Stella exclaimed, distressed, but Maddy had shaken her head.

'I want to earn my living, like you do. But what can I do? Nothing – except maybe work in a shop.'

Maddy's words came back to Stella's mind now, as she sat at Dottie's washstand working away at her ass's head. She thought of the lovely materials downstairs, found and chosen by Maddy and sent over from France, and at the same time she remembered the woman she and her sister had met on the Plymouth bus not long ago. Jennifer Tucker, that was her name. She was a senior sales assistant in Dingle's – perhaps she would know of something Maddy could do. Maddy knows about fashion, Stella thought, and didn't Miss Tucker say that Maddy had the looks to be a fashion model?

She made up her mind to go to Plymouth on Saturday and ask her. Surely a big, smart shop like Dingle's would be pleased to have someone like Maddy working for them!

'Saturday?' Felix said thoughtfully, when Stella suggested a trip to the city. 'I'm sorry, I can't – I've promised to go to Dorset to see my uncle. Perhaps we could go another week.'

'I suppose we could,' Stella said a little reluctantly. 'Maybe I'll just go on my own. It's not your favourite idea of a day out, I know.'

Felix grinned. They had been to Plymouth together before, and enjoyed walking up the Hoe and down to the Barbican where all the fishing boats brought in their catch, early in the mornings, but he was like any other man when they went to the shops, although his natural good manners prevented him from showing just how bored he was. 'I must admit, I'd rather spend my time off out in the country,' he said. 'But I don't mind going with you, if you really want me.'

Stella shook her head. 'I'll go by myself.' She hadn't yet mentioned her reason for going, and decided not to. There was no point in talking about it, if the idea came to nothing. 'I need to look for something to wear to Val's wedding, anyway. It would be very dull for you.'

'Won't Dottie make you a new dress?'

'Dottie's going to be too busy making Val's wedding-dress and the bridesmaids' frocks. I could make my own, but I don't think the sewing-machine's ever going to be free. Anyway, I thought I'd splash out a bit. There are some lovely new summer things coming in now.'

She set off on the morning bus, having decided to make a day of it. Jennifer Tucker might only work on Saturday mornings – or maybe not at all – but someone at Dingle's ought to be able to give her a message, and Stella could think of no other way to contact the other woman. She got off at the bus station and walked up to Royal Parade, thinking how smart and wide it was. She had never known Plymouth before the war, but Dottie and others had told her how narrow and cramped the streets were before the Blitz had destroyed them, and how the city planners had taken the opportunity to rebuild in modern style. The rebuilding was still going on, but Dingle's, and the other big department store, Spooner's, were both open, along with a number of other shops along the new streets, and Stella thought that Plymouth people must be very proud of their city, rising like a phoenix from the ashes.

Occupied with these thoughts, she went in through the big glass doors and stood for a moment getting her bearings. The ladies' fashions were on the first floor, and there was an escalator leading up, so she stepped a little gingerly on to that and found herself in the middle of a vast array of women's clothes displayed on racks and models.

For a while, she wandered amongst them, vaguely looking for something that would be suitable for the wedding and wishing that Maddy could be there to advise her. At the thought of Maddy, she remembered her other reason for coming, and looked around for Jennifer Tucker. Eventually, she approached a sales assistant and asked her.

'Miss Tucker?' The woman was middle-aged, with a rather supercilious expression and dressed smartly in a black skirt and white blouse, making Stella feel like a country bumpkin in her cotton frock and cardigan. 'Does she know you're coming? Perhaps I can help you with whatever it is you want.'

'No, but she said to call in at any time.' Stella was determined not to be bullied. 'It's a personal matter.'

The assistant looked even more disapproving. 'Staff are not supposed to attend to personal matters during shop hours.'

'I'm sure they're not,' Stella said with a smile. 'And I know Miss Tucker is a senior assistant here, so I expect she's busy. But I won't take up much of her time. If you could just tell me where I might find her . . . ?'

The assistant looked for a moment as if she might refuse, but at last she said grudgingly, 'She'll be having her coffee-break at the moment, so I suppose it's all right to disturb her. I'll send one of the juniors.' She lifted her hand to summon a frightened-looking girl of about fourteen who was folding jumpers in a corner. 'Go into the staff canteen, Miss Jenkins, and tell Miss Tucker there's a lady here to see her. On a personal matter,' she added with a frown.

The girl scurried off, and the assistant moved away as if she had more important things to attend to, although Stella noticed with some amusement that they didn't seem to include folding the jumpers. Instead, she began to shift some dresses on a rack, keeping an eye on Stella at the same time.

I hope Miss Tucker remembers me, she thought with sudden anxiety. It was a few weeks ago that they'd met, and the invitation could well have been one of those things you say out of politeness and then forget. And it was Maddy she really noticed. By the time the junior returned, followed by a puzzled-looking woman in a crisp blue suit, Stella was beginning to wish she hadn't come.

To her relief, Jennifer's face cleared as she caught sight of Stella, lurking amongst the dresses, and she came quickly forward, smiling. 'You're one of the girls I met at Burra-combe. The two sisters who found each other after years apart. How nice to see you again. Is your sister with you?'

'No, it's only me. I – I wanted to talk to you – to ask you something. I'm sorry to disturb you at work. I didn't know how else to find you.' Stella looked at the assistant who was hovering nearby and Jennifer's lips twitched.

'It's all right. It doesn't matter at all. Look, I have my lunch-hour at twelve – why don't you come back then and we'll go somewhere together? I'll meet you at the main door.' She gave the assistant a cool glance. 'Thank you, Miss Smith. It was kind of you to send Miss Jenkins to find me. It's a private matter so we won't take up any more time now, and since there are just a few minutes left of my coffee-break, I may as well not bother to go back to the canteen.' She guided Stella through the maze of clothes and said, 'I'm senior to her really, but she's never been able to accept it – she's been with the company for years and is rather officious. That poor little junior is terrified of her!'

'So was I,' Stella said. 'She made me feel as if I ought to have worn my best clothes just to come through the doors.'

'Luckily, not all the assistants are like that. Most of them are very friendly and helpful. Now, you just browse around and I'll see you at twelve.' They parted at the top of the escalator and Stella descended, making up her mind to go to British Homes Stores or Marks & Spencers for her shopping. Dingle's was lovely, and she would still look around the store, but the prices were beyond her budget.

Jennifer came out promptly at twelve and suggested a café down the road. They walked there together and found a table by the window. When they had both ordered shepherd's pie and rhubarb crumble, they looked at each other a little shyly.

'I hope you don't mind me coming to see you,' Stella began. 'Only I wanted to ask your advice.' She explained about Maddy. 'It would be lovely if she could find something she's really interested in, and could live near Burracombe. Or better still, in the village itself. What do you think?'

'There might be something,' Jennifer said thoughtfully. 'She's a very pretty girl. And there's some talk of our starting up a sort of fashion show in the restaurant – girls wearing our clothes, showing them off while people eat their lunch or afternoon tea. Your sister would be ideal for that. It's only part-time, of course, and the girls we'll be employing will probably be from a model agency. Would she be interested in that, do you think?'

'She might be. But I think she'd rather have a job in the store – something like yours, perhaps. She knows quite a lot about fashion. I know she'd have to start as a junior – maybe as a sales assistant – what do you think?'

'I'll find out if there are any openings,' Jennifer said. Their shepherd's pies arrived and they began to eat. Then she said, 'And how is everyone in Burracombe?'

Stella looked at her with some surprise. 'I didn't realise you knew many people in the village. Or did you say you had relatives there? I'm sorry, I don't remember exactly what you said.'

'I don't think I did say much.' Jennifer hesitated a little. 'I've met the Tozers and the vicar. And Mr Prout,' she added after another slight pause. 'Do you know him? Jacob Prout.'

'Oh, everyone knows Jacob! He's a dear old man. I don't know what the village would do without him. Do you know him well?'

Jennifer didn't answer for a moment. She seemed to be concentrating on her shepherd's pie, and when she spoke again she seemed to have forgotten Stella's question. Instead, she said, 'You told me about how you and your sister were separated during the war. It must have been lovely for you to find each other again.'

We've said this before, Stella thought, but she smiled and answered, 'Yes, it was. We hadn't got any other family, you see, and I didn't know what had happened to her. It was like a miracle, finding that she'd actually lived in Burracombe.'

'Families are important, aren't they?' Jennifer said thoughtfully. 'You don't really feel complete without them.'

'No. And we'd lost both our parents in the war, so there were only the two of us.'

'But at least you knew about each other. And you knew your parents, too. You knew who they were.'

'Well – yes,' Stella said uncertainly, wondering what Jennifer meant. 'But then, most people do, don't they?'

'Probably, but not all.' Jennifer looked at her as if trying to decide whether to go on. At last, she said, 'I never knew my father. Not my real one. I had a stepfather, and he was very good to me, but he wasn't my *real* father.'

'Oh,' Stella said blankly, not knowing what to say. She stared at her plate, feeling uncomfortable, but Jennifer went on without seeming to notice.

'I didn't even know until quite recently – but once I found out, I just felt I needed to know the truth. That's why I came to Burracombe.'

Stella looked up in surprise. 'You mean that's where he came from? But how did you know that?'

'I didn't know, for sure.' Briefly, Jennifer explained how she had looked at several villages before coming to Burracombe and half remembering a visit she had made there with her mother. As the waitress came and took away their empty plates and replaced them with bowls of crumble and custard, she told Stella more of the story. 'And then I felt sure I knew who he was. But when I talked to him, he told me I was wrong.' Her eyes filled with tears.

Stella felt a rush of sympathy. 'Oh, how sad. So won't you ever know?'

'Oh yes,' Jennifer said, poking at her crumble with her spoon. 'I'm going to know. I've got to, you see. I've got so far, I can't stop now. I'm going to go out to Burracombe again and see him – the man I thought was my father – and ask him to tell me the truth. He knows, I'm sure of it. And he loved my mother, I know that. I'll *beg* him to tell me.'

Chapter Twenty-Eight

The ass's head was finished at last and Stella took it to school. In the midst of all her other work, Dottie had found time to knit a cover for it in grey wool, and make two long ears, which Alf Coker had fixed on wire loops so that they stood up. Two large black buttons were sewn on for its eyes, and the whole thing fitted together over Micky's head in two halves before the grey cover was pulled over the top.

'I can't see nothing!' came Micky's muffled voice from deep within.

'Oh dear,' Stella said. 'I never thought of that. Can you breathe all right?' She had made holes for nostrils, roughly where she thought Micky's nose might be. 'That's more important – we can always push you into position.'

'It smells all woolly,' he complained, and the others giggled.

'You don't have to wear it for long,' Miss Kemp said. 'I think Miss Simmons has made a very good job of it. You look very lifelike.'

Micky started to drag the head off and Stella hastened to help him. 'You have to take off the knitted cover first, or you'll get stuck. That's why I made it in two halves – you'd never get it on otherwise.' She smiled at his red face. 'Goodness, you do look hot.'

'I'm going to boil,' he said irritably. 'Why can't one of the others be Bottom? I never wanted to be him in the first place.'

'It's too late to change now. And we needed a really good

actor for that part. Bottom is the most famous person in the play – in that part, anyway. Now, how are the rest of the costumes getting on?'

The other children produced their costumes and Stella and Miss Kemp inspected them. It had been decided that the play would be performed twice – first at the school at the end of term and then at the Summer Fair. Stella had heard that morning that Maddy would be here by then, and she had agreed to present the prizes. She was going to stay at Aggie Madge's cottage until she had decided what to do next.

Stella didn't know whether to be pleased or sorry about this news. Ever since the Easter holidays, she thought she had detected a slight cooling in Felix's attitude towards her. He and Stella still spent time together, going for walks or to the cinema, but he had never kissed her again and remained no more than friendly, whereas he was always talking about Maddy and looking forward to her return. Sadly, remembering how she had begun to grow fond of Luke Ferris last year and then been disappointed, Stella told herself that it was too much to hope for that Felix should prefer her to her pretty sister, and she too began to withdraw a little. She hadn't gone to church the day after her trip to Plymouth, and when Felix looked in at the classroom door after school on Monday, she'd told him she was too busy for a walk. It was now four days since they'd spent any time together and although she missed him badly, she told herself that it was best that way. Maddy would be here soon, and Felix must feel free to court her, if that was what he wanted.

As she walked home from school, Stella thought again about Jennifer Tucker's story. Jennifer hadn't told her who she'd thought her father was, but Stella hadn't missed her enquiry about Jacob Prout. She wondered if it could be him. There had been mention of the Tozers, too – a rather mysterious mention, now Stella came to think about it. Could Jennifer have thought Ted was her father? He was about the right age. Maybe he'd hinted that it was Jacob; or perhaps it was the other way about. Whichever it was, it was a muddled situation and one that would surely cause problems if Jennifer insisted on being told the truth.

That's why she was so interested in Maddy and me, Stella thought. It's all about families being separated and trying to find each other. It's about wanting to know who your real family are. But Jennifer Tucker did have a family – she'd had a mother, and a man she'd believed was her father, and sisters as well. Why isn't that enough? Does it really matter that another man was her real father? Does she really have to find him, even if it means trouble and heartache for other people?

Which was more important – the person who gave you your life or the one who looked after you and brought you up? In which case, who was more important to Maddy – their own mother, Kathy Simmons, who had been killed by a bomb, or Fenella Forsyth, who had adopted her, or Dottie, who had taken care of her through the rest of her childhood?

Stella shook her head. It was too difficult to decide. And before she could worry about it any more, Felix's voice jerked her out of her troubled thoughts. She looked up and saw him crossing the village green towards her.

'I thought you weren't going to speak to me,' he said as he came closer.

'I didn't see you. I was miles away.'

She looked at him a little uncertainly, trying to assess whether his smile was as warm as ever and thinking that he looked slightly uncomfortable. There was a small hesitation, then he said, 'Are you on your way home to tea?'

'Yes, we've just been rehearsing the *Dream* again. I think it'll be all right in the end. Shirley Culliford has a real talent – she's a surprising little girl. Only needed to be given a chance. It makes me wonder what other gifts the children have that we don't find.'

'If they've got them, they'll find some way of expressing

them,' Felix said. 'Do you mind if I walk home with you? There's something I need to see Dottie about.'

'Of course not,' Stella said, surprised. A few weeks ago, he wouldn't have asked; he'd have just fallen into step beside her. It just shows how far apart we've drifted, she thought sadly.

They walked along together, talking politely, and Stella felt even sadder. We're almost like strangers, she thought. However did it happen?

Once in the cottage, they were both warmed by Dottie's normal friendly welcome and the atmosphere eased. They sat in the battered armchairs, drinking tea and enjoying crisp, oaty flapjacks, and admiring the progress of the wedding-dress, and things seemed to be just the same as ever. But when Felix got up to go, their constraint returned, and there was no arrangement made for a walk or a visit to the cinema. He stood for a moment in the doorway, his head bent a little beneath the low ceiling, and they looked at each other doubtfully. Then he stepped into the sunshine and walked away down the short path to the front gate.

Stella came back in and closed the door.

'Is he all right?' Dottie enquired, her head bent over her sewing. 'He don't seem quite himself these days.'

'I expect he's just busy,' Stella said vaguely. 'There's a lot happening at this time of year, isn't there? Weddings and garden teas and all that sort of thing . . . And he's helping a lot over at Little Burracombe. The vicar there's not at all well.'

'No, he isn't, poor old man. Never properly got over that bronchitis he had backalong.' Dottie threaded a needle and bit off the end of the cotton. 'Well, so long as everything's all right between the two of you.'

'Of course it is. Why shouldn't it be? We're just friends, that's all.' Stella's voice was sharper than she intended, and as Dottie glanced up at her she flushed and bit her lip. 'Sorry, I didn't mean to snap. It's this play we're doing, it's getting me down a bit. I'll go upstairs – I've got a few things to see to for tomorrow.'

'That's right, my pretty, you do that,' Dottie said peaceably. 'I'll just finish this hem and then I'll start thinking about supper. I went into Tavistock this morning and got a nice piece of smoked haddock. And there's strawberries from the garden for afters – the first ones.'

'That sounds lovely. Give me a call if there's anything I can do.' Stella went up the narrow stairs to her room and shut the door. She stood for a minute or two looking out of the window, and then sighed and turned away to unpack her school bag.

If Stella had stood a minute longer at her window, she would have seen the local bus that connected with the main route through Yelverton pull up beside the green and Jennifer Tucker climb out.

Val Tozer was walking by at that moment, and the two young women smiled and greeted each other. They stopped and Jennifer said, 'I'm glad I've met you. I was thinking of coming up to the farm. You don't have time for a few words, do you?'

'Of course,' Val said. 'Come up and have some tea.'

Jennifer hesitated. 'Well – maybe in a minute. But I'd quite like to talk to you on our own. It's all a bit difficult, you see. I know your parents and your granny know my story, but . . . well, let's find somewhere quiet and I'll tell you what's happened.'

Curiously, Val led her along the lane and through the gate that led to the path up through the woods to the charcoal-burner's cottage. 'It's where Luke and I are going to live after we're married,' she explained. 'We'll need to find somewhere else as soon as possible, because it's not really suitable for two, especially in winter, but we don't want to wait any longer. We can talk privately there – Luke's gone to Tavistock for an interview at the school.'

'Is he a teacher?' Jennifer asked in surprise. 'I thought he was an artist.'

'He is, but he says he can't earn enough from his paintings. I don't want him to get a job – I think he ought to use all his time for painting – but you know what men are, they feel they've got to support their wives. And I'll make sure he does plenty of painting in his spare time!' She opened the door of the ramshackle little cottage. 'Come in. I'll make a cup of tea.'

Jennifer sat down in one of the wooden carver chairs, looking around. There were only two rooms – the main living-room where they were sitting, which served as a kitchen as well, and what she guessed must be the bedroom through an inner door. The only furniture was two chairs, a small, elderly settee and a kitchen table. Luke's easel stood in one corner and there were paintings everywhere, stacked together on the floor and leaning against the walls.

'I can see why you want somewhere else to live,' she said. 'There's hardly room to swing a paintbrush.'

Val chuckled. 'I know. It's going to be a bit like camping. But we've known each other a long time.' She turned from the tiny cooking-range and glanced at her visitor, grinning a little awkwardly. 'Longer than most people realise, to tell you the truth. Anyway, we just don't want to wait any longer. I'm almost thirty, you know, and if we want to start a family we've got to get on with it.' A shadow crossed her face, but she turned away without saying any more and poured boiling water into the fat brown teapot.

Jennifer accepted a cup of tea, and Val sat down in the other chair. They looked at each other and then Val said, 'Did you go to see Jacob?'

Jennifer nodded. 'That's what I wanted to talk to you about. You see, it's all turned out differently from what I expected. Your mother and grandmother – they were wrong about him.' She stared out of the open window. It looked out through the trees, with their bark green with moss, and up the hill towards the Standing Stones. A few birds fluttered amongst the branches; the two women could hear the piping voices of tits, the trill of a robin and the harsh screech of a jay. Jacob and Susan would have walked up that path, past this cottage, and done their courting within the ring of granite stones on the brow of the hill, just as countless lovers must have done through the ages, and probably still did. Tears pricked her eyes as she felt a sudden deep longing to know that she had been conceived there, in love and happiness, but the longing was swiftly followed by the sorrow of knowing it was not true; and the lonely desolation of perhaps never knowing the truth.

'I don't understand,' Val said after a few moments. 'How do you mean, they were wrong about Jacob? Wasn't he Susan's sweetheart after all?'

'Oh yes. They were sweethearts – he told me that. He really loved her, Val, you can see it in his eyes even after all this time. It broke his heart, what happened. But he's not my father.' She turned her head and met Val's startled gaze. 'He says he couldn't possibly be my father. They never went that far, you see.'

'But – but Mum says he was home at the right time. He'd been wounded, hadn't he?'

'Yes, she's right about that. But then he went away again. And it must have been soon after that that it happened.' Her voice was low. 'Someone else came along and – well, I suppose she was lonely and upset, and whoever it was didn't have the same scruples as Jacob. Oh, Val!' she burst out. 'I *liked* Jacob! I wanted him to be my father! I still do – I felt as if I *knew* him, even though we'd never met before. But instead . . . he's no relation to me.' She fell silent for a moment, then added tonelessly, 'I feel that if we could have found each other again, it would have made up, somehow, for all he'd lost. All they'd both lost. And now – well, I'm back to the beginning again. Worse than that, I've upset that nice old man. I wish I'd never started it.'

She buried her face in her hands, while Val watched helplessly. After a moment, she moved across and knelt beside the other woman, putting her arm across Jennifer's shoulders, patting her gently. At last she said, 'And didn't he ever find out who the man was?'

Jennifer dropped her hands and lifted her eyes towards Val's face. Her cheeks were wet with tears, and Val felt for a hanky to give her, but she shook her head and took her own from her pocket. 'He wouldn't say. And I couldn't ask him – not then. It was all such a shock, for us both. But I think he knows who it was, Val.'

'Do you think he'd tell you? Do you still want to know?'

Jennifer didn't answer at first. She stared out of the doorway, as if still thinking about it, and then she nodded slowly.

'Yes, I do. Whoever it was – and however it happened – it's still part of my mother's history, and mine. I won't feel easy until I know.' Her lips twisted wryly. 'I may not feel easy then either, but at least I'll have found out all there is to find out. I'll have done what I set out to do. The thing is, *will* he tell me? I just don't know, Val. I can't upset him any more than I already have. I can't *make* him tell me. But I feel I've got to ask him, just once more.' She drew in a deep, shuddering breath. 'That's why I was coming up to the farm. You see, I don't know how it might affect him. I thought I'd ask you and your family before I go to see him again.'

'I see.' Val moved away and returned to her chair. 'I don't honestly know what to say,' she confessed. 'I've known Jacob all my life, and he's always seemed a very steady sort of man – not the sort to get upset easily. Unless it's with Jed Fisher, who lives next door,' she added with a grin. 'They're always at loggerheads! But apart from that, he takes life as it comes.

I've never seen him in this sort of situation, of course,' she added.

'What about when his wife died? Do you remember that?'

'Not really. It was during the war – I was away from home. Mum wrote and told me about it, of course, but by the time I came back, it had been over for ages and Jacob seemed to have settled down to being on his own again. I'm not really being much help, am I?'

'I can't expect anyone to help me, really,' Jennifer said despondently. 'I wonder sometimes if I'm being selfish. What good is it going to do to anyone for me to dig up all these old stories? They can still hurt people, you see, and I don't think I'd ever realised that before – not completely. What's the point, except to satisfy my own curiosity?'

Val thought of her own story, and her talks with Basil Harvey on whether the truth should be told, even years later. He had guided her towards the decision that if it were only to result in pain for other people, it might be better kept secret. Was it the same in Jennifer's case?

'The thing is,' she said, 'you've done it now. You've brought it to light for Jacob, and now he knows that Susan didn't die all those years ago. There might not be anyone else he can talk to about it – only you. All his memories might be welling up – he may really need someone to talk them over with. And you're the only one who can tell him about your mother – Susan – during the last thirty-five years. I think you should go to see him, Jennifer. Not just to ask him your questions, but to let him ask you his.'

Jennifer stared at her. Her face was pale and there were fresh tears in her eyes. She shook her head slowly.

'I must be the most selfish person on earth,' she said. 'I never even thought of that. I knew I didn't want to upset him, but it never occurred to me that he would want to know about my mother. It never occurred to me that he might need me to talk to.'

‘So will you go to see him?’ Val asked quietly, and she nodded.

‘I’ll go now. I won’t ask him who my father was – not yet, anyway. I’ll just let him talk, if he wants to. I’ll try to get to know him before I go any further.’ She began to get to her feet. ‘I’m not going to cause poor Jacob any more pain. But I still hope he’ll tell me. I’ll always want to know who the man was, Val. I can’t help wanting to know that.’

Chapter Twenty-Nine

Jacob was lying back in his armchair, his feet up on his mother's old sewing-stool and Flossie on his lap, when he heard the knock on the door. For a minute or two, he didn't move, then, slowly and reluctantly, he lifted the cat down to the floor and heaved himself up. Whe he opened the door and found Jennifer standing there, he hardly knew whether to be glad or sorry.

'Jacob,' she said quietly, 'can I come in?'

The old man rubbed his eyes and forehead with the back of one hand. For a moment, he seemed about to refuse, then he stood back a little and made a small gesture. 'Come you in. I was just having a bit of a rest.'

'I don't want to disturb you—' she began, but he shook his head.

'You've come all the way out from Plymouth special, I dare say. Sit down –' he shifted two or three newspapers from the other armchair '– and I'll make a cup of tea.'

Jennifer did as she was told and looked around the room. It was less tidy than on her last visit, with papers on the table, dust on the dresser shelves and dirty dishes beside the sink – more than Jacob would have used for one, or even two, meals. Scruff, the dog, came over to sniff at her, wagging his stumpy tail, and she bent to fondle his ears, feeling anxious. She'd caught only a glimpse of Jacob before he'd turned away, but he didn't look as if he'd shaved that morning. Her impression of him before had been of a man who took care of himself and his surroundings. Now, he and his home looked slightly unkempt.

Jacob shuffled over in his socks and put a cup down beside her. He went back to his own chair and sat looking at her, and Jennifer fidgeted uncomfortably.

'Well?' he said at last. 'You've come to ask me summat, I suppose.'

'No,' she said quickly. 'I haven't. It was my reason in the first place, I've got to be honest about it – but I've had second thoughts.' She faced him. 'Perhaps I should never have come here at all, but when I found that my father was a different man from the one I'd always thought – a man I didn't even know existed – I felt I had to know who he was. I tried to forget it, but I couldn't. It was on my mind all the time – day and night. In the end, I had to do something about it. I looked in a lot of different places, and eventually I came to Burracombe. And I found you.'

'And I told you—'

She lifted one hand and he fell silent, still watching her. 'You told me you weren't my father. It was a shock, Jacob. I felt, when we met, that there was some strong link between us. I *wanted* you to be my father. I really believed you were. But—' Her voice broke and she shook her head, unable to go on. Jacob filled the silence.

'So you've come to ask me who he was.'

Again, she shook her head. 'No. I don't think it's right to make you go over it all. I've caused enough upset for you. I've come because I thought you might want to talk to me about my mother. I thought you might want to know what her life was like, after she left Burracombe. And – and if you can bear it, I'd like you to tell me about her when she was young. Because there's no one else who can do that – not in the way you can.' She met his eyes. 'I won't ask you about – about *him*. And if you don't ever feel you can tell me, then that's an end to it.'

There was a long silence. Scruff settled down at Jacob's feet and Flossie climbed back on to his lap. He stroked her absently, his fingers moving slowly down the soft, tortoise-shell back. His eyes were veiled as he looked down at the cat, and Jennifer waited with a thumping heart. If he told her to go now – if he said he didn't want to go over those old memories and open up those old wounds – then that really was an end to her search. She would never know who her father was. Nor – and, to her surprise, this suddenly seemed more important – would she ever really get to know this man whom her mother had loved.

''Tis good of you, maid, to come and talk to me like this,' he said at last. 'I won't say 'twasn't a shock to see you, and hear that my Susan had been alive all these years. It's taken a bit of getting used to, and I don't seem to have had the heart for much else these past couple of weeks. But you'm right. It *has* brought back old memories – and there hasn't been no one I could share them with. Maybe it'll be a good thing to chew 'em over with you. Otherwise, seems to me they'll just keep turning round and round in me own head, with nowhere else to go.'

Jennifer let out her breath and relaxed a little into her chair. Jacob had stopped speaking, but she sensed that he still had more to say. She waited, quietly, wishing that she too had a cat to stroke. After a few minutes, the old man spoke again.

'But you'm wrong to think I can't tell you who your own father was. Seems to me, if we'm to be able to talk about these things honestly together, we both got to know the truth from the start. It'll never be satisfactory if there's a secret between us. Not a secret like that, anyway. It'll stand in the way all the rest of our lives.' He raised his eyes and looked at her, and she knew that she was about to hear the truth of what had happened all those years ago.

'It isn't summat I finds easy to talk about,' he said in a dry, rusty voice, 'so you got to bear with me if I don't put it well.

And I dare say there be more to the tale than even I knows. Things that only *he* knows – and I wouldn't trust him to tell them, neither, not honest and truthful. He don't know the meaning of the words.' He caught himself up, hearing the bitterness in his own voice, and his mouth twisted. 'But there – 'tis of your father I'm speaking now, and I got to remember that. But we been at odds for years now – ever since it happened – and old habits die hard.'

Jennifer stared at him. Little as she knew of Burracombe and its inhabitants, she had heard enough to suspect what Jacob was about to tell her. She felt a dread settle over her heart, and almost cried out to him to stop, she didn't want to hear the name, didn't want to know the truth. But she had come too far now and couldn't turn away because it was harsher than she had thought.

Jacob leaned forward a little, and she leaned automatically towards him in turn. In a quiet voice, and turning his eyes towards the wall of the adjoining cottage as he spoke, he said, 'The man who took advantage of my Susan and fathered her babby – fathered *you* – lives next door. We grew up together, living side by side, and we'll live side by side until one or t'other of us dies. You saw him, last time you came here. His name's Jed Fisher.'

Jed Fisher. She thought of the scrap of paper, the last few words of the letter Jacob himself had written to her mother. The initial J that was his and hers – and, by heartbreaking coincidence, her father's as well.

The man who had stared at her with such hostility, who had ranted at Jacob in the front garden, who was dirty and unkempt and repellent, and apparently disliked by the whole village – that man was her father, whom she had thought of, dreamed of and sought to complete her own life story.

A sick, dizzy feeling swept over her and she put her hand to her forehead. She felt Jacob's big, strong hand on her arm, steadying her and then on the back of her head, pushing it down between her knees. After a moment or two, the dizziness faded and she sat up, trembling a little. He held the cup of tea to her mouth.

'Have a sip of this, maid. It's been a shock for you, and no wonder. Maybe a drop of brandy – I got some in the cupboard, for medicinal purposes.'

'I'm all right now.' She sipped the tea and then gave him a shaky smile. 'Sorry about that.'

'Bless your heart, maid, there's no need to be sorry. Seems we gives each other shocks.' He gave her a wry smile and she gave him a faint one back. 'That's the trouble with telling the truth. It ain't always what folks wants to hear.'

'No,' Jennifer said. 'We always think it's going to be something better.' She looked at him again. 'I really did want you to be my father, Jacob.'

'Ah,' he said, nodding slowly, 'and I wanted it, too. But 'twasn't to be, maid, and us got to accept that. And I'll tell you something else, too.' Jennifer looked at him enquiringly, and he went on with a heavy note to his voice, 'Right's right, and if we'm going to do this thing proper, to my way of thinking we got to go the whole way. 'Tidden easy for me to say this, considering how I've felt about it all these years, but that old so-and-so next door – begging your pardon – has got his rights, too, whatever he done. He may not deserve to be, but he'm your father and seems to me he got a right to know it. Now, you don't have to agree with me, and to tell you the truth, I'll not be sorry if you don't, but you got to think about it, at least. Do you tell him, or don't you? That's the next thing to look at.'

Once again, there was a silence. Jennifer thought of the choices that lay before her. She could take her quest no further; ignore Jed's existence, pretend that he had no part in her life and build up a relationship with Jacob himself, telling herself that his love for her mother was enough. Yet how was that any different from the relationship that she and her mother had had with her stepfather, Arthur Tucker, whom she had believed for years to be her father? If she had been satisfied with that, she would never have started on this search.

'How do you think he'll take it?' she asked at last. 'He might deny it – pretend nothing ever happened. He might say you're lying.'

'Well, us'll be no worse off, in a sense, if he do,' Jacob said. 'And whatever else happens, maid, you and me'll be friends. If that's what you wants.'

'Yes, it is,' she said at once, and simultaneously they reached across the hearthrug and shook hands.

'Well, then,' he said with a smile that showed he felt more at ease now, 'what do you want to do next?'

'I want us to talk,' she said. 'I'll think some more about what you said about Jed. I know you're right, but I'm not quite ready to talk to him yet. All this –' she waved a hand '– all this has come so suddenly. But I want you to tell me about my mother, when she was young. And I'd like to talk about her to you, too, if you'd like that.' She returned his smile. 'We've got thirty-five years to catch up on! We'd better start straight away.'

They talked for hours. Jacob made more tea, and then he noticed the time and realised that his visitor must be hungry. There was an enamel dish in the larder with some bacon and four thick sausages – 'Cokers' – in it, and he fried these along with some mashed potato left over from his dinner and some tomatoes from his garden. He cleared the papers from the table, apologising again for the 'mess' and laid it with a red checked cloth and old, bone-handled knives and forks. 'These were my granny's,' he said. 'Look after 'em right and never put the handles in water and they'll last for ever.'

They sat down to their meal, still talking. While Jennifer kept an eye on the sausages, he had shaved at the kitchen sink, using a cut-throat razor, and then he slipped upstairs and came down in a fresh, clean shirt. 'I'm ashamed you found me like you did. Been letting things go, I have.' He glanced around the room, noting the dust on the dresser. 'I'll give this place a good go tomorrow, get it back up to scratch.'

Jennifer didn't ask why he'd been letting things go. She felt a pang of guilt, realising that her sudden arrival in his life had brought back painful memories, and understanding that he had been tormented by his own conscience during the past fortnight, knowing that he must tell her the truth. If it had been anyone but Jed, his enemy . . . But when she mentioned this, Jacob shook his head.

'Jed and me were pals up to then. Always together, when us was little tackers. Well, us would be, wouldn't us, living next door to each other and our parents friendly as they were. But he were always a bit wilder than me, Jed was, and as us got older things started to change. Didn't go to chapel any more, and I didn't like his way with the maids. Didn't seem to have proper respect for 'em, somehow. And then, when the war broke out and he wouldn't join up – managed to get exemption on account of *flat feet* or some such excuse – I'll be honest with you, Jennifer, I was proper riled about that. His feet had never stopped him doing nothing before that!' He took a bite of sausage and chewed fiercely. 'And I used to think even then that he had an eye for my Susan. Not that I thought she'd ever fancy *him*, but I didn't like the way he looked at her.'

'And then you came home and found she'd gone. That must have been dreadful.'

'Ah, it were a bad time.' He told her the story he had told Basil, about his visit to Chagford and the fight with Jed. 'And since then, I've done me best to pretend he's not there, but it's not been easy and for the past few years we been snapping and snarling at each other like bad-tempered dogs. I ain't proud of it, but there you are, 'tis the truth. I reckon it got worse when my Sarah died,' he added thoughtfully. 'Seemed to bring it all back, being on me own again. I don't say I wasn't proper fond of my Sarah, I was, but I couldn't help wondering sometimes if me and Susan would still have been together, if things had been different. And I'm not very proud of that, neither,' he added.

They finished their meal and Jennifer helped him wash up. It was getting late now and she looked at the grandmother clock that stood in his front room and said, 'I'd better be going. I'll have to walk out to the main road to catch the Plymouth bus.'

'I'll walk with you, maid.' He hesitated. 'You won't be calling on him next door now?'

'Not tonight. I'll have to come out again. I can't do it until next Wednesday, though – that's my afternoon off, when the shop's closed. I'd come on Sunday but I don't know how he'll react . . . I wouldn't want to cause trouble in the village then.'

Jacob nodded with understanding. 'There's no knowing what line he'll take, and us hears his voice shouting the odds enough during the week. He generally do keep it down a bit of a Sunday, ever since the minister had a word with him after he went over to Arthur Culliford and started effing and blinding, if you'll excuse the term, about their eldest boy kicking his football over Jed's fence.' He gave Jennifer a sharp look. 'I don't say as he'll do that to you, maid, but I reckon it'll be a good idea if I'm about when you comes.'

'You don't think that would make him worse?' Jennifer asked doubtfully, wondering whether she really wanted to go through with this encounter.

Jacob folded his lips together and nodded. 'I dare say it might, at that. All the same, I wants to be on hand. Tell you what, maid, I'll be here indoors and keeping an eye and an ear out, and if I thinks you need a bit of help, I'll come out. Otherwise, I'll keep to meself. How's that?'

'That sounds ideal,' she said gratefully. 'I have to admit,

I'm not looking forward to this. But I do think I've got to do it. I've got to talk to him – no matter what he did, he's my father and I'll never be able to rest if I haven't looked him in the eye at least once.'

Jacob nodded again and took his jacket down from the hook behind the door. 'I'll walk up to the main road with you now and see you on the bus. And –' he hesitated for a moment '– I'd just like to say, whatever happens with him, you'm always welcome here. And I hope you'll come out and see me, regular, if you feels like it. You'm my Susan's babby, and you'm special to me.'

Jennifer felt the tears prick her eyes. Impulsively, she leaned forward and kissed him on the cheek. 'You're special, too, Jacob,' she said tremulously. 'I'll come out to see you whenever I can – whatever happens with Jed.'

They walked through the lanes in the gathering dusk, to reach the main road where the Plymouth bus was already in sight. Jacob stuck out his hand and the big vehicle pulled in and stopped. Jennifer began to climb aboard, then paused and turned back to give him a hug.

'I meant what I said,' she told him. 'I'm glad I found you.'

Jacob stood at the side of the road, watching as the bus disappeared into the twilight, then turned to walk back through the lanes that he and Susan had known so well, towards Burracombe. And Jennifer Tucker, the woman who ought to have been his daughter, stared unseeingly out of the window as the bus took her back to the city where she had grown up.

Her feelings were in turmoil. She wanted desperately to be able to think of Jacob as her father, yet she knew that the truth was very different and stemmed from a tragedy that had begun before she was born. It was up to her now whether she took it any further, and revived more memories – and a truth that would be painful for both her and Jacob himself.

I don't have to do it, she told herself. I could stop now. I don't have to go any further.

But she knew that she would.

Chapter Thirty

'There's a letter for you from France,' Dottie said as Stella came through the door the next afternoon. 'It's Maddy's writing on the envelope.'

'Oh, perhaps it's to say when she's coming home.' Stella seized the envelope and tore it open eagerly. She scanned the sheet of paper inside. 'She's coming to England at the weekend! She'll be staying in London first for a few days, then coming here. We must see if Aggie can put her up again.' She laid down the letter. 'It's such a shame she can't come here.'

'Well, I could go over and stop with Aggie for a day or two—' Dottie began, but Stella shook her head.

'Of course you can't! We can't push you out of your own home. Anyway, we don't know how long she means to stay. It could be for good!' She read the letter again. 'She doesn't say anything about that. Just that she's coming as soon as Fenella and her husband get back from their honeymoon. Oh, Dottie, won't it be lovely to see her again! I wonder what she plans to do. I know she'd like to have a job of some sort, but I don't suppose there's any hurry. We could spend the whole of the summer holiday together!'

'It'll be a treat to have her about the place again,' Dottie said, her round face beaming with pleasure. 'I hope she don't find anything too soon. She'd have to go away again, for certain – I can't think what there'd be for her to do in Burracombe. None of the shops needs anyone, as far as I know, and there's only the pub, or one of the big houses, and I don't think they'd suit her neither, not after the life she's led.'

'Well, let's hope we needn't think about that just yet,' Stella agreed. 'I'll go over and see Aggie straight away, and see if she can give her a room. I hope she hasn't got any other visitors coming!'

She dropped her school bag on a chair and hurried out of the cottage and across the village to Aggie Madge's house. Felix will be pleased, too, she thought, with a little less pleasure, and wished again that Maddy could be staying at Dottie's. But there really wasn't room, and Aggie Madge was the only one that Stella knew of who let her spare room. All the same, Stella found herself hoping that she had already booked in some holidaymakers. In that case, Maddy could go and stay at the Barton, where Hilary Napier had told her she was always welcome.

Felix came to the door, smiling, and before she could speak he said, 'I know why you're here. Maddy's coming! It's good news, isn't it? You must be delighted.'

Stella stared at him, feeling a little deflated. 'I am. But how did you know? Has she written to ask Aggie for the room?'

'Not really, although she does ask that. She wrote to me.' He stood back to let Stella enter, and waved a sheet of paper at her. 'I had a letter this morning. I was going to come and meet you from school, but I had to go over to Little Burracombe and see Mr Berry. He's ill again and I'm taking Sunday services for him.'

'Oh dear. I'm sorry.' Stella was diverted, but only for a moment. 'Maddy wrote to you? But why? She must know I'd tell you.'

'Well, she does write to me now and then, just a friendly letter, you know. And as I say, she did ask about the room as well.'

'Yes, I see.' Stella was silent for a moment. 'And can Aggie take her? She hasn't got anyone else coming? I know she has a couple who come quite regularly each summer.'

'They're not coming this year – they wrote a few weeks ago to let her know. So she can take Maddy for as long as she wants to stay. A long time, I hope,' he added, beaming. 'You must be hoping that, too.'

'Yes, I am.' But there was none of her previous enthusiasm in Stella's voice. 'Well, it seems as if that's all settled, then. I needn't have rushed over.'

'Of course you need! You know I'm always pleased to see you.' He looked at her uncertainly. 'There's nothing the matter, is there?'

'No. What could be the matter? I expect I'm just a bit tired, that's all. It's a busy term, what with Sports Day and the play, and the classes all thinking about moving up after the holidays. The top class will be leaving, you know, and going on to Tavistock, and then we get the babies coming in. There's a lot to think about.'

'I know there is.' He took her arm and guided her towards a chair. 'Sit down and rest for a minute. I'll get Aggie to bring us some tea. And then maybe we could go for a walk before supper.'

Stella shook her head. 'No, thanks. I've got to go back. I promised to go up to the Tozers' farm to see Val – Dottie wants her to come down for a fitting. And I've got to do something to Micky Coker's head – his ass's head, I mean – it got a bit knocked about during the rehearsal yesterday.' She was already turning back towards the door. 'So I don't need to write and tell Maddy it's all right about the room, then, do I? I expect you'll be doing that yourself.'

'I certainly will,' Felix replied cheerfully. 'And I can't wait to see her. We've got a lot to talk about.'

'Yes,' Stella said, opening the front door and stepping out on to the path. 'I expect you have.'

The June sunshine seemed a little less bright as she walked

back to Dottie's cottage. And her pleasure at the prospect of seeing her sister again had also dimmed.

Maddy arrived at Tavistock station on the one o'clock train from London, and Felix took Stella in the car to meet her. Once again, she was surrounded by a huge pile of luggage and together they hauled and squeezed it into the seats and luggage space, until there was barely room for Felix. He inserted himself into the driver's seat and grinned at them as he set off back to Burracombe, promising to return in an hour or so.

'Honestly, I could just as easily have got a taxi,' Maddy said as they walked down the steps to the town. 'It's silly for Felix to do all this ferrying back and forth.'

'He likes to think he's doing something for you.' Stella led the way to their favourite tearoom. 'He's really pleased that you're staying at Aggie's again.'

'So am I. After Dottie, she's the person I'd rather stay with than anyone in the whole world. I've promised to go and see Hilary, of course, but I don't really know her all that well. She and Stephen were away so much when Fenella and I used to stay at the Barton. Stephen's coming home on leave sometime this summer, did you know that?'

'I think I heard something about it,' Stella said vaguely. She had met Stephen Napier a few times before he joined the RAF to do his National Service but hadn't seen him now for some months. 'What are you having? Just a pot of tea?'

'Goodness, no! I'm having a full cream tea – scones and strawberry jam and lots of cream. You can't get this sort of thing at all in France, you know.' Maddy leaned her elbows on the table, rested her chin in her hands, and gazed round with satisfaction. 'It's *so* good to be back. The last few months have been just frantic, getting ready for the wedding and then sorting everything out afterwards. You know, I think I could set up in business organising big society weddings. I don't suppose there's much call for that, though.'

'There might be. Not just weddings, but big events. Someone has to do it, and I don't suppose the people who hold them are always that experienced. You'd be really good at it, Maddy.'

Maddy shook her head and laughed. 'Well, I'll bear it in mind. But I might be doing something else.' Her eyes sparkled and when Stella looked at her questioningly, she pressed her lips together and shook her head again. 'No, it's a secret at the moment – just in case it doesn't happen.'

'You're not thinking of being a fashion model, are you? Jennifer Tucker said you'd be good at that, too. Or doing the sort of job she's doing, at Dingle's. In fact, she told me she'd look out for any openings for you.'

'That's nice of her, but I don't think I'll need to do that. And it's no use looking at me like that, Stella, I'm not going to say another word. It's not just my secret, you see. Now, tell me about everyone in Burracombe. How's Val Tozer getting on with her wedding preparations? I don't suppose she needs any help with the organisation, does she?' She laughed at Stella's expression. 'I'm only joking!'

'It all seems to be pretty well sorted out.' Their tea arrived and Stella began to pour milk into the cups, hiding her disappointment. What was so secret that Maddy couldn't share it with her? And who was the other person whose secret it was? She thought of Felix and his delight at knowing Maddy was coming home, his insistence on coming to meet her, the warmth of his kiss when they'd met, and her heart seemed to weigh more heavily within her.

For the rest of the hour, Maddy chatted eagerly about Fenella's wedding, about her journey from Paris and the time she had spent in London, staying with friends. She had been to the theatre to see Moira Lister in *The Love of Four Colonels* and to Covent Garden to see *Coppelia* and *Giselle*. 'It was simply wonderful,' she said. 'I'd love to take you to see the ballet. Tell you what, we'll go to London during your summer holidays. The Festival Ballet's doing *Giselle* and *Nutcracker* at the Festival Hall in August. We could stay with my friend Alison, she's got a spare room, and I could show you round some of the sights.'

'I saw the Festival Hall last year, when we took the children on the outing to the exhibition,' Stella said. 'We didn't go in, but it looked lovely.'

Maddy nodded. 'It is. And London's looking so much better now that they're doing so much rebuilding. You'd hardly know there'd been all that bombing. Have you got any other plans for a holiday?'

Stella shook her head. 'I was just going to stay in Burracombe. There's always plenty to do there – I haven't explored half the places around. And Felix—' She stopped suddenly, then went on rather lamely, 'Felix was talking about going on walks and picnics when he has time, but I don't know if . . . ' Her voice trailed away.

Maddy looked at her thoughtfully. 'Don't you think he meant it? You do spend quite a bit of time together, don't you?'

'Well, up till now we have, but – well, there's nothing serious in it,' she said quickly. 'We're just friends, that's all.'

'I see.' Maddy split the last scone and spread the two halves with strawberry jam and clotted cream. 'Here, share this with me. So that's settled. We're going to London for a few days in August.' They heard the sound of a car drawing up outside the café and looked out through the window. 'And we'd better finish this quickly, because if I'm not much mistaken, that's Mirabelle and Felix now!'

Felix bounded over the low door of the sports car and met them on the pavement, his face alight with pleasure. 'There you are! I thought I was going to have to come in and hoik you out. Where are you going to sit? Stella, d'you want the front seat?'

'No – let Maddy sit there. I'll squeeze into the back.' She clambered into the dicky seat and the other two arranged themselves in front of her. As they drove along the main street of the market town and through the big square, with the impressive stone-built town hall on one side and the imposing church on the other, she looked at their two heads, so close together – Felix's hair a darker blond than Maddy's shimmering gold – and felt a mixture of happiness at having her sister back and sadness at the loss of something that had perhaps never really been hers. I imagined it all, she thought. The happy times we've had together, the day he kissed me, the look I thought was in his eyes sometimes – they were all in my imagination. It's Maddy he loves, and because I love them both, I just have to step back. And be happy for them.

She didn't even have to wonder what Maddy's secret was – or who the other person was who shared it with her.

Val was on her way up to the Barton when she saw Felix's sports car round the corner into the village, filled with laughing faces. She waved and the car came to a halt beside her. Maddy leaned out.

'Hello, Val. I'm back again, like the bad penny. I hear your wedding's all arranged now.'

'Yes, and you're invited,' Val said, smiling. 'I hope you'll be here then.'

'I wouldn't miss it for the world. How's everyone at the farm? And at the Barton? I must go and see Colonel Napier and Hilary sometime – Fenella's sent some presents for them.'

'I'll tell them you're on your way. Stephen's coming to the wedding, too,' Val added. 'He's getting a fortnight's leave at just the right time.'

Felix put the car into gear and they roared away again. Val

continued up the drive to the Barton and found Hilary in the stable yard, just dismounting from Beau, her bay gelding. She rode him as often as possible, frequently using him to visit tenants or parts of the estate that were more easily reached on horseback than by road.

'There's a good chap,' she said, patting his white nose. 'Can you hang on, Val, while I give him a rub-down and pop him into the field?'

'Of course. We can talk while you do that. I just saw Maddy Forsyth coming home. She was in Felix's car – he and Stella had been to collect her from Tavistock.'

'Oh, that's good. Stella will be pleased to have her sister back again. She always strikes me as being a bit lonely.'

'She hasn't been lately,' Val observed, fetching a brush from the stable. 'She and Felix have been seeing quite a lot of each other.'

'Mm.' Hilary had been the one to see quite a lot of the curate the previous year. 'He's a nice man, but I'm not sure he's serious. I think he just likes to have a girl to take about in that flashy car of his.'

Val raised her eyebrows a little. 'That sounds a bit sharp, Hil.'

'I didn't mean it to.' Hilary had finished rubbing Beau down and began to lead him through the yard. 'It's just that he got a bit keen on me last year, but he didn't seem all that upset when I turned him down. Some people are like that, you know – they think they're serious, but they're not really. I hope Stella realises that.'

'I'm sure he wouldn't do anything to hurt her,' Val said. 'Mind you, he did look rather pleased to have Maddy beside him in the car. Maybe you'd better get Stella and Stephen together while he's here, just in case her heart gets broken.'

'Oh, I think Stephen's even worse!' Hilary said with a grin. 'He seems to have a different girlfriend every week, from what he says in his letters. Anyway, it's not for us to interfere.

Have you had any news about a house or anything since I last saw you?'

Val shook her head and held the gate open while Hilary walked Beau through and unclipped the lead rein. 'No, we're staying in the charcoal-burner's cottage for the summer, but we really will need to find somewhere else then. I'm having to leave almost all my stuff at the farm as it is. Luke's waiting to hear if he's got the job in Tavistock, so if he does we'll start looking there, too.'

'Well, that wouldn't be too bad.' They watched as Beau tore up mouthfuls of grass and then collapsed in the muddiest patch he could find and began to roll, kicking his legs in the air. 'Honestly, I wonder why I bother . . . It would be a shame not to have you in the village, but Tavi would be better for you than Plymouth.'

'Oh yes. We might be able to rent one of the Bedford cottages. They're quite nice, especially the ones by the river. Luke could paint lots of river scenes from the garden! And I could carry on working at the hospital for a while. I don't see any point in giving up until I have to.'

'Nor do I. You'll need all your savings when the family starts coming. How's Dottie getting on with the dress?'

'She's nearly finished mine and it's lovely, Hil. I had a fitting yesterday and couldn't believe how beautiful it looked. And the bridesmaids are going to look sweet. Well, Patsy and June are – I'm not so sure about our Jackie!'

Hilary turned away from the gate. 'Don't be silly. Jackie's a pretty girl. And she's bright, too. She really ought to be doing something more with her life. Is she still writing to Roy Pettifer?'

'Oh yes, but I don't think she looks on him as her boyfriend any more. She's been out a few times with a boy from Yelverton. I don't think it's serious – she seems to have learned her lesson there.'

The two women looked at each other with understanding,

knowing the fright Jackie had had last year over her romance with Roy. She'd had a lucky escape, Val thought; she wasn't likely to make that mistake again.

'And how are things with you, Hilary?' she asked. 'Has your father come to terms with you managing the estate yet?'

Hilary shrugged. 'As much as he ever will, I suppose. We've come to an arrangement now – he looks after certain things and I do the rest. He can drive the car again, so he can go round and visit the tenant farmers. And listen to this – he's thinking of writing a book about the family! It started when he did that village archive last year – he got interested then and started looking out old documents, and he's decided we need a family history. It won't be published or anything, of course, but he's thinking of getting a few copies printed and bound, just for family members.'

'That's a wonderful idea,' Val said. 'It'll keep him busy and interested without putting too much pressure on him, and it'll be something he can be really proud of. How far back can you go? Did your ancestors come over with William the Conqueror or anything like that?'

'Well, they might have done, but the name Napier isn't Norman. It's what's called an "occupational" name – like Butcher or Baker.' Hilary laughed at Val's expression. 'Not nearly so upper-crust! But even the Normans must have had butchers and bakers, so who knows? Anyway, "napiers" would have looked after the table linen in a great household. The linen itself was called "napery" you see.'

'And little bits would be called "napkins"!' Val exclaimed. 'Isn't that interesting!'

'Well, I don't know if everyone will think so,' Hilary admitted. 'But I hope Dad will put it in, because I think that's the sort of thing people like to read, more than long lists and family trees and things. Anyway, as you say, it will keep him busy and be a nice thing to pass on to future generations. If there are any,' she added, pulling off her riding-boots at the door. 'Can't see much likelihood of that at present.'

'You'll meet someone one day,' Val said. 'You're bound to.'

'Maybe I won't want to. I quite like the independent life, you know. I certainly don't need a man to keep me, anyway.' Hilary led the way indoors. 'I think it'll be up to Stephen – he's got the name. Even if I did have children, they wouldn't be Napiers.' She went over to the kitchen sink and filled the kettle. 'Why the sudden interest in matchmaking? In the past half an hour you've discussed the marriage prospects of half the village – me, Stella Simmons and Maddy, anyway! It must be because you're getting married yourself. You just want to drag everyone else in with you.'

Val sat down at the table and laughed. 'I'm not dragging anyone! But maybe you're right. It's because I'm happy. I want all my friends to be happy, too.' She leaned her elbow on the table, cupped her chin in her hand and gave her friend a dreamy smile. 'I never thought it would happen to me, you know. But it did – so I don't see why it shouldn't happen to you as well.'

Hilary took a biscuit tin out of the cupboard and placed it on the table.

'You're getting maudlin. Have one of Mrs Ellis's flapjacks and talk about something sensible, for goodness' sake!'

'There is nothing,' Val said with dignity, 'more sensible than getting married and being happy. Nothing in all the world.'

Chapter Thirty-One

For Jennifer Tucker, there was nothing more important now than resolving the question about her father.

Until she had faced Jed Fisher, she felt she would never be quite sure. Although Jacob seemed to have no doubts that it was Jed who had fathered Susan's baby, she still felt that he might not know the whole truth. She knew she couldn't voice these fears to Jacob himself, who would have been even more hurt by any further slur on Susan's name, and she knew in her heart that Jed was the most likely culprit. If he were her father, she had to talk to him, even if he refused to listen.

It was the middle of June when she came out to Burracombe again. The fine weather had given away to cloud, and as the bus trundled out on to Dartmoor she saw the shadow of rain falling over Princetown. It seemed several degrees cooler when she got off at the village green, and she shivered and pulled her raincoat closer around her as she set off towards Jed's cottage.

She had written to tell Jacob that she would be coming this afternoon and he had agreed to stay indoors and be ready to come out if she needed him but otherwise keep out of the way. As she passed his window, she caught a glimpse of him inside but made no acknowledgement. Jed might be watching, too, and the situation was delicate enough without giving him cause for another tirade.

She paused for a moment before pushing the rickety gate open. The patch of front garden was an even wilder tangle of weeds now, and brambles caught at her legs as she walked up the path. She knocked on the peeling front door and waited, her heart thumping so hard that she thought he would hear it above the sound of the knocker. For a moment, she hoped he wasn't in.

A scuffling noise from inside dashed her hope. She heard a muttering, and then the sound of a bolt being drawn. The door creaked open and the old man's face peered at her with rheumy, suspicious eyes.

'What be you after?'

'I'd like to talk to you for a minute or two, if you've got time,' Jennifer said, her voice shaking a little. 'Could I come in?'

'You selling summat?' The door began to close again in her face. Jennifer put her hand against it and spoke quickly.

'No, I'm not selling anything. I just want to talk to you. It's a personal matter,' she added desperately as the door pushed against her hand. 'Please, Mr Fisher. It's about . . . it's about Susan Hannaford.'

The door stopped moving. There was a long pause. At last, the gruff voice said, 'Susan Hannaford? Her that lived up at Whinberry Cross?'

'Yes,' Jennifer said. 'She was my mother.'

The door opened a little wider. She could see his face now, grimy and unshaven. He gave her a distrustful stare.

'Susan Hannaford died years ago, and her babby with her.'

'No, she didn't. I've got her papers here.' Jennifer took an envelope from her bag. 'Her birth certificate and her death certificate. And her marriage lines,' she added.

'Marriage lines? You mean her got wed?' He seemed to be having difficulty in taking it in, and Jennifer gave the door another gentle push. 'But her died of the 'flu years ago—'

'Please let me come in,' she repeated gently. 'I don't want to talk about it on the doorstep. Please, Mr Fisher.'

For another long minute, he stood irresolute; then, to her

relief, he pulled the door wider open and turned back into the cottage. 'Come you in then, if you must,' he said brusquely, and she followed him into the disordered room, trying not to wrinkle her nose at the smell of dirt, neglect and cigarette smoke.

Jed dropped into an old, sagging armchair with cushions that looked as if they hadn't been washed for years, and waved a grudging hand towards the one on the other side of the fireplace, which was cluttered with old Woodbine packets and other rubbish. He picked up a cigarette that was smouldering in an old saucer beside him.

'You can sit down if you wants to.'

Jennifer looked dubiously at the chair and perched on the edge. For a minute or two, they regarded each other with caution, and then he said in a hostile tone, 'I seen you before. You been in next door a time or two, cooking up some fiddle or other with that old schemer Jacob Prout. What's it all about, eh? What you trying to get out of me? I ain't saying nothing.' He began to haul himself out of the chair, already waving one arm threateningly. 'You better get out. Go on with you! Out of my house!'

'Please, Mr Fisher!' Jennifer forced herself to stay where she was. 'You must listen to me. It'll only take a minute. I promise you, there's nothing going on, and I'll leave straight away if you want me to, if only you'll listen to what I have to say. Please.' She saw him hesitate, and then, terrified that he might once again order her out, or even that he might strike her, she added desperately, 'I think you may be my father!'

Jed Fisher froze. She saw his face turn pale under the grime, and his upraised arm dropped slowly to his side. His body trembled and she half rose, afraid that he might fall. Then he sank slowly back into his chair, staring at her. He took a long puff of his cigarette and then stubbed it out in the saucer.

'You think *what*?' he whispered at last, hoarsely.

Jennifer relaxed slightly against the cushions, then remembered the state of them and sat up again. Slowly, quietly, she repeated her words: 'I think you may be my father. Susan Hannaford was my mother. She left Burracombe almost thirty-six years ago, when she was pregnant.' Jennifer paused. 'She was pregnant with me.'

Jed's eyes never left her face. He shook his head slowly. 'You ain't nothing like Susan.'

'I'm like her mother. My grandmother, Liza Lilliman. Minnie Tozer says that's who I look like, and—'

'Minnie Tozer?' he broke in. 'You been discussing my private business with they Tozers?'

'I didn't know it *was* your business,' she pointed out. 'When I talked to the Tozers, I didn't know who I was looking for. I didn't even know for certain if my father came from Burracombe. And they had no idea it might be you.'

'No,' he muttered, lighting another Woodbine, 'no more they would. There wasn't nobody that knew.'

Jennifer stared at him. 'So it's true?'

'I never said that,' he countered quickly. 'I wants a bit more information from you before I starts giving any out. If Minnie Tozer didn't know nothing about me, how come you fetched up at my door?' As he stared at her, she saw comprehension dawn. 'It's that old bastard next door!' he burst out. 'That's who sent you here! Sticking his nose into my private business!' He began to get to his feet again. 'I'll tell him! I'll give him what for! I'll—'

'Mr Fisher, *please*!' Even now that she was almost certain he was her father, Jennifer couldn't bring herself to address him in any other way. 'Please, let's just talk about this. I haven't come to cause trouble—'

'If you didn't want to cause trouble, you shouldn't have come at all. What else did you think it would do but cause trouble? Didn't it never cross your mind that there'd be trouble?'

The old man was off again, but Jennifer had had enough. Rising to her feet, she stared down at him and, every word hard with anger, said, 'All right, Mr Fisher, I won't ask you again. I'll go. I wanted to talk to you, that's all. I wanted to find my father. Well, a lot of people told me I might regret it, and now I know they were right.' She half turned towards the door, tears of disappointment welling up in her eyes, and then turned back. 'But you might just remember this. It isn't me who's caused any trouble about this. The trouble started thirty-six years ago – and it was *you* who caused it. You, and nobody else!'

She held his gaze. Like a dog being scolded, he tried to look away, but had to look back. At last he said in a gruff, quiet voice, 'You'd better sit down again, maid. I thought all that was over years ago, but since you'm here, us might as well have it out. I suppose the Tozers sent you to Jacob Prout, thinking it was he, did they?' He uttered a short laugh, entirely without mirth. 'Well, I bet that put a bit of tarnish on that shiny halo of his. No wonder he ain't been out much lately – too ashamed to stick his nose out of his own front door!'

'Jacob has nothing to be ashamed of,' Jennifer said angrily. 'And if he hadn't thought, like everyone else, that my mother and I had died, he would have gone to find her and married her – even though I wasn't his child.'

'Well, *that* weren't my doing, any road,' Jed snapped. ''Twasn't me put that story out. That were *her* father, old Abraham Hannaford. Told everyone she were dead, he did, but wouldn't say a word about where she was or where she were buried. I'd have gone to see her grave if I'd knowed that.' His voice dropped and there was a sadder note in it as he added, 'I'd have took flowers.'

Jennifer gave him a curious glance. 'Were you really fond of her, then?'

'Fond of her?' He snorted. ''Course I were fond of her!

Always had an eye for Susan, I did, only she never took no notice of me, 'twas always Jacob Prout for her. Even when he first went away to war . . . I used to ask her out then. Just for a bit of a walk, or maybe some dancing in old man Tozer's barn. But no, her had to stay true to *him*.' He jerked his thumb at the wall. 'My only hope was that he might get hisself killed. Well, and why not?' he demanded as Jennifer drew in her breath. 'All's fair in love and war, ain't that right, and us *was* at war. He'd have been a hero, got his name on the village cross and all, and I'd have had Susan. Seemed fair enough to me. Anyway, it never happened, so it don't matter.' His head drooped and he seemed to sag in his chair. For a moment, Jennifer seemed to glimpse his life through his own eyes; wasted and endured, all because he had lost the girl he loved; because the one chance he might have had with her had been misused and resulted in heartbreak.

Yet Jacob had lost her, too, and Jacob hadn't wasted his life. He had overcome his sorrow, gone on to make a happy marriage. He was loved and respected throughout the village. Why had one man achieved so much and the other so little?

'I really didn't come here to upset you,' she said at last. 'If you want me to go, I will.'

He sighed and shook his head. His lank hair looked unwashed and straggly, as if he cut it himself with a knife and fork. His skin had a yellowish tinge and seemed to have tightened over his skull, as if he were shrinking. She felt a sudden regret for his poorly spent life, and wished it could have been different.

'No, you'd better stop now,' he said. 'Us can't wind back the clock. You can tell me a bit about Susan, now you'm here. When did her die, if 'twasn't back in 1917?'

'It was just a few months ago,' she said. 'Not long before Christmas. She had a happy life, I think. We were a happy family, at least until Dad – my stepfather – died in the war.'

'That were the chap she wed?'

'Yes. I was about two then. I always thought he was my father until I found the papers after she had died. Then I realised that there'd been someone else, and I wanted to find him. I wanted to meet my real father.'

'And this other bloke,' he said, the words coming out slowly and painfully, 'did he treat her right?'

'Yes, he did. They loved each other very much.'

Jed was silent for a while. Jennifer looked around the room, noting the piles of yellowing newspapers on the windowsill, the cobwebs in the corners of the dirty windows and hanging between the beams of the ceiling. Through the door she could see the scullery, little more than a cubbyhole with a deep sink, chipped and smeared with grease, a few used dishes stacked carelessly beside it. Her pity grew, mixed with disgust, but although part of her wished she had never started on this quest, another part knew that she could not abandon him now. Finding her father, she thought, seemed to bring with it responsibilites she hadn't imagined.

'And she never gave you no hint that he weren't your proper dad?'

'No. I think she brought me here once, when I was little. The first time I came, I felt as if I recognised the green and the oak tree. But that's all. And she had other children, too. I've got two sisters – half-sisters, really.'

He nodded. 'Her always wanted little 'uns, Susan did.'

Jennifer waited a moment or two, then asked, 'Can you tell me what happened, Jed? After Jacob had gone away that time? Did it start then, or were you and Susan already—'

'No!' he said with sudden vehemence. 'No, 'tweren't nothing like that. Us were friendly, like, but never no more. You got to remember, maid, I got exemption from the Army, and that didn't go down too well with folk round here. It were different in the Great War. Men were supposed to volunteer, and if they didn't, folk thought they was cowards. You got spat on in the street, and women walked about with bags full of white feathers to hand out to any young chap who wasn't in uniform. If you went to see the music hall down in Plymouth, the women singers and dancers would shout out for volunteers and chaps'd feel forced to go up on the stage and sign their names. I never tried to get out of it. I went along same as all the rest and had me medical when it first started, but the Army doctor said I had a weak chest. I didn't know if it was true or not, it'd never given me no trouble, but that's what he said. But folk didn't like it. Someone put it about that it was flat feet got me off, and I just let 'em think that, if that's what they wanted. Seemed to me, if they couldn't be bothered to listen to the truth, I wasn't bothered to tell 'em. Susan Hannaford was the only one who'd give me time of day then. Reckon she knew what it was like to be treated like an outcast.'

Jennifer listened in dismay. Nobody had given her this picture of Jed, a young man told he wasn't fit to serve his country and then treated like a coward. She tried to imagine him, returning to his village to be spat upon and handed white feathers. No wonder he had turned in on himself.

He spoke again, smoking and staring into the cluttered fireplace as if gazing down the years. 'But it weren't till after Jacob come home with his broken leg and then went back again that it got really bad. There was him, going back to fight even after he'd been wounded, and me safe at home with nothing wrong with me. Didn't matter about me chest when it come to doing a good day's work, but I couldn't put me nose out of the door without someone passing some remark, and folks even started to turns their backs on my poor old mother. I had enough of it then. Got a job over Chagford way and left the place.' He paused. 'I was on me way when I run into Susan, and her stopped to tell me how sorry she was about it all. And somehow or other, it all just seemed a bit too much for me. I'd always fancied her, but it were Jacob Prout she'd got her heart set on. *Jacob Prout!*' He spat suddenly into the fireplace and Jennifer started back, shocked. 'Couldn't do no wrong, could he! Blinking golden boy, he was – went off to war, come home a hero and then bloody went back for more. The whole village turned out to see him off, but did anyone give *me* time of day? Not them. They just turned their backs. And he'd got Susan, too. It was all too much for me,' he repeated heavily, and then, in a voice so low that Jennifer had to bend close to hear it, 'God knows I never meant to do it. I was brought up God-fearing chapel. I never meant to hurt her.'

There was a long silence. Jennifer felt the tears hot in her eyes. She thought of Jed, walking away from his home bitterly resentful, spurned by all those who had known him all his life, doomed to unfavourable comparison with his boyhood friend. She thought of him meeting the girl he loved but could never have, and she tried to imagine the sudden welling up of all his anger, his bitterness and frustration, into an uncontrollable passion. That girl was my mother, she thought. And that was the day when I was conceived.

'Well,' Jed said at last, 'now you knows. I dunno what you wants to do about it.'

'No,' she said quietly, 'neither do I.'

Chapter Thirty-Two

They talked on through the afternoon. At one point, Jed got up and made tea, but although Jennifer accepted the cup that he washed cursorily in the sink, running his fingers round the inside in an attempt to remove the stains, she let it go cold. Now that Jed had begun to talk, it seemed that he didn't know how to stop, and all the bitterness and regrets of thirty-five years poured forth in a torrent of disappointment and misery. It was as if he had held it back all this time, and now the dam had burst.

'I knew straight away I'd done wrong,' he said. 'It was in her face – in her eyes. She looked at me as if I was dirty – as if I'd made *her* dirty. I reckon that was how she felt, an' all. And nothing I could say made any difference. I told her I was sorry. I tried to tell her what it was like for me, but her couldn't understand. I don't blame her for that, mind,' he added quickly. 'How *could* her understand? Her just an innocent maid, and me – me the village outcast.' He paused, remembering the scene on the lonely moor, with the gorse in flower close by and the Standing Stones looming on the skyline. 'I said I'd see her home, but her wouldn't have it. Ran off, her did, ran off sobbing her poor innocent heart out, and left me there to think about what I'd done. I'd sinned,' he said, meeting Jennifer's eyes. 'I knew that. I'd sinned in the eyes of my Creator, and I never went in the Chapel again if I could help it. I didn't have the right.'

'But you look after the Chapel graveyard, don't you?'

'I does whatever I can,' he said, 'but it'll never be enough to make up for what I done to Susan.'

There was a short silence. Then Jennifer asked, 'Did you see Susan again after that?'

'Once,' he said. 'Her come up to me when I were working out in the fields, and told me her was going away. I'd got her into trouble, and her father had turned her out. Didn't want no more to do with her. I said I'd stand by her – offered to wed her. It was what I wanted, after all. But no, her wouldn't have that, and I knew she wanted to wait for *him*, if he ever come back.' Jed jerked his head towards the adjoining wall and gave a snort of mirthless laughter. 'I dunno what he'd have made of it, mind, taking on my by-blow. Begging your pardon,' he added, remembering that Jennifer herself was the by-blow. 'But I dare say he'd have done it, if only to spite me. Anyway, that was the way of it, off her went to Plymouth and the next thing us knew was that her'd died of the 'flu, and the babby with her. Not that Abraham admitted there *was* a babby,' he added bitterly, 'until I went and asked him straight out, and then he told me both of 'em had gone. Blasted liar!'

Jennifer could find nothing to say. The tragedy of the unkempt and unlikeable old man before her seemed greater, at that moment, than the sadness she had felt for Jacob himself. How different might life have been for him, if he had been allowed to stand by her mother? And how different for Jennifer herself? She glanced around the dilapidated cottage, realising suddenly that this might have been her home. Either of these cottages might have been her home – and either of these men, for all she would have known, might have been her father!

Jed had fallen silent, but suddenly he was overtaken by a fit of coughing and Jennifer gazed at him in alarm. This was the coughing Jacob could hear through the walls, and she wondered if he was there now, listening and thinking of her in here with his enemy. She half rose from the chair, anxious to do something to ease the racked body, but Jed waved her away and she sank back.

'That's a terrible cough,' she said, when he subsided at last and lay back in his chair, his chest heaving. 'Have you seen the doctor about it?'

Jed snorted with contempt. 'Nothing he can do! Had it for years. It's what they said at the medical – a weak chest. They were right, see. Nothing nobody can do about that.'

'Has he said so?' Jennifer persisted. She wanted to suggest that he smoked less – he had lit one Woodbine from another ever since she had come into the house – but she knew that he wouldn't take kindly to her interference. His daughter she might be, but you needed years of companionship before you could start to criticise your father's way of life. 'Have you seen him lately?'

'I never goes near him,' he growled. 'I told you, the Army said I had a weak chest and so I have. There ain't nothing doctors can do about it. It'll carry me off in the end, and I don't reckon that's all that far off now.' He started to cough again. 'Every time it gets a hold of me, I thinks maybe this time's the last,' he wheezed eventually.

'Jed, you mustn't say that! I'm sure the doctor could help. Would you like me to—'

'You keep out of it!' he rasped, and she shrank back again. 'I knows you're my girl, but that don't give you the right to come telling me what to do.' As if his own words had brought the truth home to him, he stared at her and said in a lower voice, 'My girl. That's what you are – my own flesh and blood.' His eyes, which had watered freely during his coughing bouts, grew moist again. 'I never thought to see the day.'

Jennifer swallowed her distaste. She thought of the neat cottage next door, the man who took such pride in his work and himself, and with whom she had felt such rapport. If only he could have been her father . . .

Instead, she had found this scruffy, uncombed and bitter man; yet, repellent as he was, she couldn't find it in her heart to reject him. Whatever he was now, he was her father, and had become so through real passion. Despite the dreadful ordeal he had put her mother through, Jennifer still felt an unexpected compassion for him; he had given way to a rush of feeling, made up of the rejection by the people he had grown up with, the resentment of being called a coward and compared with the shining Jacob, and the hopeless love he had felt for Susan Hannaford. It was almost impossible for Jennifer to imagine what it must have been like; she could only accept him as he was. She had set out on this quest and must take the consequences.

'I shall have to go soon,' she said quietly. 'I have to walk out to the main road to catch the bus back to Plymouth.' She realised that she had told him almost nothing about herself, and felt in her bag for a scrap of paper and a pencil. 'I'll leave you my address. If you want to get in touch—'

'Ain't you coming again, then?' He looked up at her with sudden anxiety. 'I suppose now you know who I am and what I'm like, you won't want to know me no more.'

'Of course I do!' The assurance came swiftly, without need for thought. 'You're my father, Jed,' she said, and reached out for his hand. It felt as thin, as bony and as dry as a chicken's foot. 'I know it hasn't been easy, having me come to the door without any warning. You'll have a lot to think about. But if you want me to come again—'

'You'm my maid,' he said. ''Tis only right.'

There was a short silence. Jennifer released his hand and stood up. Jed made no effort to rise, no offer to walk to the road with her; he sat with his head bowed, his cigarette packet beside him. Then he looked up again and she saw in his eyes the pleading that belied the brusqueness of his words.

'I'll come again next week,' she said softly, and turned to let herself out of the cottage.

At the gate, she hesitated, wishing she could go to Jacob. But she knew that Jed would be peering, narrow-eyed, through his own grimy window, and with a small shrug of regret she passed along the twilit lane, and set out on the walk to the main road.

As she walked by the window, she saw a flicker of movement within Jacob's cottage and knew he had been watching out for her.

Dottie Friend happened to glance out of the window, too, as Jennifer Tucker passed by. She paused for a moment and said, 'There's that young woman who's been coming out here to Burracombe lately. Didn't you say you'd met her in Dingle's?'

'That's right.' Stella craned her neck to see out past Dottie's plump figure. 'Yes, that's her. She's nice. I wonder—' She bit back the words. Jennifer hadn't asked her to remain quiet about her quest to find her father, but Stella still felt it would be wrong to discuss it, even with Dottie. Particularly as Stella had no idea as to who the man might have been. She remembered wondering if it could have been Val Tozer's father, or Jacob Prout. No, it was better to say nothing. 'I wonder where she's been at this time of the evening,' she finished lamely.

'Well, 'tis none of our business,' Dottie said comfortably, returning to her sewing. She began to fold up the blue material that Val had chosen for the bridesmaids' dresses. 'I'll have to get Patsy and June to pop in soon to try these on. Then there's only Jackie's to make and they'll be finished. I might get some material for a frock for myself then. A nice flowery print, I thought, and then it'll do for a Sunday dress for the rest of the summer.'

Stella sat down by the window. It had been a warm day and Dottie had kept it open, but once the evening started to close in and the lamps were lit, she had shut it to stop insects flying in. The room was still full of the orange-blossom scent of the philadelphus, which had thrown itself like a green-and-white coverlet over the garden fence, and the sweetness of honeysuckle from the mass of soft golden flowers that climbed up the walls of the cottage. The front garden was filled with roses, their perfume vying with the others so that it was as if the room held a huge, unseen bouquet of summer flowers. Even with the window closed, Stella could still hear the evening song of the blackbird in an apple tree across the lane, and of its rival the thrush perched on a gate-post as it waited for snails to come out of their cracks in the stone walls.

'And where have Maddy and Felix been off to today, then?' Dottie enquired, packing away the last of the shimmering blue satin.

Stella turned and looked at her in surprise. 'Maddy and Felix? Well, Maddy was talking about going to Exeter on the train, but I don't know about Felix. Wasn't he going to visit his uncle in Dorset?' Not so long ago, she thought regretfully, she would have known exactly where Felix was going on his day off, but they seemed less likely to confide in each other these days.

'Exeter?' Dottie repeated. 'No, maid, I think you've got that wrong. They went off together in that little car of his, not long after you went to school. I saw them when I was on my way to the pub, to clean through. I suppose he could have been giving her a lift to Tavistock, but they didn't go in that direction. Didn't her say nothing?'

'No, she didn't,' Stella said thoughtfully. 'I expect she just changed her mind – you know, they were probably talking over breakfast and she decided to have a day out with him instead. Or maybe he offered her a lift as far as Exeter. They're probably both home by now, anyway.'

Again, Dottie shook her head. 'The car wasn't there when I popped over to Miss Bellamy to borrow some blue Sylko. And there was no lights on in the front of Aggie's cottage.

Not that I noticed particularly,' she added quickly, in case Stella thought she was being inquisitive. 'You just see these things, don't you?'

'Yes.' Stella glanced towards the window, now a square of deepening twilight. Where had Felix and Maddy been until this time, if they'd set out at nine o'clock that morning? And why had neither of them mentioned their outing to her? 'I expect Maddy'll tell us all about it tomorrow,' she said. 'She's coming to the school to see the dress rehearsal. The play's next week, you know, on Sports Day. I hope you'll come and see it.'

'Wild horses wouldn't stop me,' Dottie declared, getting up and putting her sewing away in the cupboard. 'Now, it's a bit warm for cocoa tonight – shall us just have a glass of homemade lemonade and some of they strawberries I picked this afternoon for our bedtime snack? And then I'd better boil up what's left of the milk, or it'll turn sour overnight for certain. We can have the top of it on our cornflakes in the morning.'

Stella smiled but shook her head. 'I won't have any more now, thanks, Dottie. I'll just have a glass of cold water and go to bed. I'm rather tired.'

She filled her glass at the sink and went up the stairs. It was true that she did feel unaccountably tired, yet when she climbed into bed between the cool white sheets she could not drop off to sleep. Instead, she lay staring through the open window at the stars. Try as she might, she could not get that question out of her head: where had Maddy and Felix been all day, and what were they doing?

Chapter Thirty-Three

Basil Harvey was wondering about his curate, too. The young man was a good clergyman, but he did seem rather susceptible to female charms. I hope he's not going to get himself into a tangle over those two nice young women, the vicar thought as he went over to the church to lock up a day or two later. It would be a good thing if he could marry one of them and settle down – but which one? Perhaps that was his problem, trying to decide between them.

As he came out of the church, he noticed Jacob Prout leaning on one of the flat tombstones in the far corner, smoking his pipe. The aroma floated down through the dusk like perfumed woodsmoke, and Basil hesitated, wondering whether to approach the old man. As he paused, Jacob turned and waved his hand, and Basil climbed the sloping churchyard towards him. Scruff ran to meet him, sniffing at his trouser turn-ups.

'Evenin', Vicar.'

'Evening, Jacob. How are you these days? We don't seem to have had much time to talk lately.'

'No, to tell you the truth, I ain't been all that sociable.' The gravedigger cupped his hands round his pipe and drew on it until a tiny red spark glowed in the depths of the bowl. 'Had a lot to chew over in me mind.'

Basil murmured something and waited, knowing that if Jacob wanted to tell him what was on his mind, he would take his own time in doing so.

'It's about that young woman that came out here,' Jacob said at last. 'That Jennifer Tucker. Her come and talked to you first.'

'Yes, I remember. And then she came to you. A sad story, I thought.'

'I suppose that's one word for it. Sad for anyone to find out they'm related to that old scoundrel next door to me. Told you about that, didn't I, Vicar?'

'You did, Jacob.' He waited again, and eventually Jacob gave another snort and decided to continue.

'I had to tell her. 'Twasn't no way out of it, see. I had to break it to her that I wasn't her father, nor no kin at all when you comes down to it, and I had to tell her who was. It come as a shock, I could see that. Her'd made up her mind, see. Her didn't know what to think after that. Proper upset, her was.'

'Yes, I see.'

'Anyway,' Jacob said after another long pause, 'her come out again day before yesterday. Never come to see me, though. Didn't even knock on the door. Went in to see *him*.'

'I suppose she felt she had to,' Basil ventured.

'Oh, I knows that, Vicar. I knowed she were coming. Told her I'd be handy, just in case her wanted me, and so I was. Stopped in all afternoon, never even went out in the garden, for all it were a warm day. Stopped in and done a few jobs round the place, and just kept me ears open.'

'And did she call you? Did she stay long?'

'Stopped till it were nearly dark,' Jacob said, shaking his head in wonder. 'I saw her leave, just as the sun were going down. I thought her might come in then – might ask me to walk to the main road with her, seeing as *he* obviously wasn't going to, but her never did. Just walked past the window as if us had never said so much as a good morning to each other.'

Basil could hear the hurt in his voice and felt sorry for him. 'Perhaps she felt she couldn't come to you straight after talking to her— to Jed. And I expect she had a lot to think about.'

'I dare say her did,' Jacob said. 'Her'd only seen Jed Fisher the once, but that were enough to show her what he were like. And I don't like to think what it's like inside that dump of a cottage of his now. I'm just surprised her managed to stop there as long as her did.'

Basil was quiet for a moment, and when Jacob seemed to have nothing more to add, he said, 'I expect she'll come out and see you again, Jacob. She didn't strike me as the type of person who would drop someone she felt was a friend.'

'Maybe not. That's if her *do* look on me like a friend, after what I had to tell her.'

'That was hardly your fault. You told her the truth. It was what she was looking for.'

'That's as maybe. Her didn't know how the truth was going to turn out, did she! Her might have rather I never said nothing. After all, I could have done, couldn't I? – there's nobody but me and Jed knows the truth. I could have just let it lie.'

'I don't think you could, Jacob. I'm sure she realised that you knew. And I don't think you would have felt easy, keeping it back from her.'

'I don't feel easy now,' the old man said morosely. 'So I don't know as that would have made all that much difference.'

'Well, we can't take it back now,' Basil said. 'I think you must just wait patiently, Jacob, and hope she comes again. I'm sure she will. I don't think she'll leave matters now. She'll come and see Jed again, I expect, and this time she'll probably call on you as well.' He thought for a moment. 'I wonder if you ought to talk to Jed yourself.'

'Me, talk to that cantankerous old blackguard? And what would I have to say to him, Vicar? Wish him a happy birthday? I'm sorry to say it to you, being as I've always had respect for you, but that's daft.'

‘So it may be,’ Basil said mildly, ‘but it may come to that in the end. If you both have Jennifer’s interests at heart . . .’

Jacob sighed heavily and pushed himself away from the tombstone. His pipe had gone out and he stuffed it into his pocket and turned towards the lychgate. The sky was almost dark now, the first tiny pinpoint of a star showing in its depths, and Basil could no longer see his expression. After a moment, he spoke in a gruff voice.

‘I can’t speak for him, Vicar. Nobody can. But I can say this: I’ll always have her best interests at heart. Her might not be my daughter, not by blood, but if wishing could make her so, her would be. And her’s my Susan’s maid, and that’s the next best thing as far as I’m concerned, no matter who fathered her. By all the rights there are, her ought to have been mine.’

He walked slowly down the path, Scruff at his heels, and Basil fell into step beside him. He could feel the old man’s turmoil like an aura around him; his bewilderment, his sorrow, his struggle to understand. And he felt his heart go out to them all – to the two men who had competed all those years ago for the love of a young girl, to the girl herself and now to the young woman who was trying to pull together the ends of this heart-rending triangle.

I don’t think there can ever be a happy ending to this story, he thought, bidding Jacob goodnight and turning his footsteps towards the vicarage. It was doomed from the very moment one young man went off to war and the other stayed at home.

Jacob could, in fact, have contacted Jennifer without waiting for her to come to Burracombe again. She had given him her address in Plymouth and he knew that she worked at Dingle’s. When he went home, he took the piece of paper she’d given him from his mother’s old writing-bureau, where he kept all his bills and important papers, and turned it over between his fingers. A letter wouldn't do any harm, surely. Just a few lines, hoping she was as well as it left him now and might see her way clear to calling in next time she was out this way . . . The sentences formed in his mind as if he were writing them down. Then he sighed and put the paper away again. He would have to be patient for a little longer. Give the poor maid time to get over the shock of finding that Jed Fisher was her father. That's if she ever could!

Scruff ran over to his water bowl and drank noisily, while Flossie raised her head from her cushion and opened a sleepy eye. Jacob bent to rub her head and then went out to the scullery to make himself a cup of cocoa. The cottage was as neat and tidy as ever, and he felt ashamed of his lapse into neglect. The maid must have thought he was as bad as old Jed, he reflected, filling the kettle. He wouldn't let that happen again. Next time she came, she'd find the place spick and span, neat as a pin. He wouldn't let himself be lumped in with Jed Fisher and his slovenly ways. Not in front of Susan's girl.

When the cocoa was ready, he took it into the living-room and settled himself in his armchair to drink it. The two animals curled themselves close to him, and he felt warmed and comforted by their presence. At least I made a decent life for myself, he thought. I had a good wife, I've made myself useful, and I've been no nuisance to nobody. That's more than him next door can say.

It was very quiet in the cottage. Darkness had fallen and only one lamp cast a pool of glowing light on the table beside him. His library book lay open, ready for him to read a few pages before he went to bed, as he always did, but he was too deep in thought to pick it up just yet. He drank his cocoa, finding comfort in the hot drink, and leaned back against the cushion of his chair.

The coughing startled him from a light doze. He jerked awake, almost spilling the last few drops of cocoa, and put the cup down hastily on the table. It was Jed next door, sounding worse than ever. Jacob listened uneasily as the racking noise went on. It seemed to fade once or twice and he relaxed a little but then, as if Jed had paused only to draw painful breath for a fresh onslaught, it started again. My stars, Jacob thought, if he goes on like that he'll blow the roof off. And then, with an unexpected pang of pity, it sounds as if that hurts, and hurts bad. I wonder if I ought to do summat?

As he sat there, trying to decide what to do, the coughing stopped and there was silence. That was even worse, he thought. Suppose the old pest had had a stroke or a seizure or something and was laying there on that dirty floor of his, breathing his last? Jacob got to his feet and stood staring indecisively at the party wall. I'll have to go in, he decided at last. It's a flaming bloody nuisance, but I'll have to go and see if he's all right . . .

He was halfway to his front door when he heard a movement and then another bout of coughing. Thankfully, it didn't sound as bad this time, and after it had stopped, he heard heavy footsteps on the stairs that went up beside his own. The old misery was going to bed. Well, that was all right, then. Best place for him. If he died in the night, at least he'd die decent in his own bed, and be no further bother to anyone.

Feeling slightly ashamed of this thought but blaming Jed for being the sort of person you'd have such thoughts about, Jacob made his own preparations for bed. He took out his teeth and gave them a good scrub before putting them in a glass of clean water, where they grinned at him from his bedside table, and then he changed into his pyjamas and got into the iron-frame bed he had shared with his wife, Sarah. Then he turned out the light and settled himself for sleep.

A final cough from next door brought back the irritation he always felt at the reminder that Jed was so close, and his last thought as he drifted off was that if Jed's cough didn't get better soon, someone was going to have to do something about him.

Chapter Thirty-Four

'We ought to be thinking about this wedding,' Alice Tozer said when all the Sunday-dinner dishes had been washed up and put away. 'There's a lot to decide. So far, it seems to me the frocks are the only things anyone's given a thought to.'

'Oh, come on, Mum,' Val protested. 'You know I've booked the village hall for the reception, and Dottie and Mrs Dawe are going to help with the food—'

'Mrs Dawe!' Tom interrupted. 'What are we having, a school dinner?'

'Don't be dafter than you can help,' his sister admonished him. 'Mrs Dawe's a good cook. And Dottie's going to ice the cake, which I made weeks ago, if you remember . . .'

'Oh, was that your wedding cake? I thought you were just getting ahead with next year's Chrismas puddings.'

'If you go on like that, you won't be invited. There are three tiers—'

'I expect we'll all be in tears.' Tom ducked as Val aimed a cuff at his head. 'All right, all right, I'm sorry. Anyway, you won't need me here, will you? I don't see that I can be any help.'

'You never are, so that's no change. But you can't go away. You're going to be the chief usher.'

'What, like at the pictures?' He caught her eye and subsided, grinning. Joanna came to Val's rescue and put her hand over her husband's mouth.

'Take no notice, Val. He's overexcited because he's never been an usher before.'

'What do ushers have to do, anyway?' Jackie enquired, and answered before her brother could speak, 'I know, they say "ush" when people talk in church! Well, our Tom won't be much good at that. He never shuts up.'

Alice rapped on the table. 'Isn't there anyone here who can talk a bit of sense? Look, I've got some paper and a pencil here and I want to get a few things written down. First of all, has everyone sorted out what they'm going to wear?'

'Well, I have,' Val said. 'And so's Jackie. I don't know about the rest of you.'

'I suppose I'll have to wear my best suit,' Ted said in a tone of deep gloom. 'And a tie.'

'You'll all have to wear your best clothes. Tom, you're all right, you can wear the suit you had for your own wedding. What about you, Joanna?'

'I thought I'd borrow that marquee we used for the teas at the pageant last year,' Joanna said, looking down at her swelling figure. 'I'll be enormous by then. I don't want to be in any photographs, Val, all right?'

'You could stand at the back of the group photos and look over people's heads,' Tom said helpfully. 'Nobody will see how big you are then.'

'Well, I certainly can't stand in front!' She caught her mother-in-law's eye. 'It's all right, Mum, I am taking it seriously, honest. I'll wear that nice maternity dress I had with Robin. The one with flowers on that Tom said made me look like a municipal park.'

'You looked very nice in it,' Alice said, frowning at her son. 'What about Robin?'

'He can wear those dark-blue shorts and the little blazer I got in Plymouth. And a blue tie – I got one at the same time. He looks so grown-up, and it almost exactly matches Jackie's dress.'

'And I've got that lovely costume I bought at Sweet's,' Alice said. 'It's fuchsia-pink, so it won't clash with any of the bridesmaids. I hope Luke's mother doesn't wear the same colour.'

'When are they coming?' Ted enquired.

'The day before the wedding. I wish we could meet them beforehand and get to know them a bit, but his father can't get away before that.'

'He's very busy,' Val said. 'But you'll like them, Mum. They're really nice people.' She had been to visit Luke's family two or three times now and felt at ease in their company. 'And they're staying over the weekend. They want you to go and have lunch with them at the Bedford Hotel on Sunday.'

'Well, that seems to be all right, then.' Alice put on her glasses and peered at her list. 'Now, you've got the bellringers all sorted out, have you, Ted?'

'They're queueing up to ring. And we'm going to have the handbells, too, while the bride and groom are signing the register. Vicar suggested that and I think it's a good idea.'

Minnie nodded. 'I'm arranging some music specially.'

'Not the "Wedding March", I hope,' Tom said facetiously, and Alice sighed.

'That'll be for the organ to play. What about the flowers?'

'I'm having a bouquet of deep-red roses,' Val said. 'And the bridesmaids are having pink posies.' She and Alice had been to Tavistock the day before and looked at several different styles. 'And guess what? Miss Bellamy stopped me in the village street the other day and said I can have whatever I want from her garden for the church! Wasn't that kind of her?'

'She's a good soul,' Alice said. 'And that garden of hers is a picture. Us'll have to make time to go and see what there is a few days beforehand, Val, and then get them all picked and arranged on the Friday.' She frowned again. 'That's going to take a bit of time.'

'I could do that,' Joanna offered. 'And I'm sure Miss Bellamy will help. We can do the arrangements together.'

'That'll be a help. Now, Ted, is your Norman going to get that friend of his over Walkhampton way to do the photos? And how's our Val going to get to the church? You'll need to scrub out the pony-trap well if her's going to use that.'

'Can't she walk?' he asked. ''Tis only a footstep to the church from here.'

'Of course her can't walk! And what if it's pouring with rain? She'll look like something the cat's dragged home.' Alice threw down her pencil indignantly and everyone laughed. 'For goodness' sake! Am I the only one who's taking this wedding seriously?'

'No, of course you're not,' Val said, still giggling. 'But you don't need to worry about the trap. Hilary says I can borrow their gig, the little black one that Mrs Napier used to go to church in. And the bridesmaids can have the bigger pony-trap. She's going to have them all polished up and decorated with flowers and ribbons.'

'Well, isn't that kind of her!' Alice exclaimed. 'That'll look lovely, Val. Well –' she looked at her list again '– I reckon that's just about it, don't you? I'll talk to Dottie and Annie Dawe about the food. It'll be ham salad, and some nice puddings for afters. Ted, you'll need to sort out the drinks – sherry for when people arrive, and then cider or lemonade with the meal. And, Tom, you can make yourself useful and see to the chairs and tables. Us'll need plenty of white sheets for tablecloths, and plenty of china and glasses too – I'll have to see who can lend us some. There's only a few old cups and saucers in the hall cupboard, for teas.'

'It's time they got crockery and stuff down there permanent,' Minnie observed. 'People are going to want to use it more for weddings and parties.'

'Perhaps some of the money they raise at the Summer Fair could be used to buy some,' Val suggested.

'Well, perhaps it could, but that's for the committee to decide and it won't help us with the wedding.' Alice drew a line on her sheet of paper. 'Now, does everyone know what they've got to do?'

The family nodded and scraped back their chairs, eager to bring the meeting to a close. Tom pulled on his boots and Joanna went to fetch Robin from his afternoon nap, ready to take him for his Sunday-afternoon walk. Ted disappeared into the front parlour, where he would pretend to read the *Sunday Express* and fall asleep within minutes. Jackie slipped out to meet some of her friends, and Val wandered away to find Luke, who had talked of going somewhere along the riverbank to find a new subject for a painting.

'It's going to be a lovely wedding,' Minnie said to Alice as she stumped to the back door to sit in the garden. ''Tis going to be a pleasure to see our Val settled at last.'

'Yes, it is.' Alice followed her mother-in-law with some cushions to lay on the wooden bench where she would sit and enjoy the sunshine for an hour or so. 'I don't mind telling you, a year ago I was wondering if she would ever be really happy again. But now, you only got to look at her face to see that she's found the right man. I just hope they don't move too far away, that's all. 'Tis a problem knowing where they're to find somewhere to live.'

'You don't want to worry about that,' Minnie said, leaning back and closing her eyes. 'Something'll turn up. Something always turns up, in the end.'

Alice looked down at her. Minnie was well into her eighties now and had lived through two world wars, as well as the Boer War. She had seen enormous changes in the world, some good and some bad. She had seen tragedy in her own life and the lives of others. Yet she could still, on this quiet Sunday afternoon, sit in the sunshine in her own garden and say that 'something would turn up'.

Us ought all to learn from her, Alice thought as she went indoors to fetch a bit of sewing to do. Worrying never solves anything. If you can't do nothing about it, just let it be. Something will turn up, in the end.

Luke had walked quite a long way before Val found him at the old stepping-stones, almost a mile from the village. He was sitting on a moss covered rock, his easel propped up in front of him, looking thoughtfully at a large gorse bush that was overhanging the tumbling water. The rocks in the stream glittered in the sunlight, and as Val came round the bend she saw the brilliant-blue flash of a kingfisher.

'You've frightened him away,' Luke said, putting out an arm to draw her against his side. 'Never mind, he'll be back if we keep quiet. He's got a nest over there – see the hole in the bank?'

'It could be a she, then,' Val said, settling herself on the rock beside him.

'Could be. But they both look after the nest and the young. Look – there he is again. Or she,' he added with a grin.

They both watched as the bright bird flew like an arrow up the stream and came to rest on a low branch. It was carrying two small fish in its beak, head to tail, and turned its head, peeping from side to side to make sure it wasn't observed, before diving into the hole Luke had pointed out. A moment or two later, it emerged, minus the fish, and shot off again.

'Oh, how lovely!' Val exclaimed softly. 'It's got babies. Or maybe the other parent's inside, sitting on eggs. Did you know it was here, Luke?'

'I had an idea there was a nest the other day. I've walked along this stretch of the bank quite a bit lately and I noticed a lot of coming and going. I hope they'll get used to seeing me here – I want to paint that gorse bush over the river. The sun catches the gold of the flowers and the ripples in the water so well.'

'It'll be a lovely picture,' she agreed. 'Oh, Luke, I wish you didn't have to get an ordinary job. Your paintings are so good, you shouldn't be wasting your time doing anything else.'

'It's no bad thing to be teaching other people to paint, though. I owe my own teachers a lot – I think it'll be rather satisfying to pass some of it on.'

'Mm. I suppose so.'

'And I'll still have time to paint. Evenings and weekends, and holidays.'

'I know. But it's not just that.' She slid down to the cushiony moss and leaned her back against the rock. 'Look at what you've been doing this week – coming out here at all times of the day to see just when the sun catches the gorse and the water in just the right way. You won't be able to do that if you have to be in school in Tavistock all week.'

'I'll be able to bring home a proper wage, though,' he said, and bent to kiss the top of her head. 'That's important, too.'

'A wage-slave! That's what you'll be. I want you to be *free*, Luke, as an artist should be.'

Luke was silent for a moment. 'It's not going to be a real problem to you, is it? Me being a "wage-slave", I mean? You won't think less of me?'

'Of course I won't!' She spoke more loudly than she had intended, and the kingfisher, which had just come to perch on its branch again, flew off in alarm. 'Oh, I'm sorry – I didn't mean to shout, and now I've frightened him away. Don't take any notice of me, Luke. I'll love you whatever you do, you know that. In fact, I'm very proud that you're prepared to give up your way of life because of me. I just wish you didn't need to do it.'

'Ten years ago,' he said, 'men were having to go to war, and their wives were wishing they didn't need to do it. Going to Tavistock to teach children to draw and paint doesn't seem all that terrible to me.'

'No, it isn't, when you put it like that,' Val said soberly. 'Look, he's coming back. I'll be quiet and watch, while you start your painting.'

They were still there an hour later, Val half asleep in the sunshine while Luke stared first at the scene before him and then at the painting that was taking shape on his canvas, when Felix and Maddy came along the path. They stopped when they saw Luke and Val, and sat down on the rocks to watch the kingfisher and talk for a few minutes. When they went along their way, Val and Luke looked at each other.

'And what do you suppose is going on there?' Val enquired. 'I thought Stella was rather keen on the curate.'

'So did I.' Luke frowned uneasily. His friendship with Stella the year before had left him with a protective feeling towards the young schoolteacher. 'I hope she's not going to get hurt.'

'Felix isn't the type to play fast and loose,' Val said thoughtfully. 'And I'm sure Maddy wouldn't do anything to hurt her sister. But people don't always fall in love to order, do they? And none of us can help what we feel.'

Their eyes met as they thought of their own story, begun so many years ago when passions had run high and falling in love had certainly not been 'to order'. And then Luke shrugged and said, 'There's nothing we can do about it, anyway. They'll have to sort out their own lives – we've got our own to worry about.' He started to put away his paints. 'Come on. Let's pack up now and walk home the long way round. Your mother's not expecting us for tea just yet, is she?'

'Not today. She's just putting out sandwiches and cakes and things for everyone to come and have whenever they're ready.' Val stood up and stretched her arms above her head. 'It's such a lovely day, it seems a crime to go home at all. Let's stay out all night!'

Luke, kneeling on the ground to fasten the straps of the rucksack he used to carry his painting gear, looked at her and felt his heart quicken. He stood up and took her in his arms.

'Not long now, my darling,' he murmured into her hair, 'and we'll be able to stay out all night, every night. We can sleep under the stars for the rest of the summer, if that's what you want. I don't mind what we do – or where I work – so long as we can be together.'

Felix and Maddy strolled slowly on along the riverbank. They had had Sunday lunch at Dottie's, but when Felix had suggested a walk, Stella had shaken her head and said she had some work to do for school the next day. They'd come out alone, saying they'd be back by five as Felix was taking evensong in Little Burracombe.

'It's a shame Stella wouldn't come,' Felix remarked. 'It's too nice an afternoon to be stuck indoors. She's working too hard, you know.'

'It's the play,' Maddy said. 'It's getting close now and she's so anxious that it should go well. I know it's only a short scene, but Shakespeare isn't easy for young children. I've told her they ought to try something simpler next time – a pantomime or something.'

'Miss Kemp will never agree to that. They always do a nativity play for the Christmas term. Poor Stella! If this one's a success, she'll get roped in for that, too. Mind you,' he added thoughtfully, 'I wouldn't mind trying a pantomime with some of the older villagers. I was in an amateur-dramatics group myself once, and it was great fun. Mrs Warren started one a while ago, but they haven't actually done anything yet.'

'That's a good idea. We could do plays as well.' Maddy turned to him eagerly, and then shook her head. 'Except that we might not both be here! Oh bother.'

'Well, who knows where we'll be?' They looked at each other and laughed. 'Shall we tell her soon?' he asked.

'I think we'd better!' Maddy giggled. 'She's beginning to suspect something. I hope she'll be pleased about it.'

'Of course she will,' Felix said. He put his arm round Maddy's shoulders and gave her an affectionate squeeze. 'All Stella wants is for you to be happy. You know that.'

'I know. All the same . . . she might not be happy about me not being in Burracombe. Still, I never said I'd stay here for good. And she knows I've been restless since Fenella got married.'

'It's all going to work out beautifully,' he said with confidence. 'I'm just glad I was here when you came home again. It's been a lovely few weeks, Maddy.'

'For me, too,' she said, and they stopped. Maddy turned to him and stood on tiptoe to give him a kiss. 'Thank you, Felix.'

'What for?' he asked in surprise, and she laughed again.

'For – oh, for everything. For just being here, on this lovely afternoon. For helping me to be happy . . .'

Chapter Thirty-Five

'I been thinking about writing to you,' Jacob said. 'I weren't sure you'd be coming out to Burracombe again. Not after you'd been in next door.'

'Of course I've come again,' Jennifer said. 'He's my father. And I wanted to see you again, too.'

Jacob gave her a sharp look. 'That true, is it? Well, I been wanting to see you as well. I sort of hoped – well, even though things haven't turned out the way either of us might have liked them to, I hoped us might keep in touch.'

'I hope so, too,' she said quietly. They were sitting in Jacob's front room, drinking tea. 'That's why I've come in to see you first. I didn't want you to be upset that I hadn't called in the last time I was here. It wasn't because I didn't want to. It just – well, it didn't seem right, somehow. And I had a lot to think about.'

'I'm sure you did, after being in that dump,' he said grimly. 'Mind you, I ain't been in there meself for years, not since the old lady died, but I can guess what 'tis like. You only got to look at the front window. I don't suppose he's done any cleaning since his poor old mum passed over.'

'I don't think he has,' Jennifer admitted. 'I don't think he's had the heart for it.'

'Heart! That old misery ain't got no heart!' Jacob bit back the words and shook his head. 'Begging your pardon, maid, seeing as he'm your flesh and blood, more's the pity, but it's true. Never cared a tuppenny damn for nobody except hisself, that's Jed Fisher all over.'

'I don't think that's quite true,' Jennifer said gently. 'You were good friends when you were younger, weren't you?'

'When us was tackers and didn't know no better.'

'And when you were older – when you were young men.'

'We got along all right,' he allowed grudgingly. 'Most of the time, anyway.'

'There must have been something for you to like, then.'

'What *is* all this?' he demanded. 'Got you on his side, has he? Even when you seen what he's like and how he lives? Even after what he done to your own mother?'

'Well, I wouldn't be here if he hadn't done it,' Jennifer said, and then added quickly, 'Not that that makes it right. But I'm not sure that you really understand—'

'There isn't nothing to understand! He took advantage of her – there's no other word for it. Well, there is, but 'tis not one I'd want to say with a lady present. And he done it when he knowed her were upset because I'd gone away again, and already been wounded once. *In action*,' Jacob added fiercely. 'Which was more'n he was ever likely to be, with his flat feet or whatever he got the medical men to say was wrong with him. Flat feet!'

'It wasn't flat feet. It was a weak chest, and—'

'I don't care what it was!' Jacob was on his feet now, his mouth working with rage. 'He stopped at home when better men went off to fight for their country, and he took advantage of my Susan when her was upset and got her into trouble so that old bully of a father of hers chucked her out, and all these years I thought her was dead, and the babby along with her. And that was all Jed Fisher's doing, and he can cough his weak chest inside out for all I cares, and next time I hears him I'll just stop in here and listen, and be glad of it! I *will*!'

Jennifer stared at him, shocked, and after a moment or two he sat down, breathing heavily and looking shamefaced. 'Well,

I don't suppose I will, not when it comes to it,' he muttered after a while. 'I was in two minds whether to go over to him the other night, to tell you the truth. I thought he was going then. I couldn't just listen to him die, in all Christian charity I couldn't.'

'No,' Jennifer said, still shaken by his outburst, 'I don't think you could.'

'What I don't understand,' Jacob said after another pause, 'is why you'm sticking up for him. You say he'm your father, and I know that's true, but that don't mean you got to have any loyalty towards him – not the way it come about. Do it?'

'Well, it depends how it came about, doesn't it?' Jennifer said, feeling her way. 'I know what you believe happened, but—'

'He haven't managed to persuade you she done it willingly!' Jacob burst out. 'Not my Susan! Because I'll never believe that, not if you sits there for a hundred years!'

'No, I don't think it was like that. But I do believe he truly loved her. He told me he'd always been fond of her, but it was you she wanted—'

'That's true enough. Even he couldn't deny that.'

'He doesn't. That's what I'm saying. He always knew it was you—'

'And he was jealous.'

'Well, probably he was. But that wasn't—'

'So why did he do it, then?' Jacob burst out again. 'Why did he have to do that to an innocent maid like my Susan? I had more respect for her than that – why couldn't he?'

Jennifer didn't reply at once. Then she said, 'If I tell you what he said, will you listen to me? Really listen? And try to imagine what it must have been like for him, how you would have felt yourself, in his place?'

'I wouldn't never have *been* in—' Jacob began, then caught the look in her eye and sank back into his chair. 'Oh, all right, then. Go on. I'll listen – but don't expect me to be sorry for him, because I won't. He don't deserve it.'

Jennifer took a deep breath and began to tell Jed's story. She told it as briefly as possible, knowing that Jacob would resent any attempt to guide his thoughts and emotions towards sympathy for Jed. When she came to the end, she said simply, 'I think he's lived with a bad conscience ever since. I think that's why he's gone the way he has, and wasted his life.'

Jacob was silent for a long time. At last, he said, 'I dare say you'm right about that. A bad conscience'll turn anyone sour. But look at it this way, he had plenty to feel bad about.'

'Yes,' she said. 'He did.'

When she left Jacob at last and went next door, Jennifer was struck even more by the contrast between them – the one so neat and tidy, the other so neglected. It seemed to epitomise two very different attitudes to life itself, and she wondered whether Jed would have ended up like this if he had not been rejected for the Army, or if he had not had that encounter with her mother. He might have been killed and had his name engraved on the village war memorial as a hero, she thought. And either way, I would never have been born.

Jed opened the door and peered at her in his usual suspicious manner. His skin looked even more sallow, she thought, and the dull colour had even seeped into his eyes. He seemed to have lost weight even in the short time since she had seen him last.

'Hello, Jed,' she said quietly. 'Can I come in?'

'I s'pose you'd better,' he said, turning back into the dim recess of his room, where even the afternoon sunlight had difficulty in bringing light through the dirty windows. 'I didn't think you'd bother coming again.'

'I said I would.' She sat down gingerly on the edge of the armchair and began to unpack the shopping-bag she had brought with her. 'I thought you might like a few bits and pieces. Some biscuits, a nice Victoria sponge, a packet of tea, half a dozen oranges, a few bananas and a piece of cheese. I hope you like the tasty sort.'

He stared at her. 'All that's for me?'

'I didn't know what you liked,' Jennifer said apologetically. 'Just tell me if there's anything you'd rather have. Oh, and I've got something for your cough.' She pulled a bottle of dark liquid from the depths of the bag. 'How is it now?'

The old man shrugged. 'Same as always. Chemists' jollop ain't going to make no difference to that. I've had it too long.' As if to prove his point, he began to cough and Jennifer watched in alarm as he heaved and retched, the blood suffusing his face and eyes. When she went to help him, he waved her away angrily, and when the attack was over, he lay back in his chair, panting.

'I really think you should see the doctor,' she said at last, when he was able to take notice again. 'That's more than just a cough.'

'And what would he do, eh? Put his stethyscope on me chest and tell me to take more care of meself. He can't do nothing for what I got.' His thin, claw-like hand was spread across his chest and Jennifer's anxiety grew.

'Why? What do you think it is?' The dreaded word 'tuberculosis' passed through her mind. In the conditions in which Jed lived, any germs could multiply. 'Jed, I'm sure he could do something. You ought to be in hospital—'

'I ain't going to no hospital!' His voice rose, but she realised that even when he shouted, he lacked the strength she had heard when he'd abused Jacob, the first time she had ever seen him. 'Wire me up to a lot of machines, that's what they'd do, and I'd die just the same. Go into hospital and you never come out again, not when you're like me.'

He might very well be right there, Jennifer thought, but she didn't say so. Instead, she said gently, 'Would you like me to make you a cup of tea? You could have a piece of sponge cake with it – I made it myself.'

He stared at her, and she realised that he had probably not had a cup of tea made for him for years. Her eyes suddenly wet, she got up and took the groceries out to the cluttered scullery. I ought to have brought some cleaning things as well, she thought, filling the rusty kettle, but he might have been offended. It can't be good for him to live like this, though. He's killing himself.

'Have you got any milk?' she called, not liking to open cupboard doors without his permission. He might live in dreadful conditions, but he still had a right to his privacy.

'In the larder. By the back door.'

The larder was surprisingly large and had its own window, with a deep sill. As might be expected, it was cluttered and untidy, but there was an array of tinned foods on the shelves and a jug of milk on the windowsill. Jennifer found a bag of sugar and opened her own packet of tea. The teapot was full of swollen leaves, and as she took it outside to empty it, she wondered if he simply put in more each time he made a fresh pot, without bothering to tip out the last lot. Either that or he liked it extremely strong.

While she was waiting for the kettle to boil, she surreptitiously wiped the kitchen sink, but it was too greasy to benefit much. It wants some really hot water and carbolic, she thought. In fact, that's what the whole place needs, including the man who lives here!

At last the tea was ready and she carried it in. She had found a dinner plate for the sponge cake, and two smaller plates, and after she had cleared a space on the table, she cut a couple of slices of cake and gave one to Jed. He looked at it as if he'd never seen cake before.

'You made this for me, special?'

'Yes. I hope the crumbs don't make you cough,' she added anxiously. 'What sort of cake do you like best?'

'My mother used to make a good fruit cake,' he said, lifting the slice of sponge and turning it this way and that, as if he wasn't entirely convinced that it was real. 'Mind, I dunno if me teeth would stand up to it now. She used to put a lot of nuts in it.'

'I could make you one without nuts,' Jennifer offered, and he gave her one of his narrow looks.

'Why? Why should you do that? Hoping I've got a fortune to leave you?'

'Of course not! I don't want anything. I just want to do something for you. You're my father.'

'More's the pity,' he grunted. 'I dare say that's what you thought, anyway, when you found it 'twas me and not that Holy Joe next door.'

In all honesty, Jennifer couldn't deny this, so she said, 'It's best to know the truth. I think so, anyway.' She paused and went on tentatively, 'Are you sorry I found you, Jed? Would you rather I hadn't come at all?'

He took a noisy slurp of tea. 'Never thought about it. You come, and that's all there is to it. No use being sorry.'

'I hoped you might be pleased,' she said a little wistfully, but he shrugged. Perhaps, she thought, he had forgotten to feel any emotion other than bitterness, and she remembered her comment to Jacob about a 'wasted life'. Whatever the rights and wrongs, it was a sad thing to see.

She stayed with him for over an hour, telling him about her life with her mother and her sisters and asking him about Burracombe. He seemed to listen to her stories, but talk of his own home village only brought out more bitterness and she veered away from it. He had another coughing fit just before she left, and once again she tried to persuade him to see the doctor.

'I told you, he won't do me no good. Only give me more medicine, and I won't take it, I tell you that now. It tastes horrible.'

'I'm sure he could help you more than that,' she began, but he shook his head.

'He'd send me to hospital. I told you, I'm not going to no hospital. I'd rather die!'

At least you'd die clean and in comfort, she thought wryly, but all she said was, 'He might not do that. He could send in the district nurse to look after you.'

'And I know what her'd do, as well. Clean me up, that's what. I don't want no district nurse round here, telling me I got to have a bath and clean the place. I'm all right as I am.'

Jennifer saw that it was no use arguing, and left it, but as she walked back through the village she made up her mind that she wouldn't let it go. She couldn't pretend that she felt any love, or even affection, for Jed, but she did feel a tie that couldn't be ignored. He was her father, and couldn't be left to cough himself into his grave with nobody to care for him.

Jacob wasn't in his cottage as she walked by, but she heard the church bells ringing and remembered that he was a ringer. He was probably in there now, pulling on his rope; a part of the village community and its activities that Jed had never been.

Compassion grew within her heart for the life that had been so wasted – and yet had given her her own life. It was very hard to understand, but knowing what she must do was simple enough.

Her quest had been to find her father, but there was another side to this. For Jed Fisher, his 'wasted life' had brought him a daughter.

Chapter Thirty-Six

'Why don't we go over to Little Burracombe with Felix for evensong?' Maddy suggested as they sat round Dottie's table having their tea. It was salad, with the first crisp lettuce, radishes and spring onions from Dottie's vegetable patch and hard-boiled eggs from Constance Bellamy's hens, which were laying at the moment as if they'd been charged with sustaining the entire population of the village. 'Mr Harvey won't mind, and it'll make a nice walk.'

'That's a good idea,' Felix said eagerly, and as Stella began to shake her head he added firmly, 'You're to come as well! You've been stuck indoors all afternoon.'

'Yes, you can't possibly have any more work to do,' Maddy agreed, and Dottie joined in with her own opinion.

'You need some fresh air. You'm looking proper washed-out.'

'Well, thank you!' Stella said with a laugh. 'All right, I'll come. It's a nice idea.' But she still sounded less than enthusiastic, and the others looked at each other with some concern.

'You're not feeling ill or anything, are you?' Maddy asked. 'Dottie's right, you do look a bit pale.'

'I'm fine, honestly. It's just that this is such a busy term, what with the play and Sports Day and everything. And I have to do reports on all the children in my class who will be moving up into Miss Kemp's next term, as well as the ordinary end-of-term reports. And then there's—'

'You definitely need some time off,' Felix interrupted. 'So that's settled – we're walking over to Little Burracombe as soon as we finish tea . . .

'It'll be a good thing when this term's over,' he added later as they set out for the footpath down to the Clam. 'You need a break. I'm glad Maddy's taking you to London for a few days.'

'Yes, I'll enjoy that,' Stella said tepidly.

The other two glanced at each other. Stella caught the tail of their glance and felt her misery deepen. What had they talked about that afternoon? she wondered. They'd come back with bright eyes, wind-blown hair and the air of a secret. Whatever it was – and she thought she could guess – she wished they would come out with it soon. The sooner she knew the truth, the better, even though she felt certain she wasn't going to like it.

They must never know how I feel about it, she told herself. I've got to keep it to myself for the rest of my life. They mustn't ever know how unhappy they're making me . . .

Little Burracombe, sitting close to the river on the other side of the valley, was not much more than a handful of cottages clustered round its ancient church. Like Burracombe itself, it had once been a mining village and there had been almost as many pubs as houses, but now there was only the Rose and Crown, almost next door. The vicarage was on the other side and Felix knocked on the door to let Mrs Berry know he had arrived.

'Oh, hello, Felix,' she said, and smiled at the two sisters. 'How nice of you to come. John's rather poorly today, I'm afraid – I won't ask you to come in after the service, if you don't mind.' She looked anxious, despite her smile, and Felix laid a hand on her arm.

'Don't worry about that, Mrs Berry. I wouldn't want to disturb him. Just let him know that I'm here, and if there's anything he needs to know about, I'll slip in and tell you afterwards. Otherwise, we'll just go straight home.' As the three of them went back down the garden path, he said, 'I'm afraid the poor old man's fading away. He looked like a ghost the last time I saw him – almost transparent against his pillows. He doesn't seem to be suffering much, though, which is something to be grateful for.'

'Poor Mrs Berry,' Stella said. 'I wonder what will happen to her if he dies? Will she have to leave the vicarage?'

'Probably, but I don't think that'll be a problem. They've got a niece in Ashburton – she'll probably go and live there. She talks about it quite practically, but it's obviously going to be very sad for her to lose him.'

They went into the church. Felix walked round to the vestry while Stella and Maddy found seats near the back. Quite a few people had already gathered for the evening service and there were nods and smiles from those that knew them. The church door was left open and they could hear birdsong rising above the soft notes of the organ. When Felix emerged from the vestry, clad in his white robes, a shaft of evening sunlight beamed through the west window and turned his hair to the rich gold of ripe corn.

Stella knelt to say her prayers, and thought about the happy times she and Felix had enjoyed together – the walks and the picnics, the drives in Mirabelle. It seemed that they were about to end – in truth, they already had ended. There would still be walks, picnics and drives, but it would be no longer she and Felix alone. It would be Felix and Maddy, with Stella invited to join them only some of the time. Felix would still be a part of her life – but as a brother; not, as she had begun to hope, as a lover and a husband.

I've got to stop thinking about myself, she told herself, and think about them. I love them both and I always will. I want them to be happy.

Perhaps here, in the small, quiet church with the organ

sounding softly in her ears and the song of the birds drifting in on the scented air, she would find the strength she needed.

'Let's sit here by the river for a while,' Felix suggested. 'It's too nice an evening to go back yet.' He led the way along the riverbank to where a large slab of rock made a seat large enough for the three of them, and sat down in the middle. The two girls sat on either side of him and they watched the water break into showers of glittering spray over the rocks.

'We used to come swimming down at the Clam,' Maddy observed. 'There's a deep pool quite near the bridge, but it can be dangerous. I remember a little boy being drowned once in a whirlpool, after we'd had a lot of rain.'

'Oh, how sad. Were you there?'

'No, and Dottie never let me go swimming there again. Everyone was very upset.'

'So they would be.' Stella stared at the water, which had looked so beautiful a moment ago but now appeared threatening and treacherous, and Felix gave her a quick glance and squeezed her arm.

'It's no use letting yourself grieve over everyone who's ever died, Stella. The Reverend Berry, small boys – it's always sad, but it's natural as well. You know that.'

She nodded, but could find nothing to say. Despite her prayers and despite the beauty of the evening and the company of the two people she loved best, she felt shadowed by sadness. I'm just a selfish person, she thought bitterly, thinking of myself all the time. It's no wonder Felix loves Maddy instead of me.

'Shall we tell her now?' Maddy said suddenly, and Stella turned her head. Her sister's face was alive with excitement, and Stella felt a sudden sinking of her heart. The moment she had half dreaded, half longed for, if only so that she could know the truth, had arrived.

'I think now would be a very good time,' Felix said softly. 'She knows there's something in the wind, anyway.'

'Weren't you ever told that it's rude to say "she"?' Stella asked, rather more tartly than she'd intended, and Maddy laughed.

'Mummy would have said that. She'd have said, "*She's* the cat's mother"! Wouldn't she, Stel?'

Stella felt a sudden pricking of tears. The occasions on which she and Maddy reminisced about their childhood and their parents had brought them closer together, but they hadn't yet reached the stage of bringing them into the conversation casually. She stared at the rock beneath her hand and didn't answer, and after a moment Felix went on.

'You tell her, then, Maddy. It's your news, really.'

'Only because of you.' But Maddy leaned over and touched Stella's hand. 'It's good news, Stella. At least, I hope you'll think so.'

'I'm sure I will.' Stella looked up and smiled at her sister. 'Come on, then. Tell me what it is – as if I couldn't guess.'

'You can't. Not in a month of Sundays.' Maddy took a deep breath and then said, 'I've got a job!'

The news was so unexpected that Stella didn't take it in at once. She stared at the bright face, then looked at Felix as if asking him to interpret. Both he and Maddy burst out laughing at her expression and she felt a momentary irritation.

'You're teasing me,' she said. 'What do you mean, a job? What sort of job?'

'I don't know why you're so surprised,' Maddy said, pretending to be hurt. 'You're not the only person who can earn her own living, you know. Anyway, you knew I was looking for something.'

'I know, but I thought—' Stella stopped herself before she could say what she'd thought. Whatever this job was, it didn't mean her suspicions were wrong. 'Well, what is it, anyway?'

'I'm going to be a secretary,' Maddy said importantly. 'I'm going to be secretary to the Archdeacon of West Lyme!'

Stella stared at her. 'The Archdeacon of West Lyme? But—'

'My uncle,' Felix said. 'You knew he was an archdeacon, didn't you? I'm sure I've mentioned it.'

'Practically everyone in your family is an archdeacon or a bishop or vicar of somewhere,' she told him. 'Is this the one in Dorset?'

'Well, since West Lyme is in Dorset . . .'

'All right! You can stop laughing, both of you. It's just come as a surprise, that's all.' She looked at their faces. 'You both look very pleased with yourselves. I suppose this is why you've been making all these secret trips to Dorset . . .'

'Only two,' Maddy protested.

'Well, it seems like more. And you went to Exeter one day.'

'We did meet him there as well,' Felix admitted. 'He was coming to the cathedral for a special service and it seemed like a good opportunity for me to introduce him to Maddy. I knew he needed someone, and I thought she'd be ideal, with all her experience with Miss Forsyth. And he thought so, too.'

'Being companion to an actress is a bit different from being an archdeacon's secretary,' Stella said.

'Oh, I don't know,' he said thoughtfully. 'The Church and the theatre have quite a lot in common . . . But it's mostly all the social arrangements – travel and meetings and so on – that he needs Maddy for. There's not much difference there.'

Stella was still struggling to come to terms with the news. 'But where will you be living? West Lyme's quite a long way away.'

'Not all that far. You can get there in a couple of hours by train. We'll be able to visit each other. You can even come to stay.'

'To stay? Have you found lodgings?'

Maddy shook her head. 'I'll be in the Archdeacon's house.

It's quite big – I'll have my own little flat, with a spare room for visitors. You can come as often as you like.'

Stella looked at Maddy's bright face and reached across Felix to take her hand. 'I'm really pleased,' she said warmly. 'It sounds ideal and I'm sure you'll be good at the job. And as long as you're not too far away . . .'

'I'd never go too far away from Burracombe,' Maddy said softly. 'There's too much here to make me want to go very far.'

As Stella lay in bed that night, looking at the night sky through her open window and breathing in the scented air, she tried, as she always did last thing at night, to organise her thoughts about the day that had just passed.

It doesn't mean they're not in love, she thought. Just because Maddy's going to be living in West Lyme . . . It's only a couple of hours on the train – or by sports car . . . And she's going to be working for Felix's uncle – living in his house . . . They can still see each other often . . . It doesn't mean I was wrong . . .

Unable to lie still, she got out of bed and sat by the window, gazing out into the night. The moon was rising over the horizon, shedding a cool pale light over the rolling moor and throwing the Standing Stones into dark silhouette. Beneath her, the white flowers of the philadelphus bush gleamed like snow and the scent mingled with that of the honeysuckle on the wall and a cluster of tobacco plants just below. The hollyhocks had begun their annual climb towards the roof of the cottage, and as she leaned out of the window she heard the hoot of an owl and saw the pale glow of its wings, like a giant moth, drift across the garden.

This time last year, she thought, I was happy here, living in Dottie's cottage and getting towards the end of my first year at the school. All I wanted to make my life complete was to find my sister again. It was my one dream, and it came true.

And if Maddy and Felix are really in love, they'll stay in my life. I'll have a brother as well as a sister.

She climbed back into bed, once again reproaching herself for her selfishness.

What right did she have to feel sad now?

Chapter Thirty-Seven

'I got the doctor off me own bat,' Jacob said. 'I couldn't stand it no longer, hearing him coughing and hawking in here. It sounded too bad. I couldn't have lived with meself if he'd died in here all by hisself, and nobody to give him a bit of comfort, the old misery.'

'You did the right thing,' Jennifer said. She was standing with Jacob in Jed's living-room, while Charles Latimer was in the room overhead. Jacob had telephoned her at Dingle's and she'd left work straight away and caught the next bus, arriving within an hour.

'How long has the doctor been here?'

'Come five minutes before you did. He were out on his rounds when I went up to the house, or he'd have been here sooner. I rung you as soon as I'd been there and then come straight back.' Jacob shook his head. 'He's in a poor way, mind. Didn't make no fuss when I told him he oughter be in bed. Well, it shows how bad he is that he even let me through the door.'

'Oh dear.' Jennifer looked at the chair she usually sat in, wanting to sit down now but thinking of her business suit. 'I wonder what the doctor will say. Jed hates the thought of going to hospital.'

'Well, none of us wants to finish up there,' Jacob said, as if it were prison. 'I don't see what else he can do, though, if the old misery's really bad. There's no one to look after him, and I don't reckon he'm fit to look after hisself. To tell you the truth, maid, I had a shock when I saw him. I ain't laid eyes on him for the past fortnight and he seems to have shrivelled up in that time. He looks just like a peanut.'

'A peanut?' Jennifer echoed, startled, and Jacob nodded.

'One in its shell, I mean, all pale and wrinkled up.' They both turned as the doctor came down the stairs and looked enquiringly at Jennifer.

'I'm Jennifer Tucker,' she said, holding out her hand. 'Jed's daughter.'

'His *daughter*? I didn't realise . . . ' Charles Latimer looked from one to the other and decided not to ask any questions just now. 'Well, Mrs Tucker, I'm sure you realise that your father's quite ill. He's been going downhill for some time, I'm afraid, and he's not been looking after himself at all well.'

'I know. I've been trying to get him to come and see you but he wouldn't.' She hesitated. 'Will he have to go to hospital?'

Charles Latimer sighed deeply. 'It would be the best place for him – he'd get proper care there, certainly. But I'm not sure there's anything anyone can actually do to help him, other than that. The illness has progressed too far. And when I mentioned it, he got very upset.'

'He says if he goes into hospital he'll never come out,' Jennifer said, and the doctor looked at her thoughtfully.

'I'm afraid he's probably right, although not for the reasons he believes. Mrs Tucker, may I speak freely?'

'Yes, of course,' she said. 'But I'm not Mrs – I'm Miss.' She flicked a look at the ceiling, wondering how much Jed could hear. Jacob saw her glance and interpreted it correctly.

'Why don't we all go next door to my place?' he suggested. 'Nobody won't overhear us there, and we can all sit down decent.' He indicated Jed's chairs and the doctor smiled.

'That's a good idea. Do you want to let Jed know?'

Jennifer shook her head. 'I'll come back as soon as we finish.' They followed Jacob out of the door, through the tangled garden and back into his own neat abode. Jacob pushed Flossie off his chair and gestured towards the others.

'She don't sit on those – you won't get hairs all over your clean clothes. So what do you have to say, Doctor?'

'I'd rather know the truth,' Jennifer said quietly.

'Well, as I said, it's not good news. I haven't seen Jed professionally for a long time, not since he cut his arm rather badly with a sickle, but of course I've seen him about the village and I've been aware for some time that he's not a well man. All the same, I'm shocked by his condition now. He seems to have gone down so suddenly.'

''Tis the way he lives,' Jacob said. 'Never cleaning the place up or washing hisself properly like a Christian soul should, and feeding out of tins all the time. I don't reckon he's ever cooked hisself a proper meal, ever since his mother died, poor old lady. Stands to reason a body'll go downhill, living like that.'

'I'm afraid you're right. But there's more to it than that. I think Jed has a serious illness.'

'Is it TB?' Jennifer asked. 'All that coughing . . . '

The doctor looked at her. 'No, I don't think it's TB. I think he has cancer. Lung cancer.'

The room seemed very still. 'Cancer' wasn't a word you spoke out loud. It was something to be talked of in hushed whispers, something that nobody could do anything about. Jennifer had known a woman once, one of her mother's friends, who had had breast cancer – a 'growth' as people more usually termed it – and stubbornly refused to go to her doctor until it was too late. She could have been saved, Susan had said, because the doctors could cut off a breast. But could they take away an old man's lung? And what if it had attacked both lungs?

'Isn't there anything . . . ?' she began, but the doctor shook his head.

'I really don't think there is. As I say, he could go to

hospital where they'd make him as comfortable as possible, but they couldn't really do any more than could be done for him at home, if he had someone to look after him. And the upheaval of taking him there, especially if he were to be taken against his will – well, that in itself could kill him.'

'How long do you think he has?' Jennifer asked in a low voice. She was surprised by how upset she felt. Unlikeable though Jed was, he was her father, and the tie she'd been aware of seemed even stronger than she'd thought.

Charles sighed again. 'It's impossible to tell exactly. But in his poor condition – undernourished and weak – and by the signs of jaundice in his skin and eyes, I'd say it's no more than a matter of weeks. And not many, either. Two weeks – a month at most.' He turned to Jacob. 'If it hadn't been for you calling me this morning, it might only have been days.'

'I oughter have called you before,' Jacob said heavily. 'I've heard him in there night after night coughing and moaning, and I've never done a thing about it. I oughter have done something, even though we've been at loggerheads for the past thirty-five years or more.'

'You mustn't blame yourself,' the doctor said. 'We've all known Jed wasn't well, but nobody could force him to seek help.'

'And I tried to make him come to you only last week,' Jennifer said. 'He wouldn't hear of it.'

They sat in silence for a few moments, each lost in thought. Then Jacob said, 'So what shall us do now? Be you going to take him to hospital, Doctor?'

'You can't,' Jennifer said. 'You heard what the doctor said, Jacob. It would kill him.'

'Seems like he's going to die anyway,' Jacob began, but she shook her head and turned back to the doctor.

'Dr Latimer, is there anything else we can do? What about a district nurse?'

'Nurse Petherell could come in each day, certainly,' he

agreed. 'But Jed really needs someone here all the time. This last attack has left him very weak. The disease is accelerating, you see. I doubt if he could manage to do anything for himself now.'

'Then I'll come myself,' Jennifer said decisively. 'I'll get leave from the shop. I've got my summer-holiday leave allowance coming up, and I can ask for extra. I'll come and live here and look after him for as long as he needs me.'

Jacob stared at her. 'What, and live in that dump? You can't mean it, maid.'

'Of course I can. What else can I do? He's my father.' She saw the flicker of pain in Jacob's eyes. 'I'm sorry, Jacob,' she said softly. 'But it's the truth. I have to do it.'

Charles Latimer looked from one to the other. There was something here he didn't understand, a story he knew nothing about. But it wasn't his business just now, and he was relieved to think that Jed Fisher, the most unpopular man in the village, had someone to care for him at this last, desperate time of his life. All the same, he felt he had to warn Jennifer of what lay ahead.

'It won't be easy. Jed's small and frail now, but he'll still be surprisingly strong. He may be in a lot of pain and he'll probably become delirious. Nurse Petherell will help with bathing and lifting him, but he'll need a lot of nursing the rest of the time. You need to be very sure you can manage it.'

'I know. I nursed my mother through her last illness not long ago.' Jennifer met his eyes. 'So long as I can have help, I think I can manage. And if I really can't – well, then I suppose he'll have to go to hospital. But I'll do my best to see that he spends his last days at home.'

'And I'll be around to give you a hand,' Jacob said gruffly, and she turned to look at him in surprise. 'It's all right, maid. I know we been at each other's throats all these years, and you and me both knows why, but I wouldn't be able to call meself a Christian if I couldn't put that on one side while he'm dying. You can come in to me any time you needs me. Just knock on the wall, that's all you need do.' Their eyes met and he put out his hand towards her. 'It seems a funny business, but it's like it's the last thing I can do for my Susan, to help her maid when her needs me. Even if it do mean helping that old misery as well!'

Jennifer went straight back to Plymouth, first to Dingle's to arrange her leave, and then home to pack a case. Before leaving Burracombe, she had gone back to Jed, venturing up the stairs to his bedroom, to tell him what she meant to do.

'You'm coming to look after me?' he wheezed painfully. Like Jacob and the doctor, she was shocked by the change in him, even in the few days since she had last seen him. I ought to have realised how ill he was, she thought remorsefully. I ought to have insisted he saw the doctor then.

Not that it would have made any difference. Dr Latimer had explained that the course of the illness was already irrevocably under way, and had been for some time. Nothing could have been done for him other than what was being done now. And at least the old man had the pride, such as it was, of knowing he had kept his independence until the last possible moment.

Now, however, it seemed as if he'd given in. Lying on an old iron bedstead between thin grey sheets, he looked half the size he'd looked before, the yellow, wizened skin of his face shrunk back against his skull. His eyes were sunk back into dark hollows, and his almost colourless hair lay in thin, greasy strands across his head.

Gazing down at him, Jennifer could well believe that he had only days to live.

'Yes, of course I'll look after you,' she said gently. 'I have to go back to Plymouth to collect some things and let them know at the shop, but I'll be back by teatime. I won't leave you on your own now.'

'I dunno where you be going to sleep,' he grunted. 'There's only my old bed in t'other room but there be a lot of other stuff there, too, stuff I didn't want to throw out.'

Jennifer could believe that, too. She would have been surprised to find that Jed had thrown out anything at all during his entire life. Old newspapers, tins, bottles, jars, a broken radio set that looked as if it had been homemade sometime before the war, and tattered clothes lay everywhere. The smell of neglect permeated the whole cottage.

'I think some of it will have to be thrown out now,' she said. 'Or at least shifted about a bit. Will you mind very much if I clear out the other bedroom so that I can sleep there?'

He shrugged a thin shoulder. 'Do what you like, maid. I'm fed up with the lot of it.'

'I'll need to tidy up downstairs, too,' she warned him, hoping that he would not take instant offence. 'And clean round a bit as well. I don't suppose you've felt much like it, just lately.' She didn't want him to feel that his home was being taken over, but she knew that she couldn't possibly stay in the cottage as it was.

This time, he didn't even bother to shrug; he simply closed his eyes and turned his head away. He's exhausted, poor soul, she thought. He's past caring what anyone does now.

By the time she returned from Plymouth, Jed was awake again and Alice Tozer was in the cottage scrubbing the sink. She turned as Jennifer came through the door.

'There you are, maid. I've give him his tea and I thought I'd just try and get a bit of the grease off this sink. I don't reckon it's been cleaned in years. Filthy, the whole place is.' She caught sight of Jennifer's suitcase. 'You'm not planning to stop here, surely?'

'Of course I am,' Jennifer said. 'I can't leave him alone in that state. He needs someone here all the time.'

'Well, I know that,' Alice said, 'but the thought of you

sleeping here . . . Have you seen that room upstairs? It's not fit for a pig to sleep in.'

'I'll clean it up. I've brought some of my own sheets for the bed.'

'You'd have done better to bring a mattress as well,' Alice said grimly. 'Nothing but a nest for mice, that one be – that's if you can find it at all under all the mess and rubbish he's piled on top of it. Listen to me, maid, you come and stop up at the farm tonight and me and Val will give you a hand doing a bit of spring-cleaning.' She wrinkled her nose. 'It wants proper fumigating, but we can bring along some carbolic and disinfectant and a couple of scrubbing-brushes. And we can shift the rubbish outside – Ted'll bring the tractor along and take it down the dump.'

'I don't think we ought to do too much without Jed's agreement,' Jennifer said. 'It's his home, after all. I don't want him too upset, while he's so ill.'

'Well, maybe you'm right about that,' Alice allowed. 'But you still can't sleep in that bedroom until it's had a proper turn-out, and this kitchen's unhealthy the way it is now. I'd be frightened to eat anything made here. Now, we'll never get that room sorted out by tonight, so why don't you come and stop with us, like I said, and we'll sort it out in the morning? Jed won't hurt for one more night. Doctor popped in again while he was having his tea and said he'll most likely sleep now he's got some decent food inside him.'

Jennifer hesitated, but as they were talking Jacob had come in and stood listening. He said, 'You could stop in with me, maid, if you likes. I don't get many visitors, but there's a spare bed, and 'tis clean. And you'll be close enough to hear the old blighter if he starts coughing in the night or calls out. You could be round here in a couple of minutes.'

'That sounds a good idea,' Jennifer said gratefully. 'Thanks, Jacob, I'll do that. And thank you for your offer, too,' she said to Alice. 'If you really don't mind giving a hand with the cleaning—'

'Bless you, my bird, of course I don't. And Val's a registered nurse, you know, so she can give you a hand when Bet Petherell can't be here. We'll all rally round, never you fear.' She came closer and laid her hand on Jennifer's arm. 'I know old Jed haven't been the best-liked man round here, but he'm one of us just the same, and there's nobody would see him suffer on his own, not like this. And I hope you don't mind, but Jacob here told me what 'twas all about – you know, about your poor mother and him. Seeing as we already knew some of the story, as it were.'

'That's all right,' Jennifer said, feeling the tears in her eyes. 'I'm glad he told you. In fact, I don't mind if everyone knows now – do you, Jacob? I'd rather the truth was known.'

Jacob hesitated, and she wondered if she'd upset him. He might not want the old story brought to light again, a subject for gossip in the cottages and pub.

'It's your story, too,' she added gently. 'Alice won't spread it around if you don't want it.'

'No,' he said after a moment. 'I think you'm right, maid. 'Tis best for it to be out in the open. I don't suppose many folk will care that much, anyway. They'm too interested in their own concerns. Nine-day wonder, it'll be.'

Alice nodded. 'They'm bound to be a bit curious about Jennifer and why she's suddenly turned up in Burracombe.' She finished scrubbing the sink and dried her hands on a scrap of towel she had obviously brought with her. 'If there's nothing else you needs me for now, maid, I'll be getting off home. There's the family supper to get . . . Now, you'm welcome to call up at the farm any time you wants to, and Val and me'll be along in the morning with our scrubbing-brushes. Do you want to come up a bit later on for a bite to eat? I've put a few eggs and some butter and a jug of fresh milk in the larder, along with a loaf of bread. Ted's mother made it.'

Jennifer shook her head. 'That's really kind of you, but I think I'll stay here. I've got enough for supper tonight and breakfast, and I'll do some shopping in the morning.' She sighed, looking out of the window at the untidy garden. 'It seems such a shame that anyone can let themselves go like this. I know he's not an easy man, but I would like to make these last few weeks a bit more comfortable for him, if he'll let me.' She smiled ruefully. 'I hope he'll let me wash his face, at least!'

'Bet Petherell will see to that,' Alice said. 'She won't stand no nonsense. And it won't be just his face, neither. I have to say, I don't envy you that!' She unwrapped her apron and stuffed it into the shopping-bag she had brought with her. 'Well, I'll be on my way. Now, you know where we are, and us'll be expecting you to drop in, so don't wait to be invited, will you? And Val and me'll see you in the morning. Goodbye, Jacob. You look after her, now.'

'I'll do that,' he said as the farmer's wife bustled out. 'As if her was me own daughter.' And then, with a surprisingly shy glance towards Jennifer, he added in a mumble, 'I know you'm not, maid, and I know you've got *his* blood in your veins, but seems to me you'm as *close* as a daughter.'

'Yes,' Jennifer said. 'It seems like that to me, too.'

Chapter Thirty-Eight

It took only a day or two for the news of Jed's illness and Jennifer's arrival to spread round the village, and she was astonished by the number of visitors who began to knock on the door. Most were genuinely concerned, admitting that Jed had been deeply unpopular, but still ready to help Jennifer in her difficult task. Most were also, she realised, as curious as they were concerned – the sudden appearance of a daughter in Jed's life, and the reawakening of an old story involving one of the most well-liked people in the village, was enough to provide food for gossip for well over the nine days Jacob had predicted.

Even Joyce Warren and her husband came along one day, arriving while the doctor was there. The three of them stayed in Jed's bedroom for some time, while Jennifer and Alice gave the kitchen a thorough spring-clean. By the time they came down, it was as near gleaming as a kitchen, undecorated for at least twenty years and equipped with what looked like museum pieces, could be. Joyce Warren looked around in disbelief.

'It's hard to imagine that anyone could have managed in a place like this! You're saints, both of you, to take on such a job.'

'It's got to be done,' Alice said, wiping her hands on a roller towel Jacob had hung on the back door. ''Twasn't healthy the way it was. I'm surprised Jed didn't poison himself years ago.

How is he this afternoon, anyway? Must be in a chatty mood. Visitors don't usually stop with him that long.'

'He's certainly not very well,' Joyce said. 'It's very sad to see someone in that condition. So you're staying here to look after him?' she added to Jennifer. 'I must say, I do admire you for that. And you didn't even know him until quite recently?'

'That's right.' Although she had said she wanted the story known, Jennifer found it embarrassing to talk about it, especially to this woman who was so different from the villagers she had met so far. 'I couldn't leave him on his own.'

'Well, he's very lucky to have you,' Joyce said, and turned as her husband and the doctor appeared. 'I'm just saying how lucky Jed is to have his daughter to look after him.'

'He is indeed.' The doctor ducked his head to come through the door. 'I've been meaning to ask you, Miss Tucker, have you sent word to the Methodist minister? I'm sure he'd want to see Jed.'

Jennifer nodded. The minister, who looked after two chapels, lived some distance from the village. 'He came yesterday. He's very concerned. He says Jed didn't go to chapel much, but he always looked after the graveyard.'

'In a manner of speaking,' Alice said grimly.

'He's coming again tomorrow,' Jennifer went on. 'Jed seemed a bit easier in his mind after he'd talked to him for a while.'

Henry Warren, a quiet, grey-haired man in spectacles and a business suit, nodded. 'He seems well enough in that respect. Just very tired and obviously not at all well.' He turned to his wife. 'I'm afraid I have to be going back to Tavistock now, I've got a number of matters to attend to in the office . . .'

'Yes, dear, we'll be on our way. I'm sure these two good ladies want to get on with their work. There's certainly a lot to be done here.' She glanced around with an expression of distaste, and then smiled kindly at Jennifer. 'I really do admire you, coming here like this and making such sacrifices.'

Jennifer returned her smile but said nothing. Henry Warren nodded and said goodbye, and the doctor stayed for a moment.

'Mr Warren was right about Jed's state of mind. He's well enough at the moment – understands all that's going on, even if he doesn't like it. But I'm afraid that will start to change soon. He's going to suffer quite a lot of pain, and the drugs I give him will make him very drowsy.'

'I know,' Jennifer said. 'It's all right, Doctor. I know just what to expect and I'll do my best for him.'

'You'll get help from Nurse Petherell, of course.'

'And me and Val,' Alice said. 'She'll not be short of helpers, Dr Latimer.'

He nodded. 'I'm sure of that. Burracombe wouldn't be the village it is if people didn't rally round in times of need. Well, I'll look in again tomorrow, Miss Tucker, but call me if you're at all worried.' He let himself out.

'Well!' Alice said, turning back to her cleaning. 'I wonder what that was all about.'

'All what? I know the doctor's a bit anxious about how I'm to manage, but—'

'No, not that. I mean that Mrs Warren and her husband coming to see Jed. She never had a good word to say for him, and you hardly ever see Mr Warren around the village, he'm always so busy.' She came closer and lowered her voice. 'If you want my opinion—'

Her voice was drowned by a sudden fierce knocking from upstairs. Jed was banging on the floor beside his bed with the knobbly walking-stick Jennifer had found in a cupboard.

'Well, the old termagant hasn't started to feel drowsy yet, that's for certain,' Alice observed. 'I'll tell you something else, too – he hasn't taken long to get used to being waited on, either. That old busybody Mrs Warren was right about one thing – you'm a saint, and he's lucky to have you.'

*

'It's not Jed they're helping,' Val said later, when she came in to help Jennifer get her father ready for the night. 'It's you. Not that they wouldn't help him, I'm not saying that, but I don't think he'd get quite so many visitors if he hadn't had a long-lost daughter turn up to look after him.'

'You mean it's just curiosity?'

'Well, a large part of it is. It's only natural – all the older ones knew Jed and Jacob when they were younger, but nobody ever knew what really happened to Susan. There was talk about a baby, but no one knew if it was true, and they'd have all thought it was Jacob's. It's bound to have caused a lot of interest, to know what really happened. And you coming just when Jed's in such a poor way—'

'They don't think I'm after his money, I hope!' Jennifer exclaimed, and Val hooted with laughter.

'What money? Has he got a sockful under his mattress? Well, I suppose there are always one or two who've got nasty minds, but you don't need to take any notice of them. Anyway, if there was any money – which I'm sure there isn't – I'd say you were earning it now. It's not the most pleasant of jobs, looking after someone like Jed.'

'I suppose you're used to it,' Jennifer remarked. 'Are you going to go on working at the hospital after you're married? It's not long now, is it?'

'Three weeks! We had the banns called for the first time last week. I'll go on for a while – there's not much point in stopping, really. There's not much housework to do at the charcoal-burner's cottage! We might as well have the money while I can earn it. Dad doesn't approve, of course, he says a man ought to be able to keep his wife, but I tell him if I stop nursing he'll be asking me to help out with things on the farm, so I'll still be working but not getting paid! That shuts him up.'

Jennifer laughed and they went upstairs to give the invalid his final wash, a drink and the medicine that Dr Latimer had prescribed. As he had foretold, Jed was now beginning to suffer more pain, and the sedatives were starting to have effect, but he was still aware enough to know what was happening and to protest at the indignity.

'I ain't been seen in me underwear since I were a babby. It isn't decent.'

'Don't be silly, Jed,' Val said firmly. 'I'm a nurse and Jennifer's your daughter. There's nothing indecent about it. And these are pyjamas, not underwear.'

'I had that nurse round here this afternoon, bathing me as if I were a babe in arms,' he continued indignantly, although his voice was weakening. 'I'd have showed her the door if I'd had the strength to do it. Taking advantage of a poor old man!'

'I don't think anyone's likely to take advantage of you,' Val told him. 'Now, let me prop you up while Jennifer gives you this drink. It'll help you sleep.'

'What is it? Milk?' He made a face of disgust. 'Can't a bloke have a pint of beer in his own home no more? That old skinflint up at the pub would send one down in a tankard if you paid him. Here, and that's another thing –' he reared up in bed so that Jennifer almost spilled the cup she was trying to hold against his lips '– he've got my old pewter tankard up there, the one I always has me beer out of when I goes in there. If I can't go in there no more, I want it back. You go up straight away and fetch it.'

'Not tonight,' Jennifer said. 'They'll be closing soon. I'll fetch it tomorrow and you can have all your drinks out of it.'

'Not milk,' he said, sinking back and allowing her to feed him at last. 'I wouldn't give it the insult.'

After that, he seemed to recede into a muddled, half-dreaming world of his own, rambling and incoherent. Eventually, he drifted into sleep and the two women went downstairs, feeling exhausted. The living-room was reasonably clean and tidy now, though the distempered walls and bare floor gave it a bleak and inhospitable air, and Jennifer made cocoa for them both. They sat down in the armchairs, their old covers thrown away and replaced by clean blankets Jennifer had brought out from Plymouth, and gave each other a little sigh of relief.

'I hope he sleeps well tonight,' Jennifer said. 'He's had dreadful nights just lately. I really do feel sorry for him. I think if Jacob hadn't called the doctor and got in touch with me, he could have died here, all by himself with no one to care.'

'It's a horrible thought,' Val agreed soberly. 'Yet I expect a lot of people would say it's no more than he deserves. He really has been an unpleasant man, all his life from what I can make out.'

'I don't know – even Jacob says they were friends when they were young. I think what happened to him in the war, and what happened with my mother, just turned him in on himself. He hated himself for what he'd done, and he hated everyone else for treating him as a coward. And he must have felt as if he was responsible for my mother's death, too. It was cruel of my grandfather to tell those lies.'

Val looked at her thoughtfully. 'It seems strange to hear you talking about them as your father and grandfather, especially when you've had other relatives. Doesn't it feel peculiar to you?'

'Yes, it does. I think about it a lot. I'll always think of my stepfather as my real father, in a way. And his parents were my granny and grandad. Nothing will ever change that. But with Jed, it's a different feeling. I can't think of him in the same way, but I can't pretend he doesn't exist. I feel a sort of tie. I can't just walk away and leave him to die alone. And then there's Jacob. He *ought* to have been my father, yet if he had been, I wouldn't have been me!' She shook her head. 'It's all so complicated, it makes my head ache so I've decided to stop worrying about it and just do whatever feels right. And that means looking after Jed.'

'And what about afterwards?' Val asked. 'Will you stop coming out to Burracombe then?'

Jennifer looked up and met her eyes. The room was almost dark, and they could only just see each other across the small space. She reached out and lit the old table lamp beside her.

'No,' she said. 'I'll never stop coming to Burracombe. I'll always want to see Jacob.'

Chapter Thirty-Nine

Jed died in the early hours of the morning, four days later. His decline, once begun, was rapid and after his remark about the pewter tankard, he did not speak coherently again. Jennifer was by his side almost all the time, sleeping only when too exhausted to stay awake and only when someone else could be with her father. She had been in her own bed for less than an hour when Jacob, who was sitting beside his old enemy, woke her up.

'You'd better come, maid. I think this is it.'

She was up almost before he had finished speaking, pushing her feet into slippers and pulling her dressing-gown around her. Together, they went into the next room, where the frail, shrivelled body was shifting restlessly, the bony, yellow fingers picking at the sheets. A voice that sounded quite unlike Jed's was mumbling on and on, as if commentating on an endless procession of events, and sometimes he sobbed. Every now and then a harsh rattle sounded in his throat, and Jacob gave Jennifer a significant glance.

'That's the death rattle, that is,' he muttered. 'Won't be long now, maid. You don't have to stay if you don't want to.'

'Of course I will.' She took the chair by the bed, and Jacob moved round to the one they had placed at the other side. She picked up one of the restless hands and held it, stroking the thin fingers gently. 'Jed. Can you hear me? It's Jennifer.'

'Jennifer,' he muttered. 'Don't know no Jennifers.'

'Yes, you do.' She took a breath. 'I'm your daughter, Jennifer. Susan's girl. You know me.'

'Susan? My Susan?'

She heard a sharp intake of breath from the man on the other side of the bed, and gave Jacob a swift glance. 'Susan Hannaford,' she said steadily. 'My mother.'

'Susan,' he whispered. 'Sweet little maid, her was . . . I were sorry after . . . I told her I were sorry . . . I'd have gone after her, but 'twas no use . . . Where's my tankard? I told that woman I wanted my tankard.'

'It's here. Would you like a drink?'

'I got to go to work.' He began to struggle, his feeble body suddenly strong, so that it took both of them to hold him in the bed. 'Job over Chagford way. I got to go, Mother.'

'It's all right, Jed. You don't have to go.'

'Hens to feed . . . Lambing-time . . . I got a grave to dig.' He began to struggle again. 'Bury my Susan.'

'Jed, it's all right.' Jennifer leaned close and spoke in his ear. 'There's nothing you have to do. You can rest now. Rest easy. Rest . . . ' She spoke in soothing whispers, hoping that the tone of her voice at least would penetrate his confused mind. 'Just lie quiet and rest, Jed. Just let yourself rest . . .'

Whether he understood her or not, she couldn't tell, but his breathing, shallow and ragged as it was, grew very slightly easier and his struggles eased. He lay flat in the bed. He was so shrunken now that the bedclothes barely rose above him. He kept turning his head restlessly from side to side, his free hand still picking endlessly at the sheet. As the hours dragged on, every breath seemed to pain him more and the rattle sounded more and more often in his throat, frequently ending with a cough that threatened to tear his body to pieces. Once or twice, Jacob got up and went quietly downstairs, returning with a cup of cocoa for them both, and once Jennifer asked if they ought to call the doctor again. He shook his head.

'Nothing he can do for him now, poor old sod. 'Tis just a matter of time.'

'It seems to be taking so long. He's so frail, I can't understand how he can go on breathing.'

'The body don't want to let go. Us'll do all us can to stay alive, that's what it is. I seen it before, when my old father went, and again when it were my Sarah. Not many of us has it easy.'

She nodded and stroked Jed's forehead. It was cold and clammy, as if he were half dead already, and she wondered if he had slipped away while they were talking. But the breath was still coming, so shallow that it was a wonder it got as far as the destroyed lungs, and as she looked down on the skeletal face, the hollow eyes opened suddenly and looked straight at her.

He knows who I am, she thought. He's lucid again.

'Jennifer.' A shaking hand reached up to her face. 'You'm my Susan's maid.'

'She weren't never your Susan!' Jacob burst out, unable to restrain himself, and the yellow face turned to him.

'Be that you, Jacob Prout?'

'It be,' Jacob growled. 'I been here these past three days, on and off, only you never knowed it.'

'Wanted to be in at the death, eh?'

Jennifer gasped in shock, but Jacob shrugged his shoulders. 'Maybe. I was there at the start, might as well be here at the end.'

The dying man was silent for a moment. But he still seemed lucid as he whispered in his painfully grating voice, 'I were proper fond of her. I never meant to hurt her.'

Jennifer glanced at Jacob, and since he seemed unlikely to answer, she said, 'I know. We both know. It's all right, Jed.'

'And if it isn't,' Jacob said, 'you'll have someone bigger than us to answer to, before the night's out.'

Jed closed his eyes and Jennifer wondered if they should

have called the minister. He'd been in that afternoon and spent an hour or more with Jed; if he'd been a Roman Catholic, she thought, he would probably have given him the Last Rites. Perhaps the minister's visit would have had the same effect, leaving Jed at peace. To make sure, as best she could, she said quietly, 'My mother forgave you, Jed. She never bore any grudge against you.'

'Susan?' he whispered, his senses failing fast again.

'That's right. Susan. And so do I.' She touched his papery cheek. 'Go to sleep now, Jed. Go and rest.'

The hollow eyes looked into hers. Slowly, the bony head turned, and he cast a last look at his childhood friend and enemy. Then Jed Fisher gave one last, tremulous sigh and one last faint rattle, and his eyes closed as if in sleep. The room was suddenly silent. 'He've gone,' Jacob said after a moment, and Jennifer nodded. Her eyes were filled with tears.

'I know.'

They sat quietly for a few minutes and then, taking a deep breath, she folded the dead man's hands on his chest and drew the sheet over his face. Jacob rose to his feet, still looking down at the bed.

'He were a miserable old sod,' he said. 'But us had good times when us were tackers. I reckon that's what I ought to remember.'

'I think so, too,' Jennifer said. 'He didn't start out bad. It was what happened to him.' Her voice broke suddenly. 'Oh, *Jacob*!'

'There, there,' he said, moving round the bed to put his arms round her shoulders. 'Don't take on, maid. 'Tis the natural way of the world, and you did your best for him.'

'It seems such a waste,' she wept. 'Oh, Jacob, I never thought, when I started looking for him, that it would end like this.'

'I don't suppose you did,' he said thoughtfully. 'The thing

is, are you sorry you done it? Are you sorry you started to look in the first place?'

Jennifer took her hands away from her face and looked up at him, the man she had thought was her father, the man who she still felt *ought* to have been her father, and she shook her head.

'No. I'm not sorry. Because I've made things right for him now. I've found you – and we've both found out the truth. I'll always be glad I came to Burracombe.'

Chapter Forty

The Church of St Andrew was packed when Val Tozer finally walked up the aisle to marry Luke Ferris. They had been welcomed by the silvery pealing of the six bells, captained today by Jacob Prout, since Ted Tozer was occupied with giving his daughter away, but all the ringers were in their best suits and filed into seats at the back as soon as they had finished ringing. Everyone was invited to the reception in the village hall.

Stella was there with Maddy, sitting halfway back behind the Tozer family and keeping a place for Dottie, who was in the porch putting the finishing touches to the dresses. She scurried up the aisle just before the signal was given to the organist to strike up with 'Here Comes the Bride', and slipped into her pew. Then the bells stopped, the music started, and Luke – who had been fidgeting anxiously in the front pew for the past ten minutes with his brother, Simon – stood up and turned to greet his bride.

As the congregation caught their first glimpse of Val, tall and slender in her drift of pale blue-grey, a sigh of pleasure ran round the church. Her rich brown hair was caught in a veil of lace, cascading down beneath it in a tumble of gleaming curls. She looked proud and happy, her face glowing as if she were walking into a dream, and as she came to stand beside Luke and they looked into each other's eyes, it was as if the promises to be made between them were encompassed in that moment and the rest of the service no more than a formality.

Basil Harvey was taking the service, with Felix standing close by. Stella gazed at him, standing tall behind the short, rotund vicar, his corn-gold hair lit by the sunlight that flooded through the windows, and thought wistfully of the hopes and dreams she herself had had. Since that evening when the three of them had sat by the river and Stella had heard for the first time about Maddy's new job with Felix's uncle, she had had very little time alone with him. School had taken up so much of her time, and Felix had spent more and more time at Little Durracombe, where John Berry was failing fast. Maddy herself had been in West Lyme for the past fortnight, learning about her new duties from the Archdeacon's present secretary, who was leaving to get married, and had come home for the wedding before taking Stella to London for the promised holiday, after which she would be moving to her own apartment. It was all changing, Stella thought; all except her own life, which looked like going on just the same. And that's good, she told herself fiercely. It's what I wanted. I've got *everything* I wanted . . .

Jennifer Tucker was sitting on Stella's other side. She and Val had become close friends as they tended Jed together, and she was staying with Jacob, who had told her that the spare bedroom was now hers whenever she wanted it. 'You can't stop in that dump next door,' he'd told her bluntly. 'Wants stripping out and starting all over again, that do.'

The wedding was the second big event in the village in the past week or so. Jed Fisher's funeral, held in the Chapel, had also been well attended – better than anyone who had known him could have expected. Jennifer suspected that many of them might have come out of curiosity, having heard the story of herself and Jed, and those who had already met her were present to lend her their support. But there were others, especially the older villagers, who seemed to have come for a different reason. Perhaps they remembered Jed from his younger, happier days; perhaps they felt a vague guilt at the way he had been treated; perhaps it was just because he had been a part of their lives and of the village for so long that they felt compelled to wish him goodbye.

Jacob himself had dug the grave. He had never dug a grave in the chapel graveyard before, since Jed himself had done that, but although the minister could have asked a gravedigger from another village to do the job, Jacob had gone to him the day after the death and asked for it.

'Us lived next door to each other all our lives, and us were pals when us were youngsters,' he said. 'I'd like to see to the old misery's last resting-place.'

'Like to make sure he's properly buried, that's what he really means,' some of the other villagers commented on hearing this, but the minister agreed to Jacob's request and he was a pall-bearer as well.

Jennifer, as chief mourner, had felt a deep sorrow at the passing of this sad old man, whose life had been poisoned by bitterness and regret. She gazed at the coffin, standing before them as they sang their last hymn, and thought how prejudice and false assumptions had started the poisoning. Who was really responsible – bullying old Abraham, her own grandfather, who had driven his daughter away and then lied so cruelly about her death? Those who had scorned Jed for being rejected by one over-zealous Army doctor? Or Jed himself, for allowing the bitterness to rot his soul? Well, there was no way of knowing now, and all anyone could do was learn from his wasted life – if anyone ever did learn from someone else's mistakes. All our mistakes are our own, she thought, unique to ourselves – can we ever learn from someone else's?

Today was a happier day, however, she reminded herself as she watched Val turn to hand her bouquet of cascading deep-red roses to her sister, Jackie. Ted, having handed her over to the vicar, stepped back to stand in the front pew beside Alice, resplendent in her fuchsia-pink suit and hat. She was glad to feel a part of the Tozer family and their celebration, glad to feel a part of the village. It was strange to think that what had happened to Jed – what had seemed a wasted life – had brought all this about for her. There really was no understanding it, and all you could do was get on with life as it happened to be.

Hilary Napier was sitting just in front of them, with her father and brother, Stephen, who had managed to 'wangle' his leave to coincide with Val's wedding. Tall and handsome in his RAF uniform, he had given Maddy an interested glance as he passed her to enter his pew. They knew each other, of course, since Maddy had often stayed with the Napiers when she had been with Fenella Forsyth, but it was some time since they'd met and clearly Stephen was impressed by the changes he saw in her.

Hilary noticed the smile that passed between them and murmured, 'She's very pretty, but I don't think you've got a chance – she's been seen about with the curate rather a lot just lately!'

'Are they engaged?' he whispered, and she shook her head. 'Not as far as I know.'

He sat back with a wicked grin. 'All's fair in love and war, then! And I think my uniform's better than his!'

Hilary stifled a giggle. She was feeling especially happy today. Her father had made a start on the family book and become almost completely absorbed in it, leaving her free to administer the estate as she wanted to. He spent his mornings in his study, his head buried in old documents and photographs, and in the afternoons he either accompanied her on a visit to one of the tenants – taking the opportunity to acquire more old tales – or took the dogs out on the moor. Charles Latimer had told him that steady exercise was good for him, and he would walk for hours as the dogs dashed around looking for rabbits.

There was another reason for Hilary to feel cheerful today. Arnold Cherriman and his wife had come to dinner a few evenings before, to play bridge, and Arnold had announced that he had at last decided to move back to Plymouth. 'We're converting the old house into flats and building a new house in the garden,' he'd said. 'The whole place is too big for us now. There's over an acre of garden, you know – plenty for Evelyn to play about with, and to give us privacy. There's a big demand for decent homes in the city now, so I'm going to retire. Play a bit of golf, enjoy the fruits of my labours all these years.'

Hilary's heart had leaped. 'How long do you think it will take?' she asked, thinking of Val and Luke. What news she would be able to give them at their wedding!

'Oh, a year or more. Builders are all pretty busy, and we've got to get an architect to draw up plans and all that. So we'll be wanting to stay on in the estate house for a while yet. But you'll need to be thinking about new tenants, and I may be able to help there—'

'Oh no,' Hilary said hastily before her father could show interest. 'I think we'll be able to find tenants, thank you, Mr Cherriman.'

A year or more, she thought. Would Val and Luke be able to manage for that long in the charcoal-burner's cottage? It was so small and not at all suitable for winter. They'd hoped only to have to live there for the summer . . . But even if they had to move into Tavistock, where Luke was to take up his teaching post in the autumn, it need only be until the Cherrimans moved. They would know that they'd soon be able to move back to Burracombe.

The bride and groom were making their vows now, and everyone concentrated on hearing their voices. Sometimes a bride spoke so quietly that you could barely hear her, and even the grooms almost lost their voices at this moment. But Val's voice was clear and strong, and Luke's deep and firm. They obviously meant their vows to be heard by all present, a confirmation of their love and determination, and the silence after they spoke their last words was broken only by a small sob from Alice and another from Luke's mother. Tears were on many other cheeks, too, but no other sounds were heard and Basil's voice rang out as he lifted the clasped hands and made the exhortation. 'Those whom God hath joined together, let no man put asunder!'

While the register was signed, the handbell-ringers filed out to the chancel steps and rang Minnie's special adaptations of 'Ode to Joy' and 'O Perfect Love'. Then the ringers hastened back to the ringing-chamber at the back of the church, the organ pealed out the notes of the 'Wedding March', and Val and Luke, husband and wife now, emerged beaming from the tiny vestry and led the procession of families down the aisle, smiling and nodding at all their guests as they came. There were more tears on many faces as they gazed at Val's radiant face and the pride with which Luke bore her on his arm, but by the time everyone was out in the sunshine, milling about the churchyard and trying to get in – or out of – the photographs, the tears had dried and there was nothing but laughter.

'It's a wonderful wedding,' Stella said as she stood with Jennifer and Hilary, sipping a glass of sherry in the village hall. 'The first I've been to in Burracombe. Are they all like this?'

Hilary laughed. 'Some of them! Others are smaller and people have the reception at home, just for their family. But the Tozers are such a big family, and so well known that they couldn't really have it anywhere smaller.'

'Well, I'm really pleased to have been invited – after all, I've only been in the village five minutes. They didn't have to ask me.'

'Or me,' Jennifer said. 'I don't even live here.'

'You'd have been almost the only ones left out. Well, along with the Cullifords and a few others, perhaps! How are you, by the way? You must be looking forward to the holidays –

the summer term's a busy one, I know. I enjoyed the play, by the way.'

'It went quite well in the end,' Stella agreed. 'It was a shame that Sports Day was the only wet day in the whole month, but we managed to have it last week, and it did give us a bit more time for rehearsals. The children worked very hard to get it right, although my heart was in my mouth when the ass's head tipped over sideways.'

'Has Felix said anything to you about starting up a dramatic society?' Hilary asked. 'He was talking about it the other day when we met over at Little Burracombe – Father and I had gone to see poor Mr Berry. He seems quite keen and I'd rather like to have a go. I loved acting when I was at school.'

'I know he's been thinking about it,' Stella said, 'but I haven't seen much of him lately.' She looked round as Val and Luke came up to them, hand in hand and wreathed in smiles. 'You two look very pleased with yourselves.'

'And so we should,' Val declared. 'It's the best day of our lives.'

'So far,' Luke added. 'Unless you mean it's going to be all downhill from now on!'

'I don't mean that at all!' She slapped his arm. 'I can see I'm going to have trouble with you.'

'I've got some news for you,' Hilary said, and they both looked at her expectantly. Stella and Jennifer started to move away, but she gestured to them to stay. 'It's not private – at least, I don't think it is – but it's very good news.' Her voice bubbled with excitement. 'The Cherrimans are going back to Plymouth! That means you'll be able to have the estate house after all. Not straight away,' she added as Val turned to Luke with an exclamation of delight. 'They're building a new house in Plymouth so it'll be at least a year. But even if you move into Tavistock in the autumn, you'll know it needn't be for long. You'll be back in the village by the end of next year.'

'Oh, that's wonderful,' Val cried. 'We'll stay in the cottage as long as we can in the autumn and look for something in town – it won't seem nearly as bad moving to town if we know we're coming back so soon.'

'But you don't have to do that,' Jennifer said suddenly, and they all turned to stare at her. 'You don't have to move into Tavistock. You can have my cottage.'

'*Your* cottage?' Val said blankly. 'But which – do you mean *Jed's* cottage?'

'Yes. He left it to me. Mr Warren came one day and made out his will – you remember, Val, your mother was there and we wondered why the doctor had brought them along. I didn't even know he was a solicitor. I didn't know anything about it until after the funeral. But it was quite true – everything was left to me. I suppose he had no one else to leave it to,' she added a little sadly.

'But won't you want to live there yourself?' Val asked.

Jennifer shook her head. 'Not yet. I'm sure I will eventually, but I don't want to rush into anything. Jacob says I can come and stay with him any time I like, and I need to be in Plymouth for my job. And I do have my sisters and their families there, as well – I've rather neglected them lately.'

'And we really could rent the cottage from you?' Val asked, dazed.

'Yes, of course. But it needs an awful lot doing to it. You wouldn't be able to move straight in.'

'That doesn't matter. We could do it ourselves, during the summer holidays. Then it will be ready for us by winter – the charcoal-burner's cottage is so tiny, and with no running water or proper cooking facilities it would be dreadfully uncomfortable then for two people. Oh, Jennifer, that's lovely! It's made a perfect day even perfecter!'

They all laughed, and the ushers began to move them towards the tables that had been laid for the wedding meal. Dottie and Mrs Dawe, with a small army of helpers, had been busy all the previous day and again this morning, and it looked, as Alice herself had said when she came that morning to take a look, as good as a dining-room in any fine hotel.

Val and Luke and their families seated themselves at the top table. Jennifer was with Jacob, and Hilary with her father. Stella and Maddy found themselves seated with Felix between them, and Stephen on Maddy's other side.

'It's a great day, isn't it?' Felix said cheerfully, passing a bowl of steaming new potatoes to go with the ham salad. 'Nice to see two people so happy.'

'It is.' Stella smiled at him, determined not to let her own personal disappointment show. 'I wonder who'll be the next in the village to get married.'

'Who knows? Life is full of surprises.' He helped himself to half a dozen potatoes. 'And now that the term's almost over, maybe you'll have a few yourself.'

'What do you mean?' She looked at him in sudden dread. Please don't let them announce it now, she thought. Not today, not here amongst all these people. 'Has Maddy planned something special for our holiday in London?'

'I've no idea! Well, that's not quite true. There is something special planned, but it's not Maddy who's been planning it. It's me.'

He grinned at her, but Stella could only gaze back in dismay. Hastily, she said, 'Don't tell me now, Felix. Save it for later.'

'But I want to tell you now. I've been keeping it to myself for too long – you've been so wrapped up in school things for the past few weeks I've hardly had a chance to talk to you on your own. And once this meal's over we'll have to listen to speeches and drink toasts, and then there'll be dancing and I might not get another chance. I've got to say it now, while you're trapped here and can't get away from me.'

'Felix—'

'Be quiet,' he said. 'Eat your nice salad and listen to me.

And there's to be no arguing, understand?' As she gazed at him, mute, he went on with a touch of drama in his voice, 'When Maddy takes you to London, you're not going on your own. I'm coming with you!'

Stella stared at him. 'You? But—'

'Even curates are allowed to have holidays, you know,' he said. 'Maddy and I have been talking it over, and she wants me to come, too. You see, Fenella Forsyth, or whatever her French name is, is coming to London just then, and wants Maddy to spend a few days with her. And Maddy doesn't want to leave you on your own, so it seems the perfect solution.'

'But—' Stella began again, and he put his finger to her lips. She felt her cheeks colour and turned her head away quickly. 'Felix, don't.'

'I want to,' he said quietly. 'I want to touch you. I've wanted it for so long, but these past few weeks you seem to have drifted away from me. Tell me it's all right, Stella. Tell me everything's the same between us as it was that day I kissed you on the bridge.'

Slowly, unbelievingly, she turned back and met his eyes. With doubt in her voice, she said, 'But you and Maddy . . .'

'Maddy and I what? What do you mean?'

'I thought you and Maddy . . . I thought you . . . I didn't think you wanted me any more. I thought perhaps you never had.'

Felix stared at her. 'You thought that? But I thought you were still in love with Luke!' He glanced towards the top table. 'That day we met them up by the Standing Stones – the way you looked at the cottage when we walked down the hill . . .'

'I was thinking how lucky they were to have found each other,' she said. 'That's all. I got over Luke long ago.'

'And have you got over me?' he asked.

Stella shook her head, knowing that this was a moment for truth. 'I don't think I'll ever get over you, Felix.'

'Nor will I get over you,' he said softly, and felt for her hand beneath the table. 'Oh, how I wish I could kiss you now! But that's something I really will have to save for later.'

'I'll look forward to it,' she whispered, curling her fingers in his, and they both smiled. Then she said, 'Although I'm sorry, in a way, that it isn't you and Maddy after all. You'd have made a very nice brother-in-law!'

Felix chuckled. 'Well,' he said with a nudge, 'you may find yourself with one who's equally nice.' And as she looked past him at her sister, who was openly flirting with Stephen Napier, Stella laughed with amusement, relief and an overwhelming rush of love.

A sudden sharp rap from a gavel on the top table brought them all to attention. Luke's brother, Simon, was on his feet, and the speeches were about to begin.

'Here's to Val and Luke,' Felix murmured, touching his glass to Stella's as Ted Tozer rose to his feet, red-faced and clutching a sheet of paper. 'Here's to love and marriage. And here's to us.'

'To us,' Stella echoed softly.

available from

THE ORION PUBLISHING GROUP

- ☐ **Goodbye Sweetheart £6.99**
  LILIAN HARRY
  978-1-8579-7812-4
- ☐ **The Girls They Left Behind £6.99**
  LILIAN HARRY
  978-0-7528-0333-3
- ☐ **Keep Smiling Through £6.99**
  LILIAN HARRY
  978-0-7528-3442-9
- ☐ **Moonlight & Lovesongs £6.99**
  LILIAN HARRY
  978-0-7528-1564-0
- ☐ **Love & Laughter £6.99**
  LILIAN HARRY
  978-0-7528-2605-9
- ☐ **Wives & Sweethearts £6.99**
  LILIAN HARRY
  978-0-7528-3396-5
- ☐ **Corner House Girls £6.99**
  LILIAN HARRY
  978-0-7528-4296-7
- ☐ **Kiss the Girls Goodbye £6.99**
  LILIAN HARRY
  978-0-7528-4448-0
- ☐ **PS I Love You £6.99**
  LILIAN HARRY
  978-0-7528-4820-4
- ☐ **A Girl Called Thursday £6.99**
  LILIAN HARRY
  978-0-7528-4950-8
- ☐ **Tuppence to Spend £6.99**
  LILIAN HARRY
  978-0-7528-4264-6
- ☐ **A Promise to Keep £6.99**
  LILIAN HARRY
  978-0-7528-5889-0
- ☐ **Under the Apple Tree £6.99**
  LILIAN HARRY
  978-0-7528-5929-3
- ☐ **Dance Little Lady £6.99**
  LILIAN HARRY
  978-0-7528-6420-4
- ☐ **A Farthing Will Do £6.99**
  LILIAN HARRY
  978-0-7528-6492-1
- ☐ **Three Little Ships £6.99**
  LILIAN HARRY
  978-0-7528-7707-5
- ☐ **The Bells of Burracombe £6.99**
  LILIAN HARRY
  978-0-7528-7804-1
- ☐ **A Stranger in Burracombe £6.99**
  LILIAN HARRY
  978-0-7528-8277-2